SACRAME
SO-AUI-570
828 I Street
Sacramento, CA 95814
02/21

Jo Spurrier was born in 1980 and has a Bachelor of Science, but turned to writing because people tend to get upset when scientists make things up. She lives in Adelaide with her husband, two young sons and a formerly feral cat, and spends a lot of time playing with cars and trains ... although she still occasionally daydreams about snow.

Jo's first novel, *Winter Be My Shield*, was shortlisted for the 2012 Aurealis Award for best fantasy novel.

Also by Jo Spurrier

CHILDREN OF THE BLACK SUN TRILOGY

Winter Be My Shield (1)
Black Sun Light My Way (2)
North Star Guide Me Home (3)

A CURSE OF ASH & EMBERS

TALES OF THE BLACKBONE WITCHES

JO SPURRIER

HARPER
Voyager

Harper*Voyager*
An imprint of HarperCollins*Publishers*

First published in Australia in 2018
by HarperCollins*Publishers* Australia Pty Limited
ABN 36 009 913 517
harpercollins.com.au

Copyright © Jo Spurrier 2018

The right of Jo Spurrier to be identified as the author of this work has been
asserted by her in accordance with the *Copyright Amendment (Moral Rights)
Act 2000.*

This work is copyright. Apart from any use as permitted under the *Copyright
Act 1968*, no part may be reproduced, copied, scanned, stored in a retrieval
system, recorded, or transmitted, in any form or by any means, without the
prior written permission of the publisher.

HarperCollins*Publishers*
Level 13, 201 Elizabeth Street, Sydney NSW 2000, Australia
Unit D1, 63 Apollo Drive, Rosedale, Auckland 0632, New Zealand
A 53, Sector 57, Noida, UP, India
1 London Bridge Street, London, SE1 9GF, United Kingdom
Bay Adelaide Centre, East Tower, 22 Adelaide Street West, 41st floor, Toronto,
    Ontario M5H 4E3, Canada
195 Broadway, New York NY 10007, USA

A catalogue record for this book is available
from the National Library of Australia

ISBN 978 1 4607 5633 1 (paperback)
ISBN 978 1 4607 1031 9 (ebook)

Cover design and internal decorations by Darren Holt,
    HarperCollins Design Studio
Typeset in Sabon LT Std by Kirby Jones
Author photograph by Simon Ankor
Printed and bound in Australia by McPherson's Printing Group
The papers used by HarperCollins in the manufacture of this book are a
natural, recyclable product made from wood grown in sustainable plantation
forests. The fibre source and manufacturing processes meet recognised
international environmental standards, and carry certification.

For Liam

CHAPTER 1

I sat on the rough stone wall, gazing down the dusty road and grinding my heel against the rocks. The hobnails in my boot squealed against the stone, making me wince, but in truth the sound was a fine match for my mood.

Somewhere behind me my stepfather cursed, and there came the rattle of a bucket as it was kicked across the yard. I couldn't help but tense, one hand gripping the wall, the other crushing the letter I clutched.

That wretched letter. I couldn't decide if it was a lifeline or a sentence of exile. Could it be both? For months I'd been dreaming of leaving this place, but at the same time I'd been riddled with guilt at the mere thought. Leave my sod of a stepfather and his endless hen-pecking? I'd do it in a heartbeat — if only it didn't mean leaving Ma and my little brothers and sisters behind as well.

Now I had no choice. I scowled at the letter, the thick, creamy paper and the broken wax seal. *Where did you come from? I don't understand any of this.*

Boots crunched in the dust behind me, and I clenched my teeth.

'Well look at you,' Lem sneered. 'Sitting 'round on your arse while other folk get on with the work. Typical. You're not going to last two weeks in this new position, Elodie, you mark my words.'

Slowly, I turned to look at him. 'You told me to sit on the wall and wait for Yosh.' Normally I guarded my expression around him. It didn't take much to set him off ranting about my insolence, my hateful face. Sometimes it didn't take anything at all. But I didn't have to put up with him anymore.

His stupid red cheeks twitched with rage. 'After you get your chores done, girl! Do I have to tell you every little thing? Lord and Lady, if you talk to your new mistress like this she's going to beat you black and blue, and you'll deserve every bit of it!' He started towards me, fists clenched, shoulders hunched — and then Ma's voice rang out from the house. 'Lem! Lem! Do come and help me, sweet!'

He didn't look around, not until I slipped down from the wall, tucking the letter in my apron pocket and wiping the grit from my hands. 'I'll come, Ma!'

'You stay right there,' he growled. Then he turned on his heel and marched back into the house. It was oddly quiet, the house and the yard both, what with all my younger siblings absent. They'd been sent off to the river for the day, supposedly as a treat. I knew the real reason was so there'd be no fuss and fanfare to see me off.

Lem was sweet as pie to Ma, and he fair doted on my little sisters. He was more gruff with my brothers, but he gave praise when they earned it, and if it was scant they valued it all the more for its rarity. No, it was just me that he hated.

'What do you expect, Dee?' Ma had told me the night the letter came, and I was in shock and tears over being sent away. 'He's not your father, as you're so fond of pointing out. You can't expect a man to love another fellow's child as he loves his own. Now, he's found you a position as a servant; good, honest work, and you can't even say thank you.'

The slam of a door startled me. I jumped, and turned to see Ma bustling towards me with a cloth-wrapped bundle in her hands. 'Here you are, Dee,' she said. 'Tuck that away in your basket, quickly.' She glanced back over her shoulder, checking if Lem had seen her. It was a couple of pies, still hot from the oven, wrapped up in one of my spare dresses, one Lem had deemed too good to take to my new life as a maid-of-all-work. We bundled it into my pack-basket and put my old, worn blanket back in place on top.

Ma gave me a bright, brittle smile, and pulled me close for a hug. 'You take care, Dee. Make sure you mind what your mistress says, and watch that tongue of yours, all right?'

Feeling her arms around me, wondering how long it would be before I felt them again, I couldn't help myself. I began to cry. 'Ma—'

'Hush, hush, sweet. You're nearly seventeen, Dee, lots of girls your age get sent away for work.'

'But, Ma ...' I pulled away to look her in the face. 'You still haven't told me how it all came about. When did you even send away for the position?'

She blinked at me a couple of times, her face blank. Then she gave a little laugh. 'Oh, it was probably at the market, I suppose. It must have been. Wasn't it?'

I huffed a sigh of frustration. 'I don't know, Ma, I'm not allowed to go to the market anymore, remember? But *why*? You've always said that I can't even think about leaving the farm until all the little ones are grown. Lem wouldn't even let me go to school and now you're sending me away for work? Why? I just don't understand!'

She gave me that same blank look, and then patted my arm. 'Dee, lots of girls your age go away for work.' she repeated, as though she hadn't just said that same thing moments before. 'It happens all the time.'

'But why did you change your mind?'

She didn't answer. She just looked past me, down the road. 'Oh look! Here comes Yosh. Lem! Sweet! Yosh is here!'

While she turned away, I bit my lip, hard, and reached into my apron pocket to touch the thick paper once again. I guess I'd hoped that she'd admit that I deserved better than this, a life of endless cooking and cleaning and looking after children, work that was somehow never done well or quickly enough, work that never got a thank you, and was never worth the cost of keeping me. And yet work that was somehow so essential that I couldn't be spared to go to school, even though the fee was paid by charity since my real father was dead.

Why had they suddenly changed their minds and sent me away? *Why?*

I just had to accept that I wasn't going to get an answer. My ride was here. A team of oxen hauling a heavy cart had appeared amid a cloud of dust, and at Ma's shout Lem had gone striding out to meet the teamster, who plodded along beside his beasts.

To my eye the fellow wasn't exactly overwhelmed with joy to have Lem shaking his hand vigorously, like they were old friends. There was a smaller figure, a lass in a long dress, walking with him, and she hung back to eye Lem with uncertainty.

Lem was prattling to the teamster as Ma took me by the arm and steered me towards the wagon.

'You haven't met Elodie, have you, Yosh?' Lem said as I drew near. 'She should have been called Melody, but she's so dang careless she lost the em years ago!' Lem laughed fit to burst, slapping his thigh, but the expression on Yosh's face reminded me of the look our boss dog gave the pups when they were making pests of themselves. Lem went on, oblivious. 'Make sure she lends a hand when you pitch camp. She will actually do some work so long as you stay on her back about it. Ain't that right, girl?'

Ma interrupted before Lem could demand that I reply. 'Brought your daughter along this time, Yosh?'

The lass, a few years younger than Lucette, was watching Lem with a perplexed expression as she silently plied her spindle.

'Oh, aye,' Yosh drawled. 'Usual when folk send a daughter off for work her da or her brother goes along to make sure she gets there safe. Since she's travellin' alone I thought it best to have another lass along. Tongues'll wag, otherwise.' He gave each of them a hard look at that, Lem first and then Ma. Lem seemed not to hear, but Ma dropped her gaze, her cheeks turning pink.

Yosh came over and offered a broad hand. 'Nice to meet ya, Elodie, and this is my eldest lass, Sal.' He gestured to the girl, who gave me a merry smile. 'Off to earn some money for a dowry, are ye?'

'I hope so,' I said, cutting a sly glance at Lem as I hefted my pack-basket.

Lem scowled. 'You'd best send your pay right back here, girl, you've no idea how to handle money. You'll be cheated out of it as soon as it's in your pocket, or else spend it on some useless tat. Not that I expect you'll get much of it. You won't last out there in the real world.'

I stopped to glower at him. If he'd been closer, I'd have kept my mouth shut, but I was well out of reach. And I was about to be free of the wretch. 'You know, for someone who hates having me around you seem to be awful keen on having me come back. And as for my pay, you'll never see a penny of it.'

'Dee!' Ma snapped. 'You watch your mouth! Sorry, Yosh, I warned you, she's got a frightful temper.'

Yosh was looking at me from under beetled brows, holding out his huge hands, ready to heave my basket up into the wagon. I passed it to him with a flush spreading over my cheeks. 'Sorry, sir,' I muttered. 'And thanks.'

Lem's face had turned a deep scarlet. 'Well you just remember this, you little tart — if you end up with a baby in your belly don't you dare show your face back here, or I'll beat you black and blue and turf you out on your ear. Got it?'

'Hey now,' Yosh said, his face turning stony. 'My lass don't need to hear that kind of language. And yours don't, neither.'

Lem gave him a wide-eyed look, and then turned on me again. 'You hear that, Dee? You'd better watch that mouth of yours, or else Yosh will leave you by the side of the road to beg your way home.'

I could feel myself flushing a deep pink and I turned away, ignoring his words. Ma was standing right there, silent as usual, but when she met my gaze she threw her arms open and came close to wrap me up in a hug. 'I wish you two could be civil to each other for five blessed minutes,' she said, tears in her eyes. 'It wouldn't have to be this way if you could just be the bigger person and not bite back every time he snipes at you.'

'He's older than me,' I said. 'Shouldn't he be the bigger person?'

'Why do you always have to argue? I don't want to have a fight when you're about to leave.'

I hugged her tight. 'Promise me you won't do too much,' I said. 'Make sure Lucette does her share to help you, and Janey, too, she's old enough now. And promise me you won't let him be mean to the others, now I'm gone.'

'Oh, Dee, don't worry about that. It's hard on a man, raising a child that isn't his. It'll be nice to have some peace and quiet, instead of the kitchen turning into a battlefield every time you two cross paths.'

That stung, deep in my chest, but I shoved it down hard. My heart was beating hard now, and my belly clenched and churned under my stays. It was really happening. I was leaving.

But even so, if Ma changed her mind and said I could stay, I'd agree in a heartbeat.

'All right, all right,' Lem muttered. 'Yosh is a busy man, let him get on his way.'

'Promise you'll write,' Ma said, squeezing me tight.

I heaved a sigh. 'Ma, you know I can't.'

She pulled back, dabbing at her eyes with her apron. 'Oh ...'

I'd been supposed to go to school. She'd promised it over and over again. But somehow it was always the wrong time — she'd just had another baby and needed my help, or harvest-time was coming up, or lambing season. And then it was too late, I was too old. It would look ridiculous to send me when all the others would be half my age. Instead Ma was supposed to teach me at home, or Lucette or one of the others would do it, but there was never any time for that, either. There was always something more important to be done.

That last thought helped keep my eyes dry. Ma was twisting her apron between her hands.

'Come take the seat, lass,' Yosh said. 'You too, Sal, up you hop.'

I turned my face away as Yosh stirred his bullocks into motion with a click of his tongue, and this time there was nothing I could do to stop the tears from spilling. *Well, Dee, you've always said you wanted to*

be free of your wretched stepfather, and here you are.
Happy now?

It was lonely on the road, plodding towards the mountains. Yosh and his daughter Sal were pleasant folk, but quiet, and I was used to the noise of my family — the singing, the arguments, the dogs barking and the cats crying for pats. Out on the road it was almost silent, aside from the creaking of the wagon and the farts of the bullocks. Sal showed me how to get comfortable on the bales and sacks in the wagon bed and I slept long hours, or just lay back watching the clouds drift across the sky.

Yosh tried to ask me about my new position, but there wasn't much I could tell him. All I knew was the name of the place: Black Oak Cottage. Lem had told me nothing except that I'd find out when I got there. I showed Yosh the letter, but, after reading it through, he just handed it back to me with a shrug. I wanted to ask if there was anything strange about it, anything that might explain its arrival, so unexpected and so against every plan Ma and Lem had for me, but I didn't dare. It had always been driven in to me how little I knew about the world, and how dangerous it was for someone like me, with no education, kept sheltered at home.

Yosh seemed to think so too. 'Let me give you some advice, lass,' he said as I tucked the letter away again. 'When you get your coin, squirrel it away, a little here, a little there. Put some in your shoe and some in the hem of your skirt, don't keep it all in one place. And don't send it home to your folks, you'll never see it again.

'Work hard, even if you don't like your mistress, and keep your ear to the ground for a better position. Folk who see you workin' hard for a bad mistress will be happy to hire you themselves. Don't go back home if you can help it. That sod Lem will soon miss all the work you did, and he won't be so keen to let you leave a second time. And if you find a young lad to turn your head, make him marry you sooner rather than later, if you take my meaning.'

'Oh, I won't go down that road,' I said. 'Don't trouble yourself on that account.' Da never ran off on us, he died of lockjaw after an accident out in the woods, but it was much the same to me and Ma. I was very young when it happened, but I still remembered how hard it had been after he died.

'Good lass. But don't let all the tales of hard masters and mistresses get to your head; most folk are good and will treat you as well as you treat them.'

It was interesting to hear him say so. All I'd heard from Ma and Lem was how hard and cruel the world was, how evil people were and how lucky I was to have a home like the one they gave me. I tucked Yosh's words away inside my head and nodded to make him think that I agreed.

That night, after Yosh and Sal had fallen asleep, I lay awake, restless after dozing so much during the day. I pulled out the bit of cloth I'd found hidden within the dress Ma had given to me. It was a kerchief, embroidered all over with flowers and leaves, though the colours had long since faded — Ma's wedding scarf, the one she'd worn when she married my da. I'd found it once at the bottom of a basket of fabric scraps. When I'd brought it to show her, certain it must have been put in the wrong place, she'd shushed me and quickly tucked it away again.

It smelled like home, and as I ran a fingertip over the interlaced threads my mind kept going back to the talk I'd had with Ma, the night before I'd left.

'He'd never send Lucette away like this,' I'd said as I folded up the one spare set of clothes Lem said I could take.

Ma had no answer for that. Everyone knew Lucette was his favourite. She'd be the beauty of the village in a few years' time, with her fair curls and her wide blue eyes. It was a miracle she'd kept a sweet temper through all his doting.

Instead of denying it, Ma just sighed. 'I swear, Dee, if you could just curb your temper and not bite back—'

'I tried that,' I muttered. I truly had, years ago, swallowing my pride and trying to be the good girl Ma always urged me to be. It had made no difference; in fact, it had goaded him on to try harder to get a reaction from me. I had realised, that summer, that Lem didn't care what I said or didn't say. I could be as dumb as a fence post and he'd still make it my fault if he stubbed his toe on the way to the market.

'Look, he's not a bad man,' Ma said.

I snorted at that, not looking up.

'He's not! Lord and Lady, Dee, do you remember that winter after your father died?'

I stopped, letting the badly folded skirt fall in my lap.

'Do you?' she demanded.

'I remember the coat you made me,' I said. 'Out of the old horse blanket. I remember how it smelled.' I also remembered how the other children had teased me for it, until old Mrs Waxcomb took pity and washed it, letting me stay in her kitchen where it was warm until the wretched thing dried.

'Do you remember how hungry we were? I had chilblains so bad they would crack and bleed. We lived off scraps and rubbish, well, you did. I lived off air and snow, and let me tell you, if you ever go hungry like I did, maybe then you'll understand. Lem took us in, he gave us warm beds and put food on the table — but you've never shown him the smallest hint of gratitude for it. Well, have you?'

I scowled down at the crumpled skirt. 'He wouldn't send Lucette away to empty some old woman's chamber-pots and scrub her floors.'

Ma sighed. 'Lucette is his daughter. You can't expect him to treat you the same.'

'Lucette will get a dowry and a big fancy wedding.'

'And you'll get to leave the home of the man who's provided for you for most of your life,' Ma snapped. 'You can travel far away and you'll never have to see him again? Isn't that what you've always wanted?'

I couldn't reply. I was at war with myself. *Yes, I want to leave. I need to leave. But not like this, leaving everyone I love behind.*

Now, I balled up the wedding scarf in my fists, crushing it between my fingers, before I drew a deep breath and smoothed it out again and then folded it carefully to tuck away once more. *Do you still remember him, Ma? Will you remember me? Or will you send the last reminders away with someone else some fine day?*

In all my life I'd never been further from home than Riverton, but we passed by the town without even stopping and turned towards the mountains, which seemed impossibly far away.

When we stopped at noon to water the beasts, we met another traveller, a young fellow with a spavined horse and a rickety two-wheeled wagon. One of the wheels had gone awry and sat cockeyed on the axle. He seemed to have no idea how to fix it, and as the oxen drew near he looked up with a hopeful expression and Yosh gave a sigh. 'I'd best see if the lad needs a hand; there but for the grace o' the gods, and all that. Sal, Elodie, see to the beasts, would ye?'

In the end the rickety wagon had to be unloaded before Yosh and the fellow could get the wheel seated properly, and then we helped load it up while the fellow thanked Yosh over and over again. He had an odd way of speaking that sounded very funny to me. I fancied it might be some city accent, but I held back from asking. It had been years since I'd been allowed to leave the farm and talk to anyone from the outside, and I wasn't eager to make a fool of myself by asking stupid questions. 'My good fellow,' the young man said to Yosh. 'I simply can't thank you enough for your assistance. Would it be at all possible for me to, well, travel along with you a ways? It seems to me that keeping together would be a jolly good idea. Safety in numbers, as they say.' He'd stripped down to shirtsleeves to put the little tip-cart to rights, but now he pulled on a rather shabby-looking jacket and a ridiculous velvet cap, which immediately tipped over to one side. He had a patchy beard that he'd tried to groom into a point, without much success.

Yosh rubbed his bristling chin. 'Well that depends, lad. Where are you headed? Up to Overton?'

'That's right. I've not left the city before, you see, and one hears all kinds of stories of what happens out on the roads.'

'Well the Overton road's safe as houses, ain't no bandits along this stretch. But I don't suppose you'd go any slower than us, even if you ain't going any faster.' He looked over to where Sal and I waited by the wagon. 'What's your trade, young master?'

'I ...' the fellow glanced around. 'I'm a wizard,' he said.

Yosh burst out laughing. 'A wizard! Well I never! Shame you didn't learn any spells for fixing wheels, isn't it?'

Next to me, Sal giggled, and I hid a smile behind my hand, while the young man flushed and looked down. 'I guess so,' he said. 'Unfortunately they don't teach anything like that at the University. My specialities are prognostication and medicinal charms, although I do dabble in alchemy as well.'

'Alchemy? Like turning lead into gold?'

'Well, yes, although to be honest that's not so hard, it's that, economically—'

'Well fancy that,' Yosh interrupted. 'Sure, lad, you can come along with us a ways, if it suits you. Just let me tell you this, you meddle with my lasses here and I'll knock you on your arse and set your wheel back the way I found it. Understood?'

The wizard blanched. 'Oh, yes, sir, absolutely. I'd never dream of trifling with your lovely daughters. And I'm just ever so grateful for your help.'

'It's naught, young man. Today you, tomorrow me, that's the way it is for us country folk. What's your name?'

'It's Brian, sir.'

'Brian, is it? The Great Brian? The Astounding Brian?'

The fellow had such a mournful look on his face that I almost felt sorry for him. 'Just Brian, sir.'

'I ain't no sir, Brian. Just call me Yosh. Now let's get movin', daylight's wastin'.'

I hoped the new addition to our little party would provide some distraction from the boredom of travel, but I was sorely disappointed, at least until we pitched camp that evening. Then, while Yosh tended the beasts, Sal and I collected wood for a fire and water for our kettle. When Sal went to fetch flint and steel, I watched the young wizard sidle over to the fire and sprinkle a pinch of powder over the little pile of kindling. He followed it up with a sprinkle of water as I frowned, wondering what on earth he was doing — then, with a *pop* and a hiss and a gout of black smoke, the kindling burst into crackling flames.

Up on the wagon, Sal's head shot up with a bounce of her blonde braids. 'Oh,' she said, and hurried over to tend the flames. She didn't so much as glance at the young wizard, and I saw him sag in dejection at the lack of response.

When it was time for dinner Yosh offered to share our meal, and the wizard jumped to offer his own contribution; though it turned out to be nothing but bread and cheese, the cheese quite good though the bread was very stale. It made a good rarebit though, with a sauce made from the cheese and some of Yosh's ale.

'I do hope you're not just living off bread and cheese,' I said to Brian as we ate. Looking at his pallid skin and sunken cheeks, I suspected he was.

'To be honest, miss,' he began, 'I'm not very good at cooking. I bought a big sack of dried beans because I'd heard they were good for travelling but I just can't seem to get them to cook right. The woman in the shop said they just need to simmer for a few minutes.'

Sal laughed in a long peal, and I scowled and kicked her foot with my toe, though Brian was already as red as a beet. 'There's no need to be so rude,' I snapped at her, forgetting for a moment that she wasn't my little sister. 'That woman was having you on,' I said to Brian. 'It takes a lot longer than a few minutes, more like two hours. Or you can set them soaking the night before to make it faster.' He nodded attentively, and thanked me most politely.

'I take it a lot of folk like to give you lads a hard time,' Yosh said, once the discussion was done.

'It's true, sir, and there are so many charlatans about that I can't fault folk for being suspicious. And unfortunately, while true wizardry is seen to be a prestigious career, there's just not a lot of work for new graduates.'

'So what do you do for coin, young Brian?' Yosh said.

'Well, as I said, my speciality is prognostication ...' he trailed off, looking at us across the fire. 'Fortunes,' he said. 'I tell fortunes.'

'My ma says fortune-tellers are all swindlers and thieves,' Sal said.

Yosh broke into a laugh that he quickly turned into a cough, before composing his face. 'Young lady,' he scolded. 'You've been told once to mind your manners! Off to bed with you if you can't be civil.'

With a roll of her eyes, Sal slammed down her bowl and stalked off.

Brian hurriedly scraped up the last of his meal and stood as well. 'I'll, er, I'd best ... I think I'll just go and note down those instructions you gave me, miss. Many thanks, and good night.' He slunk off into the darkness behind his wagon.

I looked over the abandoned dishes with a sigh. 'I'll just clean all this up, shall I?'

The next day, as we continued trudging towards the mountains, I kept looking back at our little wizard trailing behind the oxcart in his rickety wagon. I'd never met a wizard before — never even imagined one, really; and if I had, he was not what I would have expected. I couldn't help but feel sorry for him. No one believed in his powers — Lord and Lady, I didn't truly believe in them myself, even after the trick he'd pulled with the fire — and everyone mocked him. I felt cross over the way he'd been tricked with the beans; how many hungry nights had he had because of one person's sport?

I didn't mean to be obvious about it, but Yosh soon noticed, and pulled me away from Sal for a quick word. 'Found something to catch your eye, young Elodie?'

I knew at once what he was getting at, and felt myself flush. 'What do you mean?'

'I may be old, lass, but I'm not an old fool. You've been eyeing that young lad up all day.'

I could feel my cheeks getting hotter by the minute. 'I have not!'

He just gave a dry chuckle.

'No, really,' I protested. 'I don't know what you've heard from my stepfather, but I'm not a fool. For one thing, anyone can see he's as poor as a church mouse, he's got no means of keeping a wife. For another, I've blessed well only just met him! And for a third, well, he's kind of pathetic.'

Yosh laughed out loud at that. 'Well, he is that, lass, I can't fault your thinking there. But I can see you're a kind-hearted girl, and I've seen many a sweet young lass like you try to rescue broken-winged birds and lame hounds, only to find themselves saddled with a bird that can't fly or a dog that won't hunt.'

'I know that,' I muttered. 'I'm just trying to imagine where he's come from, what his life must be like, roaming around in that wagon that's going to fall apart if it hits a stiff breeze.'

'And what do you think of it?'

'It's got to be a cold and lonely way to live, for the sake of knowing a few bits of magic that everyone thinks is trickery anyway. Is it worth it?' I gave him a sidelong glance. 'Do you believe in it?'

'*Believe* in it? I don't know about that, lass. But I've seen some things. I really have. Whether that young fellow has any real power is not for me to say, but some of the others ... let's just say I've seen things I hope never to see again. You've got a job a-waiting for you with a roof over your head, a warm fire and food in your belly. That's worth a cursed lot more than the freedom to starve and shiver under the open blessed sky.'

I looked down at my feet. 'Don't worry yourself about me, Yosh, I've done my share of starving and shivering. But ...' I bit my lip, glancing up at him. *Why couldn't Ma have married someone like him, instead of that fat-head she calls a husband?* 'But what's wrong with having a bit of curiosity?'

'Curiosity killed the cat.'

'But satisfaction brought him back,' I retorted. 'When am I ever going to meet a wizard again? I've been at the farm most of my life, and soon enough I'll be slaving away in another blessed kitchen. Why shouldn't I enjoy a bit of freedom while I can?'

'Why indeed?' Yosh said with a shrug. 'You're a sensible lass, Elodie.'

We left it there, but the whole exchange left something of a sour taste in my mouth. *Sensible.* That's what Ma always called me, when Lem wasn't around to object to the hint of praise. I'd always been the sensible one, while my little brothers and sisters got to run around playing the fool.

At midday we stopped again to water the beasts and have some lunch. As I was buttering bread, I heard Yosh make a concerned noise and I looked up to see a dust-cloud heading towards us along the road.

'Someone's in a big damn hurry,' Yosh muttered. 'Must be a messenger or some such.'

'Isn't that cloud a bit too big to be from one horse?' I said.

'Aye, it is. But not big enough for a stage-coach or the like. Could be a man and a couple of guards. Well, they're movin' quick, should be past us by the time we hit the road again.'

The cloud drew closer and closer, and Brian came over to confer with Yosh, although he didn't know anything more, even with his big-city background.

Then, before they'd even finished talking, the cloud was upon us. The dust was kicked up by three riders, each one on a beautiful black horse, so alike they could have been cut from the same cloth. The riders matched too — each of them wrapped in a black cloak, with hoods drawn forward to hide their faces.

The riders slowed, and then halted in the swirling dust. They stopped in a neat formation, each of them a precise distance apart. Utterly still and facing dead ahead along the road.

Something about the sight of them made my chest grow tight, and after a moment I figured out what it was — that stillness. The horses didn't toss their heads or stamp their feet. They didn't so much as twitch an ear or swish a tail.

Then one of the men turned his horse towards us and kicked it forward.

I took a step back towards the wagon. The men hadn't spoken. They'd stopped a few horse-lengths apart, with no milling together, no conversation, no agreement for one man to approach. There was something deeply unnatural about it. About all of it.

Next to Yosh, Brian made a small noise, like the whimper of a puppy.

'I think I'd best go see what they want,' Yosh said.

'No,' Brian said quickly. 'No, Yosh. Stay with your girls. I'll go.' Before Yosh had time to reply, the young wizard went striding out to meet the black rider.

Yosh didn't argue, and made no move to follow. Sal came over to us, and I caught her by the shoulder to draw her back behind the wagon and out of sight. But at the same time I couldn't bear to look away as the first rider bent down in the saddle to talk to Brian. Behind him, the two on the road stood as still as statues. The horses, too.

'What are they?' Sal asked in a worried voice.

'I don't know,' I said. 'Let's just stay back here out of sight.'

After a few minutes, the rider wheeled his horse and, with a touch of his heels, the beast set off at a gallop once more. The other riders spurred their horses forward too, without any signal that I could see, moving in perfect unison.

As the dust-cloud moved away from us I breathed a sigh of relief. 'Lord and Lady, they're going.'

'But what *were* they?' Sal said. 'Da?'

'Don't pay them any mind, sweet,' Yosh said. 'No mind at all. They're just some lord's messengers, I'd say, going about their business.'

Sal frowned. 'But what about him then?' she said, pointing. 'What's *he* doing?'

Brian was still standing in the spot where he'd spoken to the rider, shoulders hunched, head bowed, cap in his hand like a servant speaking to his master. He stood there, frozen and still.

Yosh sucked in a breath. 'Get back on the wagon, Sal. You too, Elodie.'

'What's wrong with him?' I said.

'Elodie, I said—'

I shook my head. 'Something's not right. He's sick, or hurt ... or something.'

Yosh's lips twitched, but he didn't argue. He started towards our companion. 'Brian? You all right there, lad? What did they want?'

I followed Yosh over. Brian made no response. He just stood there, completely still.

Yosh laid a hand on his shoulder, but there was no response. 'Brian?'

Heart beating hard, I touched the wizard's forehead. It felt normal, no fever, though his skin was beaded with sweat. He blinked, and as I circled around him I could see his skinny chest rising and falling with his breath. 'Brian?' I said, softly.

Nothing. Not even a twitch of his eyes.

Yosh and I exchanged a glance.

I took hold of Brian's hand, and met no resistance. He moved at the slightest pressure, and when the pressure ceased, stayed where I'd pushed him.

'What on earth ...' Yosh began.

'They did something to him,' I said. 'Those riders.'

'All they did was talk to him,' Yosh muttered.

I chewed on my lip, thinking. *Brian knew something about them*, I thought to myself. Since we'd met him the day before, he'd deferred to Yosh in everything, except this. He knew something about them, and had gone to speak to them himself. Why? To spare Yosh this fate?

I took Brian's hand again, and tugged him forward. He followed me obediently.

'Maybe we should get moving,' I said to Yosh. 'I can drive his wagon if you help me get him up into the seat.'

Under a haze of dust, Yosh looked over our little rest-stop and then surveyed the road before us and behind. 'Yeah,' he said. 'All right. That seems sensible. The pace those ... gentlemen ... are setting, there's no danger of us catching up to them.' With a clenched fist, he drew a circle over his heart, using the sign of the gods to ward off evil. Then he took Brian's other arm. 'Come on now, lad. Let's get you up into your seat.'

CHAPTER 2

The way Brian sat beside me on the wagon seat reminded me of my sisters' porcelain dolls, posed still as statues until the girls came to play with them again. I talked to him as we plodded through the settling dust, the same way I'd talk to an anxious beast or a fussing baby. For hours there was no response at all but eventually he was able to turn his head and look at me, and reply with sighs and wordless sounds.

We stopped and pitched camp as the sun was sinking. Since Brian was still lost in whatever it was that had ensorcelled him, I saw to his horse, and once I'd finished watering and grooming the poor beast, just as the sun dipped below the horizon, I returned to the fire to find the young wizard shivering like he was palsied, and looking around with wild eyes.

I hurried back to his side. 'Brian? Are you all right?'

He was shivering too hard to speak, so I fetched a blanket and wrapped it around his shoulders while he stammered his thanks. Hearing him speak, Yosh hurried over as well. 'So you're back with us, lad? Glad to see it, I was starting to think you were off with the fairies for good.'

'What happened to you?' I said.

He shook his head. 'No,' he said. 'I-I-I-I c-can't.'

'Hush then,' I said. I still had it in my head that he was a nervous animal to be soothed. 'Don't speak of it if it upsets you. I'll make you a nice cup of tea, all right? My ma always says it's the best thing for an attack of nerves.'

'Does she?' Yosh said. 'Mine always swore by a nip of whisky. You fetch him your remedy, Dee, and I'll fetch him mine.'

After a couple of swigs from Yosh's bottle, a cup of tea sweetened with honey, and then some food in his belly, Brian had stopped trembling so badly. He went to check on his horse and all his gear, and I followed him over. 'I hope you don't mind, I had a look in your wagon to see if there was any feed for your horse.'

'Oh,' he said. 'No, I'm afraid not. I didn't have enough money left for that. And the folks I bought him from said he'd stay fat on grass but I suppose that was another lie, wasn't it?'

I didn't answer that. 'You said you make medicinal charms, is that right?'

He nodded in silence.

'You should make one for him, if you can.'

He looked at me in surprise. 'What for?'

'He's spavined. Look here.' I brought him close to the skinny gelding's hindquarters and ran a hand over the horse's hocks. 'See these bony lumps? Touch them, they're quite warm.'

'Spavined?' he said. 'Someone else told me that, but I don't know what it means.'

'Like when old folks' knuckles swell up and ache,' I said.

'Oh! You mean arthritis?'

I shrugged. 'I guess so. He's going to have a hard time hauling your cart once you get up into the mountains, but if you've got some charm that will help him ...'

'Maybe. Maybe I could sell them more easily if folk can see that they work. But I don't think I'll be going to the mountains. That's where ... that's where the warlocks went, isn't it?'

'Who?' I said, and then I understood and felt stupid. 'The cloaked riders?'

Brian nodded and shivered. 'They're evil. I could feel it, as soon as they drew close. We were warned about folk like that, back at the University. Good gods, I wasn't sure I believed it ...'

'What did he want?'

He looked away, sucking in his cheeks. 'I, I don't know. I don't remember. But I don't want to risk running into him again. I'm going to find a different road, go somewhere else. I've heard the mountains are all witches' territory, anyway, it's no place for a civilised man.'

Witches? I almost said it aloud, and I was glad I hadn't — it would have come out as a sneer and the poor fellow had had enough of that already, to my mind.

'Miss Elodie,' he said, taking off his velvet cap. 'I can't thank you enough for your help. If this happened back in the city I'd have been robbed blind. I wouldn't even have the clothes on my back.'

I frowned. 'Is that really what it's like in the cities?' I'd been told as much, but I'd never believed it, on the principle that I couldn't trust any of the rot that came out of Lem's stupid mouth. 'Most folk out here aren't so bad. Like Yosh said yesterday, today you, tomorrow me.'

'Today you, tomorrow me.' He said the words back as though they were strange and unfamiliar. 'I see. How interesting. But you must allow me to find some way to repay your kindness, miss. Perhaps I ...' He flushed. 'I know you don't believe in it, but, well, perhaps I can change your mind. I could tell your fortune, if you wish?'

I frowned. I'd seen fortune-tellers at the market, back when I was still allowed to go. Even then I'd wondered about the folk who wasted good money on them. 'I haven't any coin,' I told him. 'None at all.'

'Of course, my dear, I wouldn't dream of charging you.'

'Well then, I suppose — wait.' I had a thought, of the letter tucked away in my carry-basket. 'I just need to go fetch something. I'll be right back.'

When I returned, Brian had brought out a little wooden trunk, and carefully set it down in the dust beside his cart, giving us an illusion of privacy even though Yosh and Sal sat beside the fire only a short way away.

I settled down across from him and handed him the letter.

'What's this?'

'My letter of employment.'

He looked puzzled. 'Oh, you want to know if your new master or mistress will be kindly? Perhaps if you will find love?'

I shook my head. 'No, no. I want to know where this letter came from.'

He pursed his lips. 'My dear, I'm afraid I don't understand.'

'My stepfather said that I'd never leave our farm. I was supposed to stay there and look after him and Ma forever. He'd never have sent off to find a position for me. So who did?'

'Perhaps your mother?'

That made me sit up straighter as a little thrill rippled through me. Perhaps it *was* Ma. Perhaps she did want more for me than a lifetime of drudgery.

But the feeling ebbed away as quickly as it had come. Ma never went against Lem. She'd never sneak around behind his back like that.

I didn't want to go airing my dirty laundry in front of Brian, though, so I just shrugged. 'Maybe. Would you see it, if that's the case?'

'Most likely. Let's take a look, shall we?'

From the box he took out a piece of painted cloth and laid it ceremoniously on the ground. It was decorated with a many-pointed star, and all around the edge were strange symbols and words.

Brian reached into his shirt and pulled out a pendant on a long chain that hung around his neck. He lifted it over his head and held it by the very end of the chain while the pendant swung to and fro below. It was carved from a purple stone, not flat like most pendants but a glittering, faceted spike.

'Now, in a matter like this it is best to proceed with questions that may be answered definitively with an affirmative or a negative ... uh, I mean, a simple yes or no,' Brian said.

'Don't you have to, I don't know, light some candles or some incense?' I said, resting my chin on my fist. 'Summon some spirits?'

'Well, I could, but good candles are expensive. And I'm still feeling rather weak ...'

I straightened. 'Oh, I was just teasing. I don't need all that frippery.' To be truthful, though, I was a little disappointed. This was nothing like what I'd glimpsed inside the fortune-teller's tent years ago, all hung with rich velvet and silk, and lit by coloured lanterns. On the other hand, it wasn't costing me a penny, so I supposed it was silly to fuss.

'Ah. Well, let us begin.' He leaned forward, focusing on the pendant, which swayed gently over the painted star. 'Was the young lady's employment arranged by her stepfather?'

The pointed stone was swinging gently at the end of the chain, but now the arc grew larger, faster, and the line of it changed until it was swinging firmly across the precise middle of the cloth.

'Well that seems quite clear,' Brian said.

'It does?'

'It says no, you see?' He gestured to a word painted beside those points on the star.

'Oh,' I said. 'I'm afraid I can't read.'

He glanced up in surprise. 'Oh! I thought everyone learned to read, nowadays.'

'Not me!' I said brightly, hoping that would be enough to dissuade him from prying further. 'Was it my mother, then?'

We both peered intently at the stone. There was no change. The answer was no.

'Was it someone known to Elodie?' Brian said.

The swinging line didn't change.

'Perhaps we should ask a known affirmative to be certain the calibration is correct,' Brian said.

His convoluted way of talking was starting to annoy me, but I guessed at what he meant. 'Am I sixteen years old?' I asked.

The arc of the stone grew gradually smaller, and instead of swinging back and forth it started to circle briefly, and then it settled into a new arc, crosswise to the first. 'It says yes,' Brian said. I refrained from rolling my eyes. Just because I can't read, doesn't mean I'm stupid.

'Will her new mistress be kind?' he said, before I could think of another question.

The swinging of the stone slowed, and it started to circle once more. I held my breath, waiting for it to return to *no*, but it didn't. It just kept swinging in a haphazard circle, sometimes large, sometimes small. 'What does that mean?'

'I'm afraid the answer is unclear,' Brian said with a frown. 'Perhaps that wasn't the best question to ask. Will she find happiness, and perhaps love?' He gave me a sly look, wriggling his sparse eyebrows, and I couldn't help but giggle.

The stone swung back to *yes*, making my chest feel tight and breathless. 'So,' I said. 'My mistress will be mean, but I'll find myself a beau?'

'No, no, not mean. If she were mean it would have answered no. Instead, it gave us no answer. To be fair, it was a bad question to ask, pendulums don't do well with subjective questions. For example, I could ask if the weather will be good tomorrow, and it might say yes even if it will rain, because the farmers around us will be glad of it.'

'I see. Can I try asking some questions?'

'By all means,' he said.

I leaned close to the stone. I wasn't sure why. 'Will I ever have to go home to Lem again?'

I held my breath.

The stone circled, and then settled onto *no*.

My heart was beating harder now. 'Will I be free?'

The stone slowed, circled, and settled to *yes* once again.

I could feel Brian's eyes on me, but I didn't meet his gaze. Strangely, it felt like he wasn't really there, he wasn't a part of this experience except to hold the chain and act as a guide here and there.

There was one more question burning in my mind. Perhaps it wasn't the sort the pendulum could answer, but I had to ask it. I might never get another chance. 'Who sent the letter?'

The stone slowed. Circled. And then it fell still. Utterly still, hanging straight down to point at the centre of the star.

I lifted my head to meet the wizard's gaze, and then there was a *pop*, and with a muttered curse Brian winced and pulled his hand away, shaking it as though it smarted.

The pendulum had fallen. It lay on the cloth with the chain pooled around it. I bit my lip as Brian gingerly picked it up, examining the stone and then the chain for damage.

'What happened?'

'I, I'm not sure. That was ... that was very strange. Very strange indeed.' With a grimace, he tucked the stone away. 'I think we ought to stop there. In my experience nothing good comes of prying too deeply into things we are not meant to know.'

I wanted to argue with him. Oh, how I wanted to argue, but he was looking poorly once again and I reminded myself sharply that he'd had a difficult day. I still had no idea what the black rider had done to him, and here in our lonely camp under a black sky I wasn't sure I wanted to know.

'Well,' I said, folding up the letter and gathering my skirts, ready to stand. 'Many thanks for the reading. You were right, I didn't believe in it at all, but now ...' Even as I said the words, I was wondering if I'd merely heard what I wanted to hear. Surely not, though, or he'd have told me I was going to serve a wealthy mistress who would die peacefully and leave me all her fortune. 'What was it Yosh said yesterday? The Astounding Brian? Well, consider me astounded.'

He gave me a shy smile. 'You are too kind, miss. And I truly am grateful for the companionship I have been shown these last two days. I wish you the best of fortune, miss, but I'm afraid in the morning we must part ways. I will not risk crossing paths with that, that *creature* again. Now I really must find my bed. Goodnight, Miss Elodie.'

'Goodnight,' I said.

Early next morning, while we were all still abed, I woke to the sound of the wizard driving away, his rickety cart rattling and squeaking behind the skinny horse. I truly was sad to see him go. I kept thinking about him and his pendulum, turning the questions and answers the stone had given me over and over in my mind as we started the slow climb into the mountains.

It was a little after midday on the fourth day that Yosh called to his beasts to stop and let the heavy wagon ease to a halt. 'Well, lass,' he said, pointing to a road-marker, a large stone engraved with a set of letters. 'That points the way to the village.'

Black Oak Cottage lay on the other side of the village of Lilsfield, according to the letter. Yosh had read it to me again that morning, and then quizzed me on it, like I was some idiot child, to make sure I knew the way.

'I'm sorry we can't see you there proper,' Yosh said, 'but we'll lose a full day taking you there and headin' back.'

'I don't mind the walk,' I said, heaving my pack-basket down and jumping after it. After so long on the wagon I'd be glad to stretch my legs. 'Thanks for seeing me this far, Yosh.'

'All the best to ye, girl.' With a click of his tongue, he got the oxen moving again. Atop the piled wagon, Sal gaily waved. I waved back at her but she was already turning away, watching the road ahead.

With a sigh, I heaved my basket onto my back, settling the leather straps on my shoulders, and eyed the road-marker. Lilsfield, was it? I knew a few of the letters, but not all. Underneath them were another few symbols — one of them was a number; *six*, I thought. Which meant the ones after it must read miles. Wonderful. I'd best get walking, then.

Back home at the farm the land was flat and dusty with more grass than trees, but this landscape was more like where we'd lived back when my Da was still alive — from what I could remember from so long ago, at least. The road was bordered by thick forest with only the occasional open field; the bare earth was dark and moist, not pale and sandy like the roads at home, and the ground beside the track was thick with ferns, lush and green.

I didn't pass anyone on the road, but I did stumble over a very strange set of tracks. They looked like the prints the hens left in the dust back at home, except they were sunk a full six inches into the damp earth, and were easily as long as my arm. I frowned at them for a few moments before going on my way with a roll of my eyes. Young lads playing a game, no doubt. Still, there was worse mischief they could get up to than cobbling together giant chicken feet to play tricks on travellers.

It was well past mid-afternoon when I finally reached Lilsfield, foot-sore and weary, and it too struck me as alien and strange. Back home the houses were built of costly stone or cheap rammed earth, with roofs of thatch. But here the buildings were all made of rough-hewn logs stacked together, roofed with wooden shingles and with heavy shutters on all the windows. Most of them were tightly closed. Lilsfield was nestled into a little valley, and though there were some fields and gardens behind the buildings clustered around the main road, beyond them stood a wall of trees.

I made straight for the well, and had to pick up my skirts to keep them out of the mud around the well-head. My little water bottle had run out long ago. I balanced it on the wall to fill it with the dipper and then wet my spare handkerchief to wash my face and my hands.

The water tasted different to that of home, too. I drank slowly while looking around. The road had been deserted, but there was a little more life in the village. I heard a hammer ringing out from a building sign-posted with an anvil, while a lad riding one pony and leading another ambled up the road towards it. He stared at me, unblinking, as though I were some peculiar beast with two heads. I crossed my eyes at him, but he seemed not to notice.

Nearby was a laden wagon halted beneath a sign painted with a boar's head with an apple in its mouth, and across the road from it another sturdy wooden building, sporting a sign with a picture of scissors and a spool of thread — a general store. Somewhere nearby I heard the muffled sound of a baby grizzling with tiredness and a woman singing the little one to sleep, and I felt a pang of sadness for my little brothers and sisters back at home. By the time I saw them again they'd be well past naps and singing, and who knew how many more babies Ma might have. Lucette would have to help her look after them now. I only hoped she could find the patience for it.

I rested a little longer beside the well before picking up my basket once again. The village had one main road, with a smaller fork leading northward — at least I thought it was north; it was hard to tell with the winding of the road and the sky now hidden by clouds. I knew I was supposed to take the westward path, but the letter had neglected to mention how far the cottage lay beyond Lilsfield. I turned my face towards the path, only to hesitate. The folk who lived here must know how far I had to go. It couldn't hurt to ask, surely?

I crossed the road to the general store. It had one big window displaying a couple of bolts of cloth, a spinning wheel and some glass lanterns. The door struck a bell as I opened it and inside it was very dark, smelling of lamp-oil and beeswax.

The chime of the bell brought a woman, quite tall, wearing a matched skirt and jacket with her hair pinned up so that not a wisp came free. She was so neat and trim that I felt very much the country girl with my dirty boots, my skirt hiked up into my belt and my hair coming loose from its braid. I stood as still as possible to keep from shedding mud on her floor as the woman looked down at me over spectacles perched on the tip of her nose. 'Who are you?' she demanded.

Her lack of manners made me stutter. 'G-good afternoon, ma'am, my name is Elodie Forster. I've been hired to Black Oak Cottage ...' I'd made a good start but the ache of my shoulders and my tired legs scrambled my thoughts before I could get to the end. 'Could, could you tell me how much further I've got to go? Please?'

'Black Oak,' she said, scowling. 'You've been hired to Black Oak Cottage.' Her voice was flat and her gaze made me wither.

'I ... yes, miss, I mean, ma'am.'

'Where have you come from, lass?' she demanded, still scowling.

'From Burswood Farm, ma'am, though that's a fair way from here, down past Riverton—'

'What about today, where have you come from today?'

She asked with such an odd intensity that I stammered to reply. 'F-from the sign to Lilsfield, back on the big road.' I jerked my thumb over my shoulder in the rough direction. 'That's where the teamster let me down.'

The woman huffed and rang a bell on the counter beside her with a rapid, incessant chime, though she didn't take her eyes off me.

'Coming, coming,' a man's voice grumbled from the back of the store. The fellow who appeared looked exactly as I'd pictured a mountain man, with a thick grey beard halfway down his chest and his sleeves rolled up to his elbows. His arms bore an impressive thatch of hair well gone to grey, as did his head. He made me think of a bear from my siblings' books, with his broad shoulders and the bulk of his belly hanging over his belt. He gave the woman an exasperated look. 'What's the matter?'

The woman gestured at me. 'This lass says she's been hired to Black Oak Cottage. She's just walked down from the Overton road by herself. All six miles of it, on her own.'

The man looked from her to me. His eyebrows were long and tufted, and they climbed to his bushy hairline.

'It's not that far,' I said, though my sore feet disagreed.

'And she's got another four miles to go to Black Oak,' the woman said, as though I hadn't spoken. I winced inwardly. 'She'll be expected. If she doesn't arrive, and someone comes *looking*—'

'Yes, yes, I see the matter,' the man said. 'Not enough time to get there and back before dark, not on foot. Even on a horse'd be pushing it.' He rubbed his chin. 'I think I saw Attwater head into the tavern after he delivered those furs. He's camped out that way. I'll see if he's still here.' With that he strode outside, leaving the door to smack into the bell again as it swung closed behind him.

I suddenly felt very uncertain. 'I'm sorry if I've done something wrong, ma'am.'

'No, no,' she said. 'It's not your doing. But you should have had someone with you, it's irresponsible to let a young girl travel so far from home alone. I'd like to have words with your father, though I suppose beggars can't be choosers.' She bit her lip, and I realised what I'd taken for disapproval was more likely concern. 'Did you see anything out there? No, I don't suppose you did or you wouldn't be ... well, unless you're already an apprentice?' She raised her eyebrows, looking at me expectantly.

I felt completely lost. 'I ... Ma'am? Forgive me, but I don't understand.'

'You don't? You don't know what's going on here? Well, not that any of us do,' she muttered, 'except for the one out there in the cottage.'

'Ma'am,' I pleaded. Every time I thought I couldn't get any more bewildered, she kept opening her mouth.

'Is this your first job, lass?' She pursed her lips so tight they looked like the mouth of Ma's drawstring purse.

'It is, ma'am. But I don't understand what you're saying. Is there something dangerous out there?' I suppose this countryside was a lot wilder than what I was used to at home, but I hadn't felt at all uneasy on the walk. Now the shopkeeper had me worried that I should have been. Then I remembered the footprints I'd tripped over in the road, but I quickly dismissed them again. It was some lads' prank. It had to be.

'You'd best ask your mistress,' the woman said. 'She ought to be able to explain it.' She muttered something else under her breath. I didn't quite catch it, but it sounded as though she said, 'Then maybe you can tell us.'

She looked as though she were about to say something more, but her gaze shifted to the door at my back. 'Ah, good, here comes Grigg with Mr Attwater. Nice to meet you, Miss Forster. Farewell. Good luck.'

The man called Grigg opened the door, '... some little lass from down on the plains. Here she is.'

If Grigg reminded me of a bear then Attwater — *what kind of a name was that?* — brought to mind a hound. He was tall and thin with long, lank hair and a sorrowful look on his face. The most interesting thing about him was his bright blue eyes. He smelled of beer.

'Miss Forster,' he said, looking me over. 'I hear yer headed for Black Oak Cottage.'

I nodded. 'My name's Elodie.'

He nodded. 'Well, we'll get ye there by sundown so long as we get moving smartly. Night comes on fast here in the hills.'

'Attwater will see you there safely,' the shopkeeper said. 'He's a good man.'

'Thank you, ma'am, sir,' I said, and realised then that Attwater was already striding away. With a hasty nod I hurried out the door after him.

He checked his stride after a dozen paces, when he realised I couldn't keep up with his long legs. He'd slapped a ragged leather hat onto his head as he left the store, and carried a stout walking stick. On his back was a pack-frame with a leather bag lashed to it, mostly empty from the look of it, and his clothes were a mix of leather and much-mended cloth. He looked like the sort of man Ma would have ordered me to stay away from back home, but the shopkeeper vouched for him, for what it was worth.

'Thank you for showing me the way,' I said.

'No hassle,' he replied. 'I'd be heading right by it.'

'And I'm sorry to pull you away from the tavern.'

He chuckled. 'Ne'er mind that either. Ye've saved me from drinking away all me coin.' He fell silent for a moment, sucking on his teeth, and then glanced back at me from under the floppy brim of his hat. 'Do you know who it is ye'll be servin' at Black Oak?'

I shook my head. 'No, sir.'

'Don't call me sir,' he said. 'We're all equal before the Lord and Lady, ain't we? Well, I don't suppose many folk would agree, but that's the way I see it. P'raps that's why I'm happier running trap-lines out in the woods than livin' here in town.'

I kept my head down, trudging along. In the time I'd spent in the shop, the day seemed to have turned from mid-afternoon to late. There were clouds building, and the shadows around us were growing long and cold. 'Attwater? What can you tell me about this place?'

'Lilsfield or Black Oak?'

'Either,' I said. 'Both.'

'Don't know that there's much I can tell. All I know is some strange things been goin' on. But let me ask this, how'd ye get this job?'

That question again. I scarcely had any more answers than I did when I'd left home. And anyway, at the pace he was setting I didn't have the breath to try and explain it. 'Don't rightly know,' I said. 'A letter came to say I'd been hired, but I didn't even know Ma and my stepfather had sent off for the position. It must have been at the market a few weeks ago, I suppose.'

'Which market is that?'

'Down at Riverton.'

'Down on the plains?' he asked. 'That's a fair way to go to find a hireling for up here.'

I had no idea why that hadn't occurred to me before. Were there no girls nearby who could be taken on? It seemed very strange. 'I guess none of the local girls would be interested,' I said, keeping my voice light.

'P'raps not,' Attwater said. 'And if that was a few weeks back, well … there's a few things that have happened since then. A fair few things.'

He meant something by that, I could tell it in his voice. But I had no idea what and I was sick of trying to wring information from those who were of no mind to give it, so I didn't bother to ask. Instead, I said, 'What's she like, the mistress of Black Oak Cottage?'

'Ye don't know her name?'

I shook my head.

'The old one was a nasty piece of work,' he said. 'But she's gone now. The new one, Aleida, she's a little better, so long as ye don't get on her bad side.'

I mulled on that for a few minutes. The impression I'd got from Lem and Ma was that I'd been hired by an old woman, someone who needed a strong young back to help with the day-to-day. But come to think of it, when

Yosh read the hiring letter to me there'd been no mention of the kind of work I'd be doing.

'Do you have witches down Riverton way?' Attwater said.

'Witches?' If I hadn't been minding my manners so carefully, I might have scoffed at him. 'No. There's an apothecary in Riverton, though, and I met a wizard on the way here.'

'A wizard, hey? A real one?'

'Oh yes. He has a degree from the University and everything,' I said.

'Well,' he said. 'How about that.'

I knew full well when I was being condescended to, and scowled down at my feet. I couldn't blame him, anyway, I'd reacted the same way when Brian introduced himself.

'What are you saying?' I said. 'My new mistress is a witch?'

'And what would ye say to that?'

'I'd say you must think I'm some little girl to be scared of fire-side tales.'

'No, lass. If ye were, ye wouldn't have made it six miles from the big road all on yer lonesome. I just don't like the fact that ye've been sent all this way without a clue what ye're getting into.'

'And what am I getting into, exactly?'

'I don't rightly know. Or else I'd tell ye meself, Elodie.' There was honesty in his blue eyes. 'Just have a care. Keep yer wits about ye, all right?'

'The shopkeeper,' I cursed myself for not learning her

name, 'she asked if I'd seen anything as I walked into town. What's out here?'

'Don't rightly know. There's just been some tales.'

I resisted the urge to roll my eyes. Attwater seemed a nice fellow, but getting anything out of him was like pulling teeth. 'But you're a trapper, right? You're out on your own all the time.'

'That's right.'

'You haven't seen anything?'

'I've seen plenty. Earth torn up, trees pushed over, ripped out of the ground. Things howling in the night.'

I pursed my lips. 'Big things? Things that could leave tracks six inches deep and longer than my arm?'

He gave me a glance from under the floppy brim of his hat. 'What'd ye see, lass?'

'Just footprints,' I said. 'Looked like they were made by a giant chicken. I figured it was boys playing around.'

'Ah, that one. Up towards the Overton road, ye say? He gets around, then.'

I watched him with narrowed eyes. He was playing tricks on the new lass, surely. 'You're not worried, camped out here on your own?'

'Nope. I got a little cave. It's even got a crack in the roof to let smoke out. Whatever's out here, from what I've seen, they're too big to get in.'

'But you walked all the way into town anyway.'

He shrugged. 'Man's gotta make a living. Just like ye do, young Elodie.'

The smell of beer on Attwater's breath came to my mind, and I suddenly wondered why he'd been lingering in the tavern — I'd assumed it was like the farmers in Riverton on market day, drinking their profits; but now I wondered instead if he'd been drinking down the courage to walk back along these lonely roads. Of course, that meant he had to be telling me the truth, and I had some grave doubts about that.

It was near dark when Attwater stopped at a fork in the road, not that one could really call it a road anymore. For most of the way it had been wagon tracks, two muddy ruts cut into the ground, but some way back it had reduced to a single path, more a game trail than a road. But here a smaller path branched off to the side, and the sun was too far gone for me to tell which direction the branches led.

'Ye want that one,' Attwater said, gesturing to the right-hand path. "Fraid I can't see ye all the way there, girl, I ought to press on meself.'

'Of course,' I said. 'Thanks for walking with me.'

'It's not far, just a few hundred yards. Stay on the path, an' ye can't miss it.' He held out his walking stick. 'Take this, though. Just in case.'

I wasn't sure I should. Ma and Lem had both laid into me over and over again how I should never accept gifts, how all it did was put you in someone's debt. But it was a strong, stout stick, peeled of bark and rubbed with oil. It would be a nice thing to have even if there weren't strange beasts lurking in the forests around, beasts that scared even a tough, solitary woodsman like Attwater. 'Thank you,' I said, 'but I don't know how to find you to give it back. And I don't know when my new mistress will give me leave to return it.'

'Jus' keep it,' Attwater said. 'I can make another. It'll give me something to do of an evening.'

'Then I'm grateful,' I said with a bob of my head. 'Safe journey.'

'And to ye, Miss Elodie,' he said, tugging on the floppy brim of his hat. And with that he was off again, striding away into the darkness.

With a shiver I gathered myself, clutching Attwater's staff in both hands. Hopefully my mistress would not be annoyed that I had arrived so late; with my boots and skirt splattered with mud and my plait coming undone. Thinking of a warm and cosy kitchen, well-lit by oil lamps and a fireplace, I squared my aching shoulders and marched on into the gloom.

The path was narrow and winding, leading through gnarled and twisting trees that I thought would block the road from view even in full daylight. I kept looking ahead for a light through a window, something warm and welcoming. A couple of times I thought I spotted a gleam only to lose it again in the trees' tangled branches as I felt my way through them carefully, the staff held ahead of me for fear of spiders' webs.

And then, with one final turn of the contorted path, I was there. Such as it was. It was too dark now to see much but I could make out a cottage of stacked stone, thickly covered with moss. Some of it was in ruin, the walls crumbled to rubble, and the part of it that still stood didn't seem much better. The roof, just a shadow against the dark sky, sagged in the middle like a sway-backed horse. The shutters on the windows hadn't been repainted in years, and they were firmly shut — in fact it looked like if you tried to open them they'd be more likely to fall off. There wasn't so much as a gleam of light around them or under the stout, scarred wood of the door.

I stared at the door for a long moment with my jaw hanging open, while my stomach shrivelled into a hard, sour knot. There was no one here.

No, that had to be wrong. The people in the village, Attwater — they wouldn't have sent me to a deserted house. Surely?

I looked around, trying to pick out the path that had brought me winding through the trees. It was dark enough now that I wasn't sure of finding my way back to the road where Attwater had left me, let alone all the way back to Lilsfield. Besides, I was tired and hungry, my feet hurt and it was getting cold. I didn't even want to *think* about whatever beast was out there that had the local folk so scared.

Doing my best to ignore the shiver that ran down my spine, I drew myself up, clenching my jaw and gripping Attwater's walking stick tight, and marched up to the door.

The steps that led up to it were covered with moss. My foot slipped, tearing a chunk of moss away, black in the fast-fading light, scraping my shin and making me yelp in pain. Moving more carefully, I hobbled up to the door and rapped with my knuckles. *I must be mistaken,* I thought. *There's bound to be someone here. No one would hire a new servant and then take off before they arrived. Surely. They must be saving candles or something.*

I waited, and waited, holding my breath and straining my ears for any sound. But there was nothing.

I rapped again, this time using the walking stick. Still nothing. I tried calling out, even pounding on the door with my fist, but there was nothing. No sound, no movement, no life at all.

The hard knot in my belly grew tighter and tighter, twisted up like a shirt wrung out on laundry day. My throat seemed to be closing up and my cheeks felt like they were burning in the chill night air. *They don't want me,* a little voice in the back of my head said. *Your own family didn't want you, they sent you away, and if they don't want you why would anyone else?*

Oh gods, I was going to cry. I could feel the tears prickling behind my eyes, stinging in my nose. I gulped a breath, trying to blink them away before they could spill, drawing myself up and imagining I was as cold and hard as ice, as crystal. Useless, traitorous things, tears. I tried the door one last time, pounding with my fist, shouting with a voice that cracked and broke. But, just as before, there was nothing. The night was utterly silent.

Then I couldn't hold it back anymore. My legs were too tired, my feet too sore, my shoulders rubbed and strained from the straps of my pack-basket. My legs folded beneath me and I slumped down on the doorstep. I let Attwater's walking stick fall, and pulled a fold of my petticoat up to my face as I began to weep.

What could I possibly do now? There was nowhere to go, and it was too dark to walk anywhere, anyway. I'd have to spend the night here, curled up on the doorstep like a dog. Lem had often threatened to toss me out of the house at night, but he'd never actually done it. *He'd laugh himself stupid to see me now,* I thought.

Tomorrow I could walk back to Lilsfield, but what then? I'd never catch up to Yosh, and besides, I couldn't go home. I just couldn't. *The pendulum said I'd never have to go back, it said I'd be free!* Lord and Lady, I felt stupid now for believing in the wretched thing. But the idea of returning home in disgrace made me sob even harder. *Everyone* would think that I truly was useless, worthless. Couldn't even get work as a hired girl to sweep up ashes and empty chamber-pots.

I gulped down the cold air and scrubbed at my face with my sleeve, trying to dry my cheeks, but it was a wasted effort — they kept coming faster than I could wipe them away. *Sod it,* I said to myself, *I'm not going home, I'm not going to prove them right. There must be work somewhere, there must be.* I was trying very hard not to remember the tales you always heard, the stories of young women foolish enough to take their chance in the wide world, and all the evils that befell them.

The stone of the doorstep was hard and cold under my backside. I wriggled out of the pack-basket straps and hunted inside for my blanket, then I shook it out to wrap around my shoulders. If I had a bit of light maybe I could gather some branches and twigs to lie upon, but it was too dark now — I was afraid I wouldn't be able to find my way back to the doorstep and what little shelter it gave. No, this was it. I was in for a wretched night, it seemed.

The tears eased, leaving me feeling drained and empty, and I resigned myself to the night; trying to think of anything but my empty belly and parched throat or what might be lurking out there in the darkness, which lay thick as ink around me. I stared blankly into it, wondering if the Lilsfield tavern could use a pot-girl or if a passing bullock driver would let me ride with him in return for cooking his meals or washing his clothes ...

A pale shape glided through the night and startled me out of my thoughts. It was a barn owl, flying on silent wings. Night-time stole colour from the world at the best of times, and this night was so black I felt as though I'd been struck blind, but I was sure the owl was carrying something small and round in its talons. Something that looked like an apple.

I rubbed my eyes. An owl with an apple? Seemed about as likely as me eating a mouse. Must just be my eyes playing tricks on me. And besides, it was there and gone so fast ...

I was settling back into my dark thoughts when that pale shape appeared again, gliding down towards me.

It came so fast that I didn't have time to do anything more than clutch my blanket tighter before the owl landed on the other end of the doorstep. It hopped a few times like some ridiculous, overgrown sparrow and seemed to study me, turning its head this way and that. Then, with another hop, it turned away, spread its wings, and was gone.

I stared after it, still unmoving, my mind utterly blank. I didn't know what to think.

Then, a few moments later, I heard a sound that made me sit bolt upright. Inside the cottage someone, or something, was moving about.

I tried to pull myself up, but I'd been sitting in the cold for so long that I felt as stiff as a board. On the far side of the door I heard a bolt being thrown and then the door swung open, sending me sprawling over the threshold.

I found myself at the feet of a tall, dark figure holding a lantern in one hand. The flame was only small but, after sitting in the dark for so long, it was enough to make my eyes water. I scrambled back on my hands and knees, feeling my cheeks flush, and torn between wanting to sob with relief and demanding to know why they hadn't opened the door when I'd been pounding on it earlier.

At first I couldn't see a thing, blinded by the glare of the lantern. Squinting, I made out a young matron of twenty-five or so — old enough to have a cluster of children already, back home. She would have been handsome, if it weren't for her hair being tangled like a bird's nest and her tanned skin turned an ashen, sallow shade, with marks under her eyes as dark as bruises. She had a blanket wrapped around her shoulders and was barely keeping herself upright; she clung to the door with her free hand as I struggled to my feet.

The woman's eyes were cold and imperious as she looked me over. 'Who are you?' she demanded. 'What are you doing on my doorstep?'

'I ...' I ducked my head. 'My name is Elodie Forster, ma'am. I'm here for the job?'

'What job?'

Oh no. The hard, sour knot in my belly was back. 'Y-you advertised for a hired girl?'

The woman shook her head. 'No, I didn't. Who are you, really? Who sent you?' She looked past me, eyes darting around to peer into the darkness. 'If you've come looking for Gyssha I can tell you she's long gone. If you knew that already and figured the place for easy pickings, think again.'

If I hadn't been so tired, cold and hungry I think the tears would have started up again, but all I could do was stare at her, feeling hollow inside. Lord and Lady, what was this? Some awful prank of Lem's? 'Honestly, miss, I'm here for work. I have a letter ...' I fumbled inside the carry-basket. The woman watched me suspiciously, a hand disappearing inside a fold of the blanket until I pulled out the creased, crumpled paper and offered it to her. 'Th-this is Black Oak Cottage, isn't it, ma'am? Only I was told this was where to come. A man called Attwater showed me the way. I'm sorry if there's been some misunderstanding, ma'am, but I'm cold, and hungry, and tired.'

She fixed me with a gaze like that of a hunting cat, and I felt trapped, entranced. I couldn't look away.

'Tell me your name,' she said.

I'd already told her, but I found myself speaking before I could complete the thought. 'Elodie Forster.'

'Who sent you?'

'No one.'

She pursed her lips, frowning. 'How old are you?'

'Sixteen.'

She took hold of my chin in one hand and turned my face this way and that, peering into my eyes. 'Hmm. Who wrote that letter?'

'I don't know.'

'You don't know their name? Or you don't know who put pen to paper?'

'Either,' I found myself saying. 'I don't know either.'

My eyes were watering and my head was starting to pound when she seemed to break whatever hold it was she had on me and looked away. She took the letter from my hand and I groped for the doorframe for support, head swimming as she shook the folded paper open and held it up to the light.

It seemed to take her quite some time to study it, and then her eyes cut back to me. She considered me for a long moment, then she glanced at the darkness behind me and shuffled back a few steps. 'I see. I suppose you'd better come in.'

CHAPTER 3

'Watch your step,' the woman said as she swung the door wider to let me through. 'There's a bit of a mess.'

Past the arc of the door the floor was strewn with rubble. It was hard to make it out at first in the shifting light of the lantern, but I realised that the floor was covered with books, broken pots, wooden boards and chunks of stone. My host moved through the mess in a lurch. I followed behind, picking up my skirts with cold, stiff fingers to place my feet with care. 'Uh, ma'am, are you unwell?'

She cast me a dark glance and waved me through into the kitchen without replying.

In the kitchen, I couldn't keep my jaw from dropping. It was a large room, with grey flagstones for a floor and low, dark rafters overhead; but if the hall was a mess, the kitchen was a disaster. Where presumably there had once been a table and stools, little remained but splinters.

Shelves had been torn down, with crockery and jars smashed, their contents strewn across the floor. It looked as though there'd been a brawl — or worse. Scorch-marks streaked the flagstones, as well as the plaster between the roof beams. The only thing not broken was the window, and that was doubly strange — the window was huge, set with panes of real glass that looked out into the darkness, with one side propped open a foot or so. I don't think our whole farm at home had as much glass as that one window, and I couldn't imagine how it had survived the destruction that had been wreaked on the rest of the room. I tried not to stare but she must have noticed my wide eyes.

The only piece of furniture that was largely intact was a box bed, a huge cabinet that housed a bed and could be closed in by sliding wooden doors. I say largely, because several of the panels were cracked and splintered as though something heavy had struck it with force, but it still seemed functional. It was to this that my host tottered on unsteady legs, and when she reached it she sat down hard as though she'd used the last of her strength.

I stood in the middle of the wreckage of the kitchen, my fingers laced together and my lip caught between my teeth. Something in the corner caught my eye — a metal cage, large enough to hold a person, so long as you didn't care if they could sit fully upright or stretch out their arms and legs. It was as battered as everything else in the room, dented and warped, and the door hung from one hinge as though it had been wrenched open. When I realised I was staring at it I pulled my gaze away and looked down at the floor. What in the Lord and Lady's name had I got myself into?

The silence stretched on an uncomfortably long time, and when I summoned the courage to glance up at the woman I found her still studying me with a furrowed brow.

'Well,' she said at last. 'You're not here to try and kill me, or you wouldn't have been waiting on my doorstep like an abandoned babe.'

I clasped my icy hands together 'Sorry, miss.'

'Sorry for what?'

'For causing trouble. And for waking you. Ma'am, may I ask a question?'

She gave a single nod, and I went on.

'If you didn't send for me, then who did? Someone else lived here, didn't they? Attwater mentioned her, and you said—'

'Gyssha,' she interrupted. 'She's dead.'

'I, I'm sorry to hear that.'

The woman snorted. 'You wouldn't say that if you knew her.'

I blinked at that. 'If you say so, Miss. But could she have sent for a new hire?'

'I doubt it. This isn't her style,' she said, waving the letter. 'You're a country girl, aren't you?'

I nodded.

'Thought so. Gyssha always preferred city rats to country mice.'

I lifted my head. 'Which are you, then?' I said. The words spilled out before I could stop myself.

The woman gave me a quick, fierce smile, showing lots of teeth. 'City rat, obviously. But if Gyssha didn't send for you, who brought you here? This wretched letter is about as illuminating as a candle at the bottom of the gods-damned ocean, isn't it?'

'I, I'm afraid I don't know, miss. I can't read it. I never went to school.'

She gave me a hard stare. I looked down, afraid I'd start crying again, and after a moment I heard her sigh. 'To hells with it,' she said. 'I'm too tired for games. You believe you're telling the truth, I'll grant you that. If there's anything more in there, well, it's damn well hidden and the state I'm in, anyone that skilled will get in anyway. So you might as well stay. For the night, at least. Come morning I expect you'll want to be on your way.'

There was a cold, hard lump under my heart. 'On my way where?'

'Wherever the hells you want, kid. I don't care.'

'But ...' I looked around at the wreckage and ruin. 'Please, I don't want to go home.' It was true. I was bewildered, unsettled — *scared*, I'll admit it — but I'd never get another chance to leave the farm, to have my own life. I knew it, down in my bones. 'Ma'am, maybe you weren't seeking a hired girl, but you sure could use one, it looks like. I mean, you're ill, and here you've got no fire laid, no water, no food to eat ...'

She fixed piercing eyes on me again. 'You want to stay here? With me? You know I'm a witch, right?'

I nodded. 'You ensorcelled me back there, didn't you?' I gestured towards the door.

'Yep.'

'Well, if you were going to harm me you'd have done it already. Wouldn't you?'

Her dark eyes turned sad. 'Sweet child, you know nothing about witches, do you? All right then, what's so bad about home that you'd rather stay here with a Blackbone? Aside from the fact that they apparently couldn't be bothered educating you?'

I felt my mouth open but I couldn't find the words to explain. 'I just ... I can't go back.'

She heaved a sigh. 'All right. Fine. But I don't know that I can keep you for long. Or that you'll even want to stay. I'd meant to leave Black Oak as soon as my business was done, but, well, I'll see if I can find you another position when I leave, if going home is so very bad.'

I shivered with relief, releasing a tension I hadn't realised I held. 'Thank you, ma'am! I'll start right now if you wish — would you like a fire lit? I'll fetch water if you tell me where to find it, and if you show me to the larder I'll see if I can fix you something to eat.'

She flapped a weary hand at me. 'Just settle in for the night. If you find anything worth eating, go ahead. I don't mind if you rattle around to cook, the gods-damned roof could come down and I wouldn't care. The larder's through that door,' she gestured to the far end of the kitchen, 'and that door leads out back. There's a well out there and a woodshed near the stables. Best stay out of the orchard. Really. Whatever you see out there, just don't.' She pulled herself back into the darkness of the box bed then, and as she moved I glimpsed a small, round object beside her. It took me a moment to realise it was an apple. I remembered the ghostly shape of the owl gliding past with something round clutched in its claws. 'Uh, ma'am?' I said. 'One more thing, if I may? What may I call you?'

She hesitated, one hand on the box bed's sliding door. 'Aleida,' she said. 'My name's Aleida. Goodnight, Elodie.'

'Goodnight, miss,' I said.

Even with a lantern, I didn't much like venturing out into the darkness, or even moving about the kitchen with so much rubbish over the floor. Every step carried the *clink* and *crunch* of broken pottery or the risk of tripping over splintered wood.

I wasted no time in drawing a bucket of water and hauling in a small armful of wood. I thought I could see the deep shadows of trees that might be the orchard, but I wouldn't have dared venture so far in the dark, even without the witch's warning to stay away.

In the kitchen the fireplace was cavernous — I fancied you could fit a whole ox in there if you wanted to. There was even a little bench inside of it where you could sit against the warm walls, and I hated to think how bitter the winters must be to make someone decide they needed a little seat there.

Once I had a fire lit I felt a little better, though my belly still growled with hunger. I took the lantern into the larder, and as I poked through the jars and sacks every noise seemed to ring out like the bells on temple day. From the dust that lay over every surface, I was afraid I'd find the flour full of weevils, but it was quite clean. There just wasn't much of it, or of anything, really. No eggs, milk or butter, not even any smoked sausages. But I knew how to make do. I found myself remembering the long-ago days before Ma married Lem, when it was just her and me living in the old cowshed at the back of Mrs Meecham's place. Back then we'd never had eggs or milk, and we only had treacle or molasses if someone took pity on Ma and gave her a spoonful for the sake of her little daughter. Now, hunting a bit further in the kitchen, I found a pot of lard, as well as some soda, a crock of vinegar and, best of all, a jar of honey. Good enough. I found a skillet and set it heating over the flames while I mixed up a simple batter with flour, water and lard, and a little dollop of honey, with soda and vinegar for leavening. It probably tasted pretty awful to be honest, but I ate it too quickly to notice, and my belly was happy just to have something hot inside it.

Then, exhausted and overwhelmed, I swept a patch of flagstones clear of shards and splinters, wrapped myself in my blanket and went to sleep right there on the floor.

I didn't remember falling asleep, and I didn't remember waking. It seemed that I just blinked, and suddenly the kitchen was full of light and moaning wind. It wasn't sunlight or firelight — it was a cold, frosty light, somewhere between white and blue, and the wind that stirred my hair and blanket was frigid, like a gust from the heart of winter. There were voices above the moan of the wind, too — angry voices.

I pulled my blanket tighter and rubbed my eyes, for a moment unable to remember why I was lying on cold stones instead of in my bed with little Jeb or Maisie snuggled up against me. The wind stirred the ashes of a fire, blowing smoke and grit into my face.

By the time I blinked them clear I could see the source of the light. A young man stood in the centre of the room; all white, glowing like moonlight on frost. He was tall and handsome, with thick hair and a short, curling beard, and he was angry — fists clenched, shoulders hunched, feet stepped wide. 'Help me, Ally! Why won't you help me? They need me! I can hear them crying for me, they're lost out there!'

Aleida was sitting on the edge of the bed, blanket once again around her shoulders and the heel of her hand pressed to her forehead. 'Bennett, Bennett, listen to me. They're not lost. They're dead. They've gone through the veil. They're safe there, they're waiting for you. You need to go and join them.'

'No! No! You're wrong! They're here, and they need me, but I can't do it alone. You have to help me, Ally, you have to find them. You promised me! You promised you'd help!'

'Bennett—'

'I'm not dead! I'm not! I'm not! I'm not!' The words echoed around the small chamber, a deafening noise, and I huddled down lower, wishing I could sink into the floor, wishing my blanket were thicker — a coat of armour, perhaps, or a house. Yes, a whole house between me and the apparition would be welcome right now.

Aleida's eyes flickered my way, and she made a small gesture with her hand, sweeping her fingers across the rumpled bed beneath her. *Stay down*, I took it to mean.

'Bennett,' she snapped in a voice of command. The sound made me shiver. 'Listen. I will help you. I will. But I need to get some strength back. You have to let me rest, Ben. I can't do it now, I'm too weak. Your little ones are safe, I promise you, nothing can hurt them now. When I'm stronger I'll take you to find them. Gyssha's dead, she can't do anything more to you.'

'No,' the apparition shook his head. 'No. No! NO! They're here, somewhere. I can hear them! The sound cuts me like a knife. Ally, you have to help me. You have to help me find them! Help me, Ally! HELP ME! HELP ME!'

The noise was deafening. It made my head ring like a bell but I didn't dare move my hands to cover my ears. The wind rose, the moan becoming a roar, and the wreckage of the kitchen floor began to drift across the stones. Here and there, pieces of it began to glow; splinters of wood, shards of pot, they all began to ripple with light and float off the floor, swirling around the room like a storm wrought small.

On the other side of the tempest, Aleida reached behind herself into the darkness and pulled out a club. At least, that's what I took it for — it was a stick of wood, peeled and polished and wrapped with leather. Bound to its tip was a pointed crystal; a short, squat, ugly thing, about the size of my fist. Aleida raised it and sketched something in the air, a design that hung there in floating lines of light, giving off wisps of something like smoke in violet and blue. She spoke as she drew the lines, something in a low voice, hard to make out over the moaning wind and the apparition's voice, still shouting for help. Then, with the last line, the last word, everything fell dark and silent, as sudden as a candle doused with water.

In the darkness, Aleida sighed. 'You all right, Elodie?'

I felt as cold as ice and my eyes were watering, full of grit and ash thrown up by the wind. 'Y-yes, miss,' I managed to say with a trembling voice. 'W-was that a demon?'

'No, just a ghost. I've banished him for now but he'll be back. He keeps forgetting he's dead, poor soul, and I can't make him understand that I can't help him yet. But I don't suppose that time means much to the dead.'

Next to me, the remains of the fire crackled, the coals glowing again now that the ash had been blown away and they'd been fanned by the wind. They gave just enough light for me to see Aleida's shape withdraw into the box bed once again. 'If you stick around, you'll get used to it soon enough. He comes by here a lot. But we'll have a few hours peace before he finds his way back. Try to get some more sleep.'

I stayed awake for a long time, feeding splinters of broken wood into the flames one at a time to eke out the light.

But eventually I must have fallen asleep, for the next time I opened my eyes it was daylight outside. Unfortunately the light only exposed what a ruinous state the place was in, with dented pots, shattered earthenware and cracked wooden bowls and trenchers all heaped up in drifts against the walls.

As I built up the fire and fetched more water, I tried to convince myself that the ghost and the storm of icy wind were only a dream, but as I put some water on to boil I looked around the chamber and shook my head. 'Don't be stupid,' I said softly to myself. 'You know what you saw. And this is a witch's cottage, after all.'

While the fire caught and the flames rose, I went outside for a proper look around.

The cottage was built of rough grey stone with a roof of slate, and the whole thing seemed to nestle down into the earth, as though the weight of all that stone made it sink down like a cat on a feather bed. The large windows seemed strange and out of place — I say windows, for there was one on the opposite side of the back door to match the one in the kitchen, though the shutters on that side were closed. It gave the effect of wide, staring eyes, while the slate roof overhead made a heavy, glowering brow. It wasn't a big house, but a bit of mental arithmetic quickly told me that I'd yet to see half of it.

Beyond the cottage was a field, with an orchard to the left, all of it smothered under thick mist that hid everything beyond a few hundred yards in a dull grey haze. From what I could see of the trees they were ancient, twisted and gnarled.

Nearer to the house was a pair of gardens — one fenced with wicker hurdles, though from the weeds and the chewed-over leaves it was rather neglected. The other garden was surrounded by a stone wall, set with a wrought-iron gate, chained shut. I peered through the bars, wondering why it merited such protection, but aside from a few rosebushes I didn't recognise any of the plants.

Back inside, and with the benefit of daylight, I went in search of something better for breakfast than the awful hot cakes I'd made the night before.

There wasn't much that I'd missed in the pantry. I did find a mostly empty sack of beans, which made me think of Brian the wizard, and I wondered how he was faring. Any thought of him quickly left my mind, however, when I looked behind the door to the outside, to see if anything was hidden behind there.

The first thing I found was a chunk of stone, so big that I could barely wrap my arms around it. It was filthy with dust and cobwebs, and completely covered with crystals — the largest of them was as thick as my wrist, and as long as my arm. Even the smaller ones were the size of my thumb, all clustered over the upper side of the rock in a beautiful, glittering forest of stone. Or it would be, without all that dust and grime.

I marvelled at it for a few minutes before I realised it stood in front of another door — a door that led into the half of the house I hadn't yet seen.

Gingerly, I tried the handle. It wasn't locked. I hesitated then, with my hand on the knob, dithering about whether to go inside. This pantry was pitifully small — what kind of household didn't have jars upon jars of preserved fruit and produce? Where was the cheese? The strings of onions and garlic? The barrels of apples? The sausages and bacon?

Lord and Lady, I was hungry.

The door swung open smoothly, without a creak or groan. On the other side it was so dark that I went back into the kitchen for the lantern, and lit it with a splint from the fire.

The room was half the size of the kitchen and had a matching window, glass and all. But the shutters were firmly closed, and didn't let through so much as a gleam of light.

I held the lantern high. Light gleamed off jars packed tight on shelves around the walls and I felt myself smile — this was more like it. There was a fireplace in the corner, and beside it a cabinet that held a jumble of strange and convoluted glassware. Clustered around the fireplace in a haphazard jumble were cauldrons, tripods, braziers and other odd pieces of ironwork.

There were dozens of jars on the shelves, hundreds maybe. Most were pottery, a few were glass, some were even of metal. I turned to the nearest shelf where one glass jar stood level with my face. It was three-quarters full of some pale, roundish things floating in a dark liquid. Pickled eggs? They weren't my favourite but I'd still take a few of those over the awful hot cakes. I reached for it, but as I moved closer my eyes picked out the true shape of the roundish things floating in the pickling juice. *Not eggs.* That dark brown stain that covered half the orbs was not herbs to flavour the pickle. *Not eggs at all.*

In the gleam of the lantern, ox eyes stared into the darkness around me. I jerked my hand back with a gasp. With a shaking hand I raised the lantern high. More glass jars huddled on the shelf further down, the shapes contained within made all the more ominous and grotesque by the warped and rippling effects of the glass. I wasn't sure I wanted to investigate any closer. *Well,* I told myself. *What did you expect to find in a witch's storeroom?*

I picked up my skirts with my free hand and carefully retreated. When I was back in the pantry I closed the door firmly, and returned to the kitchen. The cage caught my eye again and I turned my back to it, looking out of the window instead. 'All right,' I muttered to myself. 'Hot cakes it is.'

I mixed another batch of batter, and while I waited for the water and skillet to heat I started to clean up the ruin of the kitchen. I knew how to work quietly — back at home Lem raised hell if I made the slightest bit of noise when I got up to deal with the little ones.

The first thing to do was to haul out the wrecked furniture, or at least the bits of it that were small enough to move quietly. I hunted around for something heavy enough to prop the doors open and remembered the crystal slab.

I hauled it out, rolling it over the flagstones like a wheel, and propped it against the open door. But in the early morning light it looked sad under its filthy coat.

Well, I reasoned, I *was* here to look after the cottage. I fetched another bucket of water and a soft brush, and set to work. Getting the stone completely clean would take longer than I could spend right now, but just a few minutes made a vast difference. The crystals shone as clear as pure water, and the slab beneath them was as white as fresh snow. Still wet, it gleamed and sparkled in the sun, without a doubt one of the most beautiful things I'd ever seen.

I could have stayed there all morning, just staring at it, letting it chase away the image of the ox eyes and the other grotesqueries in the dark room, but I had work to do. I had to content myself with gazing at it at every trip I made, hauling the broken furniture outside, and glancing at it as I sorted out the bits that might be remade into something useful and piled the rest up for firewood.

I'd barely scratched the surface of the mess by the time the pan was hot and the water simmering, but I could hear my mistress stirring within the box bed. When the first dollop of batter hit the oil in the pan and started sizzling, she slid the box bed door open and peered out at me.

'Ah,' she said. 'You're still here. I'd wondered if you were going to think better of this whole mess and head home while you had the chance.'

Aleida didn't look any better by the light of day, with her skin sallow and her cheeks sunken, and her hair tangled and dull. She sat with her legs tucked beneath her and a blanket pulled around her shoulders like a cloak, leaning against the door of the bed as though she hadn't the strength to sit unsupported.

I bristled a little at her words. I was too used to Lem always assuming the worst of me, I supposed. 'I'm not one to leave without giving fair notice,' I said. The words came out sharper than I intended and I winced to hear them. Ma always said I was my own worst enemy. 'And I wouldn't leave an ill person to fend for themselves. Do you wish me to go to Lilsfield and ask for a doctor, ma'am?'

'There's nothing a doctor can do for me,' Aleida said.

When the first batch of hot cakes was ready I laid them onto a wooden cutting board for want of a plate, but when I set it down for her she beckoned me to come back and pushed half of them towards me. 'Is that teapot still in one piece?' she said, nodding to a tin kettle I'd set on the shelf.

'It'll be all right if I don't fill it all the way,' I said. 'But the tea leaves are long gone.'

'There's mint growing around the well back there. Go fetch us some?'

'Let me get the next batch on, and I will.' Once the last of the hot cakes were sizzling in the pan I hurried out and brought back a handful of sprigs. She beckoned me over so she could inspect them, and with a scowl she plucked one out and threw it into the fire. 'Those are fine. Good grief, Gyssha let this place go wild. I'm afraid to look at the orchard. Best stay out of it for now, Elodie.'

'You can call me Dee if you like, Miss. Miss?'

'Yes, Dee?'

'Who was he? The ghost, last night?'

She pressed her lips together in a thin line. 'A friend of mine. My only friend, really.'

'Did the old witch kill him?'

'No. He did that himself.' Her voice was flat, her gaze drifting off to some impossible distance. I wanted to know more, to ask about what had happened here, the scorch-marks and the wreckage. From the way she held herself, she must be injured, but she'd been quite firm in saying there was no call for a doctor. But as much as I wanted to know, I decided against asking further questions; and besides, I could put the main points of it together myself. There'd been a fight; my mistress was injured, and the old witch was dead. 'What about the cage?' I said.

Aleida cast a glance at it. 'Gyssha had her fingers in all sorts of pies,' she said. 'None very savoury. But don't worry yourself over it, I let her out.'

The tea was brewed now, and I'd found two cups that were only cracked, not shattered. 'Well, miss,' I said as I started to pour, 'I'm afraid there's not much to eat around here. There's probably a bit of food in the garden, but there's only a little flour left, and with no eggs, no milk—'

'Can you milk a goat?' Aleida asked.

'Of course.'

'Good.' She leaned back into the box bed, vanishing into the darkness. After a moment, she reappeared with a little purse, bright red, which she tossed to me. 'Here's a bit of coin. I want you to go to the nearest farm — the Sanford place — take the road back towards Lilsfield, and after about a mile and a half you'll see a track branching off to the north. It'll take you right there. Ask them if they'll give us hire of a nanny-goat in milk, and a couple of hens. I don't want to buy them, I don't know how long we'll be here, but we'll need something to eat. Actually, take your basket and see what they'll sell us. Eggs, cheese, butter, that sort of thing. Or, if you want, just take the money and run.' She shrugged. 'I wouldn't blame you.'

I fumbled the catch and scowled at her. 'I told you, miss—'

'I heard. I'm just giving you the chance to get out while you can — it's more than I ever got. And it won't be the last time I make the offer.'

I stooped to retrieve the purse. It was knitted, and made from the shiniest thread I'd ever seen. Was this silk? I'd never seen such a vivid colour outside of roses in the garden. 'Shall I leave right away? For the farm, I mean.'

'Drink your tea first,' she said. 'And, Elodie? If they won't deal with you, don't argue. Just come back here and I'll think of something else.'

The world seemed a much more cheerful place with the sun shining and my hunger sated, but it was still not enough to unwind the knots in my belly. *What on earth am I doing here?* Yesterday's heavy clouds had broken up into puffy white pillows that scudded quickly overhead, and I wondered if the sky looked the same back at Burswood Farm. Everyone would be up by now. I'd be washing faces after breakfast, checking the little ones' napkins and getting their shoes on.

For a moment I thought my heart would break for missing them. But remembering them was easier than thinking about what I'd seen in the night: the ghost of a furious, frightened man and the storm he'd summoned in the ruined kitchen. And Aleida had all but promised that it would happen again. And that was only the start of it — what about these beasts Attwater had spoken of? With everything else since I'd arrived at the cottage, it had slipped my mind to ask my mistress about them.

In the pocket of my apron, the purse bumped against my thigh with every step, and I couldn't help but wonder how much money she'd carelessly tossed my way. I'd meant what I'd said about not running out on my duties, but part of me wondered if I was making the right decision. Everything here was so different from home: the steep slopes, the dense trees, the moisture in the air and the earth; the quiet of it all, without my brothers and sisters yelling and thundering around, Lem's voice always complaining about something, Ma singing as she worked. I'd never imagined how strongly I'd miss Jeb's little arms around my neck and Maisie's tuneless singing while she played near my feet.

I plodded along, trying to ignore the ache in my legs and shoulders after yesterday's long hike, when a rustle in the bushes made me stop in my tracks.

As quick as a flash, a deer ran out in front of me. She looked at me once with soft brown eyes and then dashed away, crossing the road and vanishing again into the woods, leaping as light as a feather, as fast as a thought.

I gaped after her, my mouth hanging open like a fool, one hand pressed to my chest where I could feel my heart pounding under my stays. There were monsters in this forest, I reminded myself sharply, things that had even a woodsman like Attwater shaken. And *something* had spooked that deer.

And then, before I had time to think on it any further, I heard a voice softly cursing and the sound of someone pushing through the brush. I gripped my walking stick with both hands, for all the good it would do me, as a young man emerged from the scrub beside the road, following the doe's tracks only to step back in surprise when he saw me there.

He was tall and slender in a way that reminded me of a half-grown colt. He had thick auburn hair, brown eyes and a scatter of freckles across his nose, and in his hands was a bow with an arrow nocked to the string. 'Oh,' he said when he saw me. He lowered the bow so the arrow was pointing at the ground. 'Sorry, miss, I didn't mean to startle you.'

I hastily lowered the stick. 'It was the deer that startled me, not you,' I said. 'I'm sorry for scaring it off.' Privately, I wasn't all that sorry — the fleeting sight of her dashing across the road would have been rather spoiled if she'd had an arrow in her side. But I was a farm girl; I knew where meat came from and I did feel bad for scaring away his meal. From the looks of him he needed it, and not just for the pot — his woollen jacket was riddled with holes and patches, and the sweater beneath it was laddered and unravelling.

'Never mind,' he said. 'That's what I get for hunting near the road. And I'm glad I didn't chance a shot anyway, given there was someone walking by.' He tilted his head to study my face. 'I haven't seen you before, have I?'

'I'm Elodie,' I said. 'The new hired girl at Black Oak Cottage.'

He recoiled at that, stepping back. 'Black Oak Cottage? You ... you're working for the Blackbone witch?'

His reaction made me falter. 'I ... yes. I ...' I pulled myself in; I didn't want to tell the same blasted story all over again. Instead, I lifted my chin. 'It's honest work, and I need the job.'

'Oh.' He dropped his gaze. 'I didn't mean ... of course it's honest work — for a servant, I mean. It's not a word I'd use for the witch herself. But a body's got to eat, I understand that.'

I thought about what Aleida had said as I left — she'd been afraid the Sanfords wouldn't have any dealing with me. I was beginning to understand what she meant, and a little twist of worry tightened inside of me. What if she was right? We couldn't live on mint tea and hot cakes for ever. 'I didn't know she was a witch when I took the job,' I said.

'Oh, I get it,' he said. 'I do. I didn't mean to jump on you, I'd just worry about anyone in that place. Hey, I'm Kian. Elodie, you said?'

I nodded. 'Are you from the Sanford farm? I was told it was down this way.'

'It is. The turn-off is just a little farther along, but I'm not from there. I don't like to show my face around there much. They call me a poacher.'

'Oh,' I said, my eyes tracking to his bow again. He had a quiver hanging from his belt with just a scant handful of arrows in it, and an empty knapsack slung across his chest. He was a hunter and trapper then, like Attwater. 'Well, I won't tell them I saw you.'

'I'd take it as a kindness, Miss Elodie.'

I could have walked away, then; I had an errand to run, after all, but after the comfortless night in the cottage and the strangeness of my new mistress it was nice to linger in the sunshine. With a shock I realised that this was the longest I'd spoken to a lad my own age in years — ever since that day at the fair two years ago. Ever since then Ma and Lem had decided I wasn't fit to speak with anyone outside of the household, even when it was just the neighbours' lads come by on some errand.

I planted my feet and gave Kian a smile. There was no one now to send me away. 'I've only been here a day,' I said. 'And no one will tell me what's going on here, what these monsters are or what my mistress is supposed to have done.'

Kian glanced around. 'You have to be careful what you say,' he said, slipping the arrow back into his quiver and slinging the bow over his shoulder. He came closer, dropping his voice. 'They can possess animals, you know, and use them to spy on folk. They can bewitch people, too, and force them to do their bidding. And I've heard tales of the things that grow in the orchard there, and the gardens. Things that look like trees but no birds will roost there and no animals will graze underneath.'

I found myself nodding. 'Aleida, my mistress, I mean, she told me to stay out of the orchard,' I said.

'There used to be two witches there, did she tell you that? The old one found your mistress rotting in a dungeon somewhere. Pulled her out, made her an apprentice and taught the girl everything she knows, but the young one hated her for it, and turned on her. Folk said there was a fight, but I was off running traps over the Greyback Ridge, so I don't know the right of that.'

'Oh, there was a fight, all right,' I said, thinking of the wreckage and the scorch-marks in the kitchen. 'The old witch is gone now.'

'Is she? I wouldn't be so sure of that, not unless I saw it with my own eyes. Witches like her are hard to kill — else the folk 'round here would have done it years ago.'

Somewhere in the trees came the sound of flapping wings, and Kian fell silent, raising his head like a hunting dog.

'Maybe we should walk,' I said.

'Mm. You're heading for the Sanford place, you said? I can come with you a little way. If you like.'

I nodded, feeling a shy smile come over my lips. I liked him, and even if I hadn't, he was the first person I'd met who didn't seem too scared to talk about what was happening here. Together we set out along the track. 'What about Aleida? What can you tell me about her?'

'I've heard all kinds of tales of what she used to get up to before Old Miss Blackbone took her on,' he said, darkly. 'She was a thief and a con-artist and a gutter-tramp. She's got a tongue sharp as a whip, and a fierce temper. She's good with potions. Poisons, too. Back when my ma was still alive she bought a potion off her, after she'd been sick all winter and was coughing up blood. The potion cured her, that time; but it made all her hair fall out, and it grew back white as snow. And I hear she poisoned a man in the tavern in Lilsfield a few years back. Left a wife and five children behind.' He gave me a sidelong glance. His eyelashes were dark and outrageously long. *Wasted on a boy, they are*, Ma's voice whispered in my head. *Why don't you have eyes like that, Dee?*

'I know you said you need the work, but I don't know that I'd have the nerve to live under the same roof as that creature,' Kian said.

'Oh,' I said, making my voice sound much lighter than I felt, 'I doubt she'll go poisoning me, or turning me into a frog or anything like that. Frogs aren't much good at cooking or hauling water or scrubbing floors.'

'Ha! Well, you have a point there. But you're still braver than I am.'

The words lit a warm glow inside me, but the heat quickly travelled to my cheeks, and I hastily looked down. 'What about these monsters?' I said. 'Know anything about them?'

'Not much. Haven't even seen one in person, just the tracks they leave. They're big, though. Real big. If I come across one my plan is to run away and hope I'm faster than it. I doubt these would do me much good,' he said, laying a hand on his quiver.

We'd turned off the main road now, heading along another wagon track; and as the noise of a distant axe reached my ears Kian stopped. 'I'd better head back now, before anyone sees me.'

I turned to him, clasping my hands. 'Thanks for walking with me.'

'Oh,' he ducked his head as a flush of pink swept over his freckled cheeks. 'It's nothing. Just nice to see a friendly face. Not so many of them around here.'

I drew a deep breath, summoning courage. 'Well, maybe I'll see you again? If my mistress has more errands for me to run, I mean.'

'I hope so,' he said with a shy smile. 'Nice to meet you, Elodie.' He gave a nod of his head, and strode off quickly on his long legs. He glanced back once, with another bashful smile, and then vanished into the bushes.

I gazed after him while my heart skittered beneath my stays as his words lingered in my mind: *nice to see a friendly face*. As much as I missed my family, and as strange as it was here, maybe it wasn't all bad.

I started out again, following the sound of axes, and before long I heard a girl singing as well.

I found them just beside the path, two young men cutting wood while a girl about my age helped load the lengths into a two-wheeled cart. The lads let their axes rest as they saw me and the girl started over, waving and calling out. 'Hello! Who are you?'

After what Kian had said about being unwelcome here I wasn't sure what to expect, but the girl, round of face and with blonde hair bound in two braids, had an open and sunny smile. Then again, with my pack-basket and my dusty skirts I was clearly not a poacher, or a sneak-thief after their lambs.

'I'm Elodie,' I said. 'I'm the new hired girl at Black Oak Cottage. Is this the way to the Sanford farm?'

She ignored the question, her smile fading. 'You're from Black Oak?' she glanced back at her brothers who both edged closer, one looking worried, the other thunderously dark.

I tried not to, but all the same I could feel myself scowling. 'I'm not a witch or anything,' I said, 'I just work for one. This is the way to the Sanford farm, isn't it?'

'It is,' the girl said at last. 'I'm Melly Sanford, and these are my brothers, Ed and Bruen.'

'You have some business with us?' one of the lads blurted.

The harshness of his voice made me take a step back, wishing I'd stayed talking to Kian instead. But I had a job to do, so I squared my shoulders and looked him in the eye. 'I do. My mistress sent me to buy a goat and some chickens,' I said. 'And some food for our pantry, it's all but bare.'

The three of them exchanged glances, and Melly drew a breath. 'You'd best come talk to Ma,' she said. 'I'll walk you to the house.'

'Melly!' one of the lads said.

'Oh, hush, Ed. She's just a girl, not a witch.'

'So she says.'

'*Hush*, Ed!' She gave me another smile, though this one not half as bright as the first, and stooped to pick up a basket full of mushrooms. 'This way, miss, if you please. I'll show you to the house.'

I followed her without another word to the boys; their charms rather lacking compared to the lad I'd met by chance on the road.

We set out together, her with her basket slung over one arm, me with mine on my back. 'Don't mind Ed,' she said. 'He's only in a mood because Ma won't let him go visit his lady love, what with all the strife that's going on. Have you seen them?'

'The monsters? No. You?'

Melly shook her head. 'No, just heard them, in the night,' she said and shivered. 'Now, it's only a little way. Where are you from, Elodie? When did you come to the cottage?'

Ma would have turned her nose up at her for being nosy. I wasn't sure how to take it, myself — hearing Kian talk about how he wasn't welcome on their land had got my back up on his behalf, but I made myself push that aside. I didn't want to be the new girl who was too stuck-up to talk to her neighbours, especially when I was only a servant. 'I only got here yesterday. My folks have a farm down on the plains near the river, but I had to come away for work.' I told her about Burswood Farm and the journey up here. Then, I asked her about Black Oak Cottage.

Melly pursed her lips for what felt like a very long time. 'Is it true she's dead? Old Miss Blackbone, I mean?'

'My mistress said so. What happened? I know there was a fight of some kind ...'

'It was five or six days ago. No, six or seven, now. That's when the first of the monsters appeared.' She gave me a sidelong glance. 'We don't go near Black Oak if we can help it,' she said. 'Not since our old mule got into Miss Blackbone's orchard. How on earth did you end up working for a witch? If it's not too rude to ask,' she added with a flush

'When I took the job, I had no idea,' I said. Six or seven days? That would put it at about the time the letter arrived. Coincidence? It was all so strange I wasn't sure I could believe it had happened just by chance.

'Oh,' Melly said. 'You poor thing. I must say, if it were me in your shoes I'd have a hard time not turning around and blessed well marching home again, but I suppose that's easy to say when I'm not the one miles and miles from home. Well, I suppose the old witch really *must* be dead, she'd never bother to hire herself a servant. She cursed our old mule, you know, for eating her apples. She made him go blind. We had to sell him to a miller up in Scottsdale. Pa said it didn't matter if he was blind if all he had to do was walk in circles all day. So what's she like now? Miss Aleida, I mean?'

I held my tongue for a moment, weighing what I could say. I had enough sense to know it was a bad idea to gossip about my employer. And that went double if my employer was a witch. 'She's a bit odd,' I went with, 'but she's not been well. You must know her better than I do, though. You're her neighbour, after all.'

Melly pursed her lips. 'We'd meet her on the road sometimes, but we never really talked to her. Well, they weren't here a lot of the time — Old Miss Blackbone would be gone for months and months, and Miss Aleida would go with her, of course, up until she went away.'

'Went away?'

Melly nodded. 'A few years ago they had some sort of quarrel and Miss Aleida took off. We thought it was for good. But then she came back, just lately.' She turned to me — she was very pretty, with curling hair and large green eyes, but her face was quite serious. 'Do you know why they called the old witch Blackbone?'

I shook my head.

"Cause that's all they'd find of anyone that crossed her — a little pile of blackened bones.'

I scowled at that. 'Sounds like a tale for little children, throwing fire and whatnot.'

'Oh, but they do throw fire,' Melly said, wide-eyed. 'I've seen it.'

Her face was so guileless and innocent that I couldn't believe a word of it. She had to be teasing me. 'You haven't.'

'I have so!' She drew herself up with indignation. 'When I was little, we were in Lilsfield and the Glossops' dog started chasing me. Miss Aleida threw a fireball at it and drove it away. Bruen was there too, you ask him.'

I looked down at my feet, not sure I could bring myself to believe her. *And if she told you she saw a ghost last night? What would you say to that? Who are you to call her a liar?* 'We don't have witches where I come from,' I said by way of apology.

Melly was quiet for a few moments. 'I've heard people say that some witches help people. They make medicine and deliver babies and calves, and make charms and blessings. But they must be different sorts of witches to ours.' She shuddered. 'The day Miss Aleida came back was something I'd sooner never see again. Great-granny said she'd never seen the likes of it, and she'll be eighty next year. It was black as night, like an eclipse. It was over us but it didn't reach the Greenwood place, and that's the next farm over towards Lilsfield. Folk in Lilsfield or up on the ridge could see it better — they told us it was over Black Oak Cottage to start with and then it spread up into the mountains. All our beasts went mad. I mean, we've got a cow that Pa hand-raised since she was a day old and he had to climb into the hayloft to get away from her, and Ma had to shut our cat in a chest because it would attack anything that moved.

'Ever since then there's been ... *things* in the woods,' Melly said. 'Big things. Tearing down trees, ripping up the earth, like hogs if hogs grew the size of bulls. One of them tore into our henhouse the other night. The dogs wouldn't do a thing, we found them all cowering under a wagon the next morning. Pa and Drevin went out there thinkin' to drive it off, but they came right back in and wouldn't say what they'd seen. They made us girls and the little 'uns spend the night in the cellar while they stayed on guard.' She looked across at me, lips pressed tight together. 'I don't know your mistress, though she was kind to me when I was little. Lord and Lady know, people change, but you should talk to her if you can. See if she can do something, before someone gets killed.'

I thought of my mistress, wrapped up in blankets, weak and trembling from the effort of sitting up to talk to me, and I thought of Kian recoiling when I said I worked at Black Oak Cottage. 'I don't really know her either,' I said. 'But I'll tell her what you've said. That fight knocked all the wind out of her, though. She's right poorly, and there's barely any food in the place ...' I made myself stop there, afraid I'd already said too much.

We were at the farm now, the house built of thick, stacked logs, with a garden to one side and outbuildings scattered around. A woman with blonde hair tied into a tousled knot sat on the step, working a butter churn while a toddling boy pottered around the yard, chasing hens as they hunted after some spilled grain. A black and white dog trailed him but stopped to size me up as I followed Melly into the yard.

The woman looked up at me, but didn't stop working the churn.

'Ma, this is Elodie, she's the new hired girl from Black Oak Cottage.'

'Good morning, Mrs Sanford,' I said with a bob of my head. 'My mistress sent me here to ask if you would hire her a goat and some chickens, and some pantry goods, if you have any to spare.'

The woman looked me over with Melly's green eyes. A handsome lady. Lem would have leered at her, and Ma would have scorned her for it. 'Good morning to you, Miss ...?'

'Forster, ma'am,' I said, flushing at my lapse. 'Elodie Forster, of Burswood Farm. Lately of Burswood, I mean.'

'Will you have a cup of tea, Miss Forster?'

My belly growled just at the thought. 'I'd be delighted, Mrs Sanford.'

'Very good. Melly, go and tell Tara to bring us a pot of tea.'

'Yes, Ma.'

As Melly bustled inside with her basket, Mrs Sanford gestured to the step beside her. I was grateful to get off my feet. Yesterday's walk, a cold night spent sleeping in my clothes and then this morning's efforts had left me stiff and sore.

'Have you been in Lilsfield long, Miss Forster?' she asked.

I rubbed a hand across my eyes, feeling gritty and tired. I'd splashed some water on my face but that was the nearest I'd had to a bath in days. 'I only arrived last night, ma'am.'

'And where is Burswood Farm?'

She asked about what beasts we raised and what crops we grew, and about my family and why I left. The talking and the rattling rhythm of the butter churn helped to settle my thoughts and push the strangeness of the last day and night from my mind.

By the time I'd answered her questions, another young lass had brought out a pot of tea and a little basket of fresh scones, still warm from the oven, together with jam and cream. My belly growled at the scent of them.

Mrs Sanford broke off her churning to pour the tea, and waved me towards the scones. 'Do have one. Is young Miss Blackbone feeding you well?'

I hesitated with a warm scone in my hand. 'There's no real food in the house at all,' I said. 'And Miss Blackbone is so ill she can barely stand. I don't see how she hasn't perished of hunger and thirst.'

'Oh, witches have ways about these things,' Mrs Sanford said, her voice dark and hard. 'I daresay she managed to keep herself fed.'

I thought about something Melly had said, about Old Miss Blackbone never hiring a servant, but I still had no idea what she meant. 'Well, she must have,' I said, 'but I don't see how. And not at all well. She hasn't even had a fire, and she's very poorly.' I had to try very hard not to wolf the scone down like a starving dog.

'And how did you find her? Aside from sickly, I mean?'

I frowned while I chewed and swallowed. 'Ma'am? I'm sorry, I don't understand ...'

'Is she bad-tempered? Cruel? Do you feel she'll be a hard mistress?'

Still frowning, I reached for another scone. It was the ghost that had scared me, not my new mistress. I shook my head. 'Short-tempered, perhaps, but not bad-tempered.' I remembered her pleading with the spectre before reaching for her wand. 'And not cruel. Not at all.'

'Oh?' she said. 'Indeed? Well, people change, or so they say.'

I wrapped my hands around the teacup. After everything I'd heard that morning, first from Kian and then Melly, there was a question burning in my mind, only I wasn't sure I had the courage to ask it. I glanced towards the orange cat, sitting in a patch of sunshine with his eyes closed. Something about it felt strange, but I couldn't say why. It certainly wasn't as strange as the owl last night, carrying an apple in its talons. 'Ma'am?' I said at last. 'May I ask you something?'

'You may,' she said. She had an arch manner about her, this woman. I could tell her tongue would cut like a razor if you gave her reason to turn it on you, but I could also tell that she was willing to be patient with me.

'What has Miss Aleida done to make everyone fear her so much?'

Mrs Sanford looked away. 'Nothing to me. Gyssha Blackbone gave us plenty of reasons to fear her, but Aleida ... I thank the gods that my lads were too young for her to toy with; except for Drevin, but he had the sense to stay shy of her. I don't suppose she did anything other lasses haven't done when they learn the power they have over young men, only she had witchcraft behind her. Played with them, she did, like a cat with a mouse. Never for all that long, thankfully; the witches rarely stayed at the cottage more than a few months each year. Though Aleida was never as cruel as Gyssha was, I'll grant her that. And then when she left, I thought at the time, it was the most good sense she ever showed.'

'But Melly said she helped her once, against a savage dog,' I said.

'Oh, aye, she did. She'd do that, from time to time, lend a hand when it suited her. But never when Old Miss Blackbone could see. I never thought we'd see her again, but then there was this sad business with young Bennett and his family, Lord and Lady keep them. I suppose that's what brought her back.' She gave me a measuring look. 'Do you have witches where you come from, Miss Forster?'

I shook my head. 'No, ma'am. I met a wizard on the way here, though.'

'A wizard? Well, fancy that. I can say with truth that I have never seen a wizard.'

I could tell that she was mocking me, but I held my tongue, reaching hesitantly for another scone. When she noticed, Mrs Sanford pushed the basket towards me. 'I can see there was a fight,' I said. 'The cottage is in a fair ruin. But has no one been to check on her, in all this time?'

Mrs Sanford gave me a hard, cold look, but I steeled myself and held her gaze. 'No,' she said. 'For we weren't sure who won the fight. We knew it was the witches, of course, when the sky went dark. Afterwards, Attwater said he saw Miss Aleida coming down from the mountains ... but from what I've heard it wouldn't be the first time an old witch had stolen a young body, and I had my doubts that young lass could ever be as mean as old Gyssha Blackbone.' She took a sip of her tea; she was still on her first cup while I was on my third. 'Besides, the last time I spoke to Old Miss Blackbone she said that the next one of mine who strayed onto her land uninvited would never leave again, and I wasn't about to test her. And then folk started to see strange beasts in the forest ... by the time Attwater told us what he'd found, folk were already too scared to venture far from home.'

'Strange beasts?' I said. 'You mean ... monsters?'

Mrs Sanford gave me a steady look, lips pressed together. 'If you haven't seen one yet, Miss Forster, you ought to count yourself fortunate. There's half-a-dozen of them, maybe more, bigger than the biggest bull, with eyes that glow like firelight. And everywhere they go, they tear and crush and destroy. There's naught folk like us can do to stop them — no trap strong enough to catch them, no pit deep enough to hold them. It would take an army and their great catapults to stop them, I'd say. But unless someone does something about them, it's only a matter of time before someone gets killed.'

I nodded. 'I'll tell my mistress.'

Mrs Sanford looked me over with a faint sadness. 'You're a kind-hearted girl, Elodie Forster, but you ought not to get yourself involved in things you don't understand. The best thing you could do is turn around and head back home to Burswood Farm. If you were my lass I'd rather have you home than tangled up in these affairs.'

I caught my breath, thinking of Ma and Lucette, of little Jeb and Maisie. But I couldn't go back. I'd never get to leave again. 'I don't want to go home.'

'Whatever fights you've had, your family loves you, I can promise you that.'

It was true. Maybe not in Lem's case, but the rest of them ... But the good couldn't cancel out the bad. It wasn't like a set of scales, where one side balances the other. No, it was more like a tug-o-war, where it felt like you were being pulled apart. 'Thank you, Mrs Sanford,' I said, and I could hear the tremor in my voice. 'But I don't want to go back. I need this position, I can't afford to leave it.'

'Well, you know your own mind best, I'm sure,' Mrs Sanford said. 'But there's one thing you have to understand, Elodie: those witches may have started fighting a week ago in Black Oak Cottage, but the battle isn't over yet. Your mistress still has a struggle ahead of her, and it sounds to me that she's in poor shape to tackle it. If you do decide that this is too much for you, you're welcome under my roof, and I'll do what I can to get you home to your ma.'

I bowed my head. 'Thank you, Mrs Sanford.'

She set her teacup down with a *clink* and brushed crumbs from her apron. 'Now. What did your mistress send you here for? A goat in milk, was it? We haven't any hens right now, thanks to that beast.'

'And some food for our pantry, if you have any to spare, ma'am. Miss Aleida said she'd like to hire the goat, as she didn't know how long she'd stay at the cottage ...'

'Like that, is it? Let's say instead that she buys the beast, and we'll buy it back if she's done with it in a timely manner. We just baked yesterday, so I can give you a loaf or two. I daresay you'd like some cheese, and I have some ham and sausages in the smoker. No eggs right now, but I can give you a block of butter. And perhaps a jar of jam, too?'

Even though I was quite full of scones and tea, the thought of it all made my mouth water. 'Thank you, Mrs Sanford, and perhaps five pounds of flour too? I'd be most grateful.'

'I'll have Tara put it together while I send Drevin to bring in the goats,' Mrs Sanford said, standing up. 'As for chickens, I'm visiting my sister tomorrow, and she has some hens to spare. I'm getting some for my own flock, would you like me to see if she has any others to sell to Miss Aleida?'

'That would be very kind of you, Mrs Sanford.'

'Well, it's as much practicality as kindness,' she said. 'If she gets desperate she'll likely just take what she wants like Gyssha did. Besides, if anyone's to deal with those monsters, it'll be her; and she'll need more than what little her beasts can scrounge if she's to be strong enough to do so. Wait here, if you please, and I'll get your goods together.'

What her beasts can scrounge. I thought again of the owl. Mrs Sanford knew more about it than I did, apparently.

In short order the Sanfords had laid out enough supplies to last my mistress and I for a week, so long as we were frugal and didn't mind stale bread. They also brought out a nanny-goat for me to look over. I didn't know all that much about goats, certainly not enough to feel secure in spending my mistress's money on one, but she seemed a good beast and I reasoned that I could take her subject to Miss Aleida's approval. Given how wary the Sanfords seemed of their neighbour, I thought it unlikely they'd try to cheat her. So with that I dug out the red purse and started counting out Miss Aleida's coin.

That caused a whole other kerfuffle, since apparently no one had seen these sorts of coins before. Mrs Sanford had to send for her husband, who in turn sent for his father, who brought out a little wooden box with a delicate set of scales, and there was much to-ing and fro-ing with weighing various coins and tallying up numbers scratched in the farmyard dust. In the end, when Mr Sanford told me what he thought was the fair price, I was too lost in it all to do anything but nod and accept it; though he agreed that if Miss Aleida took issue he would speak to her about it. And so, with my pack-basket loaded and settled on my back, and the goat's lead-rope in my hand, I made my farewells and started back along the road with Melly at my side, since she had to get back to her brothers to help with their work. I was a bit worried I'd have to drag the goat the whole way, but as I turned towards the gate the nanny followed me, as tame as a dog on a leash.

'Well, I can't tell you what a relief it is to know that Old Miss Blackbone is gone,' Melly said. 'I was fair terrified of her when I was little. Granny used to tell me that if I didn't do as I was told Old Miss Blackbone would snatch me from my bed when I slept. Not that it did her any good, mind you, it just made me afraid to go to sleep. Now, tell me, have you met anyone else in the area?'

Keeping my promise to Kian, I shook my head, even though I'd liked to have found out more about the young lad. My mind was still reeling with everything I'd learned, but Melly's chatter was soothing. It was nice to talk to someone my own age, and Melly prattled on like we were old friends. She told me all about the area, who farmed where and had daughters and sons our age, though I found it hard to keep the names and homesteads straight in my head. 'Oh, and I have to ask,' she said, 'or my brothers will never forgive me. Do you have a beau at home? Someone who'll write you letters about how he'll die of a broken heart if he doesn't get to see you before the next full moon?'

I blushed at that. 'No, no, I've no swains. Even if I did, they wouldn't be writing me letters. I don't know how to read.'

'What?' Melly looked shocked. 'You can't read? I thought everyone learned how to read these days ...' She realised then, belatedly, that she might have given offence and clapped a hand over her mouth.

'Everyone does,' I said. 'Just not me.'

'Oh, well, I do hope you'll be able to come a-visiting, if Miss Blackbone gives you a half-day. We could take you to meet Tamsin Greenwood, or the Copewald girls or even head into Lilsfield.'

'That'd be grand, Melly,' I said. We'd been hearing the sound of the lads' axes for a little while now, and as we rounded a bend in the road they came into sight.

'Ah, now here's Ed and Bruen,' said Melly. 'I'd best get to helping them load up all that wood. Nice to meet you, Elodie.'

'You can call me Dee, if you like,' I said, ducking my head.

Melly grinned. 'I will then. See you later, Dee!' As she hurried away the lads glanced up, looking no happier with me than they had before, but at least Melly had a smile and a cheery wave. I returned it with one of my own as I marched past with the basket on my back and the goat trotting obediently at my side.

After talking to Kian I'd been prepared for the Sanfords to be the sort of folk who have nothing but mistrust and scorn for anyone outside their tribe. But after the way Mrs Sanford had filled my belly and heard my tale, it was hard to balance what Kian had said against my own impressions. And as for Kian himself ... I wished I could have asked Melly about him. I kept thinking about him as I trudged back towards the cottage, his dark brown eyes and long-fingered hands. I knew I had to return to my mistress, but in truth I was in no hurry to get back to the comfortless hovel and all its wreckage and ruin.

As I turned back onto the main road, something caught my eye — hoofprints. They hadn't been there when I passed by earlier. They were large ones, and deep — not as massive as the monster tracks I'd seen on the way into Lilsfield, but it was clear the horse was shod with iron and had pressed heavily into the damp earth.

It's probably nothing, I told myself. *Riders must pass by here all the time.*

But then, before I was even halfway back to the cottage, I saw a dark figure on the road ahead, mounted on a big black horse, perhaps a hundred yards away.

For an instant, I froze. Then I dived off the road, hiding behind a clump of bushes. The nanny-goat, though mildly surprised by this turn of events, happily settled in to browse on the twigs and leaves.

I crouched there for a few long moments before summoning my courage to peek out again. The black rider was still there, striding along at a measured pace. He didn't seem to notice me — a wonder, that. The way my heart had started pounding, I'd have thought they'd be able to hear it clear to Lilsfield.

After cowering behind the greenery for a few more minutes, I stole another glance. Perhaps it wasn't the same man who'd sent Brian into such a state on the Overton road. There were a lot of black horses in the world, after all. And lots of black cloaks, no matter how inky-dark or how huge the enveloping hoods. But no, I knew that figure, I knew that massive, muscular horse, with the thick, flowing mane and black feather around its hooves. It couldn't be a coincidence.

Well, I thought. *Even if it is the same man, he might not be heading for the cottage.*

Oh, who am I kidding? Where else is he likely to be going? And if there's only the one of them here, where are the other two?

I should get back to Black Oak. I should warn my new mistress, but what were my chances of getting ahead of him, what with the heavy load on my back and the nanny-goat at my side? I could leave the basket and tether the goat and then run back unburdened, but what if he saw me? He'd made short work of Brian, and him a full-fledged wizard with a university degree and everything. I was just a servant girl.

On the other hand, what if Aleida had fallen asleep again? I'd shouted and pounded on the door last night for what felt like an age, and she hadn't heard me. *Mind you, she's had some decent food since then. Well, some food, anyway. And she seemed more lively this morning than she did last night. Maybe she'll have some way of sensing that he's coming. Maybe ...*

But what good will it do her knowing he's coming if she doesn't have the strength to face him?

What good would I do by getting in the way?

I bit my lip. I couldn't just sit here and do nothing.

With one more peek, I watched the rider round the bend and head out of sight, and then I scurried back across the road, dragging the goat with me. She was rather less than willing — it must have been a tasty bush.

I had only a rough idea where the cottage lay when cutting across country, but I settled on a direction that led a safe distance away from the road and set out, as fast as my weary legs and the bleating goat would let me.

Once the road was well out of sight I cast around for a handy patch of shrubs and found one that I hoped was as tasty as the bush out by the road, and tethered the nanny to it.

I was just checking the knot of the lead-rope when I heard a twig crack behind me.

Straightening with a gasp I whirled around to find a tall, skinny boy behind me, brown eyes watching from beneath a mop of auburn curls. 'Kian!' I gasped, laying a hand to my throat. 'You scared the life out of me!'

He started to smile, to make some small joke, but then he saw the worry in my face. 'Dee, what's wrong?'

'On the road,' I said. 'There was a rider … he's bad news. Really bad. He passed us on the road up here and now he's headed for the cottage.'

Kian's dark, arched eyebrows climbed his forehead. 'All in black, on a black horse?'

I nodded. 'You saw him?'

'I caught a glimpse and decided to make myself scarce.'

'I have to get back to the cottage,' I said. 'I have to warn Aleida. Kian, I know you don't like her, but she …

she truly doesn't seem that bad to me. Not like that fellow on the road. Can you help me? Please? Just point me in the right direction to get back there and warn her.'

He studied me with worried eyes. 'I'll do you better than that, Dee. I'll take you there.'

CHAPTER 4

By the time the cottage came into view, I was panting hard, my legs burning. Kian ran like a deer, fleet as the wind, feet barely touching the ground. Not like me, with my skirts flapping behind me like laundry on the line.

Kian slowed, then halted, holding up a hand to warn me to stop. 'Hear that?' he murmured.

I listened, and shook my head. I couldn't hear a thing.

'They're around the front,' he whispered. 'This way.' Bent double and crouching low, he headed around the cottage while I bunched up my skirts and followed as best I could.

I joined him in a tangle of ferns, sheltering behind a gnarled tree, bent over so that its branches nearly swept the ground.

Sitting heavy in the saddle, the man was guiding the big black horse through the same tangled path I'd crept through the night before. It made no sense to me that anyone would tackle that approach on horseback, and it seemed the rider reached the same conclusion because he stiffly, unwillingly, kicked his feet from the stirrups and slithered down.

While he was in the act of sliding from the saddle, a patch of air between him and the house shimmered, rippling like air on a hot, still day.

By the time he was on the ground, the ripple had condensed into the image of a woman — Aleida, wrapped in a gauzy black robe. It wasn't the Aleida I knew, though. Her sallow skin had turned a heartier, golden hue, and her hair had been tamed from its bird's nest to float around her like weeds in water. Her bare feet floated a good four feet above the ground. She knew he was here, then. That made me feel a little better, but it raised about a dozen new questions in my head.

'Who approaches?' she said, her voice a dark purr.

The cloaked figure stiffened, and turned. 'You aren't Gyssha.'

'No,' she said with a chuckle. 'How terribly observant. You must be powerful indeed. Truly a force to be reckoned with.'

The cloaked man looked like he didn't know how to take that. At least, that was my impression, it was hard to tell with his face hidden in that ridiculous hood. Part of me — the stupid part of me that always had very bad ideas, and to which I tried never to listen — wondered if he would even see me if I stood up and waved my arms over my head.

Mind you, I wasn't sure my powers of sight were much better. *She said she was sick. She told me she was weak, wounded, but it was a lie. And I believed every word.* I pressed myself lower into the green ferns and ground my teeth.

'I'm here to see the Blackbone,' the man said.

'You're looking at her.'

'I mean Gyssha,' he snapped. 'Gyssha Blackbone.'

'Gyssha's gone,' said Aleida. 'There's a new mistress here now.'

The man shifted his weight from foot to foot, looking uncertain. The horse tossed its head, champing on the bit. 'Very well,' he said. 'I had a deal with Gyssha. I expect you to honour it.'

'Well, that rather depends,' Aleida said, her voice like black silk. 'What was the deal?'

'For the dryad.'

I was close enough to see her chin lift, and her eyes widen. 'Ah,' she said. 'No.'

'No?' The note of strangled outrage in his voice reminded me of Lem. As much as I was scathed over my mistress's trickery, I couldn't help but smile at his indignation. 'What do you mean, no?'

'Are you hard of hearing?' Aleida snapped. 'Or do you just have worms for brains? There is no deal. No dryad. Go.'

The rider stood still, but the horse tossed its head, as though reacting to tension it could feel through the reins. 'Do you know who I am?' the man rasped.

She blinked at him like a cat. 'Don't know. Don't care. You have your answer. Leave.'

'Or what?' he snarled up at her. 'Your illusions and phantasms are nothing to me, woman. I will have satisfaction, from your hands or from your hide.' One gloved hand dived beneath his cloak and pulled out a wooden rod as long as my arm. A third of its length was studded with crystals that glittered with light, even in the gloom beneath the trees. It was like a mace, but with spikes of black glass instead of steel. He raised it high, training the tip of it upon my mistress, and said a word, a word that sounded dark and jagged and as sharp as crushed glass.

A bolt of lightning leaped from the end of the rod with a crack of thunder. I ducked my head, clapping my hands over my ears, but not before I saw my mistress vanish — vanish before the bolt of light even reached her.

With a muttered curse, the man dropped the horse's reins. He eyed off the front door where I had waited so long in the dark the night before, and then turned on his heel and marched around to the back of the house.

Hands shaking, I scrambled up and hurried to circle around the other way, trying to remember what lay around that side of the cottage, where I could find cover.

Behind me, Kian hesitated. 'Would serve him right if someone took his blessed horse,' I heard him mutter, but then he followed me, crouching low and moving fast.

The back door slammed as I rounded the house, and the rider bellowed with rage. I couldn't see a thing, though — the walled garden stood between me and them. Still crouched, I ran to the wall and pressed myself against it, creeping along to peer around the corner.

Aleida had come out to meet him. It was the real Aleida now, I thought — but then I'd thought the last one was real, too. And she still didn't look as she had when I'd left her — her hair was sleek and smooth, her skin a hearty hue.

The rider came charging around the house and met her with his crystal-spiked club upraised. He swung it at her, a wide blow, and she raised an arm to catch it. I shrank back at the sight, imagining all those gleaming points gouging into soft flesh, but the club bounced off, leaving her unscathed as though she were wearing invisible armour. I heard a *crack*, though, and a handful of gleaming shards rained down onto the grass as the crystals shattered from the impact.

With a snarled curse he rushed her, catching her by the throat and spinning her around to slam her back against the cottage's stone wall.

I dug my fingers into the rough stone, warring with myself. I wanted to do something, to help her somehow, but how? There was nothing I could do against the rider. Even without magic, he was still more than twice my size.

'Blackbone, are you?' the rider snarled into Aleida's face. 'Killed your own mother? How did a stupid young chit like you throw down Gyssha Blackbone? You're nothing, understand? You're dirt on my shoe.' One-handed, still holding her by the neck, he lifted her until her feet dangled a foot off the ground and slammed her against the stone again. 'I came here for the dryad, and I'm going to have her one way or another.'

I couldn't look away from Aleida's face. It was red, starting to turn purple, her hands gripping the rider's huge, gloved fingers. And yet there was nothing frantic in her expression. If it had been me up there I'd have been kicking him with all I could muster, hoping for a lucky strike, but her feet were still, and her eyes … I wasn't close enough to see, not really, but it seemed to me that her eyes were elsewhere, on something behind the rider's hooded head.

'I don't know what you've done with the creature and I don't care,' the rider snarled. 'You have three days to get her to me, or I'll—'

He stopped abruptly as a shadow fell over him. A huge shape had appeared behind him, moving on oddly silent feet. I couldn't see much of it from my sheltered spot — just something dark and hulking.

The rider was still frozen when the creature swiped at him with an enormous paw. At the last moment, moving faster than I ever thought a man could move, he dropped Aleida and ducked, throwing himself to the side so the swipe passed through empty air.

The creature gave a bellow of strangled rage, a sound that made my belly clench, and I threw myself to the ground.

The rider rolled away and the beast went after him, stomping with one enormous foot. The monster was huge — at full height I guessed it would stand taller than the cottage roof, but it was hunched and stooped with a rounded back and head set low on its shoulders. Its spine was a bristling ridge, its chest deep and powerful, its forelimbs long and its hind legs squat and study. Its head was like that of a bull, with massive horns, black and gleaming, and with a wet snort it swung the wicked spikes after the rider and launched forward with a kick of its muscular legs.

One horn caught the rider full in the chest and drove him into the ground. I braced myself for his scream as the beast crushed and gored him, but there was just an eerie quiet, and the sound of tearing cloth. And the thudding of my heart, like a drumbeat in my ears.

What was going on? Had the beast killed him before he could cry out? Fingers clutching the rough stone of the wall, I leaned out as far as I dared.

Aleida was still slumped against the wall, unmoving. The beast kneeled over the body of the rider, stabbing its horns into the mound of black fabric again and again. I held my breath, hoping with all I could muster that it wouldn't turn on my mistress next. A regular bull could kill a man without breaking a sweat, and this thing was easily four times the size of any bull I'd ever seen.

At last, the creature's rage was sated, and with a snort it heaved itself up. For all its head was like that of a bull, its forelegs were anything but — they bent the wrong way, as though it had an elbow in place of a knee, and the feet at the end of them were three stubby toes, each one tipped with a hoof. It stamped these hooves into the corpse for good measure, rising up on its haunches with each blow, and each time it landed it sent up a little puff of … something. Something like dust.

Finally, the beast dropped its huge head to sniff once more at the corpse, and then it turned away from the cottage, and began to amble down the green.

I stayed frozen in place. Several long minutes passed as I watched the scene: Aleida motionless, the rider's body just a crushed pile of black cloth, with everything else still. The only sound was the thudding of my heart.

At last, I managed to unpeel my fingers from the stone. I looked around, but there was no sign of Kian. I bit my lip in confusion, but then tried to dismiss the matter — he'd probably taken off when it looked like there was going to be a fight. I had to forgive him for that — in his place I'd likely have done the same thing — but I was sorry I hadn't had a chance to thank him for helping me reach the cottage so quickly.

Now, though, I wasn't sure it had done any good.

Slowly, I crept forward, keeping close to the wall. If the beast came back, I reasoned, I'd jump over the wall and take my chances with the plants inside. But I couldn't hear the creature at all, and when I crept to the other end of the walled garden to peer down the field after it, I saw it a few hundred yards away moving slowly.

It's gone, I told myself. *It's gone, and the rider is too.* Then, with a deep breath, I hurried to my mistress's side.

Aleida stirred as I crouched by her side, her eyes fluttering open and one hand gingerly feeling her throat. There were bruises already blooming around her neck. Her skin was back to that sallow hue, I noticed, and her hair had somehow grown tangled again.

'Are you all right, miss?' I said, trying to help her up.

'Me?' she said, her voice rasping painfully in her throat. 'Oh, fine. Never better.' She was trying to sit up, and gasped in sudden pain as I slipped an arm around her back.

'Sorry,' I said. 'Sorry, sorry.'

'Not your fault, kid,' she said, swallowing hard. She leaned back against the wall with a hand pressed to her side.

I looked her over, lips pressed tight together. 'You've got broken ribs, haven't you? My brother had that once, he got kicked by a horse.'

'Yeah,' she said. 'I think so. It wasn't that sad sack, though.' She nodded towards the corpse. 'It was Gyssha.'

I glanced at the body, wondering in the back of my mind how on earth I'd clean up the body of a dead … whatever he was. But then I did a double-take — I'd expected a mauled, mangled body, torn flesh and yellow bone. Instead, what I saw was a crushed pile of torn sackcloth and … chaff? Yes, it was definitely chaff, blowing gently in the breeze. 'What?' I said. His wand, or whatever it was, was there too, but the gleaming black stones had turned dull and chalky, and were already crumbling away.

'Construct,' Aleida said. 'He wouldn't come here in person, not for first contact, anyway.'

'Oh,' I said. 'I have no idea what that means.'

'Construct. Like a big doll, kind of. It's like a vehicle for his mind, lets him come here without risking his own hide.'

'I see,' I said. 'So he'll be back, then?'

'Of course,' she said. 'Didn't you hear? Three days.'

'Oh *good*. Something to look forward to.' I looked down at my feet. 'Miss, I ... I'm sorry, I should have told you. I saw him, on the way up here, he passed us on the road. *They* passed us, I mean. There were three of them altogether.' I remembered how two of the figures had waited on the road, perfectly still, while the third came to speak to Brian.

'Three, is it? Good to know. And Lord and Lady, Dee, don't look down at your feet like you've committed some grievous sin. Unless you had some reason to think he was coming here.'

I shook my head. 'No, I didn't. It's just — with everything that's happening lately, I'm not sure I believe in coincidences anymore.'

She didn't say anything, and when I glanced her way I found her studying my face. 'Hmm,' she said. 'Well. One down, two to go. Of course, he might have something else up his sleeve, that one usually does.'

'That one? You know him? But you said—'

'Do you believe everything you hear?' she said.

I scowled and ignored the jab, glancing instead over at the remains of the rider. 'Is it dangerous?'

'Could be. There should be something at the heart of it, or inside the head.' She tried to stand, one hand on the wall for support, but as soon as she gained her feet she staggered, nearly falling again. I rushed to steady her. 'Wait! Let me do it. Really, I should get you inside, first. Are you truly not hurt?'

She scoffed as I slipped around to her uninjured side and pulled her arm across my shoulders, but then I felt her wince as she leaned into me to stand, and she was trembling like a new foal. 'Lord and Lady, you're icy cold. Best you come sit by the fire, I'll sort all this out if you just tell me what to look for.' I steered her to the door without waiting for a reply. I'd best fix her something to eat, and a hot drink too. That took my thoughts back to my pack and the goat I'd left tethered to the bushes, and inwardly, I sighed. I'd have to go back to them, and quickly.

But as I helped my mistress stumble through the door, I started shivering too. 'Good grief, it's like an icebox in here.'

'Yeah,' she said. I guided her towards her bed, where she slumped onto the mattress and then hissed with pain. Squirming, she reached under her cloak and pulled out the grotesque, club-like wand I saw her wield on the ghost in the night. As she set it aside and lay back again, closing her eyes, I just stared at it, and then scowled.

'You had that with you all along, and you didn't pull it on him?'

Her eyes opened. 'Yeah?'

'But … you let him clobber you?'

Eyes closed again. 'Yeah.'

'But—' I bit the words off before I could say any more. It wasn't my place to question her.

I turned to the fireplace, only to find the ashes and coals as cold as the grave. 'Oh, what?' I said, and then clenched my teeth to keep from saying anything more.

This is a witch's cottage, I reminded myself. *Strange things happening is the normal state of affairs around here, I should think. Might as well get used to it.* In my efforts at cleaning this morning, I'd already assembled a little pile of kindling and split wood, and I grabbed flint and steel from the mantelpiece and set about lighting the fire again. 'I'll just get this lit, and then I'll go fetch my basket and the goat, all right? I was going to make you something hot to drink, but with the fire out it'll take a bit longer.'

'Sounds good,' she said from the box bed, her voice muffled by the blanket. When I'd been helping her over to the cracked cabinet, I'd noticed the cloth was every bit as worn and threadbare as mine, and on that thought I scooped up my blanket and laid it over her as well. 'You shoulda taken the money, kid.'

I ignored the comment. 'What's a dryad?'

She squirmed to free one hand, and pointed towards the corner where the battered silver cage sat. 'It's what she had in there. Forest nymph.'

'You let her go?'

'Yeah. I didn't know she planned to sell her. Not that it makes any difference.' She was still shivering, even with the two blankets.

'What about the beast? Did you call it down?'

She nodded.

'Do you control all of them?' I asked, thinking about the Sanfords' chickens and their destroyed henhouse.

She shook her head. 'No, just the one. So far. Lord and Lady, kid, you ask a lot of questions.'

I frowned at that, and clamped my mouth shut as I surveyed the room and its chill. It would take a long time to warm this place up, even if I piled all the wood we had on the fire. The box bed was not all that close to the flames, either. Aleida was weak from being cold and half-starved, the last thing I needed was for her to get a fever on top of her injuries, what with the black rider vowing to return.

I pursed my lips, looking at the box bed. It was usually the maids who slept in a bed like that, in the kitchen where they'd be close to their work. From what little I knew of Gyssha Blackbone, it didn't sound to me like she'd be sleeping in a servant's bed. And from what I gathered of Aleida, she wouldn't have crawled into her dead mistress's bed after coming home from that fight. She'd have climbed into her old familiar bed, the one she'd had when she lived here, years ago.

I added a few more sticks to the flames, and left the room.

I went back to the hallway where Aleida had let me in the night before. There, behind the planks and fallen rocks and books from the torn-down shelves, lay another door.

I fetched the lantern from the kitchen, and eased the door open to peer inside.

The first thing I saw was the glint of gold. Gilded candle-stands stood either side of the bed, gleaming in the lamplight. The bed itself was small, little more than a low, narrow cot, but it bore a coverlet of thick, soft fur, carelessly cast aside as though the bed's last inhabitant had risen in a hurry. The walls were covered with tapestries in rich colours, glinting with gold and silver thread — the only place I'd ever seen colours like those were in the storybook Lem had bought for Lucette and the other kids, the one I wasn't supposed to touch. The largest belonged in one of those storybooks — it was a picture of a garden, and a woman in an old-fashioned dress offering a golden apple to a unicorn with its horn picked out in silver. There were gold and silver platters too, huge ones that hung on the wall like a collection of rising moons, and around the edges of the room were chests and caskets, all carved or inlaid with coloured woods and mother-of-pearl. They were stacked up like children's blocks, but the ones on top — oh Lord and Lady.

They were full of gold and silver. Not just coins, but jewels as well, and ornaments and statues, wrought in metal or carved from stone. Plates and goblets and candlesticks and anything else you care to name.

I realised I was staring, mouth hanging open like an idiot, and reminded myself what I had come here for. I swept the fur coverlet off the bed, and then the sheets as well. Under them was a feather bed and then a plain mattress of blue ticking. I gathered up mattress, feathers and coverlet and hauled them all back to the kitchen.

Aleida lifted her head when I came back into the room. 'Oh,' she said. 'I should have told you that was there last night.'

'It's not for me, it's for you,' I said, settling the mattress beside the fire. I was beginning to understand why the fireplace was so huge. 'You're going to catch your death of cold like this; half-starved, no fire, that blessed ghost waking you up every hour of the night. I bet you've had no more sleep than a mother with a new babe.'

I came to fetch her out of the bed, and at first she raised a hand to ward me back. 'No, Dee, I just ...' then she paused, looking thoughtful. 'Actually, no, that is a good idea.' She struggled up, leaving the blankets behind, and tottered over to the new bed, leaning heavily against me.

I built up the fire, set a pot of water to heat, and then set off to retrieve the goat and our supplies. I was a bit worried about our nanny, actually, afraid that something might have happened to her. It was a shabby way to treat a creature that depended on me for its food, water and all its care. I was also more than a little concerned about the dark rider lurking out there, and the beast that had destroyed his construct, but I couldn't hole up in the cottage and starve along with my mistress.

I hadn't gone far in retracing my steps, however, when I came across the nanny and my basket, the first tethered safely away from the second, only a hundred yards or so from the cottage. The nanny looked up at me with soft brown eyes over a mouthful of some tasty greenery, and gave a gentle bleat.

'Kian,' I breathed. He must have gone back to fetch them closer for me. I couldn't imagine who else would have brought them here, and I hoped he didn't think I scorned him for heading off like that. He had no dog in the fight, after all, and I was nothing but grateful. I heaved the pack-basket onto my back and gathered up the lead-rope. 'Come on then, nanny. I daresay you could use a drink of water.'

I hurried back to the cottage, and by the time I drew water for the goat, found a chain in the outbuildings for her tether and carried the basket inside and unpacked it, Mrs Sanford's scones were a distant memory. I realised then that I hadn't brought Aleida that hot drink, but when I went to check on her I found her dozing, warm beneath the fur, with the fire crackling beside her and the water simmering. So I made myself a cup of tea and a scone with butter and jam, and then went back to cleaning. It wasn't even noon yet. *Quite enough excitement for one day,* I told myself.

Lunchtime passed, and afternoon tea as well, and in between I pottered around putting the house to rights. I cleaned away the rider's remains, scooping up chaff and throwing the rags on the fire. Buried in the chaff was a strange contraption of wire, gems and metal discs stamped with strange symbols. When my fingers brushed against it I *felt* the energy bound up inside — it smarted like a spark from the fire, and left my nerves tingling unpleasantly. Gingerly, I picked it up with some twigs and left it beside the doorstep for my mistress to deal with later.

Inside, I finished clearing the wreckage from the kitchen and swept the floor clean. I found some clothes I took for Aleida's shoved into a corner — a skirt and jacket, much mended and dyed to a faded black, along with leather stays just like mine. They were filthy with dirt and what looked like dried blood, and the corset was scratched, like she'd been attacked by some wild beast. I set it all aside for laundry. Next I tried scrubbing at the scorch-marks on the floor but soon gave it up as a bad job; the black streaks looked like they'd been seared right into the stone.

Of the smashed furniture, only a couple of stools were still usable so long as you were careful not to move much once you were sat upon them. The benches and the trestles and table would need some serious repairs though.

The cottage was very old, and of a simple design that woke vague memories of the house we'd lived in when Da was still alive, though that was so long ago that I couldn't remember much at all. The door through which I'd entered the night before was in the middle of the house, with rooms to each side, but at some point the rear half of the hall had been walled off to make the pantry. Remembering the jumble of things all strewn across the floor of the entryway, I decided to sort that out next.

I opened the front door for light, and sorted through the mess, making a pile of books, and a collection of interesting rocks and crystals, every one as dusty and filthy as the one I'd cleaned that morning. It wasn't a proper set of shelves that had been torn down, just planks of wood propped on square-cut stones. I took them for salvage from some torn-down building, for they bore fragments of carving. At first the decorations seemed just pretty things, until I found a twisted, demonic face peering out at me. The sight of it made me so uneasy that when I stacked them up to rebuild the shelves I turned it to face the wall. Then I realised that one of the other friezes had a gallows strung with hanging corpses, and the carvings of flowers were all things like foxgloves, belladonna and angel's trumpet — poisonous things. When I found one with two figures hacking up a corpse with axes I stopped looking too closely at the rest of the stone blocks.

I lined up the books on the rebuilt shelves, feeling thankful for once that I couldn't read the letters, and then I turned to the crystals, which I had been saving till last. They were lovely things, pink and purple, yellow and blue and grey, some shifting from one colour to another, some opaque but with such a glassy depth to them that I felt sure that if I stared into them for long enough *something* would appear. There was an ordinary chunk of grey stone that, when I turned it over, seemed to have been shattered and then all the pieces glued together with a pale, milky rock that rippled with colour and light; and there was a perfectly polished ball as big as my two fists held together, which shimmered with blue and gold when I turned it just so. I lined them all up on a shelf, fussing with them until I was satisfied I'd turned each of them with their best face outwards. I swept the floor too, kicking up so much dust that it gave me a fit of sneezes.

Then, setting the broom aside, I found myself staring at the bedroom door. *Well,* I thought, pursing my lips. *Lord and Lady know we could use some more plates and cups and such. A goblet of gold can hold water and mint tea as well as fine wine.*

I eased the door open, and crept inside. Despite the enticement of its treasures, this room made my skin crawl. *She's like some dragon from the storybooks*, I thought. *Holed up in her lair, gloating over all her treasure. But where did it all come from? From what I've heard I doubt she came by it through honest means.*

The chest nearest the bed had a cup right on top, set with purple and green stones carved to look like a bunch of grapes. I picked it up carefully, and tried to imagine where it had come from — some grand hall, glittering with mirrors and cut glass, with hundreds of candles scattered around. Ladies in silk dresses, dripping with jewels; handsome, haughty men in crisp suits crusted with embroidery. What would it be like to drink at one of those grand parties? I'd never had wine, just the small beer we brewed at home, but all the stories talked of it. Surely it must taste divine.

But when I wrapped my hand around the goblet, the cut stones dug into my palm, no matter how I turned it. With a sigh I set it down again. Somehow, that movement started a cascade of coins, heaped up too high for the lid of the trunk to close. Hastily I tried to stop the avalanche of gold and silver, only for a necklace set with a blue stone to fall into my hand.

The moment my fingertips brushed the stone a wave of gut-wrenching sadness swept over me, the breath *whooshed* from my lungs and my throat closed over with that feeling that you get when you've been crying so hard you feel like you'll choke on your tears. I thought of the night Ma had told me I was leaving, that I was being sent away, and how hard I'd cried in the darkness after everyone else had gone to sleep, terrified of leaving even though I knew I must. I wasn't sure I'd ever cried harder in my life than I did that night, but this felt worse; it was a deep, soul-wrenching sadness, an inescapable and undeniable knowing that something precious was lost forever and that nothing would ever be the same.

Suddenly my hands were shaking like a leaf in a gale, and before I could do a thing about it, while the wave of crushing sorrow was still passing through me, the stone and its fine chain slipped through my fingers and tumbled to the floor.

I stood there, still as a statue, hands still trembling, my face wet with tears and my throat still choked half-shut. The overwhelming sadness was gone, though I could still feel the effects of it. The breath in my chest hitched and gasped, as though I'd had a fit of sobbing, and I wiped tears from my cheeks with the back of my hand. *What in the Lord and Lady's names just happened?* Was it a trap, a curse of some kind that Old Miss Blackbone had left to protect her treasures? Or was it something more?

The world around me seemed to stretch and warp and then snap back into place, and at once I remembered that this was no story, with a chest of riches for the hero to find. *It's all stolen,* I thought, looking around at the gold, the jewels and the chests. *Stolen, looted, hoarded, kept as trophies.* And the sadness and despair bound up in that sky-blue gem? With a sickening twist of my gut I realised it must be another kind of trophy, a memento of grief and desolation.

I turned on my heel and marched out of the room, pulling the door firmly closed behind me. I'd rather drink from chipped cups and eat from cracked bowls than take my food and drink from treasures imbued with so much suffering. In fact, I'd rather starve.

I was working in the garden when I heard Aleida stirring. I'd left a light meal by her bed, just bread and butter with some cheese and smoked sausage, and a scone with jam. It was near the middle of the afternoon, and she came outside to eat it, joining me on the back step.

The garden had been sorely neglected, but I'd salvaged enough for a pot of soup and was sitting on the step with a board on my knees to cut it all up. Back at home my little brothers and sisters would turn up their noses at vegetables that had been gnawed by rats and rabbits, but I remembered my time with Ma, long before Lem had come along, before all the little ones had stolen her away from me. Back when we'd been just a starving widow and her child, folks sometimes took pity on us and gave us the rejects from their gardens. If I'd been older I'd have felt the shame of it, I'm sure, but back then I'd loved helping Ma cut the vegetables up, mouth watering at the thought of the soup we'd make from the wilted and chewed-up scraps.

'Is that dinner?' Aleida said, leaning over to peer into the pot. 'You've been hard at work. I can't believe you've cleared the house out already.'

I was never sure how to respond to praise. 'I've done about as much as I can inside,' I said. 'The table and benches could be salvaged, maybe, but I don't know anything about working with wood. And most of the crockery is just fit for the trash heap. I ...' I felt myself grimacing. 'I thought we might be able to use some of the things from the other room ...'

I trailed off, and Aleida raised her eyebrows. 'Gyssha's bedroom?'

I nodded. 'But I, I ...'

She chewed a mouthful of bread and cheese before she spoke again. 'Best to leave all that alone, Dee. Gyssha had some rather odd amusements. And she always liked her little mementos.'

'Is it cursed? All that treasure in there, I mean?'

'Might be. This place is covered with little traps and tripwires and curses against anyone who comes sneaking in. It's going to take me a long time to unravel everything.'

The thought of more ... *things* like the pendant all around me made me shiver, and it was a few moments before I could muster myself to speak again. In the silence, Aleida set her empty plate aside and picked up the contraption I'd dug out from the rider's body. When I set my knife down for a moment, she picked the blade up and levered the wires apart, and did something to whatever lay within. My ears popped, and there was a smell like thunderstorms and hot iron.

Aleida tossed the contraption aside and handed the knife back.

For a moment I couldn't say anything at all. I didn't want to know what she'd just done, I decided. It was none of my business. So I reached for the other matter that had been bothering me, instead. 'Miss?'

'Mm?'

'Does the cottage have a bath? Only it's days now since I've had a proper wash.' After all that time on the dusty roads, and all the cleaning today, I felt truly filthy.

She shook her head. 'No bath. But there's a stream down past the orchard. That's where I used to go, when I lived here.' She glanced up at the sky. 'Best to head down before the sun drops any lower, while the water's still warm. But I'll warn you, even at its warmest it's pretty blessed cold.'

I bit my lip. There were monsters out there, *and* the black rider and his construct. The idea of stripping off in an icy stream far from shelter had very little appeal. Aleida must have guessed at my thoughts. 'I'll come with you, I'd like to clean up, too. We can keep watch for each other, all right?'

It wouldn't be my first choice. In fact, it was a long way from my first choice, but I'd asked for a bath and I wasn't sure how she'd take it if I turned her down. Who knew when I'd get another chance, anyway? It did seem strange to stop and have a bath at this time of day, but I wasn't about to argue.

First, I went inside to fetch a change of clothes and a bar of soap from the pantry, and Aleida called after me. 'Dee! Bring my wand as well, would you?'

'Yes, miss,' I called as I hurried inside.

I stopped dead in the middle of the kitchen. The fire was out again, and once more the room was as frigid as a winter morning. I growled under my breath as I went shivering to the box bed.

After my other unpleasant surprises inside the cottage, I tried not to look too closely at what was inside the large wooden cabinet, but I failed utterly. The bed was rumpled and badly needed an airing, but that was no surprise. There was a little shelf that ran around the inside of the cabinet, and upon it were a few pieces of jewellery, some silver rings and a couple of chains, glittering at me in the dark.

Lying on the rumpled bedclothes was the club I'd seen Aleida wield to banish the ghost in the middle of the night. *No,* I told myself, *not a club. A wand.*

It was hard to think of it as anything but a club, though, its proportions were so grotesque. The head of it was a huge crystal, so short and fat that it was almost square, streaked through with dark grey wisps, like smoke. It was hafted onto the shaft with black wax or pitch and tied down further with leather thongs.

Outside, she took the wand from me and tucked it away somewhere under the blanket, then stood.

I looked her over with narrowed eyes. Last night, and early that morning, she'd been doddering on her feet like an invalid, and after facing the black rider she'd seemed even worse.

'What?' she said.

'What did you do to the fire?' I said. 'It's like an icebox in there again. Did you, I don't know, suck all the heat out of it, or something?'

'Yep,' she said, turning away. 'It's only a short-term solution, but it'll keep me on my feet for a little while. So long as I don't have to do anything else.'

'Anything else? Like, if the rider comes back?'

'Yeah.' She started walking. 'Let's go through the orchard, I haven't had a proper look at it since I came back.'

I trailed after her with my bundle of clothes. 'Uh, do you want me to fetch you something clean to wear?'

'I don't have anything else,' she said. 'Not here. I hid my packs before I came to face Gyssha, and I haven't been able to go fetch them. I might send you out for them tomorrow.'

I wasn't sure I liked the sound of that, but I didn't have the energy to argue.

For all she was steadier on her feet, she still set a slow pace, and it was easy for me to catch up to her, even if her legs were longer than mine. 'Miss?'

'Yes, Elodie?'

'What are all these trees? I mean, I can see there are apples and pears over there, and here's an almond and a walnut, but what is this one?' I pointed at a tree ahead of us, which looked something like a pear tree but not quite — the leaves were serrated at their edges, so much that they seemed frayed, and the bark was all wrong, knotted and knobbly like skin covered with warts.

Aleida glanced up. 'That one? Choke-pear. Don't touch it.'

'What about that one?' I pointed to a tree on the other side of the path.

'Hearts-blood. It's a type of apple. Guess what the juice looks like. Go on, guess.'

'Clear spring water?'

She chuckled. 'Don't touch that one, either.'

'Melly Sanford told me that their mule broke into the orchard and Old Miss Blackbone turned him blind,' I said. 'Is that true?'

'Might be,' Aleida said. 'Or it might be the poor dumb beast ate the wrong thing. As likely to be one as the other.'

The trees made me uneasy. The choke-pear wasn't the only one that looked diseased, and others were frankly menacing. One of them, a huge, gnarled and twisted thing at the heart of the orchard, looked as though it had never been pruned. Aleida stopped to look it over, scowling, and then set out again, circling well around it as though to stay out of reach, though I could see the remains of an older path that cut much closer under the low, sweeping branches. 'Stay well clear of that one, Dee.'

I wasn't game to ask why. 'What did Miss Blackbone use these for?'

'Well, some of them are medicinal, if you prepare them the right way, or work the right spells. But a lot of them are just poisons. Gyssha liked her poisons,' she added with an icy chill.

'Will you get rid of them?' I asked.

Aleida stopped again, and I wondered if I'd just put my foot in my mouth. But she just stood, her head tipped back as she gazed up at the trees. 'No,' she said at last. 'I don't think I was called back here to destroy all this. Gyssha didn't plant them all, you know. Some of these trees are older than her — much, much older. It's not for me to tear down what others have built.'

Past the orchard, the ground sloped downward, in a little valley with a stream at the bottom, exactly like she had said. There was a pool just right for bathing in, with a little dam of rocks built up to trap the water, and some larger ones scattered around to soak up the sun and dry wet skin.

I hung back, expecting my mistress to go first. Instead, she sat herself on a large rock, wrapping the blanket around her. 'You first,' she said. 'I need a rest.'

'As you wish, ma'am,' I said. 'I'll try to be quick.'

'I don't doubt it,' she said. 'That water's blessed cold.'

She sat, not with her back to me exactly, but with her shoulders twisted away and her head held high, scanning the hills and forests around us. It was a pretty spot, I grant you, with velvety green grass running down to the edge of the stream. The far slope was a little gentler than the one we'd come down and the ground was clear for several dozen yards before a dense forest took over. I couldn't help but think that anyone or anything could be up there, hidden in those trees, and I wondered if Kian was still in this neck of the woods. I reminded myself that no one would dare spy on a witch out here, not after the tales I'd heard about Old Miss Blackbone; and I sat down to take my boots off. 'What if that fellow comes back again? Or if one of those *creatures* comes stumbling by?'

Aleida cleared her throat, and pointed across the field to a stand of trees in the middle distance. I squinted where she pointed — at first I couldn't figure what she was looking at. But then my eyes picked out a silhouette under the tallest of the trees, something dark and hulking. Then I saw the horns, and recoiled with a yelp. It was the bull-headed thing that had destroyed the rider, sitting patiently under the tree like a sentry. 'Lord and Lady ...'

'It's just a construct, Dee. Think of it like a big doll.'

'A big murdering doll with horns that could skewer a cart-horse, you mean,' I said.

She chuckled. 'If you like. Hop in. Sunlight's wasting.'

The water *was* cold, even after being warmed by the sun. When I stepped in, I couldn't keep from gasping at the frigid chill of it. I couldn't imagine bathing down here at the crack of dawn.

'It's not so bad once you get used to it,' Aleida said.

Or maybe we could buy a tin bath at the general store. I'd even spend my own money on it — once I had some, that is. I'd have to fetch some more plates and cups and so on for the cottage soon, anyway. 'Who made the monsters? Gyssha?'

'Who else? Some people sew beside the fire at night, or knit socks or blanket squares. Gyssha made monsters.'

'But why?'

'For defence. Her own personal army. There's probably hundreds of them out there.'

It wasn't a pleasant thought.

I held my breath and ducked under the water to wet my hair. I came up again with another question. 'What if that fellow in black tries to take it from you?'

'He'd have to fight me for it. But he wouldn't, he'd just take another one, or two, and use them to keep it occupied. It'd be harder for him than it was for me, because I'm Gyssha's kin and he isn't, but he could do it. Probably already is.' She was leaning back on one hand and staring out at the forest with her blanket and skirt wrapped tight around her, as though she was sitting in a freezing wind instead of the warm sun.

'May I ask you something?' I said.

She laughed. 'Dee, you've been doing nothing but. But sure. Keep going.'

She had a point, there were any number of questions bouncing around in my head. 'Why did you come back? Melly Sanford said you ran away years ago, and from what I hear of Old Miss Blackbone, I can understand why. But why did you come back?'

'Someone had to put an end to it all,' Aleida said. Her voice had changed, the laughter of a moment ago gone, leaving her sounding flat and distant. 'And it was only two years ago that I left. Not all that long, though I can see it would seem that way to young Melly.' She shook her head then, and raked her hair back from her face. 'No, ask me something else.'

Her words had an air of command; at least, I didn't dare take it otherwise. I remembered what Kian had said, about her poisoning a man in the tavern in Lilsfield, and for a moment I thought of asking her about that, but good sense stopped me. 'Who wrote the letter that brought me here?' I asked instead.

'I can't answer that one either, though I mean to find out. Got another one?'

'What are you going to do about these beasts? And the black rider?'

She sighed. 'I'm working on it, Dee.'

'But are you strong enough?'

She turned to me, and I immediately worried I'd been too impertinent. 'Let's hope so.'

'If, if I may, miss ... what happened to you? I know you're ill, but if you can't heal yourself and a doctor can't help—'

'I'm not ill,' she said. 'I'm cursed. Look, I confronted Gyssha, and we fought. She lost. But we witches have a lot of power bound up in us, Elodie, in blood and bone and breath. Power is never created or destroyed, so when Gyssha died it had to go somewhere. She turned it into a curse — a death-curse. She put all she had into it. Well, that and the fact that she kind of pummelled me before it got that far.'

'And is that's why you're so weak and ill?'

She nodded.

I decided I was as clean as cold water and soap was going to get me. I clambered out of the water, wringing out my hair. 'I'm all done.'

'All right,' she said with a nod, and heaved herself up.

I knew it would be rude to stare, but I couldn't keep myself from watching from the corner of my eye. Beneath the blanket she was wearing only a shift of linen, dyed black, with a leather belt over it to hold the ugly wand. Setting belt and wand aside, she pulled the shift off over her head and left it on the rocks before wading out into the water.

I dried myself quickly with my old shift before pulling on my new one, and set to untangling my hair with my rather toothless old comb. I kept watching the hills while Aleida soaped and rinsed her hair, and I wondered what the day was like back home, if the little ones were still asking about me, and if Lucette had lost her temper yet. I wondered if Maisie's tooth had finally come through, and if Jeb had found the little wooden horse he'd lost before I left.

'Elodie?' Aleida said quietly from the stream.

I realised there were tears on my cheeks, and I hurriedly dashed them away, blinking my eyes to clear them. 'I'm sorry, miss.'

'Dee, you have to stop apologising when you haven't done anything wrong. What's the matter?'

I drew a breath, trying to steady myself. 'I just miss my family. My little brothers and sisters.'

'Ah. It must have been hard to leave them behind.'

Something the black rider had said was pressing on my mind, brought up by her comment about kin a moment ago. 'Miss?'

'Mm?'

'Was Gyssha really your mother?'

She burst out laughing at that, and I felt myself flush. 'Good grief, no.'

'But the rider said—'

She didn't let me finish. 'Ah, I see. No, that's what we call the ones who teach us. She was my mother in the craft, I was her daughter. That makes us kin in our world, I have her last name, after all.'

'So … do you have another family, somewhere?'

She gave me a narrow-eyed glance. 'Nosy today, aren't we?'

My flush deepened. 'Sorry, miss.'

Aleida ducked to rinse her hair. When she emerged, wiping water from her face, she shrugged. 'When I left Gyssha, I went to see if I could find my mother and my sisters. But they were gone, and no one could tell me where.'

'Maybe they got married,' I suggested.

Aleida gave a humourless smile. 'Oh, I doubt it. My family wasn't the marrying sort. My mother was an alley-cat, you see, and she expected her daughters to follow her trade.'

I felt myself frowning. 'An alley-cat? What's that?'

Aleida looked across at me. 'A whore, sweetling.'

'Oh,' I said, and looked down at my interlaced fingers, thinking how I must look like an idiot for not knowing what she meant. The heat on my cheeks made me think of Lem, and how he would have crowed with glee over something like this. Not knowing meant he could berate me for being stupid but if I had understood the word he would have shouted at me for being so filthy as to know such a disgusting thing. 'My stepfather used to call me those kinds of names, before Ma threw a fit and made him stop.' It was one of the few times she'd stood up for me against him. It had surprised him so much that he'd obeyed. He did love her, deep down, I thought. It was just me he couldn't stand.

'And he's the reason you don't want to go home, even though you miss your little sibs?'

I nodded in silence.

'You're not pregnant, are you?' Aleida said.

'Oh, Lord and Lady, no!' I blurted out, the flush creeping back. 'It's nothing like that! He just … he hates me, because I'm not his, you see. Everything that goes wrong is my fault, everything I do is bad, and I'm useless and stupid and lazy.'

'Oh,' Aleida said. 'One of *those*.'

I glanced up to find her looking at me thoughtfully, and had the immediate fear that she didn't believe me. 'I'm really not pregnant. I, I couldn't be.'

'Oh, I believe you. I'd know if you lied to me. But you know, if it were something like that, I could do something about it. Something about him.'

I shook my head. 'It's not that, I swear. He's just — look, you know how some beasts are just bad-tempered? They'll step on your foot if you get near them, or make their tail all mucky so they can slap you with it? That's all he is, just an ornery beast who'll shit all over himself in the hopes of getting a little of it on you.'

She laughed at that, a long, bubbling peal as she rose from the water, wringing out her hair just as I had. 'You know, Elodie, you don't talk like someone who's never had a lick of schooling.'

I didn't know how to reply but she said nothing else, letting the silence stretch out until I felt compelled to speak. 'I used to listen in when my brothers and sisters practised their lessons. Ma would help them at the table while I got on with the cooking, and if I worked quietly I could listen in. And then when I had charge of them if

Ma was out, I'd make them sit and read a page to me if they got into mischief.' We'd always had a few books, and old copies of the Almanac and such. Lem always wanted to appear educated, and his children, too. But I wasn't counted among them.

'Sneaky,' she said with a faint smile. 'I like it.'

Sneaky. I'd heard that before, usually with disdain, but there'd been none of that in Aleida's voice. Before she could ask any more awkward questions, I tried to send the conversation elsewhere. 'Is that why you decided to be a witch? So you wouldn't have to … be like your ma?'

'I never thought that far ahead,' she said. 'Ma and my sisters were always at me to bring in money, so I turned thief. I got caught and would have got my hand cut off for it, if Gyssha hadn't pulled me out of the jail. She gave me the choice, be her apprentice or stay in the cell and wait for the axe. You can imagine it wasn't a hard decision.'

She stepped out of the water and reached for her shift, shaking it out as she wrinkled her nose. 'I suppose it'll have to do. Tell me, Dee, do we have any of those scones left?'

'A few,' I said. 'They'll need to be eaten up today, or they'll be hard as rocks by tomorrow.'

'Oh, I doubt there'll be any fear of that. We'll head back to the cottage, and then I need you to light that blasted fire again. I've got an idea about our friend in the black cloak, but I need to talk to some people first. Put the kettle on, Dee, and I'll invite them around for tea.'

CHAPTER 5

I didn't ask any more questions as I bustled about the cottage, sweeping up the old ashes, lighting a fresh fire and drawing more water. Meanwhile, Aleida disappeared into Gyssha's bedroom and emerged again with clothes she must have scavenged from the old witch's things, although they didn't look as ill-fitting or old-fashioned as I'd have expected. She found her stays where I'd left them and gingerly pulled them on over her tender ribs and tightened the laces with a small grimace. When she noticed me watching from the corner of her eye she tweaked the skirts and said, 'I remembered I left some things behind when I ran off.'

'It's a wonder she didn't burn them,' I said.

'Oh, there'd be no fun in it if I wasn't here to watch.' Then she fell still, cocking her head to one side.

I immediately went tense. 'What is it? Is the rider back?'

'No, no. Just someone tripping a wire down the end of the field. I think our guests are here. Come out and meet them, Dee.'

It was late afternoon now, and the sun was sinking. The back of the house faced east, so the field was already in shadow. About halfway down, facing the house with a bow in his hands, was a familiar figure — a tall, lean man all in brown, with a floppy-brimmed leather hat. Attwater.

It took me a moment to realise that the bow he held had an arrow nocked to the string and held at half-draw.

Aleida didn't seem to notice. She paused at the doorway to scoop up the walking stick Attwater had given me and started down the meadow towards him. She was walking more slowly than she had earlier, I noted, and had started to limp. *I'd best be sure to bring in some more wood later,* I told myself.

'Attwater,' Aleida said by way of greeting.

'What do ye want, Blackbone?' the woodsman growled.

'I just want to talk,' she said. 'To both of you.' She glanced towards the orchard. 'Come on out, Laurel. I know you're there.'

There was no movement from the trees, and Aleida sighed. 'Come on. Don't make me pull on strings. This is supposed to be a friendly get-together.'

'If ye wanted us friendly ye shouldn't have put yer mark on her,' Attwater said.

Aleida turned back to him with a cool, measured gaze. 'If I hadn't, would you be standing here now?'

He didn't reply.

'I told you I'd free her, and I did.'

'And then ye branded her like some gods-damned cow.'

Aleida bared her teeth, an expression vaguely like a smile. 'You'll forgive me for having some caution. You know what I've had to deal with.'

After a moment, I saw something stir among the trees, and then a creature stepped out into the meadow.

She was all green, brown and gold, and clearly a she, if you know what I mean. Impossibly tall, and slender as a willow. Her top half looked human, if you overlooked the enormous eyes, skin speckled like the bark of a young sapling, and hair that was a tangle of leaves and supple stems. Her lower half, though ... she had the legs of a deer, and balanced on delicate hooves as she stepped lightly across the cool, wet grass. She looked like something out of a dream. Despite Attwater's words, I couldn't see anything on her that could be a mark or a brand, but then maybe it was something that *couldn't* be seen.

As she drew near, Aleida gave her a polite nod. 'Laurel.'

The dryad nodded back. 'Witch.'

Aleida turned to me. 'Dee, could you bring us some tea? For yourself, as well.'

There was an old tree stump to one side of the meadow, and a few logs scattered around it by way of seats. By the time I returned with a tray loaded with a teapot, cups and scones, the three were sitting stiffly around it. I set the tray down, and, glancing at my mistress for permission, poured a cup for each of us.

'How are you, Laurel?' Aleida said, cradling the cup between her hands.

'As well as can be expected,' the dryad replied. 'And you?' If the words seemed friendly, their tone was not. Her voice was strange, lilting and liquid, not a human sound at all, though I could understand her quite clearly.

'I've been better.'

Attwater picked up his cup, and frowned dolefully at the tea inside.

'Go ahead,' Aleida said. 'I didn't call you here to poison you.'

'Ye said ye wouldn't use that blasted mark—'

'I said I wouldn't use it unless I had to!'

'And now it's what, a week later?' He cast a sour glance my way. 'I should have walked away when Grigg Anderson asked me to see that lass out here. She'd have been better off as a pot-girl in the tavern than out here with ye.'

I knew it wasn't my place to talk, but I couldn't let that pass. 'Well I do apologise for the imposition,' I said, keeping my voice sugary sweet. 'But I'd have found my way out here with your help or without it. And where I come from we take care of our neighbours when they're ill or injured; we don't leave them to starve and thirst and freeze.'

Attwater tipped his head back to look at me. 'There's the proof ye don't have witches where ye come from, lass. Would ye walk into a lion's den to check up on the beast if ye hadn't seen it for a few days?' He turned back to Aleida. 'The lass has no idea what she's getting herself into.'

Aleida set her cup down with a sigh. 'I've tried to send her off with money in her pocket, but she won't go. And given how she got here, I'm not sure I can get rid of her. And so here we all are. Drink your damn tea, Attwater. I'm trying to be nice here, could you at least *try* to work with me? I haven't even touched this food, it came from the Sanford place this morning. You know I'm telling the truth.'

Attwater paused. 'These are Tabby Sanford's scones?'

'Every last crumb. Seriously, Attwater. If I wanted to poison you or bewitch you, I'd just do it. I don't have the time or the energy for games right now.'

He shrugged, and reached for a scone and the pot of butter. 'Fine, then. So what do ye want?'

She picked up her cup again and took a slow sip. 'I've found out what Gyssha meant to do with Laurel.'

'And?' He buttered a scone, and Laurel lightly touched his arm. Her fingers, I noted, were long and slender like twigs, studded here and there with buds like green and gold jewels. She reached for the scone he'd just buttered, and he handed it over without a word.

They were lovers, I realised, and suddenly I understood why he'd come armed and ready to shoot.

Laurel took a small bite, and then pulled a displeased face. Still, she chewed and swallowed, but handed the remains back to Attwater and reached for her teacup.

'She made a deal with some warlock from down on the plains,' Aleida said. 'He's come to collect.'

The two across the makeshift table shared a glance. 'And?' Attwater said again.

Aleida laid her hands on the stump, spreading out her long fingers. 'You might have noticed I'm not exactly in great shape. I can deal with him, but I need to get close, get inside his guard. I'm going to need some help.'

Attwater blanched. 'Lord and Lady. I think I see where this is going, and I don't like the look of it.'

Beside him, Laurel shook her head with a rustle of leaves. 'No.'

'Would you just let me—'

'No!' Laurel said. 'You want to put me back inside that cage?'

'Just as a ruse,' Aleida said. 'I'll give you the damn key. You too, Attwater.'

'And then what?' Attwater growled. 'Ye think he won't be expecting ye to betray him? Ye'll lose her just like ye lost Bennett and Rosalie—'

Aleida thumped her fist on the tree stump with a snarl. 'Don't you dare lay that at my feet! Don't you dare!' She heaved herself up, hands on the table. 'I tried to save him! I tried to save all of them, but they wouldn't listen! I told him to get out of here, I gave him all the money I had, but he just wouldn't listen. No one ever listens.' She hung her head, black hair draping across the ancient, scarred wood.

There was silence, and after a moment she sat again, gingerly, as though every movement pained her. Whatever it was she'd taken from the fire to sustain her was wearing off, I realised, and fast.

With a sigh, she pressed a hand to her forehead. 'Look, I know what happened to him. To them. After Bennett threw himself off the falls, his spirit came to tell me what happened. What she did. That's why I came back to this gods-forsaken place, to deal with her. To end it.' She tossed her hair back, lifting her chin. 'No one else had the guts to face her, to put a stop to her evil. Just me, on my own.' She scowled, dark as thunder, and jabbed a finger at the pair of them across the table. 'So don't you sit there and harp at me for throwing down a mark here and there for a bit of backup. Because I'm doing this on my own, and I've never had anyone to watch my back, all right? Not like you do.'

Attwater bowed his head. 'Sorry, lass. That was a low blow, I admit it.'

Aleida looked away with a hand over her mouth and tears in her eyes. 'He was your kin, I know. But I mourn him too.'

'The last of my kin, really. Him and the little ones. But I do know it was Gyssha's doing, not yers. Well, at least she can't hurt anyone else.'

A flicker of something crossed Aleida's face then. I couldn't be certain what it was, but I tucked the thought away to deal with later.

'So what's yer plan?' Attwater said. 'Hand her over, then punch him in the face and let her out again?'

Aleida shrugged. 'Well, she'll let herself out if I give her the key, but more or less.'

'Too obvious. He'll be expecting it.'

'Have you got a better idea?' Aleida demanded. 'One thing you ought to consider here is that if that bloody warlock manages to kill me, he'll claim this territory and everything in it.'

Attwater and Laurel shared a glance. 'But the fact remains, lass,' Attwater said, laying a hand on Laurel's delicate arm. 'The answer's no. And I *know* ye're not strong enough to force her into that cage, mark or no. It's not that we don't trust ye—'

'Not *just* that we don't trust you,' Laurel interjected.

'— It's that we don't think ye can pull it off.'

Back in the cottage, Aleida pressed her forehead to the marble slab of the mantelpiece. 'He's probably right, you know.'

I glanced up from the pot I was stirring, feeling worried. 'Don't talk like that.'

'No, it's true. A direct confrontation is what got me in this state in the first place. I need to find another way.'

My hand tightened around the wooden spoon, and I wished the knot in my chest would loosen, just a little. 'You'll think of something.' I summoned the courage to speak further. 'Aleida?'

'Mm?'

'For what it's worth, I've got your back.'

She dropped a hand to my shoulder, and squeezed. 'You do, don't you, kid? I'm glad of it. I just hope I don't get you killed as well. There's enough blood on my hands as it is.'

I slept like the dead that night — at least, until Aleida shook me awake, sometime well past midnight. 'Dee! Wake up!'

I pushed myself up with a gasp. 'What? What is it? Is the warlock back? Beasts?' Rubbing bleary eyes, I saw her sitting on her heels beside the fire, which was still burning for once.

Aleida cocked her head, looking at me with curiosity. 'No, I've got an idea. I just need your help.'

I glanced at the window. 'But it's the middle of the night!'

'Yep. I do my best thinking at night. Now get your boots on and come outside.'

It took me a few moments to pull on boots, stays and a dress, and then wrap a blanket around my shoulders for a cloak. It was chill outside at night, and very dark. The stars drifted in and out of sight as clouds scudded overhead.

Aleida was already outside — at least, I hoped that was her I could hear rattling around in the outbuildings. After dithering for a moment on the doorstep, I went back inside for the lantern, and then found her in what looked like an ancient, unused stable, cluttered with old tools, old saddlery with the leather cracked and crumbling, fraying sacks and bundles of rags, and countless other things. It was even darker inside than out, but I found her fossicking through the hoarded trash without so much as a lantern.

She threw a coil of rope at my feet where several others already lay, and then glanced up with a small frown. 'Oh,' she said. 'I forgot about that.'

'About what?' I said, still feeling half asleep.

'That you can't see in the dark. I'll take care of it, just let me duck back inside.' She picked her way back through the rubbish. 'Oh, and fetch that axe down, would you?' she said with a gesture to the jumble of tools.

The axe was resting on a couple of pegs driven into the stonework, and I lifted it down with some hesitation. Neglected tools have a habit of turning on their wielders, and from the look of it I expected the head to fall off at the first swing, but it surprised me by being quite sound and extremely sharp.

Aleida returned then, with a little ceramic pot and a tiny brush, the sort fancy city girls use for their face-paint. 'All right,' she said. 'Close your eyes and sweep your hair off your forehead.'

A moment later I felt a touch of coolness on my forehead as she painted some strange design of curved, sweeping lines and groups of dots, followed by a sweep across each eyelid. The moist touch made my eyelids flicker and twitch. 'There. That should do it. You can open your eyes now.'

I did, in time to see her replace the lid on the pot. The tiny brush held the remains of something that glittered and sparkled even in the darkness. Blinking in surprise, I looked around.

It wasn't bright like daylight, but it wasn't dark either. Everything was just ... intense. Usually at night it was hard to see the colours in things, but now it looked as though the world was painted in vivid hues, the grass impossibly green, the sky a deep, enveloping indigo, the stars, when they briefly appeared, sparkling like diamonds. There was no source of light, no shadows like during the day, instead, everything seemed to glow softly, as though lit from within.

Aleida tucked the pot and brush away in a pocket, and scooped up the ropes into a basket with a handle. 'Come on,' she said, and set out down the meadow with the basket in one hand, leaning on the walking stick with each step. 'Bring the axe!' she called over her shoulder.

'What are we doing?' I said as I hurried after her.

'I told you, I have an idea.'

'But that doesn't explain anything!'

'True, true.' She came to a stop halfway down the meadow, near the huge tree — the one we'd made a berth around when we'd walked down to the stream. She dumped the ropes out of the basket and held it out to me. 'Take this down to the stream and find me a dozen or so rocks about as big as your fist. Leave the axe, you won't need it.'

I still had no idea what we were doing, but I figured I wasn't going to get any more explanation than I already had. I laid the axe down and set off for the stream.

'Oh, and Dee?' Aleida called out behind me. 'I'm going to call that earthbeast over. Don't go jumping out of your skin when you see it moving, all right?'

I looked back at her. I couldn't bring myself to say anything, so I just turned back and went about my task.

By the time I reached the water the beast was moving, lumbering across the unnaturally green grass. The hair on my arms rose as I watched it — it moved like a puppet, one of those puppets with a dozen strings you see sometimes at fairs, only it was bigger than anything I'd ever seen move before.

I turned my back on it, looking out to the quiet hillsides instead, and I found myself thinking of Kian, with his fair skin and soft red-brown curls. I hoped he was sleeping somewhere warm and dry instead of tramping around the countryside under the direction of a madwoman.

At the stream I crouched on the bank and splashed a little water on my face, trying to wake myself up. Whatever it was my mistress was planning to do out here, it seemed best to have all my wits about me. Water dripping from my nose and chin, I gazed into the water and wondered again what on earth I was doing here, so far from home.

As I turned away from the water, looking over the rocks beside the stream, something bright and glittering caught my eye. I stopped and turned back.

It took me a moment to find it again. In the pool, within arms-reach of the edge, something shone and shimmered beneath the water. I moved closer, peering down, and saw a crystal — a chunk of stone, mostly clear but frosted white at the base. Thanks to the spell Aleida had cast on me, it glittered like ice in sunlight.

Lifting my skirts with one hand to keep them clear of the water, I edged as close as I could without soaking my feet, just the toes of my boots kissing the lapping water, and reached in to grasp the stone.

It was a perfect crystal, its point as clear as water, the facets and faces far too crisp and clean to have been in the stream for long. It was a little shorter than my hand

and half as thick as my wrist. It was, I felt certain, the loveliest thing I'd ever held. For some long moments I just stood there and gazed at it, turning it over and over to run my fingertips over its perfect faces.

'Dee?' Aleida called, her voice floating down the meadow.

Hastily I set the crystal aside and gathered up a dozen or so stones, not looking too closely at any of them. Then, reaching for the crystal again, I hesitated. Part of me wanted to put it back in the water, or hide it nearby. I could creep back in the morning, maybe, and sneak it up to the cottage. I could keep it for myself.

But no, that wasn't right. It wasn't mine. This was Aleida's land, everything it produced belonged to her.

I set the crystal on top of the stones in the basket and started back up the hill, scowling to myself. I was selfish and greedy, wasn't that what Lem always said? *Selfish, lazy Elodie, only ever thinking of herself.* I'd heard it every single day since Lem had come into our lives, until the morning I climbed onto Yosh's wagon to rattle away.

The lumbering beast was standing beside Aleida when I returned, and I offered her the basket without saying a word.

She blinked at the crystal, looking surprised, and then picked it up and ran long fingers along the faces and angles. 'What's this?'

'I found it in the stream,' I said.

Resting a finger on the point, she looked me over, and then held it out to me. 'Where do you want me to put it?' I said, taking it back.

'Wherever you like,' she said. 'It's yours.'

'I ... what?'

'You found it,' she said. 'Or rather, you were given it, not me.' Without another word, she sat down and started picking through the rocks I'd found. After a moment I laid the crystal down and joined her.

'So what exactly are we doing?'

She was sorting the ropes into lengths, and tying a rock to the end of each one. 'I've got an idea,' she said again. 'To destroy the warlock. Only thing is, it's a bit dangerous, and I'm not really strong enough to handle this step by myself. I imagine a farm girl like you can swing that axe just fine, but how's your throwing arm?'

'Um, fine, I guess?' I said.

Two minutes later, I was sorry I'd said any such thing. We stood in the orchard, looking up at the huge tree at its centre. Long vines were hanging down from the spreading branches, swaying gently in the evening breeze. At least, I told myself it was the breeze making them move, and refused to acknowledge that the night air was perfectly still.

Aleida handed me a rock. 'All right, Dee. I wouldn't be asking you to do this if I could do it myself, but, honestly, I don't think I can throw these and stay on my feet.'

I frowned at the rock, bewildered. 'What do I do with this?'

'Throw it. At the tree. Up into the branches.'

I turned my frown on her. I had an idea of what was about to happen, and I wasn't in any mood to have it confirmed.

But what would happen if I refused? There wasn't anyone else who could help her. There was only me, and hadn't I promised her that I had her back?

I threw the rock. And watched, unsurprised, as the trailing, swaying vines struck at it like a nest of snakes, thrashing, writhing, lashing like whips, until the rock I'd thrown crumbled and fell in a shower of gravel.

'Yeah,' I said. 'That's what I thought.'

Aleida cleared her throat. 'This,' she said, 'is a Demon Snakewood.'

I raised an eyebrow. 'Demon? Really?'

'Really. They're only grown by magic, and black magic at that. Gyssha should never have let it get this big, but, well, it is what it is.'

'All right,' I said. 'So what's the plan?'

She gestured to the ropes. 'You're going to throw those rocks up there until we snag a branch. Buttercup, here,' she jerked a thumb towards the bull-headed beast, 'is going to take the rope and haul back to keep the limb taut, and hopefully keep it from grabbing us. Then you're going to take the axe to the branch. While you're doing that I'll keep the rest of the vines off you.'

'Buttercup?'

She shrugged, and reached into the basket then and pulled out some other things, which I'd taken for rags. They turned out to be two pairs of sturdy leather gloves and some scarves of heavy fabric. I let her wrap the scarf around my head and face, leaving only my eyes free, and then I pulled on the gloves. 'Why do we need all this?' I said, my voice muffled by the fabric.

'The sap,' she said. 'It'll burn if it touches you.'

'Of course it will,' I muttered.

She covered her own face the same way, and turned to me. 'Ready?' I could tell by the sound of her voice that she was grinning beneath the thick cloth.

I sighed. 'Sure. Why not?'

'That's the spirit.' She clapped me on the shoulder. 'Let's go.'

There was a trick to it, she explained to me. Don't aim too close to the centre of the tree, the branches there were too strong, and even the earthbeast couldn't stand against them. Instead, I had to snag one of the outermost limbs. It wasn't enough merely to hit it, either — I had to get the rope wrapped around it, because the tree would soon realise that we were trying to drag a limb down and would let go of the rope once it figured out there was no prey within reach.

I lost several ropes because the tree grabbed them and yanked them out of my hands, hard enough that it smarted my palms even through the thick leather gloves. Other times, the rope slithered free and fell to the earth while the vines thrashed and writhed in fury, sometimes reaching towards us in thwarted hunger, other times pulling away from us as though trying to retreat. While taking a breather, I asked Aleida, 'You're completely sure it can't move towards us, right?'

'Oh, definitely,' she said. 'If it could get loose it would have taken off years ago.'

I scowled up at the huge, hideous thing. 'What's it for? You said it took magic to grow it—'

'*Black* magic.'

'All right. So who planted it? Or made it, however it came about.'

'I don't know. It's older than Gyssha, I know that much, but I don't know if Gyssha inherited all this from her teacher, or if she took it from someone else. She never told me.'

'But why would anyone make something like this?'

'Power,' she said with a shrug. 'Folk on the dark path always want power. Beyond that, who knows? It's useful for a lot of things, if you're into the black stuff. The sap is acidic, the smoke from the wood is poisonous and corrosive. Wine from the fruit will give you visions of incalculable ecstasy and prophetic dreams but also make you bleed from every orifice. And that's before we start getting into the metaphysical properties.'

That was a different definition of *useful* than any I'd ever heard. 'So why are we doing this again?'

'I need some wood,' she said. 'It's extremely responsive to magic. And, like I said, poisonous.'

'And corrosive,' I said. 'What does corrosive mean?'

'That it'll eat away at everything it touches. Ready to try again?'

I gathered up the rock and coil of rope with a sigh. 'Sure.'

I'd had a bit of practice now, and this time, with the coil of rope in my left hand and a length of it with the rock tied to the end in my right, I set the rock whirling through the air and launched it towards the tree. It felt good this time, not falling short or flying too far, and I stepped back, reaching for the axe as Aleida quickly wound the end of rope around the bull's horns. Obediently, the beast lumbered backwards, hauling the rope taut.

Up in the tree the rope jerked, and a branch began to thrash. The rope snapped tight with a startling *twang*, and for a moment the beast faltered, its huge feet digging furrows into the soft earth before it dug in again and got enough purchase to keep hauling back.

'Got it!' Aleida said. 'Now look sharp, Dee. If the tree's too strong we'll have to cut the rope and try again. Don't mind the vines, I'll deal with them, just hack off the branch, all right?'

I wound my hands around the axe's handle, my palms suddenly damp inside the leather gloves. 'A-are you sure?'

'Yes. Now! Go!'

The straining beast had pulled down a single, slender branch while the tree thrashed and writhed in fury, tendrils straining towards us. I took a few steps forward and stopped, while the beast pulled and pulled.

'Now, Dee, now!'

The branch was drawn down to the ground. It was only half the thickness of my wrist, the axe could sever it in a single blow, surely.

Do it, I told myself. *Your name is Forster, your da was a woodsman. You said you had her back, did you mean it or not? DO IT!*

I darted forward, axe raised high. Vines stretched towards me like tentacles, but as I moved I felt something settle over me, like a damp, heavy mist, and the tendrils seemed to simply slip away.

I swung the axe, and then again. The branch was tough, sinewy; it reminded me of butchering a beast and sawing away at the tendons. I felt something splatter against me, dozens of droplets, and I wrinkled my nose at the sudden stench of scorched wool.

Then, with one more swing, the branch came loose and whipped away from me as the beast stumbled backwards.

'Out!' Aleida bellowed at me. 'Out! Out!'

I staggered back, not daring to turn away from the tree, while it twisted and writhed as though in a storm. Then, once I was well out of reach I surveyed our work properly — and recoiled from that, too. The branch on the ground twitched and jerked like a headless snake, and the end where I'd hacked it from the tree wept blood-red sap that hissed and smoked where it landed on the grass. Everywhere it touched, the green grass turned black and crumbled to ash.

I tore the stifling cloth away from my face, drawing a deep breath, glad now of the cool night air. 'Lord and Lady,' I said, resting the axe head on the ground and leaning against the handle. 'Is that enough wood for you? Please tell me that's enough.'

'Enough?' Aleida said, looking it over. 'Yeah, should be enough. It'll have to be, actually, the tree will have defences up now; it's probably not safe to cut any more tonight.'

'Defences?' I said. 'Defences! You mean, more than it already has?'

'Mm-hm,' she said. 'Some plants can do that, you know, pump poison into their leaves when something tries to eat them.' She looked over the tree, the twitching branch, and the beast, unmoving now and with the rope still wrapped around its horns. 'All right, Dee, I've got it from here. Clean the axe off and put it away for me, would you?'

I looked at the axe, streaked with what looked like blood. Then I looked down at my dress, and saw that it was spotted with dozens of tiny holes, like I'd been attacked by a swarm of moths.

I turned away without a word, and strode back up to the cottage. *I've had enough of this. I'm going back to bed.*

CHAPTER 6

*I*t took me forever to go back to sleep, and when I did I dreamed of those vines wrapping around me, choking the life out of me. In the end all I had was a few more hours of restless sleep before daylight woke me.

I found Aleida in her bed, asleep atop the covers with the box bed's sliding door open. The sun would wake her soon, just as it had me. She seemed stronger than she had been when I first came here — some decent food and a fire had seen to that — but her colour was still poor, and I saw that she'd brought the walking stick inside with her and left it leaning beside the bed.

Quietly I slipped outside and set about the morning chores, fetching water and wood, milking our new goat and turning her out on a tether near the top of the orchard. Everything around us was shrouded in mist. The trees of the orchard soon vanished into the fog, and the meadow behind the cottage seemed to peter out into nothing. It wasn't eerie, though, just quiet and cosy, like the cottage and the grounds were snuggled up under a blanket, soft and calm.

By the time I returned to the house, carrying the warm milk in a cooking pot for want of a decent pail, Aleida was hobbling outside, leaning heavily on the stick.

'I would murder someone for a cup of coffee right now,' she said by way of greeting.

'Can't help you there, I'm afraid. Tea?'

'Sure.'

The branch we'd cut from the demon tree seemed much smaller by daylight than it had last night. It was a little taller than I was, but it was spindly and thin — broken up it would barely be enough to start a fire. Aleida had strung it up to the eaves of the house, like a hunter would hang a hare, and set a bowl underneath to catch the sap that dripped from the broken end.

Inside I set about making porridge with oats and fresh milk, and watched through the window as she cut down her catch. A moment later she called me out again to fetch her some water and other odds and ends. When the porridge was done I dished it out into two bowls, drizzled with honey, and brought hers out to her.

By now, she was carefully cutting the branch up into smaller pieces, but she set it aside and peeled off her gloves before taking the bowl from me, and I sat nearby to eat my own. 'Miss?'

'Hmm?'

'Can I ask ... what are you going to do with that?' I nodded to the wood. The broken pieces merely oozed with red now, instead of dripping like a fresh wound.

'I'm going to make a construct,' she said. 'Just a little one. I'll march it right into his camp and into his fire, and then ...' With the bowl balanced on her knee she mimed an exploding puff of smoke with her hands. 'Of course, I have to find him first.'

'Will it be enough?'

'Should be, if I add a few other bits and pieces. I don't want to make it too big, this stuff—' She frowned down at the slender branch. 'It has some odd properties. The smoke taints everything it touches and, sometimes ... it's the demonic taint, you see, sometimes it makes ... weak spots, I guess you'd call them. Too much would make a rift.'

'Weak spots?' I said.

'It lets things through.'

'All right,' I said. 'I don't understand at all, though.'

'No,' she agreed. 'Hopefully you won't have to.'

I scraped my bowl clean and set it aside. Aleida was still working on hers. If I'd ever taken that long to eat back home, I'd have been accused of laziness and of trying to get out of my work, but after a week of near starvation I figured it must be hard for her to adjust to proper meals again. 'Have you any particular tasks for me today? I thought I'd keep on with the garden, and our woodpile isn't looking too—'

'Can you ride a horse?' she broke in.

'I, yes,' I said. 'I mean, I used to. I haven't in a few years, but I used to ride on errands for Ma and Lem.'

She turned to me, eyebrows raised. 'Used to? But they made you stop?'

'Ma decided I wasn't to leave the house and yard anymore, so I wasn't allowed to ride after that.'

Eyeing me up and down, Aleida shuffled closer. 'I'm sensing a story here.'

I felt myself flushing.

'Come on, Dee, spill it.'

I grimaced. 'Honestly, she blew it all out of proportion. We used to go to the market every month, see? Well, they still do, but I wasn't allowed to anymore. Ma caught me, well, she caught me kissing a boy there.'

'Really?' she said, feigning shock, and then snorted. 'Oh, the horror.'

'And when Lucette was caught sneaking off with the Brampton lad earlier this year all she got was a scolding! And I got treated like I'd stolen the crown jewels or something! It wasn't like he was a stranger, either, we were friends when we were little. Ma worked for his family for a while, see, after Da died, but then, well, to be honest I think she was caught stealing from them, so we had to leave. We'd see each other there at the market every so often, and he was just so *nice*.'

'Turned out well, did he?' Aleida said, raising one eyebrow.

All I could do was nod. 'After that Ma said I had to stay home. Couldn't be trusted, she said.'

Aleida nodded, thoughtfully. 'All right. So can you still ride?'

'Oh,' I said. 'I expect so. But do you have a horse?'

'I do,' she said. 'He's been running wild for the last week or so, but I've called him back.'

'And what do you want me to do? Take a message somewhere?'

She shook her head. 'No, I need to brew a potion, and I want you to gather the ingredients for me. Oh, and collect those packs I stashed away before I came down to face Gyssha.'

'A potion? What sort?'

'For me. I don't have time to regain strength the normal way, so I have to cheat. That warlock thinks he can knock me over with a feather and I don't have a lot of time to prove him wrong.'

'You're in better shape than you were, though,' I said, eyeing her up.

'Mm,' she said. 'Not by much, I'm afraid. It'll take more than food and sleep to really get me back on solid ground.'

I grimaced at that. 'Well, spending half the night messing around with a demon tree probably isn't great for healing, but at least we haven't had that ghost back again, or we'd have slept even less.'

I realised Aleida had fallen still, staring at me with narrowed eyes. 'What did I say?'

'Bennett,' she said. 'The ghost. You're right, he *hasn't* come back. There hasn't been a single night since I came back to this cursed cottage that he hasn't come to howl at me at *least* twice ...' All at once she looked incredibly sad, her eyes an ocean away as she sat with a hand curled around her mouth, the other wrapped around her ribs, as though something inside her ached.

'Maybe he did move on, after all,' I said. 'Who was he, anyway? You said he was Attwater's kin? What happened to him?'

'Bennett?' she said, and turned away, looking over the field. Porridge finished at last, she pulled her gloves on again and picked up a piece of the snakewood tree and a little whittling knife. 'He was Attwater's nephew, well, great-nephew or great-great; I never did figure it out exactly.'

'Was he ... like you? And Attwater? I mean, something more than human?'

She gave me an exasperated look. 'I'm as human as you are, Dee. But Bennett was just an ordinary lad. Woodcutter's son. I met him the first time Gyssha brought me here. I'd never set foot in the countryside before, and Gyssha sent me out to gather something or other. I got lost, but Bennett found me and helped me. He was a sweet lad.

'Gyssha and I only ever came for the summer, the growing season, you see, for the orchard and the gardens, and time for Gyssha to cook up her plans and schemes. I hated it. I was a haughty little thing back then, very pleased with myself. Gyssha liked it that way, it makes a person easy to manipulate. Come the fall, with a wagon full of potions and constructs and odds and ends, we'd head off to a new city. Then in the spring we'd come back to this boring backwater, loaded down with silk and silver and one of those chests you saw in Gyssha's room.' She shook her hair back and slumped forward with a sigh, her elbows on her knees.

'And every year I'd come back to Bennett. I'd tell him all about it; the fancy gowns and the balls, the gold and jewels, the fights, the intrigue, the excitement of it all. I didn't understand what we were doing at first — I was just a whore's get from the Rat's Nest, what did I know of politics and war? It was a game to Gyssha, and I was a handy pawn. It was only when I told Bennett all about it that I realised what we'd done. Have you ever heard of Karolina?'

I shook my head. 'Who is she?'

'Not a she, but an it. Karolina was a city. I ... look, Dee, I've done a lot of things I'm not proud of. Karolina's the worst of them, I think. The city's gone now. There was a war. The duke was supposed to marry the neighbouring lord's daughter, but the night before the wedding she was found in bed with the duke's rival ... well, you can imagine the rest. That's what Gyssha did, and for the fun of it, too. If it was just gold she wanted she could have taken it like any other thief, but that wasn't enough for her. She had to destroy, as well. Lives, families, happiness. Cities. The more havoc she could cause the happier she was.'

'Is that why you killed her?' I said, softly.

She looked up at me from beneath strands of black hair. 'No. It's why I left, though. But that was a couple of years ago.'

She was silent for a moment after that, and I thought of prodding her to go on, but I remembered Mrs Sanford from the day before, and how she'd let silence draw my own tale out of me.

'For a time I thought I was in love with Bennett, but we both thought better of it eventually. I never wanted to stay out here, but he had the mountains and the woods in his blood. He was a country boy and I'm a city girl ... and he met someone.'

'Oh,' I said. 'Oh no.'

She looked up sharply. 'It wasn't like that. I wasn't jealous. He was my friend, I wanted him to be happy, and Rosalie was perfect for him, she was lovely.

'Gyssha was furious. She didn't want me to have any friends, let alone a beau; but it was even worse to have one and lose him. Unthinkable to let him be with someone else. When I left, I told Bennett to get away from Lilsfield, take Rosalie and move somewhere far away. I gave him money to help and I thought he'd gone ...'

'But she killed him?'

Aleida heaved a sigh. 'Worse than that. She killed Rosalie, and their little twins. Poison. A slow one. And when it was over, Bennett started to sicken as well, so he climbed to the top of a waterfall and threw himself off. And then he came to tell me.' She fell silent after that, looking out over the field and into the forest. 'That's why I came back. That's why I killed her.'

I couldn't help but think of Jeb and Maisie, and all my other siblings, too, the ones I'd held and rocked and cared for alongside Ma. I couldn't imagine how it'd feel to watch them wither away, to know who had done it, and be able to do nothing. 'Why?' I said. 'Why would she do something like that?'

'I tried to ask her,' Aleida said. 'But she just laughed and laughed ...'

I clenched my fists, digging fingernails into skin. 'I'm glad she's dead.'

'Me too.' She gave a sigh. 'Isn't it funny how things work out? I never wanted to come back here, but Bennett couldn't bear to leave. Now he's gone, and here we are.' She tossed her head. 'Maybe he did go on through the veil. Maybe ...' Throwing down her knife and the piece of wood she was whittling, she heaved herself up. 'The horse will be here in a few minutes. You should get yourself ready to go.'

Quickly I cleaned up the breakfast bowls and made sure I was dressed for tramping about the forest. I was still scrounging in the old stables for a sack without too many holes when Aleida called me out to the meadow.

There, like an apparition in the fog, was a beautiful dapple-grey horse. He was tall and lean, a far cry from the farmers' cobs that I'd known. With a deep chest, arched neck and long, clean legs, he looked like he was built for speed.

'I rode him here when I came back to face Gyssha,' Aleida explained. 'Before the fight I turned him loose, though I did ask him not to wander too far. Problem is, I left his saddle and bridle with the rest of my gear. You'll have to ride bareback to go and get it.'

'Oh,' I said, feeling myself blanch. 'I'm not sure I can manage *that*.' Perhaps I could have done it on the flat on a lazy old cart-horse, but in these hills, on a beast that had been running wild for the past week? It sounded like a recipe for disaster. I could just see myself sliding off the back of him on some steep hillside.

'It's not far,' said Aleida. 'You'll be all right, Dee; I'll keep a hand on him until you get the saddle and bridle. I haven't the strength to Borrow him the whole time you're out, but I can help you for a while.'

'Oh,' I said again. 'Well, in that case I think I saw an old halter in the stables that'll give me something to hold on to, at least.'

I hurried back to the sheds and returned with an ancient halter, knotted from rope.

'Now,' Aleida started, and then broke off. 'Oh rats, I'll have to write you a list.'

'It wouldn't be any use anyway,' I said, feeling my cheeks flush. 'I can't read, remember?'

She gave me a sharp look and it made me think of the way Ma looked at me every time I reminded her of her promise to teach me. *One day. When we have time.*

'Oh,' Aleida said. 'You did tell me that. Well, how's your memory?'

'It's pretty good.'

I wasn't sure if she believed me but she didn't question it. 'All right, here's what I need.'

The list she recited was quite long and utterly nonsensical, or so it seemed to me. She asked for three white stones from a particular pool along the stream; six twigs from six different hazel bushes, each with seven buds; five milk-thistle heads; two day-lily buds, a butterfly's empty cocoon, a splinter of wood from a tree that had fallen across a stream, a cupful of dirt from a place where one path branched into two ... it went on and on, and, though it made no sense, I listened carefully, and when she was done I recited it all back to her, ticking them off on my fingers as she nodded along.

'Good,' she said. 'Impressive, actually. Well, first you'll need to find the old hunting bothy to the north-east — cross the stream, head left until you come to a valley, then follow it back until it climbs up into the rocks. Just before you reach the granite there's a little track to the left, that'll take you to the bothy, and my packs and gear are around the back. Don't go poking in my saddlebags, there's things in there that are dangerous in the wrong hands. But you've got better sense than that, anyway,' she said with a flick of her hand.

I wasn't sure what a bothy was, but I figured I'd find out soon enough. 'What if we come across one of those wretched beasts?' I said. 'Or the warlock?'

'Run away,' Aleida said. 'As fast as you can, straight back here. I'll be with you until you reach the bothy, just in case you fall, but after that you'll be on your own, all right?'

I nodded, though I didn't feel at all sure about the matter. 'Um, is there any way I can call you? Just in case I get lost, or we run into one of those beasts, or something.'

She scowled, looking cross, and for a moment I thought she'd tell me to just get on with it, but then her expression softened. 'Oh,' she said. 'Yeah. I suppose I should. Let me think.' She turned away, gripping the walking stick with both hands. Then she hobbled over to the orchard and broke a twig off the nearest tree. Once she came back towards me she beckoned me close. 'Come here, Dee.'

She plucked a single hair from my head, scoffing when I protested at the sting of it, and then pulled out one of her own. Holding the strands together, she wrapped them around and around the twig. Then, cupping it between her hands, she breathed on it, and for a moment I saw light streaming between her fingers. 'There,' she said, handing it to me. 'If you get in trouble, snap it and I'll find you. Off you go, now; I need those ingredients as quickly as possible.'

With no stirrups I had to lead the horse over to the walled garden and scramble up the stonework to slide onto his back. Even a horse that hasn't been groomed in a week or more feels slippery and smooth once you mount him without a saddle. It was awkward at best to ride astride in a long skirt rather than a pair of my brothers' britches, but with stockings underneath I could at least hike the skirt up to mount without too much shame. I settled myself as best I could and wrapped my hands around the lead-rope that stood in for reins. Then, I looked expectantly at Aleida.

She heaved a sigh. 'Give him your heels, girl. I'm keeping a hand on him so he doesn't dump you and run, but you have to ride him still.'

'Oh,' I said, and flushed. 'Sorry.'

With a touch of my heels, the horse set out at a sprightly trot, making me hastily haul on the ropes to try to slow him down. He felt very different underneath me than the old cob I'd ridden on errands back home. That beast was a lazy sod, no one ever took him out without first cutting a switch to use as a crop, but this fellow moved as though he had places to be and no time to waste in getting there.

We splashed across the stream and turned left, just as my mistress had said, and by then we were shrouded in fog, with the cottage and orchard and even the hills above me lost from sight. The air was cool and crisp, the horse warm beneath me, and my hands chill as they clutched the ancient rope. But I felt as though I couldn't take it all in, not properly; I was too busy, keeping my seat on the horse's slippery back, trying to hold him back as his spirited, bouncing trot threatened to send me to the ground. Also, in the back of my head, I was trying not to think about what would happen if we came face-to-face with one of the earthbeasts, or the warlock in his black cloak. With my precarious perch and dubious control of the horse, I had no doubts I'd take a hurried fall; and though the grey might be fleet enough to escape, I knew I never would be.

Thankfully, nothing went awry as I found the valley and a snaking dirt track that wound through the trees. It took barely ten minutes to reach the great moss-covered boulders that I took to be the granite Aleida mentioned. Another track wound between jutting rocks, stubby, wizened trees and piles of flat, grey slates before reaching a tiny hut. *So that's what a bothy is,* I thought, looking over the stacked-stone walls and slate roof of the hut. There was a shed to one side, and everything was covered with damp, green moss. I heaved on the lead-rope to make the horse stop, and watched the hut for a moment. There was no smoke from the chimney, not even the smell of it; the lone window was shuttered and the stout door was shut — shut, but not locked, for while there was a simple wooden latch to close the door, there was no way to lock it that I could see. *A place for hunters and shepherds to shelter.*

Aleida had said her gear was around the back. I slithered down from my unstable perch, and tied the horse to a post inside the shed. He didn't seem to mind the place, though he did stamp his feet impatiently while I ducked around the back of the stone building.

I found Aleida's gear just where she had said — saddlebags and a felt sleeping-pad and, what I was most glad to see, a saddle and bridle, all of it wrapped up in a sheet of oilcloth against the damp. I carried it all back around to the shed and set about putting on the saddle and bridle, and replacing the old, brittle halter with one that seemed far less likely to come apart at the first sign of trouble. With the girth buckled, I tied the saddlebags and sleeping-pad in place and stood back to admire my work. The horse looked like a proper adventurer now, all geared up and ready to move, and I thought again about the storybook my little siblings had, the one where I made up stories to go with the beautiful woodcut pictures. There was one with a young lad who had a horse much like this, riding off to rescue a princess or something. The lad had a jaunty little felt cap with a couple of bright feathers stuck in the band. I'd spent hours thinking about that picture, when I was scrubbing pots or pounding the washing in the copper tub, imagining what it would be like to be so free, to have adventures of my own.

How strange, I thought, remembering the loneliness and boredom I'd felt on the road up to the mountains; and then the terror of Bennett's ghost in the dead of night, and the way my heart had pounded when the warlock appeared on the road to the cottage. *This isn't how I expected it would feel, at all.*

But as I was standing there, twisting the reins between my fingers, my eye caught a little twinkle of light — another crystal, as long and slim as my finger, nestled into a crack in the stacked-stone wall.

With a small frown, I plucked it out, and rolled it between my fingers. 'Why do I keep finding you fellows everywhere?' I said, and then tucked it into my sleeve. 'All right, my lad,' I said to the horse. 'We've got a job to do.'

I thought I'd be happier once I had a proper saddle to sit on and real reins to hold, but once I no longer had to put all my attention into staying on the grey's slippery back, other thoughts began to push their way into my mind, driving away the picture in my memories. This was no storybook.

Ox eyes in a jar.

The black rider with his crystal-studded wand.

The pendant filled with soul-rending despair.

A dryad in a cage, sold like goods at a market.

Huge beasts made of dark earth, eyes glowing like coals.

The ghost of a dead man, driven to suicide by the cruelty of the old witch.

A demon tree with vines that hungered and raged, twisting and writhing like a nest of snakes.

My hands gripped the reins so tight my knuckles ached, and the horse danced beneath me, head coming up and ears twitching. He could sense my nervous tension, I realised, and I drew a deep breath and tried to let the tightness go. *Lord and Lady, what am I doing here? I don't belong here, I have no idea what I'm doing.*

I bit my lip, thinking of the kitchen back home, the floor I'd scrubbed ... how many times? A thousand? More? The sink I'd filled and emptied, the dishes I'd washed and washed again, until my fingers knew every ridge and warp in the plates, every chip and every dent in every pot. For the last few years I'd dreamed of leaving, of *escaping*, but now ...

If Ma appeared on the trail ahead of me, like an apparition, and told me I could come home, what would I say? I remembered clearly how *stifling* it had felt, like I was a peach preserved in a jar, or an old cup in a cupboard. Not a prized teapot high on a shelf to keep it safe, I wasn't worth that much. No, I was like our old draught mare out in the barn, there to be worked until I dropped and couldn't work anymore.

I thought back to the long, dusty road up into the mountains, and the reading Brian had done for me;

questions I'd asked without any forethought or any faith in the truth of their answers.

I wanted to go home. I missed it fiercely, every crack in the kitchen floor, the plates stacked in the cupboard, the dim, cool pantry. I hated it and I missed it and I hated myself for missing it. *Isn't this what you wanted?* I asked myself. *You're free of it now, and out on your own. Isn't this what you dreamed of? And you didn't even have to pay a price for it. It just fell at your feet.*

I reined in, fighting the horse to a stop. 'Such a coward,' I muttered to myself. 'Run back home to Ma's skirts, then.'

Coward. It wasn't an insult Lem had ever hurled at me. Lazy, slovenly, selfish, greedy — all of those, but never coward. Maybe it was because I was a girl. *Or maybe,* a small voice inside my head whispered, *it's because he never wanted to stir you into trying to prove him wrong.*

Go home? I drew a sharp breath, and with a toss of my head, nudged the horse onwards again. It wasn't home I wanted, I reasoned. I just wanted comfort. I wanted my ma, to hear her voice and feel her arms around me. I wanted to hear her tell me that it would be all right, that I could do this, that everything would work out. *But she's never done it before. Why would she start now?*

The horse snorted, lifting his head and pricking his ears, and with a start I pulled myself out of my slump and back to the present moment.

Up ahead on the track was a slender figure dressed in green and brown — tall, skinny, with a shock of auburn curls. Kian.

He seemed to hear me at the same time as I spotted him, for he glanced around and veered quickly off the path, vanishing into a patch of brush.

My heart sank, and then I realised he likely had no idea it was me. Yesterday I'd been on foot, after all, just a servant girl with a basket on my back, and here I was on a fine horse, loaded down with travelling gear. I looked like the sort of person he would do his best to avoid.

'Kian!' I called, cupping a hand around my mouth, as though it would make the slightest difference. 'Kian, it's me! Elodie!'

There was silence, stillness, and then a twinge of pain in my chest. *Well,* I thought, *I am servant to the witch he hates. He took off on me yesterday, for good reason. I can't blame him for keeping his distance now.* I was starting to wonder if it would have been wiser on my part to do the same.

But then, after a few more steps, his head popped out from the bushes and his face split into a grin. 'Elodie? That *is* you! Lord and Lady, look at you! You look like you're off to seek your fortune, or find true love.'

It was so close to the thought I'd had just a short time ago that I had to laugh. 'Maybe if he was mine,' I said, slapping the grey's shoulder. 'But he belongs to my mistress.'

'Belongs? I doubt it. From what I know of her, she probably stole him.' He was grinning as he said it, but then his smile swiftly faded. 'Dee, I … look, I'm sorry I took off like that, yesterday. Folk like that make my skin crawl.'

'It's all right,' I said. 'Truly. That rider, the one all in black, he makes me feel the same way.'

'He does? But not the witch, though?'

When the grey reached his side I reined in and slipped down from the saddle so I could speak to him face-to-face rather than lord it over him from my perch.

'She's not so bad. I mean, she's a bird of a different feather, for sure, but she's not evil like the old witch was.'

'No?' He cocked his head to the side. 'And you've known her for, what? All of a day?'

The words could have been snide, but he said it with a faint grin, so I took it for a gentle tease rather than the jab it would have been back home. 'In my defence,' I said, 'it was a really long day.'

'They always are, with those sort,' he said. 'Don't work too hard, Dee, or she'll expect you to move mountains every day of the week.' His smile faded then, and he shifted his feet, winding a hand around the strap of his satchel, hanging empty by his hip. 'Seriously, though, how is it? I can't imagine what it must be like, leaving your family and your home, all to fetch and carry and slave away for something like *her*.'

Oh, it's fine. That's what I should say. The words were already hovering on my lips and tongue. *Oh, it's fine. I'm fine. Everything's fine.*

'It's ... it's ... it's all so strange,' I said. 'Everything's just so strange, and I don't know what I'm doing here.'

I could have stopped it. I could have kept the words back, but I needed *someone* to talk to. There had been so many strange things, all in one short day. All of a sudden it was just spilling out of me, all of it — the ox eyes in the jars, the gold and jewels in the dark room, the huge beast that had stomped the black rider's body into chaff and dust, and then stood sentinel over us while we bathed. The orchard with its gnarled and deformed trees and that one demented growth in the middle that hungered and raged with a demon's strength. I even told him how she'd dragged me out of bed in the middle of the night to tackle the monster and tear off just one small spindly branch.

We found our way to a fallen tree as I spoke, and sat on the trunk while the horse grazed at the end of the reins. Kian listened in sober silence, letting me spill it all out. In the end I was breathless from talking, and all I could do was look down at my feet.

Somehow I doubted my mistress would thank me for telling him everything, even how weak she was, how unsteady on her feet and how the slightest exertion left her trembling. But, I reasoned, this wasn't Melly, with a dozen brothers and sisters and friends and cousins to talk to. I'd liked Melly, I truly had, but I knew a gossip when I saw one. Kian was different. There was a certain kinship between us, it seemed to me. We came from very different worlds, it was true, but I couldn't help but feel that my old life, with its endless cycle of cooking, cleaning and looking after children, was every bit as lonely and isolated as his life of hunting and trapping. I had more company, perhaps, but he had the freedom to come and go as he wished, beholden to none but himself. We each had something to envy, and something to regret.

When I was done Kian drew a deep breath. 'That's ... well, strange is one way to put it. Not the word I'd use. Terrifying, maybe? Petrifying?'

'Oh,' I said. 'It's not that bad.'

I glanced up to find him regarding me steadily with his wide brown eyes. 'Honestly, Dee, are you sure you want to stay with her? Is this truly better than your home? Or, I don't know, anywhere else you could go?'

'I'm not going home,' I said, firmly. 'I'm not.'

'Really? I tell you, I wish I had a home to go to.'

'Not like mine, you don't,' I said. 'Not unless you enjoy being told every day how worthless and lazy and useless you are. Say what you like about Aleida, she appreciates what I do for her. She doesn't treat me like something she scraped off her shoe.'

His jaw dropped at that, and he ducked his head. 'Oh. Right. I guess, I mean, I only ever had my ma, but I never doubted that she loved me.'

'It must be lonely without her,' I said. 'I can't imagine ...'

He looked away, rubbing the back of his neck. His hands, I noticed, were soft and clean, not calloused and cracked like Yosh's or Lem's, or like Attwater's. 'It is,' he said. 'I think that's why I hate her so much — the witches, I mean. Ma would still be alive if only they could be bothered to help her.'

I felt myself straighten, then. 'What do you mean?'

'When Ma died, it was consumption, you see? We never had a proper house, just a little shack with a dirt floor. It was always damp, you just can't get rid of it in the winter. She got sick one year and never really got better. We got that potion once, and it helped. It helped a lot. But the next winter it came back. Ma was too sick to get out of bed, she'd pass out if she tried to sit up. She couldn't breathe. I asked them for help, and they just laughed at me. I had no coin to pay them, and no matter what I promised to do to pay them back, they just laughed at me and chased me away. And now ...' he scowled, dark as a thunderstorm. 'And now you tell me they've got a whole room full of gold and jewels, just sitting around? I had nothing! Nothing in the world but her.' He ground his heel into the dirt then, scouring a hole in the soft soil. 'It's not just me they've done this to, either. I told you about the man she poisoned, didn't I? He dropped dead in the tavern one night, just took a swig of ale and keeled over. Everyone in the district has a tale to tell about those witches. You just have to ask and the truth about them comes spilling out.'

I felt my mouth hanging open like an idiot, and forced myself to close it. That didn't sound like the Aleida I knew. It didn't sound like her at all ... but then, she'd told me herself that she'd done things she wasn't proud of. Mrs Sanford hadn't told me much, but she'd made it clear that she had little in the way of kind thoughts for my mistress. And then there were Attwater and Laurel, and the suspicion they'd brought to that pained, awkward meeting on the green. *If there's anyone here who doesn't truly know her,* I thought, *it's me.*

Kian sighed and shook his hair back from his face. 'Look, Dee, I'm not trying to make you feel wretched. I just think you've got a right to know all this stuff. And, honestly, I like you. It's been so long since I've had anyone to talk to ... and here I am, spilling my guts all over your feet.'

I glanced down, feeling stiff and cold and empty. 'It's all right,' I said. 'Honestly, it's all right. I kind of feel the same way. I mean, when I set out to come here, it had been two years since I'd set foot out of our place. Two years since I'd talked to anyone outside of our family. And you — it has to be about the same for you, right?'

He nodded, hesitantly. 'Yeah. Something like that.'

I looked around, swallowing hard against the tightness in my chest — and then I noticed the angle of the light streaming through the trees, casting dappled shade over the forest floor. I jumped up with a start. 'Oh, Lord and Lady!'

'What?' Kian was on his feet just as quickly, reaching for his bow. 'What is it?'

'How long have we been sitting here? Good grief, she's going to wonder where I've got to. I'm supposed to be hunting down ingredients for a potion for her, and she wanted them soonest.'

'Oh,' he said, and I could hear the concern in his voice. 'Oh, hells. And here I've been taking up all your time.'

'No, no,' I said. 'It's not your fault. I needed someone to talk to, someone ... someone I could trust not to spread it around.'

'Oh, I wouldn't tell a soul. She's got a frightful temper, that one. If she heard what you'd said and took anger over it, I couldn't live with myself. But, Dee, you've barely been here a day, and you don't know anything about the mountains. How are you going to find anything?'

'Oh, I …' I faltered, then. I hadn't actually thought that far ahead. 'I …'

'Let me help you,' he said.

'Oh, I couldn't. You've got your own belly to fill.' I gestured to his bow and empty satchel.

'Never mind that, I can forage as we go along. There's plenty I can put in a pot that won't be scared off by us and the horse.'

'Well, if you're sure,' I said. I schooled my voice carefully, but inside my heart was suddenly pounding. It had been so long since I'd had a real friend, any friend at all; let alone one who could make my innards quiver with a shy smile. 'It would truly be an enormous help.'

The work went quickly with Kian's aid, though he rolled his eyes at the strangeness of collecting things like the hazel twigs, and catkins from thirteen different willow trees.

Without him it would have taken me twice as long to find everything. As it was the list led us far afield, up into the high meadows where a particular kind of caterpillar spun its cocoon. By the time we were finished we were miles from where we began, or from anything I recognised. The only landmark I could see was a distant waterfall that vanished from time to time behind the slopes.

At last, my empty belly was rumbling loud enough that even Kian could hear it. But when I flushed and made apologies, he just laughed before his smile quickly faded. 'Did she send you out with something to eat, at least?'

'Oh,' I said. 'She didn't, but that's my fault more than hers, I should have packed something. To tell the truth, she barely seems to notice if she's eaten or not, most of the time.'

'Oh really? Must be nice. Well, there's a stream over this way. Let me tell you, water in an empty belly is better than nothing.'

I followed him back down the hillside, through meadow and around thicket, leading the horse until we found a clear stream running over rocks. I watered the horse first, and then tethered him to a sapling before returning to the water myself to drink with cupped hands.

There, under the water, a glimmer of light caught my eye, and I frowned at the sparkling water. Another one? I reached in, cautiously, not believing it until my fingertips felt the smooth faces and crisp edges of the crystal, smaller than the one I'd found yesterday, but if anything, more perfect. It was only when I lifted it out to sparkle in the sunlight that I wondered what Kian would think if he saw it. I didn't know why I kept finding these stones but I couldn't deny the strangeness of it, and I knew full well he had nothing but hatred for witches. I didn't want to risk having him turn some of that coldness against me, when he was the only person here I felt I could truly talk to.

Kian had wandered downstream a little while I saw to the horse, and he was kneeling on a rock overhanging a pool, peering down into the water, so it was easy enough for me to sneak the crystal out of the water and tuck it into the pocket of my apron. Then, drinking from cupped hands, I watched as he stripped off his jacket and rolled up his sleeve. As slender as he was, his bare arm was all muscle as he dipped his hand into the water and reached down into the cool depths.

For a moment, we were all perfectly still, him lying flat on the rock, me crouched on my heels at the water's edge. And then, with a splash and a crow of victory, he threw a streak of silver onto the bank of the stream — a mountain trout, flopping and dancing among the rocks.

In what seemed like no time at all, he had half-a-dozen of them there, and all I could do was gape as he lined them up on the rock and pulled out a knife to clean them. 'There we are,' he said, 'a nice bit of lunch.'

'That was amazing!' I said. 'How did you do it?'

He gave me a shy grin. 'It's a trick my ma taught me. Takes a bit of work to learn it, though. When we went fishing we'd bring a bucket and she'd put one in it for me to practice on.'

'Oh,' I said, with a wistful note. I couldn't imagine my ma doing anything like that. I dreaded it when she'd try to teach me something new, she was always so impatient if I couldn't get it right away.

'Why don't you see if you can find us some dry twigs and such?' he said. 'I'll get a fire going and have these grilled in a flash.'

As soon as I came back with an armful of wood, he lit a fire with flint and steel, and with the fish strung on green twigs, sank the ends of the sticks into the earth to hang over the flames.

Sitting there, I had an idea, and began to hatch a plan. 'Kian?'

'Mm?' he said, glancing up.

'You must have a hard time coming by any coin out here.'

He gave me a slight frown. 'I can make most of what I need, or scavenge it. You'd be amazed what folk throw onto their rubbish heaps.'

'But what if I could arrange to get you a bit of money, now and then? If you brought a couple of rabbits or a string of fish to the cottage every week or so, I'm sure I could convince Aleida to pay you for it.'

His eyes narrowed. 'You want me to have dealings with that witch? Take her money?'

'Aleida's not evil like the old one was,' I said. 'I'm sure of it. I mean, the old one's dead, thanks to her; and she says she's going to do something about that warlock, and the beasts.'

Kian snorted. 'How? I saw what happened yesterday. He grabbed her by the throat and she couldn't do a blasted thing about it.'

I remembered the wand she'd had hidden under her cloak. 'I think, I think she let that happen. I think she wanted him to think she was weak.'

'But that's just more deception, isn't it? Folk like that, they're just liars through and through. Sure it's lonely, living like this, and sure I have to make do with what I've got rather than spend coin on fancy things, but no one out here lies to me.'

I could feel the crystal hidden in my apron pocket — suddenly it felt like it was made of lead. I hoped my cheeks weren't flushing. 'Just think about it? Please? If nothing else, it'd mean I could see you every week or two.'

He stopped then, as though that was something he hadn't considered. 'Well, that's a good point. I, I'd like that. If I'm not careful, I could get real used to having your company. I'm just ... Dee, I'm afraid she's going to be just like the last one. You don't know what it's like, living next to them. If you knew the misery they've caused, the damage they've done. And now that young one is swanning back in here like she owns the place. She's no different than the old Blackbone, really. How could she be, when the old one found her, gave her power, and trained her up in her image? They're just the same.'

'I don't think so,' I said. 'I think she's different. But I don't want to keep harping on at you. If she's different, you'll soon see it. You and everyone else around here.'

'I hope you're right. But I'll tell you this, Dee. If I'm right, and she's not different; if you ever decide you need to get away, I'll help you.' He plucked one of the trout from over the fire and handed it to me, the white flesh tender and steaming. 'I just don't want to see you end up like the other poor souls who've crossed paths with those wretches, and paid dearly for it.'

CHAPTER 7

After we'd devoured every morsel, I collected the horse and made sure the packs were safely tied. 'Many thanks for the food. I haven't had fish that fresh in years.'

'You're welcome. I haven't had anyone to share it with in years, either. Now, do you know your way back home?'

I bit my lip, looking out over the hillsides. 'Um, that way, I think?'

He sighed and shook his head. 'I guess I'd better come with you.'

'I'm sorry, I know we've come miles and miles from where we started.' I glanced up at Aleida's grey. I'd hardly spent any time at all on his back, and I had a thought. 'Why don't we ride? We've just been strolling along, so he's fresh as a daisy and you don't look like you weigh all that much.'

He gave me a wide-eyed look. 'Oh, I don't know, Dee. I've never ridden a horse.'

What, never? I almost said it aloud, but at the last minute I remembered how much I hated the response I always got when folk found out I couldn't read. *What do you mean you can't read? Didn't you go to school?*

Of course he'd never ridden a horse. Poor folk didn't, and despite my patched dresses and hand-me-down boots, it had been a lot of years since Ma and me were truly poor and hungry. 'Then come and ride with me,' I said with a smile.

He looked nervous, scuffing his foot in the loose earth. 'I ... oh all right, then.'

I climbed up into the saddle, arranging my skirts as discreetly as I could manage and very glad that I had my nice stockings on, to avoid showing too much leg. Then I kicked my feet out of the stirrups and offered a hand behind my back, ready to help him up. 'Come on, then. Put your foot in the stirrup and take my hand.'

It took a couple of tries, but then he was sitting behind me, his chest against my back. There truly wasn't much of him at all, the saddle stayed firmly put under his weight in the stirrup, and his hand took mine more for balance than anything else. Then, as he settled onto the saddlebags, the grey danced beneath us and his arms wrapped tight around my waist. Abruptly, he pulled away. 'Sorry,' he said.

'No, it's all right,' I said, pulling the horse's head in to quiet his stamping feet. Any doubts I had in this plan were swiftly fading. The horse set out with a sprightly step and it seemed to me he could carry three of us and barely feel the weight. 'If you start to slip, you'd best grab for the saddle, or his mane. If you hold on to me we might both go over.'

'Ah, good point.' He had to reach around me to hold the saddle-horn, which meant that he was pressed right against my back. Part of me rather enjoyed the feel of it, but most of me just wanted to giggle and gibber with nerves. I tried very hard to squash that part down — the last thing I wanted was to make the grey think there was something here to be nervous about. I did my best to think soothing thoughts for the both of us. 'So,' I said, 'where are we heading?'

'Oh! Ah, that way,' he said, pointing, and then quickly grabbed for the saddle-horn once again.

Heading homewards, my thoughts turned to Aleida, and I wondered how she was going with the construct she meant to build, and if she was getting impatient that I'd taken so long to collect her ingredients. *Well, honestly, it's her own fault. She had to know I wouldn't be able to do it quickly. She knows what it's like to be a stranger out here, after all.*

I remembered, then, what she'd said about Bennett, and how she'd met him, and suddenly I felt very strange. That was quite a coincidence, wasn't it? She'd been in the exact position I was in, sent out into unfamiliar territory to collect things she had no idea how to find, only to come across a local lad who helped her. Once again I had that peculiar sensation, as though the world had pulled back around me and I was watching everything from a state of calm detachment, before it all snapped back into focus.

Well, no, I told myself. *It's not the same circumstance at all. And besides, what does it matter if there are some similarities? It doesn't mean anything.*

I had bigger things to worry about, anyway — like this warlock. Aleida might have a plan to deal with him, but I wasn't looking forward to carrying it out, and I strongly suspected she'd need my help. She wasn't up to doing it all by herself; and even if she said she was, I didn't like the idea of letting her go alone.

'Hey, Kian?' I said. 'You must know this area pretty well, right?'

'Pretty well? I know it like the back of my hand,' he said.

'That's what I thought. So let me pick your brains a little. That fellow we saw yesterday must be camped somewhere nearby. You wouldn't happen to know where a fellow with three horses and not much gear would find a spot to hole up for a few days, would you?'

I felt him shift behind me. 'There are a few spots I can think of.'

'Would you show me?'

For a moment there was silence. 'You shouldn't get mixed up in her affairs. Not any more than you already are.'

I didn't want to risk an argument. The morning had been too pleasant to spoil it now. 'Oh, I'm just thinking, in case she's mad that I took so long, if I can tell her where the black rider is camped she might forgive me for it.'

'Oh, right. Well, there's an old bothy near the river, but that's a bit too close to Black Oak Cottage—'

'He's not there,' I broke in. 'I was there this morning, the place is deserted.'

'Well, there's a couple of little herdsman's shelters up in the high meadows, but there'll be folk up there at this time of year, grazing their cattle.' He shifted again. 'Actually, there is a place. It's a few miles from the cottage, down a ravine. There's a cave there, big enough for a couple of men and horses, with water and firewood nearby. It's no good for herders or folks on any regular business, but it's a good place for laying low, if you know what I mean.'

'Well that sounds promising. Could we go and take a look? Carefully, I mean.'

'Oh, very carefully. I don't want that fellow turning his attention our way. But if he's there we should see it easily enough, those big horses will leave tracks a blind man could follow.'

'All right, good. If we see them, that will be enough to tell my mistress, and we should be able to get in and out without being seen. Where do we go?'

'Head back to the main road. There's a stream flowing to the south that leads into the ravine.'

We set out, picking our way through the trees and following an easy path that kept to the flat — for Kian's sake, I told myself, since he was so green at sitting a horse, though I had to admit he was doing well.

We skirted around the trees as well, since low branches were a hazard to any rider, but as we passed by one thicket I couldn't help but notice huge clods of earth scattered over the patchy grass and wet litter of the forest floor. There were dozens of them, and still more smaller chunks, scattered around as though cast by a careless hand.

I reined in to look it over. 'That's odd, isn't it?' I twisted around to look over my shoulder at him.

'Yeah,' Kian said. 'It's odd.'

I turned the horse towards the thicket, and watched his ears. He didn't seem concerned, and even with the two of us on his back, I reckoned he would take any excuse for a run. 'Everything seems quiet, though.'

'True. Take us a bit closer, maybe?'

I nudged the horse onwards, closer and closer to the thicket. There was a clear trail of loose earth, I could see it now that we'd come closer. The clods nearest the trees were largest, some bigger than my head.

Behind me, Kian hissed. 'Something came through here. Something big. Look over there, there's a print it left behind.' He pointed, and I nudged the horse closer.

The print looked like no kind of foot that I'd ever seen — it looked like some unholy combination of a hand and a foot, with either stubby, clubbed fingers or long, grasping toes. 'Good gods,' I said.

'And look, through there.' He leaned forward, over my shoulder, and pointed into the thicket. Deep within the trees was a dark patch of earth. No, a hole in the earth, dark and damp.

We edged as close as the trees would let us.

The hole was enormous, big enough to swallow the stable-block back at Black Oak. The bottom of it was littered with loose earth, while broken tree roots bristled around the walls and the saplings around the edge leaned precariously over it, as though they'd fall in at the first touch of rain or wind. 'Earthbeast,' I said. 'That's what she called them. One was born from here, I think.'

Kian felt tense behind me. 'I think you must be right.'

'I wonder how long ago?'

'A few hours, from the look of it. This morning, I'd say, maybe around dawn? But listen, the birds are still chirping. It's long gone, I'd say.'

'Well, thank the Lord and Lady for that. But I wonder how many of them are out here?' I remembered what Aleida had said, about Gyssha making monsters by firelight like other folk knitted socks.

'Gods only know,' Kian said, and I felt him shiver. 'Let's keep moving.'

'Yes, of course.'

We left the cavernous hole in the earth behind, and, a disconcertingly short time later, found the road; though to my mind it hardly deserved the name when it was little more than wagon-ruts cutting through the soft earth.

I kept watch for anything that looked familiar, any sign that we were heading back towards the cottage, but the landmarks all looked the same, and I felt like I could have been anywhere in these hills. I couldn't even see the waterfall from here.

After heading north a ways, we reached the stream. Out here in the wilderness there was just a shallow, rocky ford that the grey splashed through without hesitation. 'Turn here,' Kian said, pointing downstream. 'And keep the horse off to the side, don't let him trample any tracks.'

We didn't see any prints at first, what with the rocks beside the stream and the bracken that choked the damp ground. After a while I reined in. 'Kian, I'm not sure …'

'Keep going,' he said. 'Just a bit further.'

Biting my lip, I pushed the horse on, around a willow tree that hung across the water in a green curtain. The ground was getting rockier here and ahead of us it rose, soil giving way to rocks and rubble, just as it had when I'd climbed the slope to the bothy that morning.

As the ground rose, the stream sank, cutting through the hillside in a rock-strewn ravine. Had I stumbled across the place by myself I wouldn't have looked any further — the water filled the entrance between the rocks, and it looked for all the world like there was no point going on, just a death-trap of water and rock. But there on the sandy bank above the water were hoofprints.

They were bigger by far than the grey's rather dainty hooves, and I thought of the three black horses I'd seen on the road, their huge hooves feathered with coarse black hair. There were many prints headed in, and even to my untrained eye the prints looked old and crumbling, but cutting across them was another, newer set. I realised, frowning to myself, that I had given no thought to what had happened to the horse yesterday after Aleida's beast had torn apart the construct, but if I was reading these tracks correctly it had somehow found its way back to its master. 'All right,' I muttered to Kian. 'I think this is the place.'

'So now what?' he whispered back.

'Now we get out of here. Back to the cottage.'

I turned the horse, and at once I was facing something huge and hulking.

The earthbeast was lurking under the trailing branches of the willow, so still, so perfectly still. I had a flash of memory, the beast Aleida had tamed, standing sentinel at the foot of the field below the cottage. Well, she wasn't the only one to put her captured monster on sentry duty.

I froze. Beneath me, the horse did the same. He didn't see it, I think, but he knew from the way I went tense that something was amiss. Behind me I felt Kian stiffen with unease — and then I felt his arms cinch around me as he saw it, too.

This beast had a deer's head, kind of, if a deer was large enough to eat a dog in one mouthful. The head was topped with antlers, pale as bleached bone. Its eyes were huge, milky marbles.

I gripped the reins tight in hands suddenly slick with sweat. 'Hold on,' I whispered to Kian. 'Hold on tight.' I pulled the grey's head around just as the earthbeast finally noticed us — those foggy eyes shifted our way, somehow *sharpened* — and then with a touch of my heels, Aleida's grey was off and running.

The horse launched with a surge of power I'd never felt before, a strength I could only dream of, thundering like a storm. Some half-remembered instinct had me crouching low over his neck, hands buried into his mane while Kian hunched behind me, fighting to keep his seat.

From behind us came an unearthly bellow, a scream of pure rage. It wasn't a bestial sound at all, but something else — it had something of a crash of thunder, something of the tearing screech of a falling tree, something of the roar of a rockslide. I glanced back and saw that the beast had been thwarted in following us — those bone-white antlers had fouled in the branches of the willow tree, but in the space of my glance it tore itself free and came thundering after us on clawed feet.

'Oh hells,' I said, hunching lower, and driving my heels into the grey's sides.

Kian was shouting in my ear, and it took me long moments to realise he was calling my name. 'Dee! Dee! You have to let me down!'

'What? No!'

'Do it! He'll be faster with just you on his back, and I'm going to fall if we keep this up.'

'Kian, it'll kill you!'

'No, no, I've got an idea. Cross back over the stream and veer east, and you'll see a huge oak tree. I can climb straight into the branches and hide in the crown, I did it once before when a wild boar chased me. That thing could never climb up and follow me, and, in any case, it'll be off chasing you. You have to let me off, Dee!'

'Are you sure?'

'Certain,' he said. 'You just keep heading north until you hit the road and then go west. You'll see your mistress's orchard from the road, you can't miss it.'

I had the token she'd made for me too, I belatedly remembered. The horse snorted, his arched neck turning dark with sweat, and I swallowed hard. 'All right. Just … take care? Find some way to let me know you're safe. And hold on, we're going to jump.' I hauled the grey's head around, towards the stream. We both almost fell as he leaped down into the water, and then made a laboured leap up the bank on the far side. It bought us a few precious moments. I stole another look back when I heard the beast crash into the water behind us. The creature wasn't built for agility, it seemed, and the grey's landing had weakened the bank. It took the earthbeast several tries to haul itself out of the water, but once it did it came charging after us again with another bellow of rage.

'There it is,' Kian shouted, and I wrenched my gaze away from the beast to focus on the huge oak ahead of us. The grey wasn't interested in stopping, and I couldn't blame him, so I had to heave back on the reins with all my might.

Kian reached up as we came under the branches, and in an instant he was up and gone, pulling himself up onto the bough and straight away reaching up again to climb higher. 'Go, Dee, go!' he shouted.

I felt awful for leaving him there alone, with no defence other than the height of his perch — after all the help he'd given me, this was scant thanks. But the one thing I could do was draw the enraged beast away. I gave the grey my heels again, turning him north — or what I thought was north — and then a little bit further, cutting closer to the earthbeast to draw him away.

As skinny as Kian was, losing his weight seemed to make a difference. I'd never ridden so fast in my life — only once had I come close, when I was much younger and our old cob had taken fright and bolted while I was

riding a message to our neighbours. I'd been terrified at
first, convinced I was going to fall, dropping the reins
to cling desperately to the front of the saddle. But then,
when I didn't fall, I'd discovered the rhythm of the horse's
gallop, and found out for myself how to find the balance
of it, the calm amid the chaos.

The grey was faster than old Ned had ever been, but
I'd lost the advantage of distance for the sake of drawing
the beast away from Kian. When we reached the road
and I veered west I stole another glance back, and the
beast seemed to be only a few lengths behind.

Gritting my teeth, I unwound one cramping hand from
the reins, and fumbled in my apron pocket. The crystal
was there, bouncing heavily against my leg, but beneath
it I found what I sought — the twig Aleida had made for
me, bound with a hair from each of our heads. Fishing it
out with a shaking hand, I snapped it in half.

Nothing happened. Not for long moments as the horse
pounded along the road, the beast bellowing behind us
and my heart thudding in my ears.

Then, I heard a rough *caw* overhead, and a black
shape appeared, plummeting down to land on the horse's
surging neck. It was a crow, all black shining feathers and
beady black eyes, and until that moment, I never realised
how big those birds were. As it perched there, talons
tangled in the grey's mane, the spread of its wings was
longer than my arm. Its beak was so close to my face I
would have winced away if I'd dared straighten from my
crouch over the grey's neck. 'Well, well, Dee,' it croaked.
'Have you made a friend?'

I was too relieved to be surprised. All of a sudden, strangeness meant safety. 'I need help!' I gasped. 'I need—'

'I'm already outside waiting for you. Come through the orchard around the western side of the tree. There's a ditch between the orchard and the road, so you'd best be ready to jump.'

I didn't need to ask what tree she meant. I just nodded.

With another harsh *caw* the crow leaped up from the grey's neck, quickly falling behind as its wings clawed the air. I heard another bellow, and glanced back to see it beating around the beast's head, making the stag-headed thing falter in its stride and gaining me a fraction more of a lead. I wondered if the beast was tired now, or if it *could* feel tired. It was born out of mud and earth and bound together with magic, for all I knew it could run to the ends of the earth without feeling fatigue. *Oh Lord and Lady.*

Then I saw it. From the crest of a little hill, I glimpsed the roof of the cottage, just a flash of slate faintly sheening in the sun, and down the gentle slope the grey–green mass of the demon tree. The horse was flagging beneath me, but I kicked him on without mercy, driving him forward with everything I had. *We're nearly there. We're so close!*

If she hadn't warned me of the ditch I wouldn't have seen it, it was so overgrown and cluttered with weeds and bracken. I saw it, but the horse didn't, and I wasn't skilled enough as a rider to tell him it was there. At the last minute he saw it and collected himself for a hurried, ungainly leap and an awkward landing that bounced me out of the saddle, throwing me forward over his shoulder.

I abandoned the reins and grabbed for his neck and mane. I was so desperate to keep from falling that I didn't notice how close we were to the demon tree — not until I saw ropy, grey–green tendrils dangling in front of me.

There was a flash of light, and a figure appeared in front of us — Aleida, dressed in a plain black shift, running towards us and waving her arms to scare the horse back. With a snort the grey tossed his head and veered away, just as the demon tree's vines struck my mistress like a hunter's snare. They struck, and found nothing there, and then thrashed and writhed in thwarted fury.

I was too busy trying not to fall to see what happened next, but when I could turn back to where she'd stood, there was nothing there but a furious tangle of vines, like a nest of snakes.

'Over here, Dee!' I heard her call, and saw her at last, standing on the grass at the edge of the orchard.

Then, with another bellow, the earthbeast crashed through into the orchard behind me, hard on the grey's heels. It, evidently, had more sense than I did, for it immediately veered around the demon tree.

In the corner of my eye, I saw a patch of air shimmer and ripple, and then Aleida's bull-headed beast appeared, as though a curtain had been swept away.

Head low, it charged and slammed its huge, spreading horns into the stag-beast's side with a force that sent it sprawling into reach of the demon tree's tendrils.

I kept heading towards Aleida, the grey slowing now that I wasn't driving him onwards anymore, but I couldn't look away from the tree and the beasts. The vines lunged, whipping through the air, snapping and snarling around the stag-headed beast. At the first touch of them it seemed to panic, throwing up its head and bellowing again, feet scrabbling at the dirt and fallen leaves beneath the tree, but as its head came up more grey–green tendrils reached down and snagged its antlers.

It wasn't just the stag-beast, though — some of those vines had caught hold of the bull-like horns as well. The branches above tossed and thrashed, flailing as though caught in a storm, long trailing tendrils lashing like whips.

When I reached my mistress, I reined in hard and wheeled the horse around. The stag-beast tried to plant its feet and haul against the vines, but its forelegs lifted from the ground, and then its hind legs, too. Thrashing like an insect caught in a spider's web, the beast struggled and flailed, and then, with a *whoosh* of wind and a groan of wood, the tree hoisted it up into the air.

The bull-creature was losing its battle too — the tree had it by the horns, the vines wrapped around and around like a herdsman's rope.

I turned to Aleida. 'Can you help it?'

She turned to me with a puzzled frown. 'Help what?'

'The beast! It's yours, isn't it?'

She snorted. 'Not anymore, the tree can have it.'

'But ...'

'It's not alive, Dee. It's just a construct.' She stood there, quite unconcerned, watching as the bull-headed thing was dragged and hoisted up into the thrashing branches — and then the only sound was the rustle of leaves, a sound that put me in mind of a huge flock of birds very quietly coming in to roost.

And then, a soft patter like gentle rain, except it wasn't water that fell to the ground beneath the tree's oily green–black canopy, but little clumps and clods of earth.

My hands were shaking, my legs trembling with the effort of clinging to the grey's sides. He was exhausted too, after that run. He was breathing hard, his head hanging by his knees and his coat damp with sweat. Shakily, I managed to kick my feet out of the stirrups and slither to the ground, just as something fell from the demon tree's canopy to land on the earth with a soft *thud*, followed swiftly by another.

The noise made me startle, and the horse too, pulling back with a snort. I quickly tightened my grip on the reins, even though my hands felt weak and slick with sweat.

At the edge of the tree's reach, Aleida held out her hand. The shapes on the ground — weird, twisted things, like clumps of unearthed roots — shook, trembled, and then skittered towards her over the bare ground.

She picked them up, one in each hand, and dragged them a safe distance away before dumping them on the grass.

The things were so grotesque it hurt to look at them. In protest, my eyes started to sear and water, stinging like salt and tears and smoke; it felt the way nails on a chalkboard feels to your ears. All I could make out were bones and bits of wood twisted together with wire and leather cord and little chunks of crystal; dark, gleaming things. 'What is *that?*'

'The seed,' Aleida said. 'The charm that bound it together and brought it to, well, not life. It was never alive.' She threw one of them aside. 'If I leave it here the earth might well form up around it again. But this one ...' She pulled a knife from her belt and slipped it into the net of woven wire around a kind of rib-cage, prying and levering until there was a hole big enough for her hand. She reached in with her fingers and grasped something inside the mess and then pulled it free with a sharp tug, just as my ears *popped*, just as they had before with the warlock's construct.

Then, all of a sudden, I could look properly at the thing. It seemed like a kind of doll, but a doll made of old bones and horns and teeth, and bits of old wood and dried roots, wrapped together in the form of a skeleton. It reminded me of an old, desiccated carcass, like a beast had died somewhere too dry to rot away, so it had mummified instead.

Aleida threw it aside, a little chunk of horror on the green grass, and turned to me. 'Did you go *looking* for that damn warlock?' There was anger in her face, stone in her eyes. I faltered, unable to speak.

'Dee,' she said in warning tones.

'I, I ...' Before I could muster my thoughts, a sudden noise from the crown of the demon tree interrupted me.

Straight away, Aleida's head snapped around, just as the branches and vines of the tree began to thrash and flail as though striking at something within.

I glanced quickly to my mistress, but she stood still, frowning at the tree. Her hand dropped to the wand at her belt.

'Uh, miss?' I said. 'What—'

'Hush,' she said, without looking around. 'Get the horse, take him to the house.'

'Miss—'

'*Now*, Dee.'

I swallowed hard. My legs were shaking, my arms, too. It always surprised me how much effort it took to ride a galloping horse, and that was without having a murderous magical construct pounding at your heels. On trembling legs, I staggered backwards towards the house, while the tree still thrashed and fought with something unseen.

Aleida backed up with me, though her steps were halting and uncertain, and her eyes never left the tree.

'What is it?' I hissed.

'Nothing good. *Move*, girl.'

I didn't want to leave her. But I had no idea what was in that cursed tree, and it looked like she did. If she said to move, I'd best listen.

Then, at the edge of the demon tree, I saw it — a black shadow, a patch of pure darkness, oozing out from between the branches like a knot of smoke. The tree was still trying to catch it, but the flailing tendrils passed through it like mist. The black thing paid the tree no mind. Instead, I had the sense that it was looking at *us*, sizing us up. I felt its gaze like a chill touch, a ray of pure cold. It froze me in place. 'Aleida—'

'*Move*, Dee!'

I tried, I really did, but it was too late.

The black shadow moved faster than a thought. In an instant it was wrapped around me, and I was swept away to an empty, dark place. Dark and cold, so very cold, a cold that felt like needles dragging over my skin, a cold that pierced me right to the heart.

Then, in another instant, it was gone. I was lying on the grass, huddled into a ball, while around me a few wisps of flame evaporated into the air. The grass around me was scorched, giving off little curls of smoke, or was it steam?

Gasping for breath, I shuffled backwards towards the cottage, obeying Aleida's order at last. I'd lost my grip on the reins and hurriedly glanced back to see the horse had obeyed where I had not.

I turned back to Aleida. She was still heading up the slope, too, shuffling through the long grass and leaning heavily on Attwater's stick. Her eyes were darting everywhere, from sky to ground, from orchard to forest.

I spotted the shadow only moments before she did. It was in the air, high above us, barely visible against the glare of the sun — and then, swifter than any arrow, it shot towards her.

I saw her fall in the instant before it wrapped around her, a churning cloud of pure darkness that swallowed her up. I heard a shout, though it was heavily muffled, and it could as easily have been a shout of defiance as a cry of pain. Then, within the cloud, a flower of fire bloomed, a spreading ball of pure flame that burned the darkness away, and the black smoke-creature was gone again, moving in utter silence.

Aleida lay sprawled on the grass. Blood sheeted her right arm, though she still gripped the wand tight as she tried to roll to her knees and find her feet.

Something was wrong, though. Something was very wrong. The line of her legs beneath her skirts was *strange*, crooked. Her legs bent where they shouldn't bend, her joints facing the wrong way. And there, under the hem of her skirts, was something even stranger. Beneath the stained and frayed cloth, damp and dirty from the orchard's earth, were a pair of hound's paws; huge, hairy and studded with blunt, scarred nails.

In the corner of my eye I saw the shadow forming up again, over near the garden wall. Aleida's flames could drive it off for a moment, it appeared, but weren't doing enough harm to drive it away.

Considering how quickly it could move, there was no time to think. So I didn't. I darted back to Aleida and pulled her free arm over my shoulders and heaved her to her feet. With one hand on her wrist and the other arm around her waist, I dragged her back towards the house.

As soon as she was upright those hairy paws vanished under her skirts, but I could feel her teetering upon them, leaning heavily against me. *Lord and Lady*, I thought. *No wonder she's so unsteady on her feet.*

'The house,' she gasped in my ear. 'Gyssha has defences around it, unless she went and moved the damn things.'

Then, in that same unearthly silence, the shadow-creature shot towards us again.

Aleida tensed beside me, raising the wand, and I felt something rise up from the earth around us. It felt like walking into a spider's web in the dark, sticky and stretchy and clinging, but at its touch I felt Aleida shiver with relief.

The shadow-creature slammed into us, and again I felt the inky blackness wrap around me. This time, in the frozen, biting darkness, I felt the touch of something sharp, like teeth or claws, or knives perhaps, and I understood where the wound on Aleida's arm had come from.

But then, before the wicked edge could sink in, a tracery of light flared over the shadow-creature, glowing strands knotted together like a hunter's net.

Suddenly I was lying on the grass, my legs tangled with Aleida's, her body pinning my arm to the ground. She struggled free of me just as I did of her, and each of us scrambled back, out of reach of the thrashing black cloud pinned down under a net of light.

'Ha!' Aleida said. 'Got you.'

With her hands on the grass she got her legs beneath herself and slowly straightened, wobbling and unsteady. Once she was standing upright, she pulled a knife from her belt, and with the wand in her other hand, brought them both together. She began to speak in a language I didn't understand, saying words that thrummed in my ears, and with a tool in each hand, began to scribe a symbol that hung in the air in a glowing tracery of blue light. Then, with a final gesture, and a word that crackled like fire in dry grass, she slashed through the glowing symbol, and it shattered into myriad fragments.

The fragments blasted towards the captured shadow, and when they hit the inky blackness, they began to burn with a clear blue flame, as bright and brilliant as the summer sky.

The shadow-creature howled and shrieked, thrashing and fighting, but it couldn't escape the blue flame. In moments, there was nothing left but ash.

CHAPTER 8

Aleida staggered to the back step and sat heavily on the stone, breathing hard as she slumped against the wall.

I stayed where I was. I felt frozen. Numb. A short time ago, I'd had the thought that strangeness meant safety, but now, now I felt cut adrift from everything I thought I knew.

With an effort of will, I unstuck my feet from the ground and headed over to my mistress. She still had her wand and knife in her hands, and her right arm was a sheet of blood, dripping on the stone.

I pulled my handkerchief from my apron pocket and offered it to her, gesturing to the wound. Wearily, she lifted her head, and then waved it away with a grimace. 'No, no. No sense ruining it. I'll deal with it in a moment, I just need to catch my breath.'

I crouched on my heels to peer at her face. Her golden skin was sallow and ashen, not at all a healthy shade. 'Do you want some water?'

'Gods, yes.'

To get to the well I had to walk past the charred spot on the turf where the shadow-creature had died. I steeled myself to stride past it without flinching. I could still feel the heat left behind by the blue flames.

I brought her some water, and fetched some for the horse as well, though not so much he'd give himself bellyache from drinking his fill before he'd cooled down. I stripped off the saddle and bridle too, and felt guilty for not walking him until he'd cooled, but I wasn't game to stray too far from the cottage and its defences right now.

With the saddlebags and the sack of ingredients in my arms, I came back to the step in time to see Aleida wipe her hand along the cut on her arm, firmly, as though trying to rub off a smear of grime. With one stroke of her hand, the cut was gone, and only a faint white line in her skin was left within the smear of blood.

I set the bags and sack at her feet. 'Now *that's* a neat trick.'

'Mind over matter, kid,' she said, without looking up. 'It only really works on little things, though.' She looked down at her bloody palm and, with a shrug, wiped it off on her skirt. I started to understand why all her clothes were dyed black.

Then, her eye fell on the saddlebags, and her face lit up. 'You got them!' She started to rummage through the packs, and as she stretched her legs out for balance, the dog's feet peeked out from beneath the hem of her skirts once again.

'What in the gods' names was that thing?' I said, my voice still trembling. 'Where did it come from?'

'It's called a Nefari, not that that would mean much to you. It's a creature from the nether realms; they feed on blood and fear and pain. Looks like he buried it in the beast he captured, ready to spring out when I destroyed the construct.' She fixed me with a cold gaze. 'Searching out the warlock was stupid, Dee. Really, really stupid. Do you have any idea what he'd have done to you if he'd caught you? Man like that, you'd be lucky if all he did was kill you.' She turned back to her bags, then, and went on. 'On the other hand, if the Nefari sprung out while I was in the middle of fighting the warlock, it'd be one hell of an unpleasant surprise. So I guess you did me a favour dragging it back here like that.'

'Is it dead? That blue fire ...'

'Yep,' she said. 'Aethereal flame. It's the only way to kill them; everything else just banishes them for a time. Ah,' she said, pulling a brown leather pouch out of her packs. 'Finally!'

Inside was a pipe of dark brown wood, a pipe-tool and a pouch of tobacco. Her hands were still shaking, I noticed, as she filled the pipe.

I frowned at the sight of it. Women didn't smoke, where I was from. My da had smoked — I had a vague memory of curling up on his lap when I was a little girl, while he filled his pipe after a long day. But mostly the smell of the wretched stuff reminded me of Lem. Settling down to fill up his pipe was usually the time he started to lecture me on whatever fault he'd found that day.

Aleida glanced up and seemed to read my distaste.
'Don't like it?' she said. 'Move upwind then and you
won't smell it so bad. But I need this right now. I've had
a rough week.'

That much was true, I conceded. 'I've never seen a
woman smoke a pipe,' I said.

'Haven't you? Then I know you've never been to the
Rat's Nest in Stone Harbour. Not that it's somewhere
you'd *want* to go. You could burn the place to the ground
and the world'd be better off.' She plucked a twig from
the ground near the step. Holding it close to her mouth,
she breathed on it, and with a wisp of smoke it caught
alight. 'There are worse vices than tobacco, Elodie. Trust
me, I've tried most of 'em.'

I felt on edge, tense as a bow-string, and it took me
a while to figure out why. It wasn't just the reek of the
tobacco, though that was part of it. I felt like I didn't
know this woman sitting on the step before me. Since I'd
first seen her, slouching in the doorway with a lantern in
her hand, I'd thought of her as weak and injured. Which
she was, undeniably. But she was also powerful in a way I
couldn't comprehend. It was as though there was a slot in
my mind for her, but she no longer fit in it.

Aleida glanced up again, one eyebrow raised. 'No
more questions?'

I sat down on the grass and wrapped an arm around
my knees. 'What happened to your feet?'

She glanced down at them with a grimace. 'Gyssha's
death-curse.'

'But yesterday when we walked down to the river ... they were normal then.'

Aleida cleared her throat, and in the blink of an eye the dog's paws were gone, and a pair of normal, slightly pink human feet were in their place. Then, a second later, the hairy paws were back. 'Illusion,' she said. 'Easy to cast, doesn't take much power, but it's just for show. They're still cursed hard to walk on. Or I can nullify the effects of the curse for a little while, and they turn back properly, but that works by blanking out *all* magic, so it's not that useful. Or I could cast a spell that unravels the curse for a time, but that's hard. A lot of work, a lot of power. More than I can manage right now, and it wouldn't last long.'

'Do they hurt?'

She grimaced around the stem of the pipe. 'They ache. Like wearing boots two sizes too small.' She pulled her legs in again, flicking the hem of her skirt over to hide them from sight. 'Well, Dee, you've had an exciting morning. Learn anything useful?'

It seemed a pointed question. Lem did that sometimes, hinting that he knew about some mistake I'd supposedly made, some transgression I had to be punished for. It didn't matter what I had or hadn't done, if he made up his mind I'd committed some crime, nothing would convince him otherwise. 'I know where the warlock's camped,' I said. 'There's a ravine—'

'I know where he is,' she said with a puff of smoke. 'A little bird told me. The question is, how did *you* know it was there?'

I felt myself flushing. *Stupid.* I was stupid to think for a moment there was anything I could tell her that she couldn't find out herself, and with much less effort. 'I was only trying to help!'

She waved away my words. 'Quit it, Dee. I ought to rake you over the coals for doing something like that, but I'm tired, and like I said, better to handle the Nefari now than in the middle of a fight. If I wasn't on home turf with those defences already in place, it would have been much worse to deal with. But you need to be more careful,' she said, jabbing the pipe in my direction. 'It's all well and good to have some initiative, but trying to track down a warlock when you've got no powers and no defences is *not* the best choice to make if you want to live to see your next birthday, all right?'

I pressed my lips together, sullen, and her mouth quirked in a brief smile. 'But you still haven't answered my question. How did you know where to look?'

I looked away, and heard her sigh.

'Dee,' she said. Her voice was soft, but there were notes of iron and stone within it. 'Don't make me *make* you tell me.'

My head snapped back, eyes wide, and I remembered how she'd looked at me that night I'd arrived on the doorstep, the darkness in her eyes. She was still sitting slumped, her elbows on her knees as she held the pipe lazily in one hand, but I knew it was no idle threat.

'I asked someone,' I snapped. 'I needed help, with that list you gave me; I don't know these hills any more than you did when you came here.'

She shrugged, and nodded. 'Who was it?'

'Just some local lad.'

Her eyes widened, just a fraction, and then she laughed. 'A local lad? My, my, Dee, you *do* move quickly. Anyone I know? Not one of the Sanford boys, is it?'

I'd thought I was blushing before, but now I could feel my cheeks blazing red. 'No!'

'Good, last thing I need is Tabby Sanford rallying her whole clan to turn up on my doorstep with torches and pitchforks.'

I swallowed hard. 'He, he's scared of you. You and your old mistress.'

She flinched at that word, and I counted it a small victory at the same time as I cursed myself for prodding this woman with powers and skills I couldn't comprehend. 'Is he?' Aleida said, her voice flat. 'I imagine he had some tales to tell.'

'He did,' I said, holding her gaze. 'He said you poisoned a man in the Lilsfield tavern. He dropped dead leaving a wife and children behind. Is that true?'

She took a long draw on the pipe. And then she nodded. 'Yeah. Yeah, I did do that. To be fair, I didn't poison him in the tavern, but he did die there.' She sighed a cloud of smoke and looked away from me, out across the meadow. 'He was a drunk who liked to smack his little kids around, and one day he cracked his two-year-old's head on the side of the fireplace. Their older girl came here to beg for help. Gyssha was busy with something or other, but she told me I could try my hand on the girl if I wanted to. She was a right mess, but I managed to fix her up. Took me all blasted night and it was bloody hard work, I'll tell you. The whole time that wretched man was blubbering and weeping about how sorry he was and how it would never happen again. He swore to me that he'd never touch another drop. I didn't believe a damn word. So I told him to put his money where his mouth was — I made up a potion and told him that if he ever took another drink he'd keel over dead on the spot, and if he truly loved his family he'd drink it.'

'Oh,' I said.

'Yeah.'

'How long did it take?'

'I think it was ten days.' Aleida raked a hand through her hair and grimaced. 'I told you, there's a lot of things I'm not proud of, Dee. I shouldn't have done it. I could have made it so that the smallest sip would make him puke up his toenails, or shit his britches or spend the rest of the night thinking he's a chicken ...' She curled a hand around her face, covering her mouth as she stared out into nothing. 'But then I think of that little girl with her head cracked open, and, well, what's done is done. At least he's not going to beat those children anymore.'

'Are they still around here? The rest of the family, I mean?'

'No. After he died they moved away. I wasn't too happy with the mother, either, she used to drink with him and she never tried to protect the little ones. Of course, Gyssha thought the whole affair was hilarious. You should have heard her cackling when she heard about it.'

I frowned, knotting my fingers together as I thought. 'But the lad said that you wouldn't help, when people got sick. He said people died that you could have saved.'

Again, she nodded. 'Yeah. That happened. More than I like to think about.'

'But Gyssha let you save that little girl.'

Aleida shifted, stiffly, pressing a hand to her sore ribs. 'Look, you have to understand, Gyssha didn't serve anyone but herself. Knowing how to save someone with their head bashed in is useful. But you don't waste that skill on every peasant who comes weeping to your door. She let me do it once in a while, to learn how. To practise. And probably to get me out of her hair, so she could do something behind my back. The rest of the time ...'

'But you could have done *something*! His mother died because you wouldn't help them!'

'What did you want me to do, defy her?'

'Yes!'

'No! If I'd tried, she'd have killed the woman anyway. You don't understand, Dee, you never met Gyssha. I tried, Lord and Lady, I tried. One time I defied her I ended up with my hands in a gods-damned jar and she made me beg for a week to get them back. She could turn your mind inside-out and leave you writhing in the dirt, begging her to cut your throat 'cos it'll never be right again. She'll give you nightmares that'll make you afraid to ever fall asleep. She'll make you crave the scorpion's sting, make you long for the touch of red-hot steel like you long for a lover's kiss.'

I let the words wash over me without sinking in. I was good at that. I'd had lots of practice, back at home. 'And then you ran away. You ran and left all these people with her.'

'Yeah. Yeah, I ran, like a whipped hound. I've got the feet now to remind me of it, every damn day. Listen, little girl, you think I don't know what the folk around here think of me? You think I *care*?'

I glared at her, refusing to look away, refusing to give in and drop my head. 'He said you had a temper. He said you had a mean streak.'

'Well, maybe he does know me, after all,' she snapped. Then, pipe gripped in her teeth, she snatched up the sack, and heaved herself to her feet. 'Enough of this,' she muttered, 'I've got work to do.' Holding on to the wall for balance, she staggered inside, and slammed the door shut behind her.

For a time I just sat there, stewing. I didn't know what to think. It seemed that everything Kian had told me was the truth, just not all of it. But did that make any difference? It didn't change what happened. His mother still died because Aleida refused to help. Did *why* she refused make any difference? Not to Kian, or his poor ma.

On the other hand, Aleida knew it was wrong. She'd done *something* about it. You could call her a coward for just running away and leaving Gyssha behind, but what if she'd attacked her then and died for it? Or maybe she should have stayed and kept trying to reduce the harm that Gyssha did?

I bit my lip at the thought of that. I had an inkling of what that might be like, after all those years with Lem and Ma. As much as I loved my ma, I couldn't deny I held a little knot of scorn buried deep in my chest for the way she turned the other cheek and pretended not to hear Lem carry on about how lazy and selfish I was after I'd worked all blessed day to clean his house and wash his clothes and cook his food.

Why should I scorn Aleida for running away? I'd thought of it too. I just hadn't ever climbed the hurdle of actually *doing* it.

At least in the end she'd come back to put it right — or as right as it could ever be when a young family lay cold in the ground, for no other reason than an evil witch's whims.

I could imagine what Kian would say to that: *a pity she waited so long. If she'd come sooner, maybe Bennett and his family would still be alive.* I wondered, though, if he'd still say that if he saw what I saw. Aleida might have won that fight with her old mistress, but the cost had been high. Between the battle and Gyssha's death-curse, she had been left crippled and weak. If I hadn't come along, the gods only knew what state she'd be in by now.

I sighed and shook out my skirts. I couldn't deny she was as prickly as a cat in a thorn bush, but I reckoned she'd come by it honestly. *Who am I to say what she should and shouldn't have done, anyway?* I thought as I heaved myself up. I was just a servant girl, and there were chores to be done.

I saw to the horse, fetching him more water and brushing the sweat from his coat, and then I found a spot in the stables to stow the saddle and bridle. I took my mistress's packs inside and dumped them by the bed. Coming out again, I noticed something on the mantelpiece that hadn't been there before — a bone-white lump positioned between the teapot and our few unbroken bowls.

Frowning, I crept closer, only to jump back when the shape of it became clear. It looked like a spider made out of wood, a little larger than the palm of my hand, with legs whittled from twigs and jointed with wire, and a body that was a bundle of wood shavings wrapped up in thread. There was a stubby crystal sticking out of the plump body, and a number of tiny, sparkling beads woven into the head, which could have been eyes. Frowning, I crept closer.

The spider moved, legs jerking like a marionette as it turned around to face me and then reared up, lifting its front pair of legs wide.

I jumped back with a shriek, clapping a hand over my mouth to quiet the noise, and fled the room.

To settle my nerves, I had a bite to eat, just some bread and cheese and a couple of apples from the safe end of the orchard. While I was in the pantry, I heard strange noises through the door to the workroom and risked peeking through a knothole in the wood. Past the shelves with the grotesque stores, Aleida was erecting a complicated array of glassware, lots of strangely shaped bottles and twisting tubes linked together with some unwholesome-looking tubing.

I took my lunch out to the back step to eat, glad that I didn't have to bother with that rubbish. Once my belly was full, I set to work again in the garden.

I was there for the better part of the afternoon, pulling out weeds, tying up plants, watering wilted vegetables and picking overripe and vermin-eaten produce to haul to the rubbish heap behind the stables.

It felt good to be doing something *normal* for a while, even if I did feel terribly lonely. Back home I'd have had Ma and Lucette working alongside me. Little Jeb and Maisie would be there too, chasing each other through the rows of plants, picking off caterpillars and bugs to feed to their favourite hens. I found myself imagining what it would be like to tell them all that had happened since I'd left home, all the things I'd seen. Lucette would cover her ears at some parts of the tale, she insisted that she hated scary stories; but one of my other brothers, Matto, would listen rapt and wide-eyed to every single word. *If only I could write, I'd send them a letter,* I thought. *Lem would say it's all lies and fancies, but he can carry on all he likes when I'm not there to hear it.*

But it was a waste of time even to think such things when I couldn't read or write a word, and I wasn't likely to learn any time soon. Even if my mistress was inclined to teach me, I doubted she'd have the patience for it and, in any case, when would we have the time?

I was sunk deep into these dark thoughts when I heard a noise that made me freeze — the soft sound of a horse's hooves, snapping twigs and rustling leaves.

My first thought was of the black rider, returning to claim the dryad he'd been promised. With the garden fork still in my hands I darted towards the cottage and flattened myself against the wall outside the workroom window. For a moment I nearly called out to my mistress inside, but I soon thought better of it. She had her own ways of knowing what was happening around us, after all.

Then, a moment later there came another noise, and I was glad I'd held my tongue. A soft rustling reached my ears, and then … chickens?

I crept around the cottage just as I heard a girl's voice, talking softly. 'Whoa now, Bess. Now I wonder, is anybody here?'

I recognised the voice, just as I recognised that she was talking as much to calm her own nerves as her horse. I leaned the fork against the wall and stepped out, wiping my hands on my apron. 'Melly?'

She was sitting on a stocky bay horse with a pair of wicker baskets slung behind the saddle. Her face lit up with relief when she saw me. 'Dee, I'm glad to see you! Is your mistress around? I don't want to stray where I'm not welcome, see …'

'Miss Blackbone is in her workroom,' I said. 'I don't think we'll disturb her out here. What brings you?'

'I've brought the chickens your mistress wanted,' she said, slipping down to the ground. 'Four of them, all first-year layers. Ma picked them out herself. Where's your coop?'

The thought of fresh eggs cheered me up immensely, until I remembered that I hadn't given any thought to where the birds would live. There *was* a coop near the stables, but I had no idea what state it was in. And, given the condition of the rest of the cottage, I didn't have high hopes. 'It's over here. But I confess I haven't had any time to look at it.'

'Oh?' Melly said. 'I suppose you would have had a lot of work to do.'

A lot of work and a lot of excitement, with little of it the pleasant kind. 'Maybe we should go take a look before you get those baskets down.'

It didn't look promising at first glance. The coop had a base of stone, which was a good start, but the upper part was built of wood and covered with shingles, a number of which were split and falling off.

Melly sucked her cheeks in as she looked it over, in a way that reminded me of the teamster, Yosh. She pulled a little knife from her belt and tested the wood underneath. 'Well, the good news is that it isn't rotten. Do you have any spare shingles? There's only a few broken, it wouldn't take long to patch it up.'

'I honestly have no idea,' I said. 'Let's go and look.'

She hesitated. 'Your mistress won't mind?'

'I shouldn't think so. She asked for the birds, after all, and they need somewhere to live.'

At first Melly looked around the cluttered stables with interest, only to shrug with a disappointed face at the decidedly un-magical mess of old, rusted tools, bits of rope, splintered buckets and bundles of rags, and dozens of other odds and ends. 'Oh,' she said. 'I thought there'd be ...'

'Jars full of pickled ox eyes and glassware made by a blind madman?' I said. It was meant to be a joke, but my voice came out rather too bitter to pull it off. 'That stuff is all inside the house.'

Melly was frowning at first, but then it turned into a smile. 'Truly, Dee, what's it like in there?'

She thought I was only teasing, bless her. 'Well, it's mostly empty, now. Most everything got smashed up in the fight,' I said. 'Well, in the main room, anyway. I don't really go into the others. Exploring only turns up surprises of the unpleasant kind. Oh, here we are.' In a corner under a crumbling oilcloth I found a stack of shingles, tied up in bundles with string.

'Oh, good,' said Melly. 'And here's a hammer and a cask of nails. Are you sure she won't mind if we use these?'

'I doubt she'll even notice,' I said. 'If we use them up, she'll just have to buy more. It's not like she doesn't have the coin for it.' I winced the moment the words left my lips. I hadn't meant to say it, not really.

Melly's eyes grew wide. 'Is that so? Well, well, I always heard they were rolling in it.'

'Oh Lord and Lady,' I groaned. 'I really shouldn't have said that. Please don't pass it on.'

'I promise, Dee, my lips are sealed,' she said, her eyes bright and merry.

I found another hammer and we brought everything outside. I wasn't sure what to do with it all — back at home there were strict rules about whether something was a job for girls or boys, and anything involving a hammer was most definitely for the boys. But I watched Melly as she pried out nails and lifted off shingles, and then I started to copy her.

'So how do you like the place, Dee?' Melly asked as we set about the work. 'It must be terribly interesting.'

'Sure,' I said. 'If by terribly interesting you mean interestingly terrifying. But that's only part of the time. The rest of the time I'm just looking after the garden or milking the goat or cleaning up inside.'

'And have you, well, have you *learned* anything yet?'

The way she said it had me give her a sidelong glance. 'What do you mean?'

The hopeful look she was giving me swiftly faded. 'Oh, well, I suppose you have only been here a day or so.'

'Melly ...' I said with a frown; and then suddenly I understood. 'You think I'm going to be a witch?'

'Why else would Miss Blackbone have hired you on?'

I dropped my gaze. 'She's been very poorly ever since the fight.'

'Oh, I know that. But that can't be the only reason you were brought here. I mean, why you? And from so far away, too?'

They were the same questions that had been burning in my mind since I'd left home. Funny, though, how they'd all but dropped out of my thoughts since I'd arrived here. Mind you, I'd hardly had time to catch my breath, what with all that had been happening. *It wasn't Aleida who brought me here,* I thought. *But it wasn't Gyssha, either. So who was it?*

Melly nudged me with her elbow. 'Come on, Dee, don't tell me you haven't even thought about becoming a witch.'

I set my hammer down and straightened, looking past the stables and down to the orchard. The grey horse was still hanging close, I could see him grazing in the meadow through the trees. 'I truly hadn't given it a thought.' I frowned then and picked up the hammer to get back to work. 'Honestly, I'm not sure I'd want to. From what I've seen of it, being a witch is kind of ... dreadful, really.' I couldn't help but think of the Nefari, the demon tree that had destroyed two earthbeasts, and the odd little spider-thing my mistress had made from the branch. And the dog's hairy paws sticking out from the hem of Aleida's skirts.

Melly huffed a sigh. 'And there you go, spoiling my nice daydreams of how much fun it must be, learning how to cast spells.'

I must have given her a sharp look, because she raised her hands in a gesture of peace. 'I'm just joking, Dee!' She looked thoughtful. 'Ma asked me to tell you again, though, if you wanted to leave, we'd help you.'

'Thanks, Melly. But Miss Blackbone already told me that she'll send me on my way with a bit of coin, if that's what I want.'

'But it's not?' Melly asked. 'Even if it is a little bit dreadful?'

'Oh, it's mostly just dreadful for her,' I said. 'I'm just a serving-girl. I keep my head down and do as I'm told.' It was time to change the subject. 'Do you get a lot of visitors to Lilsfield?'

'Oh, hardly any at all, unless you head across to the Overton road. Just merchants who come through to buy our goods, or bring in wares to the store. Oh, and then there's ...' She broke off, pulling a face.

'There's what?' I said.

'Oh, Dee, we just got done talking about how awful witchcraft is, I didn't mean to bring it up.'

'It's all right,' I said. 'I did ask the question.' A thought came to me, then. 'Were you going to talk about Old Miss Blackbone's visitors?'

Melly gave me a sharp look. 'Are you sure you're not going to be a witch? Because you did just read my mind. Nasty characters,' she said with a shudder. 'You'd spot them on the road and just *know* something weren't right. If you had the chance you'd turn away and find some job to do elsewhere, but sometimes they'd want directions or supplies and you wouldn't get a choice.'

'Do they cause a lot of trouble?' I said, thinking of Brian and my first sighting of the black rider.

'I always had the feeling that they could do a lot of harm,' Melly said. 'But they never did. Ma reckons they were too scared of Miss Blackbone, Old Miss Blackbone, that is. Gran says there was one who made a lot of trouble, long ago, before Ma was even born, but Old Miss Blackbone settled her good and proper. No one was allowed to mess with us but her.' She frowned, then, looking up into the afternoon sky. 'I wonder if that'll change, now that Old Miss Blackbone is gone and we've just got the young one instead?'

I thought of the black rider, and shivered. 'Oh, she's pretty canny,' I said.

'But she's hurt.'

'Yes, but she'll get better. She just needs rest and some good food.'

'Lucky she's got you, then.'

'But you don't have any other trouble?' I said. 'Like with poachers, or thieves?'

I wasn't even sure why I said it. I certainly didn't think the question through before it left my lips. The words seemed to bubble out of my mouth unbidden.

'Poachers?' Melly looked at me with wide eyes. 'Around here?' She seemed puzzled. 'I don't know how things are down on the plains, but up here it's a fool's errand to fuss over who owns the wild game. I mean, anyone who messes with our cattle or such will get what's coming to them, but the deer and the rabbits and the other wild beasts? They belong to the mountains, not to men.'

'So you do get folk who make a living from hunting them?'

'Like Mr Attwater, you mean, or Bennett Winthrop, gods rest his poor soul? Yes, a few. Mountain folk, we call them. They'd rather live rough and wild in the woods than clear a patch of land and make a farm. Nothing wrong with that; it takes all kinds, as Pa says.'

I thought on that, as we hammered the new shingles onto the henhouse. Kian had definitely said that the Sanfords didn't like him; it didn't add up.

Maybe, I reasoned, he just *thought* they didn't like him. Or maybe it wasn't his thought at all, but his ma's. I remembered how my ma was, after Da died. For a time there she'd been convinced that folk hated her, that they looked down on her and talked behind her back, that they conspired against her. That was one good thing about Lem, as much as it pained me to say it. After he took us in, Ma was so much happier and all those dark thoughts seemed to fade away. But if things hadn't worked out that way, if it had stayed being just her and me, I might have eventually believed all she said about how everyone hated us.

'Melly,' I said. 'You've lived here all your life, haven't you?'

'Sure have,' she said.

'So if there was a boy I'd seen, who lives around here, you'd know him, right?'

Melly tossed her hair back. 'Oh, I know everyone. A boy, hey?' She grinned and nudged me with her elbow. 'What does he look like?'

'He's got brown hair with a touch of red, and curly. Brown eyes, and freckles, and pale skin. He's tall, and skinny. And he has bony wrists.'

Melly rolled her eyes to the sky, tapping a finger to her lips. 'There's a lad lives on the far side of the Overton road who looks a bit like that. He was an orphan from down on the plains but came out here to be the wheelwright's apprentice. He's not all that skinny anymore though. I tell you, he's got some lovely arms on him now, and those shoulders ...'

I shook my head. 'No, that's not him.'

'No? Well, it could be one of the Belltree boys from over the ridge, they've all got their ma's curly hair. Was he with a fat little boy or a spotted dog? The Belltree boys never go out without one or the other.'

'No, no, that's not right either.'

'Hmm. Well I know it's not my other brother, Todd, he's still laid up with a broken foot. There's Gavin Carson, out to the south, but he won't set foot out this way since Mr Greenwood caught him trying to sneak in through Tamsin's window last summer. Thrashed him within an inch of his life and told him he'd finish the job if he ever saw his face again. He doesn't have freckles, though, and if it was him you'd have mentioned his ears.' Melly shook her head. 'Anything else you know about him, Dee?'

'Well, he dresses kind of rough,' I said. 'And he carries a bow with a quiver on his belt.'

Melly slowly shook her head. 'Nope, don't know anyone like that.'

It was curious. Very curious. 'All right, thanks anyway,' I said. 'If I see him again, maybe I can ask him.'

Melly looked sombre. 'I'd have a care, Dee. Strange things happen around here sometimes ... well, not that you need me to tell you that, hey?'

'No. You know, it's a wonder there's so many folk live around here, what with the stories I've heard.'

'Oh, well,' Melly said. 'There's a reason for that, you know. It's the tax collector, you see.'

'Tax collector? What about him?'

'There isn't one. Not anymore. Old Miss Blackbone saw to that.'

'*Oh*,' I said. 'Well, that makes sense.'

We soon had the henhouse finished, and popped the new hens inside. Melly fetched some water for them while I searched for something to line the nesting box, and settled on some chaff from the black rider's construct, since there wasn't anything else available. Since it was getting too late to let the hens out I gathered some vegetable scraps for them and left them to settle in, happily clucking and warbling to each other in the cosy darkness.

We put the tools and the unused shingles away, and on our way back from the stables Melly's foot hit something hidden in the grass. Her hobnailed boots struck it with a high-pitched *chink*, and she bent down with a frown.

When she straightened, she held a little glass bottle, no bigger around than my thumb and forefinger and about as long as my palm. She held it out to me. 'You'd better have this, Dee, it must belong to your mistress.'

It was sealed with a cork and was mostly full of some clear liquid. There was a paper label pasted to the glass, and though it wasn't brand new it wasn't all faded and dirty, either. 'Doesn't look like it's been here long,' I said with a frown. 'What does that word say? Can you read it?'

'It's laudanum,' Melly said.

'Oh.' I tucked it away in my apron pocket. I knew what laudanum was. Ma had a little bottle, back at home. I wasn't sure where this one had come from, though —

maybe the old witch had dropped it, before Aleida came to confront her. Or maybe it had fallen from Aleida's packs when I'd been putting all the gear away.

'Well, I'd best head back before it gets dark,' Melly said.

'Of course,' I said. 'Thanks so much for your help, Melly.'

'Don't mention it,' she said, mounting up onto her horse again. 'But there's just one thing, Dee. If you do end up becoming a witch, I'm going to say I told you so. Just warning you now.'

I shrugged. 'That's fair enough. Safe journey.'

'You too,' she said with a wink, and turned the bay to ride away.

⁘

I milked the goat and shut her in the stables, then I brought in some wood and water and closed up the house for the night. I thought about knocking on the door to see if my mistress wanted some dinner, but after our words earlier I decided I wasn't quite game. Instead I fixed her a plate of food, with another plate over the top to keep any vermin away, and left it by the workroom door. Then I had my own dinner, sitting beside the fire in the barren kitchen. It seemed a waste to light the lantern when there was only me here to use the light, and in any case, I didn't have any handiwork to do to make it worthwhile. Back home I'd have socks to knit or mending to do or a dress or shirt to make for someone, but here I didn't even have a needle, let alone thimble or shears. Lem had kicked up such a fuss at me taking my needle-book that Ma had rolled her eyes and taken it for a keepsake. It had made me happy at the time, thinking that it was important to her to have something that I'd made and used every day, but now it meant that I was just sitting here twiddling my thumbs. It felt so strange, sitting still like this, having nothing to do, and part of me kept expecting Lem to come through the door and start berating me for being lazy. Then I imagined what my mistress would do if he did, and I smiled to myself. *Brian's reading was right after all,* I thought. *I am free. This might not be what I expected freedom to look like, but I'll take it.*

Then, since there was nothing else to do and I was weary to the bone after the last few days, I lay down on my bed beside the fire and went to sleep.

I slept well to begin with, but after a time a creeping unease invaded my sleeping mind. I found myself rousing to listen intently to the soft crackle of the fire, and other small noises that I hoped came from my mistress in the workroom. I was weary enough to settle again each time, and eventually I fell to dreaming.

It wasn't a pleasant dream. I dreamed of a spider crawling over me in arcane patterns, leaving a trail of sticky silk behind it that sank into my skin, leaving marks like tattoos. I wanted desperately to brush them away, to scour my skin clean, but I couldn't move.

Then, startlingly close, I heard a door bang shut, and the noise freed me from the grasp of sleep. I sat bolt upright, gasping, to see Aleida hobbling into the kitchen.

I think I startled her as much as she'd startled me, for she hurriedly grabbed for the doorframe as she staggered on her ungainly feet. 'Dee?' she said.

I pressed a hand to my chest, my heart beating hard. 'Sorry, miss,' I said. 'I just ... I had a bad dream. But you startled me out of it, I think.'

'A dream? What kind?'

'Spiders, crawling all over me,' I said with a shudder.

'Oh,' she replied. 'Well, I won't apologise for waking you then.' She looked around, as though searching for something to sit on, then gave up and settled onto the floor.

I was feeling rather strange myself — slow and sluggish, and faintly dizzy. Lack of sleep, I guessed, and tried to put it from my mind. 'Is your potion finished?' I said.

She nodded. 'The hard part of it, anyway. It needs to sit for a few more hours before it's ready.' She looked very weary, I thought, and too thin, with her cheeks sunken and her skin sallow with a greyish tint beneath the golden hue. When I first saw her I thought she was sun-browned, like someone who spends all their time working outside, but I was starting to wonder if it was just the way her skin was. Given what she'd said of her mother, it was quite possible her father had come from some far-flung place. 'Do you want something to eat?' I asked. 'I fixed you a plate.'

'Mm,' she said with a slight shake of her head. 'I had a bit, earlier. But I can't eat now. I have to do something about this warlock, and you can't do magic on a full belly.'

I just blinked at that, drawing up my knees and

hugging them to my chest. 'The warlock? *Now*? You can't, miss. You look like you're dead on your feet.'

'Better that than dead off them,' she muttered.

'But why *now*?'

She sighed and rolled her head from side to side, as though her neck pained her. 'You heard him the other day, Dee. Three days.'

'Yes, but that won't be up until the day after tomorrow.'

'Three days doesn't mean three days. It means sometime before three days. And you stole the beast he'd turned and set up for the attack. He has to act, soon.' She frowned down at the flagstones. 'I should have moved on him as soon as the sun went down, but I need that potion. Well, maybe this is good. He'll wonder what the hell I'm playing at. It's always good to keep your enemy confused. Of course,' she said with a grimace, 'that only works if he hasn't already figured out that I got clobbered in that fight with Gyssha.'

I slipped out of my blankets and, out of habit, put on my apron over my chemise. Then I fetched the kettle I'd set up ready for morning, hanging it on the chimney crane and swinging it over the fire. 'Well, at least have a cup of tea to warm your belly.'

She looked up, seeming surprised. 'All right,' she said. 'Yeah. That sounds good.'

I felt her eyes upon me as I prepared the teapot, and after a few moments I simply couldn't take it. 'What?' I demanded, glancing across at her.

'Oh,' she said. 'Just wondering if I should take you with me.'

'You have to,' I said. 'I doubt you'll be in any shape to walk back here afterwards.'

'Mm. But that's my problem, not yours. It'll be dangerous, Dee, after that trick you pulled earlier. He probably assumes you're my apprentice, and he'll figure you for an easy target. If he does beat me, he'll come after you next. I think it'd be best to set you up with the horse and gear and a bit of coin. If it goes well I'll send a bird for you, if you don't hear from me you can just take off.'

She was so matter-of-fact about it that I felt a chill down my back. She was calmly preparing for her own death, making sure I'd be safe. 'Do you *have* to stay and fight him? Why can't you just walk away?'

She gave me a scornful look. 'And what do you think a man like that would do if he had access to that blasted tree? In the wrong hands that demon-tainted monstrosity could wreak an impressive amount of havoc. I'm not about to walk away and let him have it.'

'Oh, right,' I said. 'Fair point.'

When the tea was brewed, I poured two cups — or at least, that's what I meant to do. At one point I found myself holding a glass bottle in my hand, but with a shake of my head I put it back where I'd found it and rubbed my eyes before finishing the task. I was so short on sleep that my mind was playing tricks on me.

I brought Aleida her tea, but she was gazing into the middle-distance, as though she couldn't see me at all, so I set it down beside her. 'Are you sure there's nothing I can do to help?'

It took her a moment to respond, and then she shook her head firmly. 'No. Look, Dee, this isn't going to be a pitched battle. I'm not stupid, I know I can't take him that way. It'll be a sneak attack. There's nothing you can do. I'm just making contingency plans, that's all.' She picked up the cup and cradled it between her hands, blowing on the steaming surface of the tea.

'You can't wait until the potion's finished?' I said.

'Nope. Not enough time. It wouldn't really help, anyway, it's more of a recuperative than an amplifier. I've got a few other tricks up my sleeve, though.' She looked around, then, taking in the barren room, and our paltry collection of cups, plates and trenchers on the mantelpiece. 'Any sign of Bennett?'

I shook my head. 'He must have moved on, after all. What did you call it? Through the veil?'

'Mm. Maybe. Why, though? Why now and not before?'

I sipped my tea, puzzled. 'Maybe he listened to you? You kept telling him to go, after all.'

She shook her head. 'No. I'd been telling him that for days. He only stopped when you arrived.' With a purse of her lips, she set her cup down and heaved herself to her feet. 'Did you find any candles when you were cleaning up? There should have been a box of them somewhere.'

I nodded and went to fetch it.

When I returned, Aleida had moved her teacup aside and had her wand in her hand. 'Set them out for me, please,' she said. 'There are marks in the flagstones to tell you where.'

I'd noticed the notches when I was cleaning, but hadn't thought much of them. The candles were only little, but they were made of fine beeswax, and I set each one on a plate or in a cup to save scraping the wax off the floor afterwards. 'Light them?' I said.

'Please.'

'Uh, miss? Are you sure this is a good idea? You were going to fight the warlock, should you be wasting your strength?'

She looked at me with an icy gaze. No, I realised, not icy. Just detached. Indifferent. 'Don't ever ignore your intuition, Dee. It's there for a reason.'

I wasn't sure what that meant, and it in no way answered my question, but I figured it was all the answer I was going to get. 'Yes, miss.'

I lit the candles with a splint, and then Aleida hobbled into the space they marked out on the floor. She stood there, leaning on the stick, and closed her eyes.

I'll admit it, I was expecting something ... more. But all she did was stand still with her eyes closed.

Then, I felt a creeping pressure seeping through the room, a prickling, icy touch that rose up from the floor.

'Bennett,' Aleida said, her voice very soft. I flattened myself to the wall beside the fireplace, and from the corner of my eye I noticed the flames were stretching taller.

Aleida's frown deepened, her hand clenching around the wand. 'Bennett.' Her voice was growing harder, more stern. The pressure grew with each moment that passed, like the air under a swift-coming storm. I could feel it now, a pull, like hunger, like thirst, a craving like cool water on a hot day. How strange, I could *feel* it, but I could tell that it wasn't calling to *me*.

'Bennett.' Slowly, she lifted the wand. It wasn't *glowing*, exactly, but it seemed to me that it glittered in the firelight, as though the crystal's glassy facets caught and reflected more of the light.

'*Bennett.*' She called one last time, her voice throbbing with power, sounding as deep and dark as the ocean.

She waited then. We both did, perfectly still, listening, waiting.

Long moments passed. A dozen heartbeats. Two dozen. Then, she let her hand drop, and, sagging, she hobbled out of the ring of candles. 'Blow them out, Dee. He's not coming.'

I did as she asked, but I didn't understand her worried, despondent air. It was good that he didn't come, surely? It meant he had gone on through the veil, or whatever she had called it. 'Miss? Didn't you want him to move on?'

'Want has nothing to do with it,' she said as she leaned back against the wall. 'It doesn't make sense—' She broke off then, as though something had just occurred to her. 'Unless ... unless it wasn't Bennett?'

'But who else would it be?' I said. Then my eyes dropped to the cup near her feet. 'Your tea's getting cold, miss.'

She barely glanced at it, and I could see it would be no easy matter for her to stoop down to get it, so I fetched it for her.

'Who else, indeed?' she said as she took it from me. 'And why did it stop when you turned up? Those are the real questions, Dee.' With that, she drained the cup in one gulp — and immediately spluttered, doubling over with a cough.

In the blink of an eye I found myself standing over her, hands on her shoulders. Gulping for breath, she let the cup fall. It shattered on the flagstones. She reached for her walking stick, but my hand was already there, knocking it out of her grip and sending it clattering to the floor.

Inside my head, my mind seemed to shut down. It felt like closing a book. The world had suddenly become incomprehensible, and my mind was having none of it. All I could do was stare at my hands, mouth hanging open like the village idiot.

Off balance, Aleida stumbled forward, hands clutching at the neck of my chemise, her face just inches from mine; and I watched as her eyes went from bewildered to enraged to sudden clarity. 'Dee,' she said, and in my name I could smell something on her breath. The mint tea, of course, and spices — but also spirits, like the whisky Lem drank back at home. 'Dee,' she said again, her voice growing slurred. 'What was in that tea? What did you give me?'

'Nothing!' I said. 'It was just tea!' *Wasn't it?* But then I remembered the glass bottle in my hand. There was a weight in my apron pocket, something round and heavy that bounced against my leg with each step. *Laudanum* — tincture of poppy in strong spirits, usually flavoured with spices. *Oh Lord and Lady. What happened? What have I done?*

Aleida shook her head, eyes drooping closed before she fought to open them again. Her legs were giving way beneath her and she sagged against me.

Hands that were no longer mine pushed her down, and she was sinking too fast to fight it. She fumbled for the wand at her belt, and quickly my foot darted out to pin her hand to the floor. Then, no matter how I fought against it, no matter how I struggled to make it stop, my body shifted its weight onto that delicate hand, and I felt bone and tendon grind under the ball of my foot.

Lying on the flagstones, Aleida gasped, struggling to pull away but sinking too fast to manage it.

Then I felt something in my throat, something dry and dusty and tasting of death. It reached up and took a hold of my tongue. 'Wretch,' it said in a hoarse whisper. 'Wretched traitor of a girl. You should have been a whore like the slut who birthed you; I should have let them cut off your faithless hand. Maybe then you'd know your place.' Aleida could hear the words — I could see it in her face, even if she didn't have the strength to respond.

'You're pathetic,' my voice whispered. 'Useless. You think that little scrap of a spider is enough to finish that warlock? You little simpleton! He'll break you like a dry twig! Didn't you learn a thing from me, you stupid girl? Well don't you worry your little head — I'll take care of the warlock. And then I'll take care of *you*.'

I was certain Aleida could hear, and then, when the laudanum finally took her, I saw that too. Her face went slack, and the tension in her neck and jaw eased away, and the hand beneath my foot went limp as the laudanum stole her away — drugged into oblivion, and dead to the world.

CHAPTER 9

I t felt like a bad dream, like a waking nightmare. I wished I could believe that's all it was, as the body that had been mine got dressed, putting on stays and skirt, stockings and boots, but I knew better. This was a witch's cottage, after all, and such easy explanations were for other people. I knew what was happening; the only way I could have been more certain was if Aleida told me herself. I was possessed, and there was only one name I could put to the thing inside me. *Gyssha*.

My apron was flung aside, and though I heard the *chink* of glass, I couldn't turn my head to look around. It was only when the body sat to lace my boots that I saw it. The flask of laudanum had rolled out of my apron pocket, the cork absent, the bottle empty. *No*, I said to myself. *No, no, no*. People died of drinking too much laudanum. You heard tales of it — babies given too much by careless nursemaids, young lads stealing it if they couldn't sneak out their father's whisky, old folks with their insides eaten away by tumours. Thirty drops was the dose for a body full-grown, and twenty would be better for someone like my mistress, as scrawny as a newborn foal.

There had to have been an ounce in the bottle Melly had found in the garden.

There was nothing I could do for Aleida now, but I'd have stayed by her side if I could.

I had no choice in the matter, though. Once my boots were laced and my skirts tied about my middle, my body heaved itself up and stepped over my mistress's crumpled form, and marched out into the night.

When I saw what awaited me — us, rather — I thought my heart would stop. Beasts. Huge and hulking in the starlight. The ghost within me didn't falter, though, and marched down the meadow to join them, standing silent and still around the tree. There were half-a-dozen of them clustered on the green, and in the dim light I could make out more across the stream. A dozen? A score?

The tree knew we were there. The vines and tendrils hung down low, stretching towards the ground and swaying restlessly, like a barn-sour beast. I wanted to curl into a ball, to close my eyes and pull the covers over my head. I wished I could be one of my little sibs and crawl into bed with the big people when it thundered in the night.

But there was no refuge anymore.

'Well?' my voice said, sharp and whispery. 'Go get it.'

The beasts all swung their massive heads my way. And then, they turned towards the tree.

It was a hard battle. So many of them were torn apart that reinforcements had to cross the stream and join the struggle. But at last a branch was torn from the demon tree, a branch so big it was the size of a small tree itself. The vines that hung from it twitched and writhed for a long while, thrashing with dying rage.

Once the worst of the twitching had stopped, my hand gestured to the nearest beast and commanded it to lay down upon the soil. Then, another construct — one with forelimbs like a bird's feet, made for grasping — sank the branch into the creature's earthy back, like a bizarre and ugly crest.

My body climbed onto the back of the bird-legged beast, and then the two of them, my mount and the branch-bearer, set out through the orchard. My hands gripped tight to the bulk of the beast beneath us — there was no smooth, sleek coat like a horse would have, just packed earth that crumbled if my fingers pressed in too hard. But the bird-beast's back was studded with sticks and twigs and pine needles in a grotesque parody of hair, and on these my hands found a grip, of sorts, while the beast pitched and rolled beneath me like a wallowing boat.

I started to tremble as the dark closed around us — from the cold, from fear. I was in the grip of an evil witch, and the only one who could help me was behind us in the cottage, poisoned by my own hand.

She's not dead, I told myself. *She's a witch, she can't be dead.* Besides, I'd heard what Gyssha had told her, before Aleida had slipped away from us: *I'll take care of you,* voice dripping with venom. *That means the old witch wants her alive.* I hoped with all I had that I was right in that. If Aleida was dead then so was I.

For a moment my hands shook like shutters in a gale but then, a moment later, something dry and cold surged through my veins, and I felt Gyssha's grip wrap around me like a strangling vine. My voice made a little growl of annoyance, and after that I couldn't move an inch, while beneath me the earthbeast plodded through the night.

How long we walked I couldn't say — it could have been hours, it could have been just a few minutes. It didn't make any difference to me; once we left the road I was hopelessly lost, with all the stars hidden under the thick cover of the trees.

Then, after an age, the beast beneath me halted, and stiffly my body struggled down from the perch upon its back, staggering on the ground.

My mount turned to face me and lowered its great head with a rumble in its throat that sounded like rocks grinding together.

My hands reached for the crown of its head and dug deep into the mud and earth that was its body, clawing and scraping it away until they found a stone. It wasn't a crystal like the ones I'd been finding since I arrived in the mountains, but just a plain round river-stone. My filthy hands kept digging and scraping until the bulk of it was exposed.

Then, I stood on the tips of my toes. My hands cupped around the stone and my body leaned close, as though to kiss it. My body drew a deep breath and then breathed onto the rock, just as my mistress had breathed onto a twig earlier that day to light it aflame.

A spark of heat blossomed deep within my chest. It rushed up my throat, searingly hot. When I breathed out, my mouth was a furnace, my breath a bellows blast, searing, scorching, full of heat and flame.

The stone beneath my hands throbbed once, and then blazed, hot as iron fresh from the forge. The damp earth of the beast's body sizzled against it, the twigs and needles around it shrivelling and smoking with the heat as the beast backed away.

Then, both of beasts, the one with the red-hot glowing stone and the one with the demon branch embedded in its back, turned away and lumbered off into the darkness. I was alone.

No, I realised when my feet began to move. *Not alone. Definitely not alone.*

I felt like a passenger in my own flesh as Gyssha Blackbone marched me off into the darkness. Once again, I started to shiver, trembling like I'd been struck by a palsy. My feet faltered and I fell to my knees. Then, once again, came that little growl inside my head, and this time when the cold, dead touch tightened around my limbs it felt like wires cutting into my skin, like a huntsman's snare cutting tighter and tighter as the beast struggled within. I heard my voice cry out with the pain of it before the ghost inside me choked it off.

She forced me to my feet again and drove me forward like a baulking beast. I could feel tears on my face as I silently wept in confusion and fear. *What is she doing? Lord and Lady, I should have let Aleida send me away ...*

Then, ahead of me, almost lost amid the pounding of my heart and the blood rushing in my ears, I heard the stamp of a hoof, and a rustle of heavy fabric.

In the blinking of an eye, Gyssha's grip on me vanished. I fell forward, not realising how hard I'd been fighting her to regain control of my own body. I landed hard, sprawling on my belly in the dirt.

When I pushed myself up, there were two pairs of feet standing by my head. They were clad in identical black boots, dusted by identical black robes. I was still staring at them in shock when I felt gloved hands cinch around my wrists and haul me to my feet.

One of them stood behind me, as solid as a brick wall at my back, his hands locked around my arms as hard as iron chains. The other stood in front of me, and behind him were the horses, barely visible in the darkness. I might not have seen them at all if it weren't for the faint red glow of their eyes.

The warlock in front of me took hold of my chin and forced my head upwards as he pulled down his hood. He looked … rather ordinary, actually. He was of middle years, not young but not old, though his broad face was weathered and his forehead was deeply lined. I saw why as he scowled at me. 'The Blackbone apprentice,' he said in a low growl.

I pulled uselessly against the hands that held me captive. 'I'm not an apprentice! I'm just a servant!'

His lips twitched, and he gave me a brief look of puzzlement. He could tell it was the truth, I realised, and he was surprised.

But then he shrugged. 'A spy, either way. Why did she send you here, girl? Talk, and maybe I'll let you live.'

Even if I wanted to talk, I had no idea what to say. *My mistress is back at the cottage, out cold on the flagstones* was not a good option. *The ghost of Gyssha Blackbone brought me here and dumped me at your feet* was hardly any better. I simply had no idea what was happening, and after all that had occurred in the last hour or so I was too overwhelmed to invent a story.

With a growl of impatience, the warlock wrapped his gloved hand around my throat and squeezed, choking off my breath. Out of instinct, I struggled and tried to pull away, but the one at my back didn't move an inch, and only held me tighter as he leaned in to whisper in my ear. 'One way or another, you *will* talk.'

Heart and head pounding, my throat burning, I saw a flare of light in the darkness. My eyes tracked to it, even with the hand around my throat and my lungs screaming for air.

After the flare of light came the noise — crackling flames, and a roar like falling rocks, together with the dull thud of massive feet on the soft earth.

The warlock's head snapped around. His hand grew slack, and I gasped a breath, my legs weak and trembling. My eyes, however, were still seeking the source of the sound, my mind trying to work out just what was going on.

Then, I saw the earthbeast charging towards us, the branch of the demon snakewood hanging over its head like a burning crown, and I understood. I was a decoy, a distraction. Nothing more.

The warlock in front of me swiftly backed away, pulling his wand from beneath his robe. The one holding me shoved me to the ground, and I'm guessing did the same, though I couldn't see. I tried to crawl away, but he planted his foot between my shoulders and pinned me face-down in the earth.

I raised my head as high as I could, to see the flaming beast bearing down upon us. That rumbling sound was coming from the creature itself, I realised — it was *screaming.*

The warlocks separated, and raised their wands as one. In perfect synchronicity they barked out a word that burned and crackled in the air, and launched two fireballs at the charging creature.

They both struck, a bare instant apart, and the creature made of earth and twigs and vines simply disintegrated under the assault. Just like the other beasts when the tree caught and shredded them with its thorny vines, this beast crumbled into chunks and clods of earth — but the main bulk of it kept coming, carried by sheer momentum, bringing the demonic fireball with it.

Oh no, I thought. *No, no, no.*

I pressed my face into the ground, wrapping my arms around my head, and prayed.

Then, the world tore in two. The *shriek* of it tore at my ears, making me scream in pain. From above me came a blast of heat, like air from a blacksmith's forge.

The sound was so loud that I couldn't think. It was a wall of chaotic noise, so overwhelming that I just wanted to curl into a ball and play dead until it was done. But then the pressure between my shoulders lifted, and somehow, over the assault of sound, I heard the warlock scream.

I glanced up to see something out of a nightmare. The calm darkness of the forest was gone. Instead, overhead, a rift in the blackness opened up into a world of red and black, a world of searing heat and scorching ash. Silhouetted against it was a creature with black bat wings, clawing at the air. It held the warlock in its claws; he was dwarfed to doll-size against the massive wings.

There were other creatures, too — smaller ones that came howling out of the red world to flap away into the cool darkness of ours. A few long, glistening tentacles reached through, groping across the ground and the remains of the shattered and crumbling beast. There were other things, too, things that whooped and hollered and chittered and screeched, and moved too quickly to be anything more than a blur in the darkness.

I'd seen enough. I'd seen more than enough. Keeping low to the ground, I scrambled away, but my skirts tripped and hindered me. I fumbled them up with one hand and hobbled away on my other hand and my knees. I heard another scream and stole a glance to see the other warlock caught between two creatures that looked vaguely like huge cats, if cats had horns like a steer and rows of spikes down their backs and a horned club at the end of their tail. Two of the horses were fighting the cat-things, but the third had gone down while another creature tore at its flank. While I watched, one of the cat-things released the warlock's leg to launch at the nearest horse. It tore the horse's neck open with huge, dagger-like teeth, but instead of blood, the cat-thing was showered in chaff. The rearing horse collapsed, crumpling to the ground like a deflated bladder. *Constructs*, I thought.

The remaining warlock was no construct, though. The cat-things had ripped his leg open, and his arm, too. The hand that had held the wand hung at a grotesque angle, not so much broken as nearly wrenched away. He screamed again as the cat-thing released him, only to take a better hold of his shoulder, stabbing him right through with those dagger-like teeth, before it began to drag him towards the rift.

I started to crawl away again, keeping as low as I could, hoping that the mud that coated me would help hide me from sight. The warlock's screams were growing fainter, but I didn't dare look back again.

Then, suddenly, the red glow from the rift went dim.

It's closing, I thought. *Thank the Lord and Lady, it's closing.*

I stole a swift glance back, and my heart faltered.

It wasn't closing at all — no, the giant bat-wing creature was squeezing back through the rift, blocking the light. It must have realised its first catch was a dud, made of stale straw and rags, and had come back for a second try.

I got a better look at it this time, for all I wished I hadn't. It had landed on the forest floor, balanced on hind legs and clawed wing-tips. Its head was a little like that of a huge bird, with a long beak curved like a scythe blade. It was naked with black, leathery skin, adorned only by a ruff of spikes like porcupine quills around its neck. Above the beak were four tiny eyes that all blinked in unison, gleaming yellow in the light through the rift. Then, clacking its great beak, it started towards me.

I didn't scream. I couldn't. I needed all the breath I had to scramble away. I stood, skirts still clutched in one hand, and ran, while behind me came a shriek and the flap of leathery wings as the creature launched after me.

I ran unseeing into the darkness, blinded by the flames and the glare of the rift. When something flitted, whistling, over my head, I couldn't see what it was or where it came from. All I could hear was the creature behind me shriek again, and then again and again as the flitting, whistling things kept coming.

A pair of strong hands caught me by the shoulders and hauled me upwards, hoisting me like a bale of goods up into the branches of a tree. I found myself face-to-face with a pair of large golden eyes, surrounded by leafy hair that ranged from gold to green to autumn red. I was already sobbing with relief by the time my weary mind put a name to the face. Laurel the dryad. Perched next to her in the tree, expertly wedged between two branches, was Attwater, he of the hound-dog features, with a bow in his hands and a quiver at his hip.

Laurel held on to me until I was steady on the smooth, curving branch, and then released me to gather up her own bow.

I flattened myself against the smooth branch, clinging tight and sobbing as they sent arrow after arrow into the winged creature's bony chest. Grudgingly, the creature fell back.

'The rift's getting smaller, isn't it?' Attwater said. 'Tell me I'm not imagining it, for the love of life.'

'You're not imagining it,' Laurel said. Her voice was calm and dry, and I took refuge in it. Attwater sounded near as tense as I felt, but if one of us was calm, maybe everything would be all right after all.

The rift *was* shrinking. The bat-thing glanced back to the red glowing tear, took one look at the three of us, perched on the branch, and then launched itself up with a laboured flap of its wings. The arrows bristling from its torso didn't seem to bother it as it flapped back to the hole and forced its way through.

After it vanished, the red gash in the night sealed shut with one last sigh of scorching air, and then everything was quiet. The only sound was the crackling of the fire that still burned around the remains of the earthbeast, illuminating the bodies of the horse-constructs, and the earth torn up by the fight.

CHAPTER 10

Between them, Attwater and Laurel somehow got me down from the tree. On the ground I collapsed, trembling so hard I thought I'd shake my bones from their sockets.

My two saviours talked over my head like I wasn't there. 'A fair few of the beasties got through,' Attwater was saying. 'I couldn't count them all.'

'Daylight will kill some of them,' Laurel said. 'We'll hunt down the rest.'

'I'd best warn folk, all the same,' he said. 'Of course, they're already keeping their doors and shutters barred against Blackbone's beasts. There's going to be a right old panic if any of these critters turn up too. Any sign of the one who did it?'

Laurel shook her head. 'If the witch is here, I can't smell her.'

That brought my head up. 'It wasn't her,' I said.

They both looked down at me. 'It wasn't her,' I said again. 'Aleida. It wasn't her.'

'No? Then who?' Attwater said.

'The old one, Gyssha.'

'She's dead.'

I nodded. 'Dead, but not gone.' I was still shaking. I didn't know much about witches and ghosts, but I had the idea that the old witch could move faster than a thought, and my mistress was still back at the cottage, either drugged to a stupor or dying. 'Aleida's in danger.'

'Young Blackbone?' Attwater said. 'I reckon she can look after herself, lass.'

'No, not now. I … I drugged her. I mean, Gyssha did. She made me do it. I need to get back to her! Please help me, please!' The words my voice had spoken rang in my head. *I'll take care of the warlock, and then I'll take care of you.*

Attwater and the dryad exchanged a glance.

'I will go,' Laurel said. 'I can be fast. You follow with the child.'

Attwater considered the matter, and then nodded. 'Be careful.'

She barely acknowledged his words with a nod before she was off, running as fleet as a deer.

With a deep, ragged breath, I tried to stand, only for my legs to give way. Attwater settled a hand on my shoulder. 'Steady, lass. Give yerself a few moments more to catch yer breath.'

'What if we don't have a few moments?' I said.

'And what are ye going to do against the ghost of Gyssha Blackbone?'

He had a point there. And truthfully, I didn't have enough breath spare to waste it in arguing with him. 'Thank you,' I gasped, instead. 'I didn't get a chance to say that before.'

'No matter, lass, no matter at all. Ye did well to keep yer hide intact. Laurel and I were tryin' to figure a way to get ye out but couldn't see how, and then ye managed to do the better part of the job yerself.'

I felt utterly drained, without even enough strength to think clearly. *I bet this is how Aleida's felt since she killed the old witch.* 'What happened out there? I mean, I know it was the tree, that demon tree, but—?'

'That tree shouldn't exist,' Attwater said with a growl. 'It can open a portal between realms. Laurel can sense the wretched thing, she knows when it's stirring an' getting riled up. Always bad news, that is, so we came out to see what was going on. We thought it was Aleida dealing with that warlock.'

'She was going to,' I said, thinking of the spider waiting on the mantelpiece. 'But she didn't get the chance.'

I looked down at my hands and forearms. They stung, like they'd been burned. My eyes were adjusting to the darkness again, enough to see that they were filthy with what looked like dirt or soot. I touched the back of my hand to see if it would wipe off, only for my nerves to spark up with a searing pain that made me yelp.

'Leave it be, lass,' Attwater said. 'The smoke from that cursed tree burns whatever it touches, and ye copped a brush with it. Don't worry over it too much, though, doubtless yer mistress has something that'll help.'

I drew a deep breath then, and tried again to stand. This time I managed it, though I felt none too steady. 'Can we get going, please? Which way is it?'

He looked me over with the same measuring gaze he'd turned on me in the street in Lilsfield two days ago. 'All right then,' he said. 'This way, lass.'

He let me set the pace, for which I was grateful. I was so weary I felt like I was slogging through molasses, and I dreaded the thought of what we'd find at the cottage. ... *and then I'll take care of you.* It should have been at least a small relief knowing the warlock was dead, but all I could think about was that dry, desiccated feeling inside my chest, and the icy contempt I'd felt when Aleida lay gasping on the floor. Gyssha had destroyed the warlock with my borrowed body and barely any magic at all. Could Aleida have done that? Despite the loyalty I felt for my mistress, I thought not. If Gyssha had done so much with so little, what else was she capable of? I had the strong sense that she didn't want Aleida dead — hadn't Aleida warned me herself that there were plenty of poisons around the house? If Gyssha wanted her dead she wouldn't have had me reach for that bottle of laudanum. No, the old witch wanted her alive. But why?

I remembered something Mrs Sanford had said, about old witches stealing young bodies, and swallowed hard, pushing the thought away. 'Mr Attwater?' I said, instead. I couldn't dwell on that idea, couldn't even consider it. Not yet, anyway. 'May I ask you something?'

'Go ahead, lass.'

'Are you ... are you human?'

He ducked his head at that, chuckling. 'Oh aye. For the most part.'

'The most part? Then what about the least part?'

He cast me an amused glance. 'Tell me, lass, has yer mistress talked about taking ye on, yet? As an apprentice, I mean?'

'Why does everyone think I'm going to be a witch?' I said. 'After tonight, I'm not sure I'd want to. I'm *really* not sure.'

'Well ye'd best make up yer mind swiftly. In or out, that's the general rule. Can't be dithering on the threshold, ye know. As for me ... how old would ye say I am, lass?'

I studied him from the corner of my eye. 'Older than you look,' I hazarded.

'Hah. What'd ye say if I said I was somewhat north of a hundred fifty?'

I bit my lip. 'I'd believe it. How, though?'

'Well, let's just say I've had an interesting life.'

'That really doesn't answer the question.'

He chuckled again. 'Now ye do sound like yer mistress. Well, young Elodie, some folks, when they come across something out of the ordinary, they turn around and walk away without e'er looking back. Let's just say I ain't one of those folks, and I don't think ye are, either.'

When we reached the cottage, the back door was open and the only light inside was from the faint flicker of the dying fire.

Attwater gestured for me to wait outside. I was torn, but I did as he said while he sidled up to the door, making a low whistle like the call of a night-waking bird.

From within came a similar call, and he ducked inside, bow strung and in his hands with an arrow nocked. After a moment he reappeared, waving me to follow.

Inside, Aleida still lay on the floor, much as I'd left her. Laurel sat on her heels nearby, head cocked to one side. Next to her was one of our few bowls, holding a bundle of dried herbs wrapped up with string, one end charred and wafting smoke. 'The old witch was here,' Laurel said as we entered. 'But I interrupted her, and the smoke saw her off. She will be back, though.'

'I don't doubt it,' Attwater said, looking down at Aleida.

At the sound of their voices, she began to stir. With a low moan she pulled her hands in, as though trying to push herself up, but she lacked the strength.

Attwater caught her under the arms, and without ceremony heaved her up and dragged her to the wall. There he set her half-upright with her back against the whitewashed stone while she moaned again, fighting to open her eyes.

'If I didn't know better, lass, I'd say ye were drunk,' he said. 'Then again, it ain't the first time I've scraped ye off the floor, is it?'

'Screw you, Attwater,' Aleida said, her voice slurred and her eyes still shut. 'Where's the girl? Gyssha, Gyssha's going to kill her.'

'The lass is here, she's safe. The old witch tried to get rid of her, but she didn't manage it.' He beckoned me forward.

'I, I'm here,' I said. For a moment Aleida managed to open her eyes, but they were unfocused and soon closed again. 'I'm sorry, miss, I truly am.'

She didn't respond. Eyes closed, her head slumped to one side.

Across the room, Laurel stood with one graceful movement, picking up the bowl with the smouldering herbs as she did so. 'Here,' she said, passing it to me.

'Thank you,' I said. Good manners out of reflex. 'What is it?'

'Protective agents,' she said with a shrug. 'Keep it smoking, and for a time it will keep the old witch away.'

'For a time?' I said. 'How long? What about when it runs out?' I wanted to protest that smoke could do any such thing, but then I remembered the red rift in the darkness, and the monsters crawling through.

'A few hours,' Attwater said. 'Long enough for young Miss Blackbone here to wake up a little.'

Laurel started towards the door then, without so much as a backwards glance. With a small shrug, Attwater turned to follow.

'Wait!' I said. 'Please, don't go. What if she comes back?'

Laurel paused in the doorway. 'She won't, as long as the smoke burns.'

'And after that,' Attwater said, 'there's not a damn thing we could do to help ye, or yer mistress. I'm a hunter, lass, I kill beasts, not ghosts. We can do more good going after the beasties that came through the rift.'

'Let them go, Dee,' Aleida slurred, barely more than a whisper. 'It's the truth.' Until she spoke, I'd guessed she'd passed out again.

I wanted to argue. I wanted to grab Attwater by the sleeve and beg him to stay. I'd have done the same to Laurel, except that I didn't dare touch her, as wild and otherworldly as she was. But instead I just clasped my hands together, and tried not to cry. 'Thank you,' I said. 'For helping me out there.'

Attwater gave a brief grin, showing rather more teeth than I expected. 'Well, lass, let's just say that ye owe me one.'

'And on that note,' Laurel said. 'Blackbone. You freed me, I freed you. We are even.'

'Yeah,' said Aleida, still slumped. 'Sure. Fine. Whatever.'

Laurel snorted, a sound like wind in the leaves, and then the pair of them were gone.

After a few moments, I stepped over Aleida to shut the door behind them. 'Were you born in a barn?' I muttered under my breath. Then I checked on the bundle of herbs, and blew on the smouldering end of them to raise another gust of smoke.

'You all right, Dee?' Aleida said.

I looked down at myself. Filthy dirty, covered with scratches, scrapes and bruises. My throat burned, my neck ached, and my arms throbbed where the smoke had scalded them. I was rather worried about my hair, too, but I wasn't game to explore that any further right now. 'Yeah. I'm in one piece.'

'Good.'

She said nothing more after that. Cautiously, I crouched down to touch her cheek, and then feel her neck for a pulse. She was icy cold, and the throb beneath my fingertips was impossibly slow. *You should probably be dead*, I said inside my head. *But I'm not going to make a fuss.*

I was cold too, cold and weary to the bone. I should fetch her a blanket, I thought, and probably one for myself, too. I should build up the fire and fetch some water. I should wash the dirt and ash from my skin.

But instead I set my back against the wall and let my legs fold, sliding down the rough plaster until I sat beside my mistress. I felt empty and dry, like a piece of charcoal thrown clear of the fire. Just ... spent.

Beside me, Aleida stirred. She tried to lift her head, but it rolled to the side instead. 'I'll be honest, kid,' she said, her voice soft and slurred. 'I figured you for a dead girl.'

'I nearly was,' I said. 'You knew it was Gyssha?'

'Soon as I tasted the laudanum. What did she do? Did she use the tree?'

I nodded, too weary to speak, and only then recalled that Aleida couldn't see me. 'Yeah.'

'Did it make a rift?'

I remembered the hole, a hole in the world itself. The hot air streaming around me, the shrieks and gibbers of the creatures that spilled through, the burning smoke. 'Yeah.'

'Warlock dead?'

'I think so? They pulled him through.'

'Oh. Oh yeah, he's dead. And now there's a gods-damned rift to clean up. Just what I need.' Her eyes were open, but only just.

'Are you all right?' I said. 'What about your hand?'

A small crease appeared on her forehead. 'Hand?'

'I, I stepped on it, remember?' I recalled all too clearly how the bones had groaned and grated under my foot. I didn't think I'd felt them crack, but that didn't mean there was no damage done.

'Oh,' she said again. 'Hah. Look, kid, you gave me enough laudanum to kill a horse. I can't feel a gods-damned thing right now.'

'Enough to kill a horse, but not you?'

'I'm a Blackbone, Dee, I've got poison in my veins; no one's getting rid of me that easily.'

I squeezed my eyes shut. 'I'm really sorry, miss. The laudanum ... I don't even remember doing it.'

'You wouldn't,' she said. 'Gyssha's good at this sort of thing. Really good. It's not your fault.'

It didn't feel that way. Every inch of me hurt, my hands and arms worst of all. How many of those *things* had made it through the rift — the rift that *I* made? And the warlock ... there was no way around it, he'd still be alive if it weren't for me. It wasn't the fact that he was dead that bothered me, really — it was the fact that I'd been used to kill him. At the time I couldn't see it clearly, I was too caught up in the chaos and confusion, but now, looking back, I could see the whole picture. Gyssha had dumped me in the warlock's path as a distraction, nothing more, while she lit up the branch of the demon tree and sent the earthbeast in. The old witch had used me, and when she was finished she'd thrown me away.

'Dee?' Aleida said, and I glanced up to find her watching me with dark eyes, her pupils huge in the dim light.

'Can't feel a thing, hey?' I said. 'I could use a little of that right now.'

Her lips quirked in the semblance of a smile. 'Kid, I'd pass it on if I could. What happened? Catch some smoke?'

I nodded, and held up my arms.

'Did you breathe any in? Get it in your eyes? Even a little?'

I shook my head. 'As soon as I saw what was coming I threw myself down into the dirt. Why? What would happen?'

'Bad things. Visions of demons and creatures from the nether; bleeding from the lungs and eyes. Good move, getting down low.' She shifted against the stone, head lolling again. 'I wish I could help you, Dee, but I still can't move. If I — wait, there is something. My packs, where did you put them?'

It felt like weeks ago that I'd set out on the grey horse. 'They're over here, near the bed.'

'Tip them out. Somewhere there's a little porcelain jar with some ointment inside.'

I looked over to the bed. It was so far away I'd almost rather forget about it. But with a sigh I heaved myself up and crawled across the flagstones to tip the bags out onto the floor.

What lay inside bore a striking resemblance to my own gear in the carrying-basket. A couple of changes of clothes, roughly bundled up, a gap-toothed comb, a few pairs of socks. But also a clouded mirror, a leather-bound book with a feather quill between its pages, and a bottle of ink. There were pouches that clinked, and bundles wrapped in rags, a few rocks and crystals and many other odds and ends. But right down the bottom I found a bundle tightly wrapped in cloth.

'That's it,' Aleida said. 'Bring it here.'

Moving gingerly, I brought it over and then paused to waft the smoke again. 'Does this stuff really work?'

'A smudge stick made by a dryad? I bloody well hope so, kid; that's the strongest you're ever going to find. Besides, you don't feel Gyssha around here, do you?'

I didn't know how to answer that, so I ignored the question. 'But what about when it burns out?'

'Oh,' she said. 'That's when the fun starts up again. Open it up, Dee.'

The bundle was a medicine kit, of sorts. A few bottles and vials, a little packet of needles and silk thread, some neatly folded rags and rolled bandages, and as she said, a little jar of salve, the wax seal already cracked and flaking.

'That's the one,' she said. 'But you're best off washing your arms first. Any water left by the fire?'

That meant moving again. I'd really rather have stayed where I was. I felt eyes upon me, and glanced across to find her watching me. 'Go on,' she said. 'You gotta look after yourself, kid, no one's gonna do it for you.'

'Yeah, yeah,' I muttered, heaving myself up. 'I'm going, I'm going.'

There was enough water left to wash my face and my hands and arms, but the touch of it set the burns throbbing again. By the time I stumbled back to the kit laid out on the flagstones my arms felt like they were on fire.

'Salve,' Aleida said, flapping a hand towards the porcelain jar. 'Put it on thick, it'll help. It's my own formula.'

The salve smelled strange, sharp enough to sting my nose and make my eyes water, but as soon as it touched my skin the throbbing settled to a prickling tingle, like pins and needles. Unpleasant still, but miles better than the raw sting of the burns.

'You'd better bandage them, too,' Aleida said. 'You'll need to keep the burns out of the sun, or they'll scorch all over again.'

'They're going to scar, aren't they?' I said, glumly.

'Not if you do what I say. Trust me, Dee, if there's one thing I know, it's potions.'

By the time my arms were wrapped from knuckles to elbow in clean linen bandages, Aleida's eyes had brightened, and she was slowly flexing her fingers in her lap.

I blew on the smouldering herbs again. The bundle was more than half gone now. 'Can I ask you something?'

Her eyes cut to me with a glare. 'Stop that.'

I flushed and looked down. 'Sorry.'

'That, too. Just spit it out, Dee, don't waste both our time asking for permission.'

It took me a moment to find the words. 'Out there, with Gyssha, she used me to set an ember burning, to light the branch. That was magic, wasn't it?'

She scowled, as though it was a stupid question. 'Of course.'

'So did that come from her or me?'

'From you.'

'But does that mean I'm a ... a ...'

'A witch? Nope. Fire's an easy one, most people could do it if they knew how. Or if they believed they could.' She rolled her head my way then, and regarded me steadily. 'You could be, though. If you wanted to.'

I started to speak. I opened my mouth, but no words came out. I didn't know what I wanted to say.

She was still watching me. 'Do you want to?'

'I ... I ... I don't know. Is it always like this?'

She laughed then, a deep chuckle. 'Like this? Gods no. Sometimes things get really hairy.' She shifted on the flagstones then, heaving herself up a little straighter as she looked over the floor. The candles I'd set out earlier were still there, I realised. 'Don't answer me now,' she said. 'Though you'd better decide soon. In the meantime, there's something I need you to do. Light those candles again, would you?'

I really didn't want to. Now that my arms finally stopped hurting, and the rush of terror from the conflagration in the forest had passed, all I wanted was to sit and do nothing. 'What if I said no?' I said, giving her a flat stare.

'Not an option. We need to move while we can. Gyssha's already got her next move planned and underway, and we need to keep up. So get up, get moving.'

'This isn't fair! I nearly died out there!'

'Yeah, well, I nearly got my body stolen by an evil witch, so I've got you beat.'

'And what d'you call what happened to me then? She stole my body too!'

'That's possession. Similar, I grant you, but she couldn't have held it for long. I bet you felt her losing her grip, didn't you? Now come on, no rest for the wicked, Dee. Up.'

Grumbling, I heaved myself up again and stumbled around, lighting the candles with a splint of wood from the fire. 'All right,' I said when it was done. 'Now what?'

Aleida heaved a sigh. 'You're not going to like this bit. Sit in the middle of the circle.'

I froze. 'Why?'

'I want to talk to Gyssha. Well, not the real Gyssha, but the echo of her. She possessed you, right? She left … call it footprints, or fingerprints, inside you. I'm going to call them out.'

'Do I get a choice in this?'

'You really don't. Sorry, kid. Sit.'

I wondered what she'd do if I turned on my heel and marched out the door. Somehow I doubted I'd get that far. 'Fine,' I snapped, and gathering my filthy skirts, stepped between the candles to settle on the flagstones. 'Now what?'

'Just sit. I'll do the rest.'

She'd recovered a lot since Attwater had hauled her up to sit against the wall, but she was still clearly under the influence of the laudanum — her words were a little slow and slurred, and her hands were clumsy. But as I sat within the candles' glow, she held out both hands with her palms up, and straight away I felt the air thicken.

Aleida closed her eyes and bowed her head, and then slowly raised her hands. I expected … I don't know, an incantation, a spell, or something. But all she said was one word. 'Gyssha.'

The air around me grew heavy and tight. I couldn't move. The candle flames grew longer, stretching up to an impossible height.

'Gyssha,' Aleida said again, and this time I felt something stir within me, like a snake entangled in my vitals. I felt it *move*, felt it slide along my spine, and I nearly retched with revulsion.

'Gyssha,' Aleida said again, and I fell forward — no, I was *flung* forward, coughing and choking, my mouth full of ashes. They spilled from my lips, gritty and grey.

Slowly, I felt my head lift until my eyes locked onto Aleida's.

'Ah,' she said. 'There you are.'

'And there you are,' my voice rasped. 'Foolish girl. On the floor where you belong. I can put you there, dead or alive. Never forget that.'

'I might be on the floor, Gyssha, but you're under it. Winning is the only thing that counts, isn't that what you taught me? I won, and you lost.'

I felt myself breathing out in a low growl, and with my breath came a cloud of smoke and ash. 'The game's not finished yet, little girl.' My mouth tasted like a charnel-house, full of burning and decay. 'I had you, until that wretched dryad interrupted.'

'Nearly won is just first loser,' Aleida said with a small smile. 'All because you couldn't even kill a servant girl. Barely a scrap of power in her, too.'

'The girl is nothing,' my voice spat. 'Less than nothing. It was the warlock I wanted — you cursed near spoiled everything when you let the dryad go! Do you have any idea how long it took me to catch that flighty beast? Or what he was going to pay for her? Of course not, but then, you always were a sentimental fool. He'd have killed you if you'd gone after him with that pathetic little puppet you made. Just how you survived two years without me, I'll never know.'

'And there's the very essence of Gyssha Blackbone,' Aleida said. 'Why use a slipper to kill a bug when you can use a hammer?'

'You're soft,' I snarled. 'Soft and weak, you always have been.'

'Maybe,' she said with a smirk. 'But I'm alive, and you're dead.'

I felt my lips draw back in a hiss. 'Not for long, you little traitor.'

'No?' she tipped her head to one side. 'So that's your plan, is it? A new body for the old witch.'

'Have you only just worked that out? You must have lost all your wits to the black smoke after you ran away from me. Oh, I know what you've been up to, Ally. Whoring around, hiding in opium pipes and bottles of rum, drifting about like trash on the tide. I saw you, always looking over your shoulder, waiting for me to come after you; so scared, so lonely. You're pathetic! All that time, and you never realised I could call you home any time I wanted.'

Aleida's half-smile faded, and her eyes turned to black stone. 'Bennett,' she said, with a voice like cold steel.

I felt my lips draw back into a smirk. 'I told you, child. I told you, time and again. Friends, family — they're nothing but a trap. A weakness. I told you years ago to get rid of the boy, or I'd do it for you. Did you think I was bluffing?'

Aleida clenched her fists. 'I told him to go! I checked on him before I left. You couldn't bind him here, I made sure of it!'

'You didn't have to. He was weak, too, bound with ties of kith and kin. Not that it would have made any difference. He could have run thousands of miles away, but when it was time to call you home I'd have found him one way or another.'

Aleida studied me with narrowed eyes, her face cold and hard. 'It was you, wasn't it, wearing his face, hounding me each night? Bennett moved on weeks ago, after he found me out on the islands. It was you waking me up at all hours, keeping me from resting. Trying to make me weak.'

'You were always weak!'

'No. You had to wear me down, didn't you?' She leaned forward, her eyes never leaving mine. 'You couldn't take me otherwise. And then Dee came along and spoiled that plan. Who is she, Gyssha?'

'She's nothing! Less than nothing! She's worthless, pathetic, just like you!'

Aleida frowned for a moment, but then her face cleared. 'You didn't send her; that much is clear. So who did?'

My jaw clamped shut, clenching so hard I thought my teeth would break.

'Gyssha,' Aleida prompted.

'I don't know!' I spat the words out, and they came with another puff of ash and smoke. 'I've looked and looked but I can't find the answer. That little wretch came from nowhere and she's been nothing but a bone in my teeth ever since! But I'll take care of her. You'll see. When I'm back in flesh and blood I'll take her apart, piece by piece.'

'Empty words, coming from a dead woman,' Aleida said. She reached into a fold of her skirt and pulled out her wand. 'I've heard enough, Gyssha. Get out, and leave the girl alone.'

I felt power thrum as she raised the wand, and as she started to draw a symbol in the air everything around me grew hot and tight. I started to cough, and then to choke, but I couldn't move and I couldn't close my eyes or look away as my mistress drew the glowing shape, all jagged angles and slashing lines. Then, with one last convulsion within my flesh, I bent double and vomited, spewing up something that looked like thick black tar, and my world went black.

CHAPTER 11

I found myself lying on the stone, feeling dazed and sore and chilled to the bone. Why was I not in bed? The fur blanket had been thrown over me, but there was only so much warmth it could offer when I lay on cold flagstones. But why was I on the floor? I rubbed my eyes, and winced at the throb and sting of my arms. With a groan I pushed myself up as the memories of the night before came seeping back — the burning beast, the warlock, the scorching smoke, the screaming, then the ghost inside me, the rot and decay. I wanted to tell myself it was just a dream, will myself to forget it with the early daylight that was streaming through the window, but I knew it was all real.

I heard the tap of the walking stick near my head, and then a *clink* of pottery as my mistress set a chipped teacup on the floor beside me. 'I figured I'd let you sleep for a while,' she said. 'Feeling better?'

It was a tie between *a bit* and *not really*. The taste of dust and ashes, the coldness deep in my chest, the invasion, the violation — they were all gone. But I was still smeared with mud and ashes, stiff and sore from the night's misadventures. 'I feel like I've been hung in a sack and beaten with sticks.'

'Yeah, it'll get you like that. Drink up, it'll help.'

I glanced at the teacup, and frowned. I'd expected the murky green of mint tea. Instead, the cup held a little scoop of summer sky, a vibrant, endless blue. I heaved myself up and took a sip, and then closed my eyes as it rolled down my throat and into my belly. It tasted like … summer. Like grass warmed by the sun, like cool water flowing over sun-baked rocks, like the comfortable drowsiness of mid-afternoon. Like sun on bare skin. 'Lord and Lady,' I mumbled. 'Is this what you brewed yesterday?'

'Yep. A nice drop, if I say so myself.' She had her own cup, and sipped slowly as she pottered about the room. I couldn't see beneath the hem of her skirt, but from the way she moved I guessed she was walking on dog's paws, not human feet. By the mantelpiece, she stopped to run a finger over the snakewood spider, and with a ripple of legs the creature turned to face her, just as it had faced me the night before. 'Poor little poppet. You'd have got the job done. Ah well, I'm sure you'll come in handy at some point.'

'Did you get what you wanted, last night?' I said. 'I really don't want to have to do that again.'

'You won't,' she said. 'I banished her. She could possess you again, of course, but you're clean for now. And yes, I heard enough. Did you?'

I rubbed my face, and winced again. Every movement of my hands and arms set the burns stinging. 'It wasn't Bennett. I remember that. It was Gyssha, keeping you weak and worn down. But why?'

'She wants to live again,' Aleida said. 'To take over my body, already trained and primed for magic. If she'd moved on me as soon as the laudanum hit, she'd probably have it now. But she had to get rid of the warlock first, fighting me for the body would have left her too weak to deal with him afterwards. If you'd died like you were supposed to — or if you hadn't sent Laurel on ahead — she'd have been able to get a good hold before the drug wore off.'

Shivering, I set the cup down long enough to wrap the blanket around my shoulders. 'What would happen to you?'

She leaned against the wall beside the fireplace. 'Well, there's two ways it could go. First is that she could kick me out, but that means I could try to take it back.'

'What's the other way?' I said.

'She swallows me up. Soul-death, basically. Guess which one Gyssha would go for. Go on, guess.'

I just grimaced. 'But what about the death-curse? She'd still have to deal with it, wouldn't she?'

She shrugged. 'Honestly, I don't know. I killed my mother in the craft, maybe surrendering my body to her is enough to lift it. Or maybe alive and cursed is just better than dead. Who knows? I don't really intend to find out.'

'And what if she decides she can't take you, and goes for someone else? How would you find her? Would you even know?'

Aleida shook her head. 'Can't happen. Not like that. Remember how it felt while you were possessed — you must have felt her grip slipping, now and then? Like you were breaking free?'

I nodded, slowly.

'The dead can't just go around stealing bodies from the living, or else every bastard'd do it. Gyssha can do it to me because I'm her kin. So don't worry about her coming after you, or your friends out here, they're safe.' She swirled the potion in her cup, looking thoughtful. 'But she'll try to kill you again. Watch out for that.'

'Oh,' I said. 'Great. Thanks for the warning.'

'It's not all bad. She already failed once. There's not many folk who can say they walked away after Gyssha Blackbone wanted them dead.'

I swallowed hard. 'She's not going to give up on getting you, though, is she?'

'What, just shrug her shoulders and slouch off through the veil?' She laughed, a dry, dark sound, and I shivered again. There was more life and energy in that laugh than I'd heard from her since I'd first arrived at the cottage. 'Nope. Not Gyssha. She expected to beat me when I came back to fight her. The fact that she lost, well, you caught a taste of it, Dee. She's consumed by rage. The old bitch lost, and she doesn't like it one bit. She'll *never* back down.'

'And neither will you.'

She answered with a fierce grin. For a moment all I could think of was the warlock last night, and the instant we'd both seen the flames approaching. I knew there was no way I could fight it, that all I could do was escape, and that's why I'd thrown myself down. But the warlock had stood his ground, ready for a fight; and because of that, he'd died. 'So what are you going to do? You're not going to go after her, are you?'

She tipped her head to one side, watching me with dancing eyes. 'That's exactly what we're doing.'

'But you're not strong enough!' I waved a shaking hand at her. 'I mean, look at you! You're staggering around half-drunk from that cursed laudanum still. And don't try to tell me you've been resting while I was lying here on the floor. You've been up all night, and all the day before. You're in no shape for this. It's a bad idea. A really bad idea.'

Aleida shrugged. 'True,' she said. 'But we're doing it anyway. We can't afford to wait.'

I scowled at her, trying to hide the fact that my heart was pounding and my palms damp with sweat. 'Are you completely mad? You can't do this.'

With a faint smile Aleida crouched down beside me — she would have been on her heels if she'd been fully human, but instead all I could see was the hairy dog's feet as she put one hand to the floor for balance. 'Let me rephrase that, Dee,' she said. '*You* can't afford to wait. Look, kid, you've thwarted Gyssha twice; once when she set you up to die with the warlock, and again when you sent Laurel back here to guard me while I was out of it. You're a thorn in her side now. She's going to try to kill you again, and this time she'll take no chances. Let's say we did hole up in here for a day or so to rest up — what do you think she's going to do? We're on her home turf! She'll rouse every damn construct she's ever made and have this cottage reduced to rubble before sundown. So yes, we're going out now, because it's our best chance to meet her on our terms instead of hers. Got it?'

I looked down at my cup, and the little piece of summer sky that remained. 'But what if you can't beat her? What if you're just not strong enough?'

'If I fail, we're both dead. So we're in this together.'

'So you're just going to go out there and see what happens? That's your plan? Aleida, I just ... I just don't think this is a very good idea.'

She watched me for a moment, and then her face split into a smile, a kind of mad, manic grin. Then she patted me on the shoulder. 'Bad ideas are my speciality, Dee. Drink up.'

I grudgingly followed Aleida outside. 'I thought you liked working at night.' The potion had helped, a little, but it had also left me feeling more strange than restored. My skin still felt cold as ice, while within me was a seething, spreading warmth, like a frozen skin over a steaming pool.

'I do,' she said. 'Trouble is, Gyssha knows it. If we wait 'til nightfall she'll have had all day to prepare. That's why I let you sleep while you could.'

'Gee, thanks.' I'd had all of, what? Two or three hours? I'd had more sleep after little Jeb was born, and it was my job to bring him to Ma for his milk and then rock him back to sleep afterwards. 'What do you need me to do, then?' I said with a sigh.

'We need wood for a fire,' she said, 'down there.' She gestured down the field, where a little patch of earth was paved with the same flagstones as the floor inside. 'I'll need you to milk the goat, too, and bring some equipment down from the house.'

'All right,' I said, resigned. 'A spot of breakfast first? Even just some bread and honey?'

'Nope,' she said, firmly. 'After last night I'm not taking any chances — and neither are you. She could have you poison yourself as easily as you dosed me. You'll get something in your belly before we set out, just not yet.'

I stifled a groan. 'Fine. Um, Aleida?'

Her eyes cut to me. '*Do not* ask if you can ask me something.'

'Umm, could you do me a favour? Maybe?'

'What?'

'When this is over, could you buy a bath? Just one of those little tin ones? I'd do just about *anything* for a hot bath right now.'

She regarded me steadily for a moment, and then her lips quirked up in a smile. 'Yeah. All right. That's a good idea.'

'I have them, on occasion.'

She snorted. 'Well for now, you'll have to make do with the stream, or a bucket from the well.' She glanced up then, looking out towards the lightening sky to the east. 'Sun's coming up. Might as well do it now if you're going to, Dee, this is going to take me a few minutes.'

She started away from me then, hobbling down the slope with the walking stick. I thought about going down to the stream, but turned to the well instead. It wouldn't be the first time I'd had to bathe in frigid water on a cold morning, and I remembered how Lem used to complain when he washed his face in the rain barrel on the way out to the barn. *Colder'n a witch's tit out here,* he'd say, but only when Ma wasn't near enough to hear it.

As I worked the winch to lift water from the well, I caught sight of Aleida wriggling out of her leather stays. She tossed it to the side, and then shrugged off her chemise, too, to stand in the chill air as naked as the day she was born. Her skin was the same golden hue all over, putting the lie to my earlier thought that she was tanned by the sun, but what most drew my eye were her legs. From the knee down — or rather, where the knee ought to have been — golden skin gave way to black fur, while her legs bent where no human leg ever should.

She held herself still for a moment, finding her balance, and then let the walking stick fall.

I leaned against the well-head, and shamelessly watched. As the sun rose and the first rays of light blazed over the far hills, she spread her hands wide, and, throwing her head back, slowly raised them up.

I squinted. Then I had to raise a hand to shield my eyes, and finally, I had to look away. As her hands raised, the light grew brighter and brighter, not the searing light of midday but the piercing brilliance of dawn, as though she was gathering it to herself, breathing it in.

It lasted only a minute or two at most — then the unbearable brightness receded to the normal soft glow of the break of day, and my mistress stood on the grass, dog's feet gone, fully human once again. Or, I corrected myself, as human as something like her ever could be.

Aleida stretched, arms overhead, as though she'd just woken, then turned back towards the house, flipping her long hair back over her shoulder before stooping to gather up her discarded clothing, and the now unneeded stick.

'Now that's a neat trick,' I called to her.

She flashed me a fierce smile. 'One day, I might teach you how. Hurry up, little girl, daylight's wasting.' She looked happier than I'd ever seen her. *Oh yes; now that there's a fight brewing you're all smiles.*

And 'one day'? I remembered what Attwater had said, and clenched my teeth. *In or out. Soon enough, you'll have to decide.* I pushed the thought from my head. *Soon, maybe, but not now.*

It took longer than I'd have liked to bathe and dress, pulling on clothes that were only clean-ish instead of clean. Then I had to salve and bandage my arms again, though Aleida helped with that, smearing on ointment and wrapping the linen strips with a firm, sure touch. 'Once this is all settled, I'll brew you another ointment for it,' she said. 'There's a few things that'll help that I wouldn't put in a general purpose mix like this one.'

'There's a lot that needs to be done once this is settled,' I said, glumly.

'One foot in front of the other, Dee. That's what I always tell myself, anyway. Now go milk the goat.'

'Yes, miss.'

I let the hens out too, and scattered some grain for them at the end of the garden, and by the time I returned with the milk pail Aleida had lit a fire on the flagstones in the field and laid a circle around it with a length of rope. Now she was bringing a cauldron and some other things down from the cottage. The effigy that had been at the heart of the first earthbeast torn apart by the tree was lying to one side, the grotesque construction of bones and wire and glittering beads curled up as though it was sleeping. It didn't hurt my eyes anymore, but I quickly looked away from it all the same.

'How much of this do you need?' I said with a nod to the pail. 'Only I'll need to set the rest of it to cool, or else it'll go bad.'

'All of it,' she said. 'Just put it down by the fire and come here.'

She was dressed more neatly than I'd ever seen her, wearing a black dress over her chemise and corset, and over that a wide leather belt that held her wand at one hip and her knife at the other, and a number of little pouches besides. But the dress, I realised, wasn't quite black. There was a subtle pattern to the fabric, and after a moment I realised they were flowers. It must have been a rather pretty floral print before it had been bundled into a pot of black dye, but the pattern was still there if you looked hard enough.

As I came to stand before her, Aleida pulled out the little pot and tiny brush again. 'Before you ask, no, you don't get a choice. I want to keep you close, and this will let you see what's happening. Close your eyes.'

I did as I was told, and this time I didn't flinch away at the cool, gritty touch of the ointment. 'Can you tell me what the plan is? Or am I not to be trusted with that much?'

I heard Aleida sigh. 'It's not that I don't trust you, Dee, it's just that, well, Gyssha got you once, she can do it again. I *could* make a ward to slow her down, but if she can't possess you she'll just kill you. There, you can open your eyes.'

I did, and then pursed my lips. 'It doesn't look any different,' I complained.

She gave me an exasperated look. 'Have some patience, kid, I haven't called them up yet.'

Tucking the little pot away, she set the cauldron over the fire. 'So, this plan,' Aleida said. 'There's not all that much to it. You were right, before; all Gyssha has to do is wait for an opportunity to strike, or *make* an opportunity if she gets tired of waiting. So I'm going to give her one. Gyssha lived here for seventy-odd years, she has all kinds of caches and power-stores hidden around these hills. I bet she's using them as a kind of fuel source. It's hard for the dead to stay in our world; naked spirits are *meant* to go through the veil, so she's fighting against the tide to stay here this long. If I start attacking her supply lines, she'll be forced to take action — or she'll just take the opportunity.'

'In other words, you're using yourself for bait.'

'That's the idea,' she said, pouring the fresh milk into the pot over the coals.

I wrapped my arms around myself and shivered. 'Are you sure that's a good idea? I mean, you're still not all that strong.' I couldn't help but think of how, just a day or two ago, she'd drained all the energy from the fire in the kitchen, and how quickly it had been spent, like water leaking from a sprung barrel. It didn't take much in the way of instinct to know that the power she'd raised from the sunrise was probably greater, but was it enough?

Then, before I even realised she was moving, she was right in front of me, her hands on my shoulders. 'Listen to me, Elodie. Listen good. Don't ever show fear. Don't ever show weakness. The things we deal with day and night will eat us alive if they see that we fear them. If they see weakness they will hammer at it with all they have until we shatter and crumble. So make sure they only see what we choose to show them, all right? We are the eye of the storm. We are the darkness behind the stars. We are the glare of the sun, and nothing touches us unless we let it.' She shifted her hands to my face, pressing her fingertips to my temples with a pressure that made me want to shrink away. 'The heart of all witchcraft is here, kid. Whatever you will, will be, if only you have the resolve to bring it about. Bodies break, skin tears, but your mind is your greatest weapon and your strongest shield. Got it?'

I felt myself shaking. 'But ... I can't. I can't do this stuff. I can't fight monsters and evil witches and demon-possessed trees and creatures from the nether realms. I can't do any of that. All I know how to do is cook and clean and change dirty bottoms and wipe snotty noses.'

She drew herself up with a snort. 'And is that all you want from your life, Dee?'

No. Gods no. I shook my head.

Aleida leaned close, her forehead grazing mine, her breath tickling my neck. 'Say it,' she said. 'Come on, kid, say it. Tell me you don't want this. Tell me you don't want this freedom to shape the world to your will. Say it!'

I closed my eyes and shivered. 'It's not that I don't want it,' I whispered. 'I just ... I don't think I can do it.'

With a sigh she let me go, taking a step back. 'Well, that's where it all falls apart.' She shook her head then, turning away, and I felt a pang deep in my chest. I wanted to take the words back, to turn back the clock and make a different choice, but what was I going to say? *Yes, I want it, make me a witch, turn me loose on those monsters and warlocks and demons?* I wasn't kidding anyone. I was about as much use as the hens fossicking through the wilting garden, or the goat nibbling around the orchard. 'I'm sorry,' I said.

She gave me a narrow look that I read as disappointment. 'If you can't, you can't. It's not for me to say, and I'm not going to try and talk you into it. Some witches do, you know, they'll back a young lass into a corner and badger her into saying yes, and nine times out of ten she's dead within a year.

'On the other hand, this is a baptism by fire if ever there was one, so maybe wait until it's settled before you make the call. And, mark my words, Dee, you will have to make it, one way or another.'

'That's what Attwater said,' I said, wrapping my arms around myself.

'He knows a thing or two, old Attwater. Just don't ever tell him I said so.'

I had to laugh at that, though inside I felt like weeping, or like gathering up all my gear and running away. The worst part was, I knew she'd let me. Hells, she'd give me some money and wish me a good trip. But where would I go? I could find work as a pot-girl or a housemaid, maybe; Aleida had offered that much the night I arrived. But as unnerving as this strange world of witchcraft and forest-sprites and realms beyond our own had proven, I also couldn't bear the thought of turning away and leaving it all behind.

With an effort I pushed that thought aside. I had a reprieve, of sorts. We had to deal with Gyssha first. And who knows? Maybe the old witch would kill us both and I wouldn't have to make the choice. 'Look,' I said, trying to keep my voice steady. 'Those fine words are all well and good, but I could still knock you down with a feather. How are you going to fight her?'

'Strength of body and strength of mind are two very different things, kid. You'll see.'

She turned back to the fire, and a basket she'd brought out from the kitchen, and to the pot over the fire she added a measure of honey and a collection of spices — curls of cinnamon bark, whole cloves, pods of cardamom and something else I didn't recognise, which looked like a flower made of wood. I was watching with a blank gaze while my mind whirled like a pinwheel.

'Aleida?'

'Mm?'

'What you said; *whatever you will, will be* — well that just doesn't make any sense. The world doesn't work that way.'

She snorted with amusement. 'Are you going to teach me how to be a witch now, child?'

'But ... but, if that's true, why did you send me out for those ingredients yesterday? You should have been able to make a potion out of anything you had at hand or out of nothing at all. And the curse, can't you just *will* it away?'

She glanced up from the fire, lips quirked in a sardonic twist. 'Why didn't you ever just convince your ma to leave your arsehole stepfather? Why didn't you *make* them send you to school?'

Her voice was soft, but the quiet force behind the words made me take a step back. 'It not that simple!' I said. 'I would if I could!'

'Exactly. What you're talking about: brewing a potion from pure water, willing away a death-curse, sure, they're theoretically possible, but they require perfection, a pinnacle of the craft. If you make it as a witch, a real witch, you might manage something like that once or twice in your life; if you hit that perfect moment when the stars align and the wind sings in your ear and you can feel the eyes of the gods upon you. The rest of the time we're just slogging through the mud, trying to make a silk purse out of a sow's ear, cobbling together something good enough to get through the day. Understand?'

'I think so,' I said. 'Have you ever had that perfect moment?'

Silently, she added a pinch of tiny tangled threads of dark orange, and the moment they touched the milk it bloomed yellow. 'Once,' she said. 'Just once. When I killed Gyssha.'

She stirred the milk, and in the rising steam I caught the scent of honey and spices. On an empty belly it was near enough to make me swoon. 'Lord and Lady, what is that you're making?'

'An offering. I'm going to call up some sprites to find Gyssha's caches and nodes. This is what's going to draw them in.'

'What about the earthbeasts?' I said. 'They're fair terrorising the countryside — will they stop once Gyssha's gone?'

Aleida looked pained. 'I don't know, Dee. I can't tell if she's woken them up or if they were just made to rouse and wreak havoc if anything happened to her. I'll have to look into it.'

'Maybe you'd better start a list,' I said.

Again, she snorted. 'No, no, can't be having with that. If I don't remember, clearly it's not important. All right, this is ready now, we'd best begin. Come give me a hand, would you?'

Together, we lifted the cauldron off the coals and tipped about half of the brew into a shallow dish balanced on a low trivet. Aleida crouched beside it to scatter a few flowers on the yellow milk. Spread out like that and steaming warm, the heavenly scent of it was even stronger, and I breathed it in with pleasure. She waved me back and pulled the wand from her belt. Standing over the steaming dish of fragrant milk, she traced a shape into the air. I felt my eyes widen as the tip of the wand left a glowing blue tracery suspended in the air, the glow of it playing over the rising steam and the golden milk. I watched her draw a complex cluster of curves and triangles and lines and dots, all marked out with dizzying speed. Once it was drawn she swapped the wand to her other hand and tapped the glowing shape with her fingertips. It shattered at her touch as though it were made of spun glass, breaking into countless fragments. They hung in the air for the briefest moment and then shot outwards and were gone.

Aleida slipped the wand back into her belt, and with a ladle she dished out two cups of the spiced milk, passing one to me. I took a sip, and for a moment thought I'd expire with bliss. Sweet and spicy, exotic and comforting, all at the same time. I licked my lips, tasting honey. 'Now what?'

'Now we wait.' She sank to sit cross-legged on the ground, sipping on her milk, and gesturing to me to join her. I did, only to wince when something pointed poked me in the backside. I knew at once what it was.

Aleida gave me a peculiar look when I set my cup down and felt across the damp earth, but her expression cleared when I found a crystal poking up through the grass, and plucked it out. It was only a little one this time, no longer than my thumb, but it was tinted purple, deepening to dusk at its tip.

Aleida raised an eyebrow at the sight of it. 'Lord and Lady, Dee, and you—'

'Don't say it,' I snapped. 'Don't say a word.'

'Oh, I wouldn't dream of it,' she said. Then she held out a hand. 'Can I take a look?'

I handed it over. 'I keep finding them everywhere. I suppose Gyssha must have buried the blasted things, like you were saying.'

Holding the stone up to the light, Aleida shook her head. 'No. No, it's not Gyssha's.' She handed the stone back to me with a faint smile. 'I think you've made a friend, Elodie. Someone likes you, he's bringing you little gifts.'

'What? Who?' My first thought was of Kian, but somehow I knew that wasn't right.

She tipped her head back to look up at the lightening sky. 'I shouldn't be telling you this if you don't want to be a witch, but screw it. This is a truth known to, well, to anyone who cares to know the first thing about witchcraft or wizardry and takes the trouble to look it up, but technically it's the first Mystery of the craft. There is another world that lies alongside this one, and over it and under it and woven through it like threads in a cloth; the world of elemental forces and the Divine. This realm is inhabited by spirits, sprites, elementals, godlings and the gods themselves. And you've been befriended by one of them; a spirit of crystals and gems, I think.'

'I have? How? Why?'

She nodded towards the house. While I'd been busy with the animals she'd propped the door open with the huge slab of crystals I'd hauled out and cleaned on my first morning at the cottage. 'Because of that, I'd say. Most witches have a few clusters like that. Spirits are drawn to them like bees to nectar. This is the same,' she raised her cup, still steaming and fragrant. 'You hauled that big cluster outside, didn't you, and cleaned it off?'

'Yes?'

'And I bet it looked right lovely, out in the sunlight? Well, you're not the only one who thought so. Some spirits love stones like that; they'll take up residence, like a cat in a patch of sunshine. When you hauled him out into the light and cleaned him up so nicely, he decided that you must like crystals as much as he does. So he keeps finding them and giving them to you.'

'I ... really?'

She nodded, and took another sip of milk. 'Ah, look, they're starting to come now.' She turned to look out over the field, and I saw something glowing coming bumbling towards us, keeping low to the ground. The way it moved made me think of leaves being tossed in a fitful wind. It seemed so strange, so counter to everything I knew about the world, that it made my skin prickle all over. I took a half-step back without really thinking about it and watched as the glowing orb came tumbling over the ground. It bounced up onto the rim of the bowl and sat there, casting a deep green glow onto the dish of warm milk.

That's a spirit? I almost said it aloud, but I didn't want to invite another withering look so I tried to think of another way to phrase the question. 'When you say spirits ... what sort are these?'

'Just spirits,' she said again with a shrug. 'Sprites, elementals — lesser elementals, I mean, not the big guys. Some folk try to divide them up into types; there's whole books written about the subject, but I've never found it to matter that much.' As she spoke a pale, icy blue orb floated down from above and seemed to be drifting purposely towards her cup. Aleida quickly shifted it to her other hand. 'No, not there, you silly thing, that's mine. Down there, down there.' She fanned it with her hand until it bumped against the dish of warm milk. As it settled, another one climbed up to the rim, this one coloured a dark, dusky purple. 'Most of them aren't too bright, either. I don't expect we'll get a huge turn-out, not after the way Gyssha treated them, but I'll let the summoning go a little longer before I close the circle.'

'What did Gyssha do to them?'

'Well, they're kind of like chickens,' Aleida said. 'You keep them for eggs, and to hunt out pests in the garden, but sometimes you want a chicken in the pot, too. Gyssha was rather more keen on the pot than the eggs, so they're a bit wary. This isn't too bad, though a few more would be welcome.'

'Can I see one up close?' I asked. 'Or will that scare them away?'

'You can go as close as you like,' Aleida said with a smile.

I crouched down, kneeling on the flagstones, and peered at the little glowing blobs on the rim of the dish. There were nearly two dozen of them now. Some really were blobs, just little formless clumps of light, but others … one looked like a little harvest mouse, except that where its ears would have been were two flowers and its tail was a stalk of grass. Next to it was perched … well, it was shaped like a weasel, but made up of repeating segments like a pill bug; it had six pairs of legs along its furry body and it sat contentedly within its green glow, sipping on the spiced milk.

'Funny things, aren't they?' Aleida said. 'They don't really have physical bodies, they tend to take their appearance from the things around them.'

'Lord and Lady,' I said as I backed away, and then I shook my head, trying to remember what we'd been speaking of. 'Spirits,' I said. 'Is that what's been hiding stones for me to find?'

'No, that's an earth spirit, of a higher order. It has a little more power than these fellows, enough to move a stone to where you can find it.'

'What does it look like? Like those ones?' I pointed to the milk dish.

'No, no, different order of spirit entirely. Here, give me that amethyst, and I'll see if I can call him out.' I pulled the crystal out of my apron pocket and Aleida touched a finger to the tip of it. It hummed faintly in my hands, vibrating for just a moment, and then a shaft of blue light swelled upwards from the glassy stone. It moved slowly, as though the space around it were as thick and viscous as honey, and then bloomed into a multifaceted shape, all planes and lines and angles, glittering like frost with a blue and purple glow. It reminded me of the paper snowflakes Lucette made for midwinter, with shapes cut from paper and then slotted together; only this was far more complex, dizzying in its intricacy. I couldn't take my eyes away from it. 'Normally he'd be by the big cluster,' Aleida said. 'But like I said, he likes you, so he's staying close by.'

After a few moments the shape began to fold back in on itself, withdrawing back into the stone I guessed, and at last I was able to look away.

'Looks like they're just about done with the milk, let's get started before they all wander off again.'

I looked around to find that the milk was nearly gone, with only a slick of it across the bottom of the dish.

Aleida gestured at me to stay where I was as she stood and moved to pull the rope in and complete the circle. Then, with the wand, she drew a stroke across the two ends of rope, muttering some words under her breath. With each word she spoke, a little puff of blue glow drifted from her lips, and as she wielded the wand it left a glowing tracery in the air.

As soon as the circle closed, the spirits gathered on the rim of the dish leaped up into the air, tumbling over each other like critters caught in a trap, throwing themselves against the invisible wall Aleida's circle had cast, like a bumblebee trying to headbutt its way through a window.

'Oh, calm down,' Aleida said to them. 'No one's going to hurt you. I have a job for you all — come here, take a look at this.'

With the spirits hovering around her in a cloud she reached for the effigy, and set it down between the fire and the milk-dish. 'Take a good look at it,' she said to the hovering spirits. 'There are other things out there made by the one who made this. Go seek them out, then come back and tell me what you've found.' She still held the wand in her hand, and as she spoke she drew another symbol, more blue lines that hung in the air as though frozen in place. Another tap with the tip of the wand, and it shattered into shards of light just as the first had, each one flying to one of the spirits and adhering to them as a little blue speck. 'Good, then,' Aleida said, and turned to open the circle. 'Go on your way, little ones, and come back when you've found something.'

When she broke the circle, they all spilled out and bumbled away, tumbling over each other in a way that reminded me of cows being let out of the barn at the end of winter. I smiled at the sight. 'How many of them will come back?'

'All of them. I cast a binding. Without that, we'd get maybe a quarter. They don't have much in the way of memory. Now we have to wait.'

My milk finished, I set my cup aside and stretched out my feet towards the fire, tipping my head back to look up at the sky, adorned with a few puffy clouds, glowing gold with the sunrise. 'It's nice here, isn't it?'

She gave me a sardonic look, one eyebrow raised. 'What, with all the monsters and the demon tree and the ghost of an evil witch and the warlock—'

'You can't count him,' I said. 'He's dead now. But yes, aside from that, it's nice here. Nice people. Good soil for gardens. Lovely clear water in the streams. And plenty to do, you'll never get bored.'

Aleida leaned back on her elbows. 'I never thought of it that way,' she said. 'But then, I'm a city rat. Never knew what to do with myself out in the countryside. I like to be able to vanish into a crowd; it's too exposed out here. And there's nowhere to buy coffee.'

'Well that certainly is a problem,' I said solemnly, and Aleida snorted.

After a pause I spoke again. 'Where were you, before you came back here?'

'Spice Islands, out to the south-west,' she said. 'It's lovely down there. It's always warm, and everything's lush and green like you wouldn't believe. There are beaches with white sand, so bright it's blinding, and the water is turquoise blue and always warm. The mosquitos are the size of sparrows, though.'

'What about coffee?'

'Every damn street corner. Black as night, bitter as scorned love. Gods I miss it.'

I turned my head to study her.

'What?'

'I can't picture you in a place like that.'

'On a bright, sunny beach, flapping around in a black dress like some great crow?'

'Well, yeah.'

She just grinned at me. 'Oh, you'd be surprised, Dee. I'm good at blending in, and folk down there look like me, with black hair and golden skin. I dress like the locals do, and you'd never give me a second glance.'

'Will you go back there? When all this is done?'

She shook her head. 'I can't. Someone has to look after this place. It's valuable, you know — not the house, but the orchard, the gardens. A lot of these plants don't exist anywhere else. And someone has to keep an eye on that wretched tree.'

'But I thought you and Gyssha went off and left them?' I asked.

'Spirits,' Aleida said with a shrug. 'She had spirits enslaved to tend the garden, and constructs she could use to make sure everything was in order. And she could draft the neighbours in when needed.'

'Constructs?' I said, thinking of the earthbeasts. But then I remembered the warlock. 'Oh, you mean like the warlock's spare bodies, not the monsters.'

'Yes, exactly.'

I glanced across at the walled garden, the plants peeking over the wall. 'So those plants will be well in need of attention by now. We'll have to get to them soon.'

'We probably should,' Aleida said with a sigh. 'And then I'll have make sure the defences won't come unravelled with Gyssha gone. I hope it won't take too long. I'll need to do something about this wretched curse, and that'll mean a bit of travel. I'll probably need to hunt down some books and maybe consult with other witches, if I can find any that'll talk to me.'

'Will that be safe? I mean, are most witches good, or are there more out there like Gyssha?'

'Witches are the same as everyone else; some good, some bad, some middling. The real problem is that the bad ones usually want you to think they're good.'

'And will they think you're easy pickings, with that curse?'

She made a face that was half-grimace, half-grin. 'Maybe. If they're wise they'll stop to think about how I came by it in the first place. And that'll be another problem; once folk find out what happened up here they'll, well, I'm not sure what will happen. Gyssha was my mother in the craft, you see, and a witch who kills her mother is the worst kind of traitor, it's the deepest betrayal of all.'

'But she was evil,' I said. 'People must know that, surely.'

'It doesn't make much difference,' she said. 'To white witches I'm still Gyssha Blackbone's daughter, and to witches on the dark path I betrayed the one who made me. But ...' She gave a shrug and lay back with her hands behind her head. 'It doesn't matter a jot what they think, so screw 'em.

'And there's another thing we have to look into — the letter that brought you here. I haven't forgotten about that.' She suddenly frowned, and then heaved herself up to sitting. 'Actually, we've got some time to kill now. Let's rattle the woodpile and see what comes scurrying out. Go fetch your letter, Dee, and bring me my runestones. They're in my packs, a little velvet bag.'

I remembered the pouch from when I'd hunted through her saddlebags last night. In a few moments I returned with both, and handed them over. She shook open the letter first, reading through it again before setting it aside with pursed lips. 'All right, let's see what the stones have to say.'

She opened the drawstring to pull out a white cloth — a simple linen kerchief. It even had lace around the edges. She laid it on the ground, and shook the bag, and I heard a tiny *clink* as something rattled within.

With swift fingers she started pulling out stones and dropping them onto the cloth, one at a time until there were nine of them laid out on the linen. The stones were black, but not the flat black of onyx — they sparkled and glittered in the sunlight and each one bore a symbol marked out in gold. Watching her, I couldn't help but remember Brian and his pendulum, and how sceptical I'd felt when he set it swinging.

'Hmm.' Sitting cross-legged, Aleida leaned forward to look down on the stones, touching one here and there with her fingertips. Every so often she would glance up at me, but her eyes were so distant I could have sworn she was looking *through* me, not at me at all. After a few moments she frowned. 'This is strange. It doesn't ... all right, no, it *could* make sense. Maybe.' She gave me another intent look, eyes so sharp I wanted to shrink away.

'What do they say?'

For a moment she didn't respond, she just touched the stones one after another, lips shaping silent words. 'It's a funny thing about stones,' she said at last. 'Cards too, for that matter. You go into them expecting to see mysteries solved, secrets revealed, but they end up mostly telling you what you already knew. This part of the reading,' she gestured to the part near her right knee, 'speaks to the past. You were unhappy, stagnating, wanting change and fearing it at the same time. Wanting escape, but fearing a leap into the dark. Here, the present: awakening. Change. Choices. More choices than you ever dreamed of. But many things are not what they seem. Here in the centre is what must be done — wits sharpened, secrets uncovered. Choices must be made; you can't sit on the fence forever, kid. But still, you must not trust unwisely. Fate is tempting you off the beaten path, but there is danger all around. There are monsters and pitfalls away from the safe road. If you make the wrong choice ...' She fell silent as her fingertips rested on one stone, bearing a symbol of a many-rayed star, each ray tipped with an arrowhead. 'Chaos. Destruction.' She stared down at the stones for a long moment, not frowning, just thinking.

'Mine?' I asked. 'Or yours?'

She lifted her eyes to mine. 'Good question. Could be either. Could be neither; it might mean the cottage. It might mean Lilsfield.' She reached for the bag and pulled out another stone, setting it beside the pointed star. 'Ah. No. Definitely a person. Someone is going to die.'

I felt frozen, like a spike of cold had pierced my heart.

'Don't worry about that one, kid,' Aleida said. 'My money's on Gyssha.'

Well of course you'd say that. 'But she's already dead.'

Aleida held out her hand palm down and rocked it side to side. 'Only halfway.'

I remembered what she'd said before about doubt and fear, and wondered if she truly felt as certain as she seemed. Maybe, like me, her guts were twisting inside her, feeling full of worms and snakes. Maybe that was why she wouldn't eat, and why she was distracting herself from the task ahead of us.

I'd watched her touch each of the stones as she spoke of them — all but one. A stone on Aleida's right-hand side had fallen face-down, the only one that had. 'What about that one?' I asked, pointing.

She turned it over. 'The hand,' she said. 'Obverse, indicating the influence is hidden, secret.' She sat back with a sigh. 'Well, thanks for that, stones. I ask why she was brought here and all you can tell me is that it was done by someone for hidden reasons or by hidden means. I already knew that much.' With a hiss of irritation, she reached into the bag and brought out another one, all but throwing it down on to the cloth. 'Good gods, I wonder why I bother—' She stopped mid-sentence as the stone gleamed and winked in the sunlight. 'Ah. Now we may be getting somewhere. Magic, it was magic that brought you here.'

'Magic? But, why? Before I came here I'd never seen a witch in my life, let alone magic. I didn't even believe in it.'

'The universe doesn't care what you believe, Dee.' She picked the paper up again and held it up to the light. She closed her eyes and moved it under her nose, drawing a deep breath. Opening her eyes again, she frowned even deeper. 'Doesn't smell like it's been enchanted. No watermark, but that doesn't mean anything.' She muttered. 'This is *very* strange.'

'Maybe it was Gyssha after all,' I said.

'Can't have been. Gyssha herself might lie, but her echo can't.' With a hiss of breath, she pulled another stone from the bag and set it down.

As soon as it hit the cloth, the fire popped with a shower of sparks, the flames leaping high above my head. Smoke swirled around us, thick and choking, and I felt a sudden pressure in my ears, a prickling across my neck.

Aleida fell still, hand hovering over the last stone, and slowly she lifted her eyes.

I started to follow her gaze, but straightaway, her hand shot out and grabbed my knee through my skirts. 'Dee,' she said quietly. 'Remember what I told you …'

Hovering above the fire was a … a shape, wreathed in smoke and firelight. My first thought was the Nefari, the smoke-creature black as night with eyes like red coals. But after the first rush of fear I realised that this did not have the same air of malevolence the Nefari had had. It still made my chest tighten, but there was no hatred oozing out from its presence. Just … power, heavy as an anvil and hot as a forge. A pair of eyes gazed down at us, or at least that's what I took them for — two blazing blue lights the size of dinner-plates.

'What *is* it?' I whispered.

'A greater spirit. It won't harm you, Dee. It's watching me,' Aleida said.

'Why?'

'Not sure. A warning, maybe.' Eyes on the spirit, she slowly reached for the last stone. With every fraction of movement, I felt the pressure upon me grow and grow again, until my heart was racing and my blood pounding in my ears.

I grabbed for her hand and pulled it away. 'Stop!' I said. 'Please, stop!'

She fought me for a moment, and then let me pull her away. Then she raised her hands in a gesture of submission. 'All right,' she said, speaking to the spirit hovering above us. 'All right, I'll put them away. I'll let the matter rest ... for now, anyway. Are you satisfied?' She wasn't talking to me at all now but casting her words up to the hollow sky.

I was shaking uncontrollably, but as I watched, the shape faded away, turning transparent and then vanishing in a gout of smoke. After a few moments, the hot, heavy feeling in the air eased away and my nerves settled with it. 'What was that?' I hissed once I could trust myself to speak again.

'I think I just asked a question I'm not supposed to know the answer to,' Aleida muttered, bundling up cloth and stones and shoving them back into the velvet pouch.

The knot in my belly and the tightness around my chest was back now, and I thought of Ma, the warmth of her arms. My siblings, too, the little ones who would cling to me when it thundered. The sense of wonderment I'd had when Aleida started the ritual was gone, and once again I felt lost, adrift in a strange place, out of my depth.

'You all right, Dee?' Aleida said.

I made myself straighten, raising my gaze. I'd been staring at my boots, the tough, scarred leather. They'd been Trev's before he outgrew them. I'd never have had such a sturdy pair otherwise. 'What does it mean?'

'It means you were brought here for a reason. Just what that reason is, we'll have to figure out as we go along.' She raised her arms over her head in a stretch, and then rolled her shoulders. 'It's time to call the sprites back. It'll take a bit of work, that little show will have scared them off. Help me pour the rest of that milk in the dish, and then go fetch a halter and rope. We'll need the horse to start with, I think. I'll call him up.'

My hands were still shaking as I went to the stables, but I drew deep, steadying breaths, and refused to look around as though I felt fearful. If I pretended to be calm, surely, eventually, I would feel that way.

CHAPTER 12

The horse must have been nearby, for he arrived within moments. The sprites were back, or most of them anyway, perched once again on the rim of the dish. Aleida was kneeling beside it, holding one cupped in her hands. The way she held it reminded me of the way Ma held songbirds she'd taken away from the cats — gently but firmly, fingers laced together to keep it from squirming away. As I drew close she set it down and reached for another.

I thought it better not to interrupt and set about readying the horse instead. She'd said halter, not saddle and bridle, and I didn't dare disobey, so I just brushed out his coat and picked out his feet instead. By the time that was done, the sprites were bumbling away, with just a few left supping up the dregs in the dish.

'Did they tell you what you wanted to know?' I asked.

'Mm. They're not very bright, but they can sense power a lot more keenly than we can. We'll need to head north along the stream.'

'Are you sure you don't want him saddled?' I asked as she took the lead-rope from me and tied the free end to the halter, turning them into a semblance of reins.

'Yep. Once we find the spot I'll turn him loose, he'll only be in danger if he stays close.'

I was about to ask how she meant to mount up without saddle and stirrups, but when she touched the horse's shoulder he immediately sank to his knees, low enough to let her swing a leg over his back. 'Come on, Dee,' she said, beckoning me to follow, and quickly I did the same, barely settling on the beast's warm back before he was heaving himself up again. Hastily, I grabbed for her waist, but as I did my hand brushed the wand hanging from her belt and I felt a sudden stinging jolt, a shock somewhere between the chill of ice and the shocks you sometimes get on dry, cold winter days.

Aleida looked down and laid a hand on the wand. 'Stop that, you,' she said. 'Behave yourself.'

'Sorry,' I said.

'Not you, him,' she said. 'He's a one-woman kind of fellow, and he's never liked me much — he was Gyssha's, before I killed her.'

'But didn't you have one of your own?' I said. I spoke without stopping to think, and immediately regretted it when I felt her tense at my words.

'I did,' she said. 'But Gyssha shattered it. Hold on to my belt, Dee, and tell me if you start to slip.' With a nudge of her heels the horse set off into the bright daylight, escorted by a handful of the sprites Aleida had summoned. A couple trailed along behind and some more were gambolling ahead of us. One seemed to have attached itself to the horse's left front hoof, and I wondered if it was enjoying the arc it made with each stride as the horse splashed through the stream and up the slope on the other side, heading towards the steeply rising mountains to the north. I just hoped we weren't going too far up those slopes — I had no faith in myself to be able to ride bareback over such rough ground. Riding pillion could only be worse.

Thankfully, Aleida kept a slow pace, peering intently into the woods around us while the horse ambled along.

'What are we looking for, exactly?' I said.

'I'll show you when I see one. This might be frightfully boring, Dee, but you'll just have to put up with it. I won't risk leaving you behind.'

'Fine by me,' I said with a shiver. 'You might be utterly mad, but I'd rather take my chances with you than alone out here.'

'Really?' she said. 'Not even a little tempted to run off and hide out with this mysterious boy you've found?'

Kian. I'd hardly given him a thought since Gyssha had taken me over and dosed Aleida with the laudanum. Immediately I wondered if he was nearby, what he'd think if he saw the two of us like this.

Well, I told myself, *he can think what he likes, it's not for me to say. But I do hope he doesn't despise me for working with a witch.* But what if I did take up Aleida's offer and let her teach me? What would he do then? What would he think of me?

I knew there were more important things to consider than the feelings of a boy I'd known for just a few days, but, still, the thought of his scorn hurt. I had so few friends, and he was the only one I'd been able to talk to about the strangeness of life in the cottage and this world I'd found myself in. Maybe I had only known him for a short time, but the thought of losing him was a pain I couldn't bring myself to contemplate. I had to push the idea away. I'd deal with it later, once all this was done. If we were still alive. 'Aleida?'

'Yeah?'

'When Gyssha came to you, did you have any doubts?'

'Doubts? Nope. Not one. I told you, didn't I? I was in prison when she came for me. Not much of a choice between escaping or waiting to get your hand cut off. At the time I was thinking I'd just bolt for it as soon as we were free and clear, but then I saw what she did to the guards to make them let us leave ... by the time the gates closed behind us I'd decided that maybe it was worth sticking around for a bit. But, of course, it was all carrot early on. She didn't show me the stick until later.'

I thought about what it would be like, being locked in a dungeon, waiting for the axe. 'I'm not scrappy, like you. If I ended up in jail like that I think I'd just sit and bawl like a lost calf.'

'Oh, there was plenty of bawling, Dee, let me tell you. And what do you mean you're not scrappy? The way you've handled yourself out here, you could have fooled me.' Aleida made a small noise in the back of her throat then, and nudged me with her elbow. 'There's one. Look, can you see it?' She pointed into the underbrush to our left.

She was pointing at a clump of ferns growing under the shelter of a fallen tree. There was nothing remarkable about it at all, as far as I could see. 'I can't see anything.'

'Look closely. There's a kind of mist hanging over it, a little plume of green. Can you see it?'

I squinted, tilting my head this way and that. How ridiculous was it, to be looking for a green haze against the lush greenery of these mountains? But then ... 'Oh,' I said. 'Yes. Yes, I can see it! Wait—' She'd made no move to stop the horse. 'Aren't we going to stop?'

'No, that's just a little one. I told you, Gyssha must have buried hundreds of constructs or trinkets around these hills, thousands maybe. I'm looking for something bigger. But now you know what to look for.' She nudged the horse on into a trot, and then, thankfully, into a canter. There might be girls out there who can comfortably ride a trotting horse bareback, but I am definitely not one of them.

We followed the stream for a ways, the ground steadily rising, but after just a few minutes Aleida slowed the horse to a walk. 'Ah. Now we're talking.'

This time I could see it clearly, a plume of sickly green, like smoke, that rose up from the ground. She guided the horse over to it and halted to hold her hand over the murky haze. 'Hmm. Another earthbeast, I think. We'll keep going.'

While she was investigating the plume, I'd been looking up, at the tops of the trees on the mountain ahead. 'Look,' I said, 'up there. Is that another one? It looks like a big one.' There was a murky green haze rising up above the trees. The plume on the one beside us was about as tall as a person standing, so this one seemed much, much bigger.

She squinted at the trees up ahead. 'Yeah. Looks promising. Let's go.'

We found it after just a few minutes, and this time when Aleida reined in she swung a leg over the horse's neck and slipped to the ground. 'You come down too, Dee.'

'What is this?' The ground had flattened out, and we were under a thick cover of trees, the canopy so dense that not even ferns grew underneath. There was just a damp, mouldering carpet of fallen leaves, and in the middle of it, an oddly smooth, pointed stone jutting up out of the ground, veined with some black mineral that glittered, even in the darkness.

'Not sure,' Aleida said, studying the stone. 'A power-store, maybe?' She shrugged. 'I'll soon find out. Stay close, now. Don't wander off.' She settled down, sitting cross-legged to face the stone, and fell utterly still.

Minutes passed.

Well, I told myself. *She did say this would be boring.* The horse was even less impressed than I was, being asked to wait patiently when there wasn't even any grass to keep him occupied. I was too tired to have any tolerance for his antics, so I tethered him to a low branch and left him there to stamp and fuss.

My belly grumbled. A cup of spiced milk was nice as a treat, but hardly a substitute for a real breakfast. After last night's misadventures I could have used something much more substantial — I felt drained and weak, and I was tempted to settle onto the damp leaves beside Aleida and close my eyes, just for a few moments.

But then I remembered that Gyssha was out here somewhere, watching us, and all thought of sleep swiftly left my mind. Instead I turned on my heel, surveying the trees around us, the green–gold canopy above. Was she here already, waiting for an opportunity to strike? I clenched my fists, digging fingernails into my palms. She must be here, I'd bet money on it. In fact, I'd bet she'd been watching us constantly, and we never even knew.

I turned back to Aleida then, watching her sitting motionless with her head bowed and her fingertips pressed to the stone. It seemed somehow *absurd* that she'd ever offer to train *me*. Boring, dull little Elodie, who'd spent all her life cleaning and cooking and wiping dirty faces and bottoms ...

And yet. And yet that letter had come from *somewhere*.

Magic, she'd said, peering at the runestones. *It was magic that brought you here.*

Something drifted through my field of vision then, something pale and fluttering. My head snapped up, my thoughts shoved aside as I tried to focus, but the thing was so strange that my weary mind could make no sense of it. There were pale feathers and gleaming, golden wire ...

And then I realised it was heading straight for Aleida's unprotected back.

With a shout of warning I started forward. Her head lifted at my cry and she twisted around — only to stop short with a gasp, clamping an arm down on her injured ribs.

The little fluttering *thing* was moving faster than I'd realised. Much faster. As I closed the gap I could see it more clearly; the feathers were wings, the body and legs made from twisted wire.

It landed on Aleida's back, and I saw her stiffen with a hiss of pain, reaching over her shoulder for it, only for her injured ribs to bring her up short again.

I reached her then, and yanked the thing away.

It was a wasp — a wasp the size of a sparrow, made of wire and glass and glittering beads. Its body was a glass vial, streaked with traces of something brown and oily. Its stinger was a snake's fang, smeared with blood.

Aleida turned and snatched it from me, its feathery wings still beating against my palm, wire legs writhing and twitching. She gave it a single glance — and then smashed it against the stone with a *chink* of shattering glass.

I grabbed her by the shoulder with shaking hands. 'I'm sorry! I'm sorry, I should have been watching, I should—'

She lifted her head, and gave me such a withering look that the words died in my mouth. 'Dee,' she said. 'Do you think I brought you here to stand between me and Gyssha? Your only job is to stay alive.' Then she glanced down at her hand. Blood flowed freely from a gash in her palm, and there was a smear of the dark, oily stuff from the vial, too. She raised it to her mouth, tasting it with a quick touch of her tongue, and then immediately spat it out again.

'Poison?' I said.

'Belladonna,' she said with a grimace. 'It causes delirium, confusion and hallucinations. All right, Dee, this is about to get interesting. Stay close.' She seized my hand in hers — the injured one was nearest, and I soon felt the blood seep into the bandages wrapped around my palm. 'Stay right here, Dee. Right here. No matter what, don't let her lead you away. Got it?'

But before I could reply, in the blink of an eye, with a single thud of my heart, the forest and the mountains and everything around me was swept away.

I was in a ballroom, full of colour and noise and candlelight. I wore a beautiful rose-hued gown, stiff with embroidery and glittering with jewels. Before me, hundreds of lords and ladies danced, spinning and circling in a dizzying display while music filled the room. Above me the roof beams were picked out in gold, while the ceiling was painted to look like a blue sky studded with perfect, fluffy clouds. Colourful, exotic birds were painted flying overhead or perched on the beams to look down at us, enthralled. Chandeliers the size of wagon wheels illuminated the room, and they too were covered in gold and dripping with crystals. Mirrors lined the walls between each candelabra, reflecting the candlelight and the dazzling display of coloured silks and glowing jewels, the women in gorgeous gowns, the men in crisp uniforms with sabres at their sides or else in long jackets every bit as colourful as the ladies' dresses.

I shrank back, fingers buried in the crisp silk of my skirts. Where was I? *Who* was I? I didn't belong here, I was sure of that. *I'm not supposed to be here.* But my rose-coloured gown was as fine as any other in the room. My hands were clad in spotless white gloves that reached past my elbows and were bedecked with rings and bracelets, resplendent in the candlelight. Cautiously, I raised my hands to my head and found my hair piled artfully atop my head, held in place with jewelled pins and decorated with long, delicate feathers that danced and swayed with every movement.

I started to push my way around the edge of the room, confused and verging on panic. This was wrong, this was all wrong. I wasn't supposed to be here. I needed to be somewhere else. *Someone* else.

At the far end of the room was a dais where two people sat — a man and a woman, dressed in white and gold and loaded with jewels that put the rest of the room to shame. The man was handsome, the woman beautiful, with gleaming blonde hair that matched the gold on her dress, and I knew without a moment's thought that they were wearing bridal clothes, and this was their wedding night. But they didn't look happy — not at all. The man held himself as stiff as a sword, staring straight ahead; his face blank and his lips pale, as though he was clenching them tight to keep from speaking. The bride looked pale and fearful, and there, by her side, was another woman, a lass with gleaming black hair and golden skin, clad in a sapphire-blue gown. She leaned in close, whispering in the bride's ear, and I saw their eyes following one of the couples on the dance-floor, and I saw the bride smile, her stiff posture soften and a blush of pink cross her porcelain cheeks.

Then, in the blink of an eye, everything changed. Now I was outside on rain-washed streets strung with bunting and garlands of flowers. I was crowded cheek-by-jowl with other folk and straining to see an open carriage driving past, drawn by six white horses and gleaming with gold. Inside sat the blonde woman from before, and riding with her, arm linked through hers, was the same girl with golden skin and black hair, a wicked gleam in her eyes and a sly smile on her lips.

I know her, I thought, as the carriage rumbled past and the crowd surged into the streets after them, cheering and calling out blessings and praise. *I know her.*

Then, another blink, and the vision changed once again. I was still in the street, but everything had changed — the buntings in tatters, the flowers rotting and mouldered. Shutters were broken, doors splintered and torn from their hinges. The cobblestones were streaked with filth, and great patches of them had been torn up to litter the streets elsewhere, as though levered out to be hurled as weapons. Plumes of smoke rose over the city, and the street was deserted. The side-streets were cluttered with splintered, broken furniture — folk had built barricades, and then had them smashed apart. In the distance I could see bodies, crumpled and sprawled and left to rot.

Another blink, and I was back in the ballroom — only this time, everything was aflame and the air was full of choking smoke. The candles were out, the candle-stands toppled, the mirrors smashed while the painted ceiling smouldered, raining ash and cinders. Through the crackle and roar of the fire I heard distant screams and shouts and the ring of metal. Something snagged my foot and I tripped, falling on my hands and knees, only to find that I'd stumbled over the body of a man in one of those beautiful embroidered coats, his throat cut from ear to ear. When I looked down, I realised my own dress was streaked with blood, torn and charred at the hem, and in my hand was a bloody knife.

There were dozens of bodies under the choking smoke, and here and there I could see fallen figures stirring, dragging themselves over the ballroom floor, leaving streaks of blood behind. Overhead, the ceiling groaned and cracked, and a massive chunk of it sagged, shedding a waterfall of sparks and cinders. Slowly, as though time had turned to honey, the roof fell, crashing down onto those crawling figures ...

The moment it hit, I was somewhere else — an elegant chamber with tapestries on the walls and carpets on the floor, gilded couches upholstered with creamy silk — all of it splattered with blood. Lying half on the couch, half slid to the floor, was the golden, beautiful bride. There was a sword driven right through her chest, pinning her to the couch while she coughed and gasped, plucking at the blade with bloody hands. On the floor by her feet was a dead man, half-undressed, his hands and chest rent with great, bloody wounds. His face, slack and still, was that of the man she'd smiled at on the dance-floor, the one who'd sparked the blush on the bride's cheeks. Behind them, the bridegroom was striding around the room, tearing at his hair with both hands, his fine clothing all splattered with blood.

There came a noise from outside and I whirled, just as he did — in time to see two men charging through the door, both of them bloodied, with swords in their hands, both of them with the same golden hair as the dying bride. Once again, I knew without thinking that they were her kin, come to save her, or avenge her.

And at the back of the room, half hidden in shadow, was the black-haired woman in the blue gown, pressed against the wall with her hand to her mouth in a gesture of horror. Beside her … beside her was a smaller figure, an old woman, all in black, though her dress glittered like the stars on a clear night. She clutched the younger woman's arm with fingers that looked like talons, and on her face was a vicious smile, eyes sparkling with delight as the bride's kin fell upon the unarmed groom, hacking him to pieces, while on the blood-soaked couch the bride gasped her last breath and fell still.

I stood frozen, overcome with the horror of the scene, the smell of blood and the stink of death. *This isn't right,* I told myself. *This isn't real. This isn't happening. This can't be happening.*

In that frozen moment, I felt someone — something — take hold of my hand. I wanted to jump out of my skin, but I couldn't move. I couldn't do anything, even as I felt the unseen figure reach for my other hand. There was something wrapped around it, something holding on to me, gripping tight, and as I felt the other hand pull mine away I didn't know if I should panic or feel relieved. I couldn't talk, I couldn't *think*, my head was full of horror, of dread and of the smell of blood and fear and smoke.

Then I felt an arm wrapped around my shoulders, and a voice whispered in my ear. 'Come on, Dee. Come on, come with me. It'll be all right, I'll get you out of here, just come with me.'

I couldn't resist. The gentle words might as well have been a command set in stone. The arm at my back propelled me forward, and the vision, the gold and blood and candlelight, all melted away.

CHAPTER 13

I tried to pull back. Something inside me knew it was wrong to let myself be drawn away. I had to stay here. It was *important*, but I couldn't remember why. There was a blank spot inside my mind, like the spots that dance before your eyes after staring into a bright light. I could see, but what I saw made no sense — it was just a blur of green and blue and brown.

But no matter how I pulled back, no matter how I tried to resist, the owner of those hands kept pulling me away, pushing me onwards; whispering soft words like you'd use to soothe a frightened beast.

The forest, I realised. *I'm back in the forest.*

Where's the city? Where's the ball? Whose clothes are these? I had a dream, I know it was a dream. I had a dream about a witch in a cottage and monsters in the woods and a boy with soft hands and tangled curls and freckles across his cheeks.

'Kian,' I said. 'It wasn't a dream. Kian.'

'You're all right, Dee. I've got you. I'll take you somewhere safe.'

I blinked, my eyes clearing. I understood now that the green and brown shapes were trees, the blue was the sky between them. Ahead of us was a river, flowing fast over rocks, and the air was full of noise, a rushing, roaring sound. My wits felt dull, I couldn't make sense of it. I just wished it would stop. 'Kian? What are you doing here?'

I pulled back to see his face, and he gave me an easy grin, the same sort of grin he'd given me the day before when I'd called after him on the forest trail, but at the same time he kept propelling me forward. Yesterday I'd been relieved to see that smile, but today .... Today something about it put me on edge.

'I saw you,' he said. 'I saw you both, heading along the river. And then, well, it looked to me like you were in trouble. Like something was wrong.'

Something *was* wrong. *He* was wrong. Kian hated witches, he was frightened of Aleida. Would he really creep up under her nose to drag me away, when she could open her eyes at any moment? Maybe. Maybe he would. Maybe, if he really did care about me. But he didn't look like a lad who'd just braved his worst fear for a girl he really liked. If he had, he'd be wide-eyed and flushed, breathing hard. Not watching me with a little half-smile, almost a smirk, on his lips, as calm and collected as ... as Aleida was when we set out that morning.

I wiped my free hand on my skirts, feeling the bandage thick against my palm. He hadn't asked about the bandages. I hadn't been wearing them yesterday. What kind of person wouldn't comment on something like that? A dark thought was unfolding inside me, a dark and terrifying thought, and I fervently hoped I was wrong.

I tried to stop. He had an arm across my shoulders, and when I pushed back he braced against me, driving me forward, until I grabbed for his hand and tried to spin out of his grip. It worked, for a moment, but then my feet tangled with his and I fell. Before I'd even hit the ground, he was behind me again, hands wrapping around my wrists. 'What's the matter, Dee? What's wrong? Don't you trust me?'

The words echoed inside my head as he drove me onwards towards the water. *What's the matter, Dee? What's wrong? What's the matter? What's wrong?* 'Kian, please let me go. Please.'

He was right behind me, breathing down my neck. Except, he wasn't. That morning, when Aleida had pulled me close, I'd felt her breath on my skin, but now I felt nothing — no heat, no air. 'Soon,' he said. 'Soon. I wouldn't worry about the little witch if I were you. Whatever she's tangled up in, it doesn't need to concern you.' Still, he propelled me onwards, marching me towards the river, hands tight around my wrists.

'Kian!' I pleaded.

I remembered the moment I'd first seen him, back on my first morning at the cottage. I'd felt so strange then, so out of place, and I'd been so glad to see a friendly face, that warm smile — and then I thought of Aleida's Bennett, and how she'd been lost and alone out here until he befriended her.

I threw myself down on the ground, a dead weight. It should at least have pulled him off balance — Kian was slender, like Aleida, he looked like he never ate enough. But he simply kept dragging me across the ground, his grip on my wrists so tight it was as though I could feel the touch of the flames all over again. I heard my own breath sobbing from the pain of it, but he either didn't notice, or didn't care.

I knew what it meant. It all added up in my mind, the pieces fitting together like the fragments of a dish, shattered on a flagstone floor. No warmth, no breath, strength far greater than his weedy frame. The way he was so often *there* whenever I ventured from the cottage, ready with a warm smile and a friendly ear. Like he'd been lying in wait. He was too good to be true. He always had been. 'You're not Kian,' I said. 'There is no Kian.'

He looked down at me and chuckled, eyes full of mirth. 'Then who am I, Elodie?'

My chest felt tight with fear, like an iron band around my ribs. All I could do was whisper. 'Gyssha …'

The thing wearing Kian's face threw back its head with a laugh. 'Stubborn little thing, aren't you?' he said, still hauling me towards the river, despite my thrashing and kicking. 'The one thing that bothers me is that I can't for the life of me — hah! — figure out where she dug you up from. Oh well, I don't suppose it matters. I had another wasp lined up for you, you know, all ready to go. I decided against it in the end — there'd be no fun in it, you see?'

We were at the river now, rocks rolling under his feet, the water rushing over smooth stones. The air was full of noise and water. I realised then where the old witch had brought me.

The thing let go of my wrists and took another grip — one hand buried in my hair, another on my shoulder, and dragged me on scrabbling hands the last few feet to the water. At the edge of the river, a couple of boulders made a little sheltered pool where the water was just rippling and swirling instead of the frothing, tumultuous flow a few yards away.

'Sure,' the thing went on, 'I could pump you full of belladonna and chase you over the falls with visions of demons and monsters, but then you wouldn't *know*. You wouldn't *know* who killed you.' It held me over the water, and I felt it lean down, its head next to mine. Our faces reflected in the swirling water, distorted but still clear enough to see — my face with wide eyes, panting lips, pale with fear, and Kian's smooth, freckled cheeks and tousled curls, as beautiful as the first time I'd seen him.

'And I just couldn't be having that,' he said in my ear while I panted with fear and pain. 'It wouldn't be right. I need you to know in your last moments. I need you to know what happens to those who cross Gyssha Blackbone. Because if you don't know, what's the point?'

The reflection changed. The sweet, kind face melted away, flowing like wax. His hair became a thatch of twigs; his brown eyes were brown river-stones. His lips, his smile — oh gods. His true face was a skull, green with moss, with shreds of flesh still clinging to the bones. The stench of decay made me choke and retch.

The hand buried in my hair forced my head to turn towards him. 'Now,' the corpse said, teeth clacking together with every word. 'It'd be an awful shame for a young lass to die without ever having her first kiss, wouldn't it? Kiss me, Elodie. Don't tell me you haven't dreamed about these lips, girl. Kiss me, my lady love!'

As the revolting face pressed close to mine, something inside me turned cold and hard. My breath was still sobbing in my throat, my heart pounding so hard it hurt, but for an instant all that seemed to pull away. *A weapon,* I thought. *I need something, anything!* Even a chunk of stone from the river would be better than my bare hands, shaking with terror. I threw myself down towards the water, shoving aside the thought of how easy it would make it for Gyssha to drown me like a rat ... but then my fingertips found a shaft of cold, crisp stone, its flat faces as smooth as glass, the bulk of it thicker than my wrist. Another crystal, the largest I'd ever seen.

I lifted it out of the water and smashed it across the grinning skull with all my strength. Then I swung it again, and again, and heard bone *crack* under the strike.

It didn't cry out. That was the strangest thing. Aside from the rush of water, the only sounds were my own grunts and panting breaths as I clubbed the awful thing again and again. The crystal broke, the perfect point cleaving off, but I didn't even care. In fact, it was probably for the best, as it had a wicked edge now, like broken glass. I stabbed it into his chest, felt it squeeze between the ribs, forcing them apart. And then, as the corpse lay still, I backed away, panting and shaking.

I'd seen enough of witchcraft now to recognise what it was: a construct, made of human bones. The rags he wore might well have been the suit the poor lad was buried in. The bones had been strung together with leather and wire and wrapped in tiny crystal beads that glittered like eyes in darkness. I remembered the day before, when Kian had sat behind me on the grey horse with his arms around my waist, and I had to choke down bile as my stomach heaved.

I raked hands through my hair and reeled back, feet slipping on the round stones. We were even closer than I'd realised to the top of the falls — I could see the edge of it, only a few feet away. I started to glance around, but then a noise made me freeze. A rattle of bones.

A demented laugh rang out, clear even over the roar of the waterfall, and the construct lifted its head, river-stone eyes fixed on me. 'Stupid girl,' it said. 'Stupid, stupid girl. Do you think *this* has a heart to pierce? A brain to crush?' It heaved itself up, broken crystal still buried in its chest. 'I don't know how my worthless daughter could think a lack-wit like you could ever be a witch.'

I backed away, two quick steps, and crouched down. There was a length of wood jammed between two stones, probably by some past flood. I got my hands under it and wrenched it up, just as the skeleton found its feet and lurched towards me.

My first swing caught it under the chin, wrenching its head up and sending it stumbling back. My second drove it back further, its rotting boots scrabbling on the slippery rocks above the falls.

On the last swing, it grabbed for the wood, fingers closing tight around the end of the bough.

It started to speak, opening that ghastly, grinning mouth.

It never got the chance. I shifted my grip on the bough, and gripped it like a lever, like a ram, and *shoved*.

For an instant the skeleton wavered on the edge of the falls. Then, it was gone, and there was no sound but the roar of the water and the pounding of blood in my ears.

'Wouldn't be my first kiss, anyway,' I spat after it. Then I stumbled to the edge of the river, and hastily scrubbed my hands and face with the cold, clean water. I tried not to vomit at the memory of those arms around me and that dead, rotting face so close to mine.

When I thought I could stand again, I heaved myself up, found another stick — not as long or stout as the one I'd lost, unfortunately — and crept up to the edge of the waterfall to peer over the side. Part of me was certain I'd find the construct there, clinging to the rocks with hands that would never tire, but there was nothing. Nothing but long scrapes through the moss where dead, fleshless fingers had scrabbled for grip. Gone. Dead? I felt myself grimace. How do you kill something that isn't alive? All I could hope for was that the fall had smashed it to pieces. 'Kian,' I felt myself whispering his name without ever willing the word to my lips. For a moment I entertained the idea that it wasn't *all* a lie, that maybe there really was a boy out there with tangled curls and warm brown eyes with freckles on his cheeks, but then I remembered my talk with Melly. No, if he was ever real, she'd have known him. It was all a lie, built just to ensnare me.

I tried not to contemplate how well it had worked. There was no time for that.

'All right,' I said to myself, trying to smooth down skirts that were once again streaked with mud, and now also soaked by the river. 'All right. Now I just have to find my way back.'

But with the roar of the waterfall loud in my ears, I bit my lip. The gods only knew how far the construct had taken me from Aleida — from the clearing where I'd left her I couldn't even hear these falls. I had no idea which way to go. I was alone out here — at least, I hoped I was — and utterly lost.

First I tried to retrace my steps, following the trail where the construct had dragged me across the damp ground. But the tracks petered out while the sound of the waterfall was still loud in my ears. I thought about just setting out and hoping to find some clue — a footprint or a shred of cloth caught on a bush — but then I shook my head. It would be beyond foolish to get lost out here; more lost than I already was, that is.

Instead I went back to the river and the waterfall, and stood on the huge rock at the top of the cliff, looking out at the mountains through the haze thrown up by the falling water. I'd glimpsed the falls a number of times yesterday, out on the horse, and I had a rough idea of where the cottage lay from here. I ought to be able to walk in that direction until I hit the trail we'd taken out that morning, and then follow that path back to Aleida. Except that I was at the top of the waterfall, not the bottom; and in any case, the remains of Gyssha's construct was down there somewhere. Even if the disgusting thing was smashed on the rocks, I'd sooner not stare into that grinning face again.

It'd take too long, anyway. With her construct gone, what would Gyssha do next? Summon something else to torment me? Or go after Aleida? I bunched my fists in my skirts, ignoring the sting of the burns on my hands and arms. I felt hopeless. The one thing Aleida had asked me to do was stay by her side, and I hadn't even managed that.

I turned away from the cliff-top with a shake of my head. It was too cold to stay up there for long, what with the spray from the falls and the up-draft driven by falling water.

As I retreated, something caught my eye — a mirror-bright flash among the round river-stones. I stopped, and then stooped to pick it up: the broken point of the crystal I'd used to bludgeon the *thing* hiding under Kian's face. 'Sorry,' I murmured, cleaning mud off the shard with my sleeve. It was by far the largest one that I'd ever seen, a true wonder; and I'd ruined it.

I held it up to the sunlight, remembering the beautiful, unfolding shape Aleida had called out of the amethyst point that morning. '*You've made a friend,*' she'd told me. Well, I really needed one of those right now. I might be lost, but maybe I wasn't alone after all. 'Um ... hello?'

I said, softly. 'I'm sorry I broke your stone, but I really am grateful you brought it to me.'

A pulse of light rippled across the crystal's glassy face. I almost dropped it in surprise. I hadn't really expected a response. 'You can hear me?'

Another flash of light mimicked the first.

I glanced around, afraid that I was imagining things. What if it was just a reflection off the water? What if …

No, I told myself. *It's real, you know it's real. You've seen it.*

A seed of hope unfolded in my chest. I had an idea. Aleida had called him an earth spirit. I didn't know much about spirits and witchcraft, but it seemed to me that an earth spirit here in the mountains would have a hard time getting lost. 'Can you help me?' I said. 'I need to get back to Aleida, quickly. Can you show me the way?'

One more pulse of light washed over the stone, and then the lights appeared in a rippling flood, just like the sun sparkling off the flowing water.

It took me some time to understand — it was like a game of blind man's bluff, but with the direction of the ripples showing me which way to go. Only, it seemed to be leading me right into the canyon.

I only held back for a few moments. When the alternative was waiting for Gyssha to come after me again, either before or after she settled her business with Aleida, I didn't see I had any choice but to trust the strange, glittering creature folded up within the stone. So I shoved my stick under my apron-ties to free my hands, and set out to follow where the spirit led.

The ripples led me along the riverbank, heading away from the falls. I *knew* this wasn't the direction we'd come, but, again, what choice did I have? There might be many things to fear in this strange world I'd found myself in, but every instinct I had said that this spirit wasn't one of them. So I went where it guided me, even when the ripples of light sent me into a canyon, past sheer, rocky walls blanketed with moss, picking my way over huge, smooth-washed boulders with water rushing white all around me.

Then, when I reached a narrow crevice in the wall, the spirit guided me into the dark. This time I didn't hesitate at all — it seemed pointless *now* to quibble over where the spirit was taking me. The shimmering glow kept leading me on, even when we left the sun behind, giving just enough light for me to see the blackness and void around me. I crept on through the dark, clutching the stone so tightly that my knuckles ached, and keeping my other hand raised over my head, hoping it would keep me from walking into a low-hanging stone in the dark. Even so, I didn't feel half as scared as I had been when Kian's hand closed around my wrists, dragging me to the river's edge and the top of the falls.

After what felt like an age, I saw a gleam of daylight ahead and hurried towards it on shaking legs. 'Thank you,' I whispered to the stone. 'Thank you, thank you.'

When I stepped out into daylight again, the roar of water was gone, and there were only the regular sounds of the forest, the rustle of leaves and the distant twittering of birds.

And then, close by, the sound of someone breathing hard.

I took one glance back, making sure there was no danger behind me, but the passage that had brought me here was gone. Utterly gone. There was nothing there but solid rock. *Well,* I said to myself. *Are you really so surprised?*

Then I saw her — her black hair had come loose from its bun and spilled over her shoulders, fallen leaves clinging to her dress. Her wand was in her hand, and she stood as though frozen, staring.

Slowly, I tucked the crystal fragment into my apron pocket, and started forward. Part of me wanted to call to her, to let her know I was here but something made me hold back. She was focused intently on something I couldn't see, but the line of her shoulders and the way she held herself reminded me of a cat, hunched and ready to attack.

But what was she staring at? An illusion? A hallucination brought on by the belladonna? I couldn't see a—

No. There was *something* there. A haze, like smoke hanging in the air.

I took one more step, and then I saw it.

Back home, in my siblings' storybook, there was a page full of strange illustrations that played tricks on the eye. There was a young woman who changed into an old hag if you looked at her just right, and a duck's head that became a rabbit, with the beak turning into the ears if you shifted your eyes just so. That's what this was like, as strange as it seems. One moment all I could see was a faint haze in the air, like smoke trapped low to the ground on a cool morning. The next moment, I saw it — the body of a young woman.

My body. Bloody and contorted, soaked to the skin and tangled in water weeds. My body, as it would have looked if Kian had succeeded in throwing me off the top of the falls.

Leaves crunched under my foot, and Aleida whirled, training her wand on me. The way she fixed her gaze on me gave me an idea of what it must feel like to be a mouse. Her intent, unwavering stare was like a hunting beast. Her pupils were huge, swallowing up almost all of the brown in her eyes. *Belladonna,* I thought. That's how it got the name — somehow, huge pupils were supposed to make a girl beautiful? It never made sense to me.

'Aleida?' I said. 'It's me. It's Dee, it really is.'

She blinked and squinted, as though it was hard to focus. 'Well, of course you'd say that,' she hissed. She tried to back away from me, only to stumble. Out of reflex I started forward, only for her to raise her wand with a hiss. 'Stay back.'

I stopped where I was, hands raised. 'It *is* me. But it's all right if you don't believe me. I'll just stay here. I won't move a muscle. Aleida, are you all right?'

She looked weary, with dark circles under her eyes. 'Belladonna,' she said. 'Delirium. Confusion. Agitation. Dysphoria. Racing heart, dry mouth. Irritability and wandering thoughts. Hallucination and visual disturbance.'

'Right,' I said. 'So, all in all, a normal day at Black Oak Cottage?'

She blinked at me. Frowned. And then she smiled. 'Dee ...'

Starting towards me, she stumbled again. I hurried forward and she all but fell against me, wrapping one arm tight around my shoulders. 'Gods, Dee,' she said in my ear. 'Where did you go? I told you to stay.'

I opened my mouth to reply — but then I saw her. A haze in the air, a wisp of fog and sunlight.

It was the spectre of an old woman, her face little more than a mask of wrinkled skin over a fleshless skull, white hair bound in a braid as skinny as a rat's tail, or the lash of a whip, arms and fingers like gnarled twigs, clad in tattered rags. She hovered like a hawk, preparing to dive.

I dodged aside, and tried to pull Aleida with me, but she refused. Like the warlock last night, she planted her feet instead, raising her wand to fight back — and the spectral figure slammed into her. The impact drove her back, into me, and sent us both sprawling on the ground, Aleida on top of me.

In panic, I looked around for the spectre, trying to wriggle out from under my mistress's body, waiting for the next attack and expecting at any moment for my corpse tangled in the water weeds to rise up and join the fight — but the other me was gone. And Gyssha was gone.

Still half-sprawled over me, Aleida squirmed and *writhed* like a cut snake. She coughed, and from her lips came a puff of ash and dust, smelling of ancient, mouldering rot.

'Oh,' I said. 'Oh no!'

She coughed again and heaved herself off me, rolling over and levering herself up. Her head lifted, eyes fixed once again on me, but Aleida's dark brown eyes were gone. Instead, her irises were a pale, watery blue. Her lips parted, but I couldn't call the expression a smile. It bared far too many teeth.

I scrabbled for a weapon. I still had the stick jammed through the ties of my apron but I couldn't get it out, I was half-lying on the thing. Aleida was crawling towards me now, hands twisted like claws, and I frantically felt around for a weapon.

My fingers found her wand, dropped when the spectre struck.

Without thinking, I closed my fist around the handle and swung it as hard as I could. I didn't want to hurt my mistress, but this wasn't her anymore — it was Gyssha, and I knew the old witch wouldn't hesitate to kill me if she could.

Gyssha caught the movement and jerked back. The point of the wand merely grazed her cheekbone, instead of striking it square-on. But that movement was enough for me to roll away from her and get to my feet.

Panting, she tried to stand, a trickle of blood on her cheek where the point of the wand had grazed her skin. 'You're dead, child,' she rasped. 'After all the trouble you've caused me I ought to flay you alive! I'd have had the ungrateful wretch days ago if it weren't for you.' She managed to get her feet underneath her, but then staggered again, and beneath the hem of her skirt I saw the black dog's paws, tottering and unsteady. Of course, she'd had no practice walking on them, I realised. Not like Aleida had.

I glanced down at the wand in my hand, thinking back to the night before, when that rasping voice had come from my own throat, and the symbol Aleida had drawn to drive her away. I have a very good memory. I remembered every line of it, and every word.

I leaped, and slammed into Aleida, knocking her onto the ground once more. Then, I scrambled on top of her, pinning her down while she thrashed and struggled, too weak to throw me off. I felt one of her hands go for her belt, pulling something free, and hastily I dropped the wand, using both hands to catch her wrist as she slashed at me with her dagger. It took hardly any effort to force her arm down, and pin it there with my knee. She really was just skin and bone.

'Idiot child!' Gyssha hissed up at me. 'I'll have your guts for garters. I'll bleed you dry!'

I paid her words no attention as I picked the wand back up.

It shouldn't have worked; I wasn't a witch, I didn't have any power. The wand didn't like me either, I could feel its hatred seeping through the wooden handle, turning my hand numb, but it couldn't stop me either. I drew the symbol and spoke the words, and each line left a glowing blue tracery inscribed in the air. When it was done, the glowing shape shattered into myriad fragments. They poured over Aleida's face, flowing in her mouth and nose, settling over her eyes. Her feeble struggles stopped, and then, with a howling gust of icy wind, Gyssha's spirit left her body, shrieking with rage.

Beneath me, Aleida coughed and choked, and then gasped a heaving breath.

And then a sack full of sticks slammed into me. It reeked like a charnel-house. I tumbled over the mouldering leaves, entangled with the *thing*, my braid wrapped around my neck, tight enough to cut off my breath.

Then it grew tighter still, and a hideous, grinning face loomed over mine. No, it wasn't my braid at all — hands, bony hands strung together with wire and sharp, glittering beads. 'Hello, lover-girl,' the construct clacked at me with stained teeth. 'Miss me?'

I clutched and scrabbled at the fingers but I couldn't peel them back — the construct was far stronger than any mortal man.

Over its shoulder I saw Aleida heave herself up, wand in her hand. She started towards me, but ducked away when Gyssha's spectre appeared again, diving towards her. Aleida turned her back on me, head tilted back to search the canopy above for the old witch's ghost.

My throat was on fire, my vision growing narrow and black around the edges. My eyes stayed on Aleida, pleading where my voice couldn't. *Help me, Lord and Lady, please help me!*

Then, my hand dropped away, abandoning the useless task of plucking at those bony fingers. I tried to pull it back — I couldn't give up. I *wouldn't* give up, not while there was any will to fight left in me. But my hand wouldn't obey, it was as though it had a mind of its own, or someone else's. While my neck burned and my heart thumped in my throat, my hand slipped downwards into the pocket of my apron, closing around the first crystal I'd found that morning, the little amethyst point I'd dug out of the earth, what felt like hours ago.

'Gyssha!' Aleida shouted, howling up into the trees. She had her back to me, like she was ignoring me, as I struggled for breath among the rotting leaves. 'Show yourself! Come on, old woman! Or are you finally ready to admit this ungrateful upstart is better than you?'

My vision was fading to black, but somehow I felt my hand clutch the crystal tight and draw another symbol on the construct's rotting flank. My lips shaped words I didn't know and had no breath to speak.

Dimly, I heard a shriek of rage from Gyssha's spirit, and the howl of spectral wind as she swooped again. And then something slammed into the construct and tore its grip away.

For a moment everything was black, and all I could do was gulp down air in great heaving breaths.

Then I felt a hand wrap around my upper arm, and I panicked, thrashing.

'Dee,' Aleida hissed. 'It's me, it's just me. Get up, quickly!'

I tried to get my feet under me, and was mostly successful, though I would have fallen if Aleida hadn't had a good grip on my arm. It seemed to me that we were holding each other up.

A few more breaths, and my vision cleared enough to see the construct on the ground, struggling to stand, just as we were. It hadn't escaped the waterfall unscathed, it seemed. One of the long thigh-bones had broken, and had been crudely splinted with a stick and some vines.

Aleida's grip on my arm tightened. 'Tell me,' she murmured. 'Is there a walking skeleton over there?'

I glanced at her quickly. Her eyes were still huge. 'Um, yes. Definitely yes.'

'Right. So it's not just the belladonna, then.'

'No. Where's Gyssha? Where—'

'Trapped. That sigil you drew on the construct is a binding.'

'Oh! I thought that was you,' I broke in.

'Well, obviously, Dee, who else? When she came at me again I cast a shield and threw her off onto bonehead, there. Now she's stuck. Until she breaks the binding, that is.' She frowned at me briefly before turning back to the construct. 'But you're not too bothered, are you, Dee? Seen ol' Boney before, have you?'

'I, um, remember that boy I told you about? The one who told me all those stories about you? It was her, all along.'

The skeleton stood and rippled, and a moment later Kian stood there, hatred in his soft brown eyes and a sneer on his lips. 'Oh, and you loved it, didn't you?' he spat. 'I bet you've never had a lad cast a second look your way in your whole life! One more day, and I'd have had my hand up those pretty skirts of yours.'

Aleida elbowed me in the ribs. 'Dee,' she hissed. 'Crystal?'

It took me a moment to figure out she was looking at the broken stone I'd stabbed him with. The point was still buried between his ribs, the end jutting out beneath his breast. But, in the same moment, I realised that the broken end of the crystal had come out of my apron pocket at some point in the fight, and lay on the ground between us.

'Dee?' Aleida said again, her voice low.

'Yes,' I said. 'It broke. That's the other half.'

'Right,' she muttered. 'I'll put him on the ground. You keep him there, I'll get the stone. Got it?'

'What?' I squeaked, but she was already moving away, readying her wand. Sometime during the scuffle, the stick had come free of my apron, and it lay just a few feet away. Keeping my eyes on Kian, I darted over, stooping to pick it up — only to fumble, and drop it again.

At least, that's what I wanted Gyssha to think.

As soon as I'd moved to the stick, Kian had dropped into a crouch, and as I fumbled the stick he roared and charged — and Aleida struck him with a blast from her wand, a great gout of flame like a dragon's breath.

It rather threw me off, I must admit. By that point I'd snatched up the stick and was charging to meet him, and was moving too fast to avoid the flame. It stripped away the illusion, revealing the stinking skeleton again, flames licking over his ragged clothes, just as I collided with the scorched, smoking, *disgusting* thing. I clubbed it with my stick, once, again, and then threw myself on top of it, stick across its neck and arms, me sitting on its shoulders.

The thing's legs came up to kick at me, but before it could land a blow Aleida threw herself down beside me, pinning them down too.

'Do you *mind*?' I snapped at her without thinking. 'I've had enough burns for one day, thank you!'

'Sorry,' she grunted. 'I tend to default to fire when I'm under strain.' Then, before I could reply, she plunged her dagger into the construct's chest and levered the ribs apart. Beneath them was a complicated weaving of wire and stones and scraps of silk and glowing charms — and piercing it all, the broken crystal.

Aleida threw her knife aside and picked up the broken tip of the crystal. She started to draw another sigil, and as soon as the first line appeared, the body beneath us began to struggle harder, roaring with fury and rage. But Aleida never faltered — she drew the symbol with quiet surety, and spoke each word with a puff of blue. Then, with the last word, the last line, I *felt* the spell release. With one last fading howl, I felt Gyssha's spirit leave the construct, felt it be forcefully pulled away — into the stone that had pierced the thing's chest.

Aleida slammed the broken end of the crystal down, like a cork in a bottle, and there was another flare of power as the break was mended.

Inside the stone, darkness swirled. Like smoke, like a storm cloud, boiling out of the air, roiling and seething. Then, the movement slowed, like air turning to water, turning to tar. It ceased and then it froze; the witch's soul was trapped inside the stone.

The crystal fell from Aleida's hands, stained black as soot now, and rolled away over the leaf litter. She threw her hands forward, trying to catch herself, and raised her head to look at me. Her lips parted, trying to speak, but then her eyes rolled back and she collapsed against me, breathless and spent.

CHAPTER 14

I caught Aleida under the arms and pulled her away from the tangle of green, mouldering bones, just far enough that we weren't touching the revolting object, and let my shaking legs give way. Aleida sagged against my shoulder, eyes closed, breath panting.

We stayed like that for a time, just resting, while I felt my heart gradually slow and the nervous energy from the fight drain away.

Finally, Aleida shook back her tangled hair and rubbed her forehead with the back of her wounded hand. The gash across her palm was a nasty one, now a mass of clotted blood and dirt. Without a word, I pulled out my handkerchief and folded it into a long strip. This time, when I gestured to the wound, she let me wrap the linen around it. 'I suppose there's some spell or potion that can get the stain out,' I said.

Aleida shrugged. 'Honestly, it's easier just to dye it

black. That's what I—' She broke off then, lips parted and eyes suddenly narrowed.

She was frowning at the skeleton. I went as tense as a hunting cat, suddenly afraid the construct was about to jump up again. But instead, she crawled towards it on her hands and knees. 'Oh, Lord and Lady. For pity's sake, Gyssha, you couldn't even let the poor soul rest in his grave!' She huddled over the desecrated corpse, her hand hovering over the green, mossy skull with its eyes of staring river-stones. She was weeping, tears falling like rain on the poor lad's rotten burial suit. 'Ben. Oh, Ben ...'

Ben? Bennett? The name hit me like a physical blow, driving the breath from my lungs. It was one thing to know Gyssha had robbed a grave to build her construct, but it was another knowing she'd used the body of a man she herself had driven to suicide. I picked myself up and came around to the other side of the construct. 'Lord and Lady, she didn't—'

'Of course she did,' Aleida growled though tears. 'Oh, Ben,' she whispered. 'You poor soul. I'm sorry I couldn't protect you and your kin. I'm sorry ...'

I crouched down to slip an arm around her shoulders. 'But she's gone now. She won't harm anyone else. And we can take him back to his grave, back with his ...' my voice broke on the last word. I had to swallow hard and try again. 'Back with his family.'

'I don't even know where they're buried!' Aleida wailed.

'But we can find them. I can ask the Sanfords, or Attwater. They'll know. They'll help us.'

She nodded, gulping down sobs. Then she threw her head back, dashing tears from her cheeks as she drew a shaking breath. 'Oh, good grief, Blackbone, pull yourself together.'

'You don't have to, you know,' I said. 'I mean, I don't know about you, but a nice little bout of hysterics has a certain appeal right now.'

She gave a brittle laugh and shook her head. 'No, no, no, that'd never do. Blackbones don't have hysterics, Dee, we make other people have them.' She sat back awkwardly, her dog-like legs splayed to one side, and shivered. 'We can't just leave him here, though. The scavengers will get to him, chew his bones. He doesn't deserve that. He didn't deserve any of this ...'

'Maybe we can bury him here, then,' I said. 'Just for now. It'll keep him safe.'

'Bury him? Dee ... I can't. I don't have the strength.' I could see it was true. She was propping herself up with one arm, and even that was taking all the strength she had.

'Well,' I said. 'Can I do it? Can I help?'

She raised her face to mine, searching my eyes. 'Is that what you want?'

I swallowed, hard. 'Yeah. It is.'

'Dee, I mean—'

'I know,' I said. 'I've made up my mind. I think I made it up a while ago, actually. I just couldn't bring myself to say the words.'

'Words are cheap,' she said, wrinkling her nose. 'It's what you *do* that counts. But you have to know, there's no going back.'

'Oh, I'm never going back. What do I need to do?'

'Just look at me, Dee.'

I met her gaze across the mouldering bones, and then I felt her slip inside my head.

Without thought or intention, I placed my hands on the dead man's chest, clothed in ragged shreds of cloth, and then I *felt* her call to the ground beneath us, the moist, rich earth, born of death and decay but full of life.

In the space of a single breath, the skeleton sank into the dark earth, embraced by the world itself.

Aleida released me, and let her head fall, black hair hanging across her face as she wiped her eyes with the edge of her cloak. For a moment all we did was sit there and breathe in the cool, damp air. 'What happened to you, anyway?' she said. 'Where did you go? I tried to find you, but that damn belladonna got me all turned around.'

'Kian dragged me away. Gyssha, I mean. Only I didn't understand what was happening until we got to the waterfall and she dropped the illusion.'

'The waterfall?' She lifted her head to give me a puzzled frown. 'That's nearly a mile from here! How did you get back so fast?'

'I, I'm honestly not sure. I found that crystal, and broke it when I was fighting the construct. Then I thought of the earth spirit you showed me and ...'

'Spit it, Dee.'

'I asked it to help me. It showed me this place, like a crack in the rock, but it turned out to be a cave.'

Aleida's eyes widened. 'A Pathway? You used a Pathway to get back here?'

'A Pathway? Is that what it's called? What was it?'

'A short-cut through the spirit realm. Can be dangerous, even if you've got a tame earth elemental to show you the way. So, you just went in? In the dark?'

'What else was I going to do?'

She laughed again, a brief chortle. 'Well, quite.'

I leaned back on one hand, glancing up at the glowing leaves overhead. 'Does this mean I'll be Elodie Blackbone?'

'It does. If you stay with me.'

'Well of course I'm going to stay with you. I was brought here for a reason, wasn't I?'

'A reason ...' she said, and tipped her head back to gaze up at the branches above. 'Yeah, about that. I think I've figured out what it was.'

I waited, but she didn't speak. Not until I snapped. 'Well? Tell me!'

'To keep Gyssha from coming back. She'd have had me there if it weren't for you, Dee.'

It was true, I had to admit. 'But that just leaves more questions! Who sent the letter? How?'

She pursed her lips. 'Well, think, Dee. Remember the spirit who warned me off pushing the reading any further?'

The shiver that ran over me was answer enough. 'What about it?'

'Whoever — or *what*ever — it was that brought you here, they have enough clout to send a greater spirit running around as an errand-boy. That means we're being watched, Dee.'

'Watched? But Gyssha must have had enemies, surely. Couldn't it just be one of them?'

'Enemies, yes. Enemies with the power and will to risk drawing her ire? Not so much. Enemies who could look into the future and see that I was about to attack her, see the way it was going to go, then find you and bring you here in time to make a difference? By my reckoning, that letter arrived at your farm the night Gyssha died.'

She kept watching me with a steady gaze, and the shiver that ran over me had nothing to do with the cooling air. I'd worked out the timing of the letter and the fight with Melly days ago, hadn't I? 'Okay,' I said. 'What does that mean?'

'Like I said, we're being watched. Watched by someone or something with far-reaching sight and a very long arm. And let me tell you, kid, that kind of attention is not a good thing.'

The way she spoke, quietly and with a kind of intense precision, made all my nerves prickle. I knotted my fingers together, wondering if the question hovering in my mind was a stupid thing to ask. 'Do you mean, something more than human?'

She nodded, once.

The idea of being watched and measured by something even more powerful than the huge being that had gazed down on us that morning was not a calming thought. 'All right. But why would they care? I mean, I know she was awful, but if you're talking about something big, bigger than us ...'

'I just don't know, Dee. Maybe they saw Gyssha could be a threat to them if she had another lifetime to gain power and hone her skills. I'd believe it. She was always hungry, Gyssha. Always wanted more. With another lifetime there's no telling how far she'd have gone.'

'Or maybe they were like you, and decided it was time to put a stop to the harm she was doing. Like putting down a dog that keeps attacking the sheep.'

From the look on her face, she was unconvinced. 'I don't know, Dee. Beings like that, I'm not sure they'd even notice.'

I smoothed out my skirts over my knees. 'Well, either way, it's done and dusted now.'

'Mm. I hope that'll be the end of it. I'm not going to look into it any further — there's no way of finding out more without getting smacked down for our trouble, and given that I've been warned off once already, they won't be gentle about it. I really hope this was just to see Gyssha dead, and now they'll turn their attention elsewhere.'

Hopefully. Then again, the job wasn't finished yet. 'What about the crystal?' I nodded towards the black stone lying on the leaf-litter, with the soul of the old witch trapped inside.

She followed my gaze. 'I'll see to it. Can't leave her in there, or some idiot'll come along in a few hundred years and let her out again. I'll need a few days to rest up, but I'll shove her through the veil and make damn sure she stays there. That should be an end to it.'

'Can I help?'

She shook her head. 'Not this time. You're a rank beginner, and I'm not taking any chances. But you know, Dee, there's a lot of paths open to you now. Don't feel that you're bound here, to this one.'

I turned to her with a scowl. 'What are you saying? You've been telling me all day that I ought to be a witch, but now ...' My voice began to falter. 'You don't want me?'

'It's not about what I want,' Aleida said, tugging on the handkerchief wrapped around her hand. 'It's about what's best for you, kid. Look, I'm not going to be a great teacher. I'm not patient, I'm not gentle and there's a lot I still have to learn myself. I've got a short temper and a mean streak a mile wide. And if you stay and become a Blackbone, every witch worth her salt will know where you came from. It'll be a long time before that name means anything but terror and despair, and you'll have to deal with it, too — Gyssha's pall will hang over you, probably all your life. And that's before we even get into the matter of my curse, or the fact that I killed my mother in the craft.' She sighed and shook her head. 'You'd be better off with another teacher, there's no two ways about it.'

'I don't want any other teacher,' I said. 'I want you. Besides, you need me. You're not capable of looking after yourself, in your state. I'm staying, and that's all there is to it.'

She drew a breath, opened her mouth — but then sagged back onto the leaves. 'I really can't argue with that.'

'Good.' I heaved myself up, stretching cautiously. 'On that note, we ought to get back to the cottage. Can you call the horse?'

'Yeah, I can manage that much.'

'And I suppose it's too late today to head into Lilsfield, isn't it?'

'Probably. But why d'you want to go there?'

'To buy a bath. You promised me, remember.'

'Oh. Yeah. Tomorrow, Dee. Take the horse — but I get to go first. Head of house's prerogative.'

I'd have to stop in at the Sanford farm, too, I mused. I'd promised Melly she could say 'I told you so'.

Through the still air of the afternoon, I heard hoof beats coming towards us and spotted the pale shape of the grey trotting through the trees. 'As long as the water's still hot, I don't care. Let's go home.'

READ ON FOR A PREVIEW OF
THE NEXT TALE OF

The
Blackbone
Witches

TO BE RELEASED IN 2019

CHAPTER 1

A man stood in the dappled shade in the middle of the road. He wore a leather hat pulled down low to shade his eyes and a printed kerchief tied around his neck. And he carried a bare sabre in his hand. The blade flashed in a shaft of sunlight gleaming through the trees, shining the light back into my eyes.

I scowled, tightening my hands on the reins. *Really?* I thought. *He's doing that on purpose. And just how long did he spend traipsing up and down this road to find the perfect spot to pose?* He was handsome, I had to admit; but the effect was rather spoiled by the smug expression on his face. I'd also bet any money he'd dressed himself as carefully as a girl going to her first village dance.

Feeling my eyes upon him, his lips parted in a wicked smile. 'I'd stop right there, miss, if I were you.'

'If you were me, I doubt you'd do anything of the sort,' I said. I dropped my hand to my side, reaching for the wand that hung there, hidden in the folds of my skirt. But before I could gather the courage to pull it out, our draught mare, Maggie, tossed her head and threw her weight back into the breeching to stop the heavy wagon. She was a gentle giant, our Maggie. Plenty of beasts would just shoulder a man out of the way, but not her. Then again, she didn't have enough sense to recognise the sabre in his hand, or what it meant. I didn't imagine for a moment that he was alone out here.

From the gleam in the man's eye, he took it as a victory. His smile deepened, crinkling the skin around his eyes, and he took hold of her bridle. I wondered what Maggie would do if I slapped the reins on her rump to drive her onwards. We hadn't had her long enough to know and, in any case, I couldn't risk him turning that sabre against her. Instead, I reached behind myself to rap my knuckles against the door at my back, trying to keep the movement subtle.

The bandit didn't seem to notice. He just rubbed Maggie's long nose and gave me a sly grin. 'Well,' he said, 'aren't you a good girl?'

Lord and Lady. 'Are you talking to me, or the horse?'

'You tell me,' he said. '*Are* you a good girl?'

I couldn't think of any way to answer him that wouldn't lead to a conversation I did *not* want to have, so I just scowled as he blatantly looked me over. I knew exactly what he'd make of me. A young woman in worn and mended clothes, brown hair coming loose from its braid, sitting on the footplate of a sturdy travellers' wagon. I looked every inch a maid-servant, but though

I was coarsely dressed, the wagon, Maggie and her harness had clearly cost a pretty penny. I could see why they thought us an appealing target. They had no way of knowing who was behind the door at my back.

Still grinning like a fool, he came towards me, sliding his gloved hand along the rein. 'You should be careful, pretty young thing like you, out here all on your own. There's all kinds of scoundrels in these woods, you see ...'

At those words, a dozen men appeared around us, stepping out from behind bushes and rocks, a few even swinging down from the trees.

'But never fear,' he went on. 'I'll protect you.'

I leaned back and this time thumped my elbow against the door. *Come* on, *Aleida.* My mistress was sleeping inside. Not too deeply, I hoped.

The bandit caught the movement with a lift of his chin. 'Ah,' he said, sheathing his sword. 'Or perhaps you aren't all alone, after all?' With that, he put one foot to the step-iron and sprang up to sit beside me. With a yelp, I tried to move away, but all I succeeded in doing was trapping my wand under me as he reached across and plucked the reins out of my grip. The other arm snaked behind me, around my waist and pulled me close. Oh, good grief, was he wearing *scent*? I'd half-expected the stink of someone who went weeks between baths and, honestly, I wasn't sure if this was any better.

'Who's inside, lass? Your father or your husband? Or your master, perhaps?'

'None of those,' I snapped. 'And if you don't take your hands off of me *right now* I swear by all the demons in all the hells you're going to regret it.' With my heart beating hard I thumped the door again. This time, there came an answering knock through the wood, and the knot of anxiety under my heart softened a little. My teacher was awake, after all.

The bandit just laughed at my bluster. 'Oh, don't be like that, honey-cake. Besides, you've got it all wrong. I promise, the only time ladies have cause for regret is when I leave.'

'I'll do my best to bear it with fortitude,' I said. 'Seriously, though. You should go, now. Before it's too late.'

The men were closing around us now, and I cast a wary eye over them. A couple of them were just young lads, close to my age. Others were older, but none of them were quite what I'd picture as hard-bitten criminals. They looked just like ordinary folk, with the usual complement of eyes, teeth and noses. *Of course, once we drive away from here, they might not be so lucky. Why didn't I draw my wand when I had the chance?* I could feel it half-pinned under my leg, and wondered if I dared try to dig it out. With this lout of a bandit pressed against me, I was terrified he'd take the gesture as something else entirely. *Aleida is never going to let me hear the end of this!*

'Now, now, sweet,' he said. 'Why would you say something like that, when I've been nothing but a gentleman to you? Well, what *do* we have inside this fine little wagon? Perhaps you and I should take a look.' He stood swiftly, catching my wrist to yank me to my feet.

That was all I needed to find the smooth wooden handle of my wand. I pulled it free and shoved the point of it towards his face. For a second he recoiled — just a second, and then he realised it wasn't a knife I'd thrust towards him, but a chunk of crystal hafted to a wooden shaft.

Looking more puzzled than anything else, he tried to snatch it out of my hand, but the moment he touched the stone there came a flash of light and a crack like thunder. The shock of it threw him back against the door, and the air was suddenly full of the smell of burning hair and scorched leather.

Before he could recover — before the men around us could react at all to what had happened — there came a piercing shriek from above.

Something huge and dark speared down through the trees, screeching like a demon. It was an eagle, huge, its wingspan wider than the reach of my arms. It came swooping down towards us, only to flare its wings and bank hard, diving under the wagon's eaves as it reached out with taloned feet, each as large as my hand.

It slashed at the bandit's face and the man screamed, flailing at the eagle as it beat about his head with its vast wings. I ducked away from the wildly swinging arms and wings, and then I had a thought. He looked awfully precarious there, balancing on the narrow footboard ...

Crouching low, my shoulder against the wall of the wagon, I shoved him with all my strength. With a strangled cry of surprise, he toppled from the seat, landing heavily in the road in a puff of dust, blood pouring down his face.

Then, behind me, the door swung open and my mistress loomed out, her black hair tousled and her dark eyes glowering, her wand in her hand. 'Get the reins,' she said to me while the eagle flapped over our heads, climbing with laborious beats of its wings, turning its fierce gaze to the man who'd taken hold of Maggie's head. The rest of the bandits were crowding around us, one of them even climbing up to the footboard where we stood.

Aleida turned to him with murder in her eyes. I left her to it. That scented buffoon had dropped the reins when he hauled me up, and they had fallen onto the shafts, down where they attached to the wagon. With a quick glance at Maggie to make sure she wasn't thinking of kicking, I slipped down to retrieve them, hearing the crackling roar of a fireball above my head and the shriek of a bandit as Aleida sent it searing his way.

She caught me by the collar to steady me as I scrambled back up. 'Get her moving! Go!'

Maggie didn't need to be told twice. I was still gathering up the reins, but it seemed the mare had decided by herself that she'd had quite enough of all this bother. With a nicker of fright, she reared between the shafts and threw herself forward, jerking the wagon into motion with a lurch that set me and Aleida both snatching for a grip to steady ourselves.

It didn't stop Aleida from throwing another fireball at the men who rushed towards us, waving their arms and shouting as though they could stop Maggie in her tracks.

'Get out of the way, you fools!' I yelled, having a horrifying vision of what would happen if they went down under Maggie's enormous hooves, or the wheels of our heavy wagon. Amidst all the confusion something hit the wood near me with a hefty *thunk*, but it barely registered with everything else that was going on, with men running towards us or away from Aleida's fireballs, as well as the eagle circling, searching for a new target.

But there was one man not moving, seeming calm amid the chaos. He had a bow in his hands, sighting at the eagle as he hauled back the string. 'Aleida!' I yelled. 'Bow!'

'I see it,' she growled, and stepped towards the edge of the footboard for a clear line to the fellow, raising her wand. The smoke-stained crystal at its tip glowed with a vivid green pinpoint of light, and I felt power flex around us, thickening the air.

The bow in the bandit's hands *squirmed*, rippled, and then burst into life. Tiny green buds split the wood, swelling to a leafy profusion, while pale white roots swarmed from the lower length of the bow-stave, questing for the ground. By the time the bandit dropped the thing in surprise, it was barely recognisable as a weapon.

Aleida sat beside me with a thump, gripping the seat with one hand. 'Give me the reins, Dee. Check behind us.'

Now that the wagon was moving, Maggie was settling into a laboured canter, determined to leave all this vexation behind. A sentiment I definitely shared. I handed the reins over and tried to stand, only to lose my balance as something pulled me back down. There was an arrow jutting from the wagon seat, inches from my leg. It had pierced my skirts and petticoats right through, pinning them to the bench.

I pulled it out, and Aleida snatched it from my hand, her face dark. 'Are they coming after us?'

This time I managed to stand on the rocking seat, and peered around the edge of the wagon to see just a few of the bandits left milling in the road. The rest had retreated into the trees. 'No,' I said, sitting down again. 'They've got the wind up them good and proper.'

She rolled the arrow in her hand, her face like thunder. 'We should go back.'

'What?' I said. 'No! Why?'

'They shot at you!' she said. 'No one shoots at my apprentice! I'll turn that little wretch inside out!'

I pressed my lips together, focussing on the road and Maggie's ears, still flat back with annoyance for the whole affair. Convincing her to stop now would be no easy task. 'Oh, let's just keep going. I reckon they've learned their lesson.'

'Mm. Maybe.' She turned to me then, and I wanted to shrink away at the anger in her eyes. 'Dee,' she said. 'Why in the hells didn't you have your wand out? You should have had it in your hand as soon as you saw him.'

I didn't ask how she knew. I just looked away, hiding behind the excuse of keeping my eyes on the road. 'You said we should keep our heads down. Try not to make it obvious that we're ... what we are.'

She snorted. 'For villages, sure. Farms, maybe. But bandits? Screw 'em, who cares what they think? If you'd pulled your wand out, that idiot wouldn't have dared get close enough to grab you.'

'For you, maybe,' I muttered.

'What was that?'

'For you,' I said. 'Aleida, you *look* like a witch. I just look like a servant girl.' I glanced down at my wand, lying beside my thigh, the crystal bound to the shaft with copper wire. I'd made it myself, under her direction, but it didn't feel *real*. It felt just like a hunk of rock tied to a wooden handle. Not like Aleida's wand of smoke-wreathed quartz. You could feel the power in that stone, radiating like heat from a fire.

'I've told you, Dee. It's not what you look like, it's how you carry yourself. Next time something like that happens, I want your wand out right away.'

'Even if I still can't really use the damn thing?'

'Especially then. It's not going to do anything if it's not in your hand.'

'But I can't—'

'And you never will if you don't *try*. He saw you as a harmless little girl because that's how you were acting. You're not a servant-girl, you're a witch. Act like it.'

'Yes, miss,' I said, scowling down at my dangling feet. 'And I'm fine, by the way,' I added, tartly.

She looked me over with flat, dark eyes. 'I know. If you weren't, those fools back there would have seen why I'm called Blackbone.'

The word made me shiver, even though it was my name now too. I didn't doubt Aleida would have turned them to ash too, if she had been pushed hard enough. I hoped I'd never see it happen. 'Sorry, miss,' I said.

She sighed and leaned back against the door. 'Next time, Dee, next time. And I suppose there's no harm done.' She gave a dry chuckle. 'Well, not to us, anyway.'

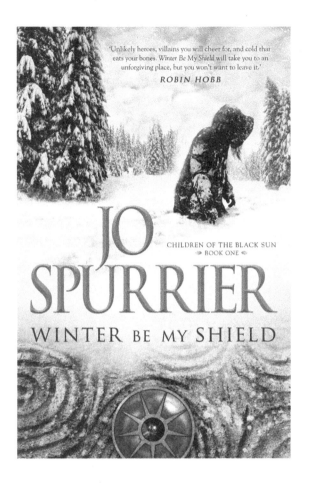

'Unlikely heroes, villains you will cheer for, and cold that
eats your bones. *Winter Be My Shield* will take you to an
unforgiving place, but you won't want to leave it.'

ROBIN HOBB

CHILDREN OF THE BLACK SUN
BOOK ONE

JO SPURRIER

WINTER BE MY SHIELD

Sierra has a despised and forbidden gift – she
raises power from the suffering of others.
Enslaved by the king's torturer, Sierra escapes,
barely keeping ahead of Rasten, the man sent
to hunt her down.

But Rasten is not the only enemy hunting
her in the frozen north, and Sierra will soon
have to decide what price she is willing to pay
for her freedom and her life …

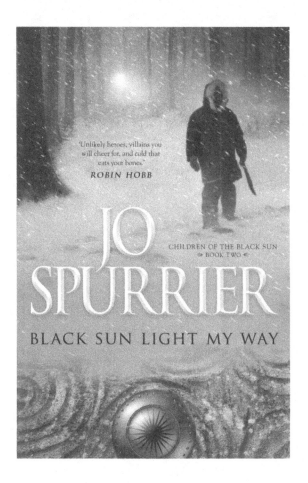

'Unlikely heroes, villains you will cheer for, and cold that eats your bones.'
ROBIN HOBB

CHILDREN OF THE BLACK SUN
BOOK TWO

JO SPURRIER

BLACK SUN LIGHT MY WAY

Sierra has always battled to control her powers, but now her life depends on keeping her skills hidden from the Akharians, as they draw close to Demon's Spire.

When Sierra's untrainable powers turn destructive, she has nowhere to turn for help except to the uncertain mercy of an old enemy. But what will Rasten do when she returns to his hands at last?

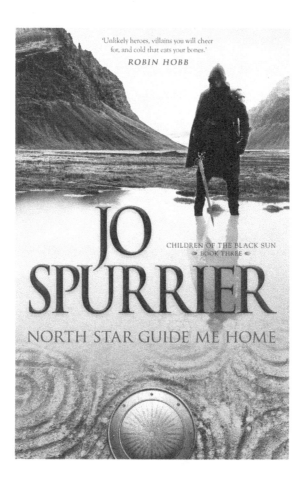

'Unlikely heroes, villains you will cheer for, and cold that eats your bones.'

ROBIN HOBB

JO SPURRIER

CHILDREN OF THE BLACK SUN
☀ BOOK THREE ☀

NORTH STAR GUIDE ME HOME

Sierra is desperate to rebuild shattered bonds with her old friends, but with one of them incontrovertibly changed and her own wounds still fresh, things can never be as they once were.

Rasten knows he cannot atone for the horrors of his past. But when the Akharians follow the trail back to Ricalan, the skills Rasten swore he'd renounce may be their only hope for victory ...